**C. A. BYFORD** is one of those people who your parents warned you about, but you didn't listen. You insisted on doing your 'own thing'. An unashamed 80s tearaway, he worked many IT roles when growing up, from service desk, IT manager, all the way to assisting huge multinationals and governments with cloud-based email and security services. After being diagnosed with Ulcerative Colitis in the mid-2000s, he underwent surgery, giving him the kick he needed to pursue writing full-time. When not writing, he can normally be found somewhere dark indulging in astrophotography, or wandering local woodland, camera in hand. On the side, he runs Unusual Type, an imprint for titles that seem a little too fringe for traditional publishing. He lives with his wife and son in Gloucester, where it rains constantly, and people tumble down hills trying to chase wheels of cheese.

**Also by C. A. Byford, writing as Christopher Byford**

The Gambler's Den Series
*Den of Shadows*
*Den of Stars*
*Den of Smoke*
*Luck and Other Deadly Things*

C.A. BYFORD

# THE NIGHT MARKET

HQ

ONE PLACE. MANY STORIES

HQ
An imprint of HarperCollins*Publishers* Ltd
1 London Bridge Street
London SE1 9GF

www.harpercollins.co.uk

HarperCollins*Publishers*
Macken House, 39/40 Mayor Street Upper
Dublin 1, D01 C9W8, Ireland

This edition 2026

1
First published in Great Britain by HQ,
an imprint of HarperCollins*Publishers* Ltd 2026


A catalogue record for this book is available from the British Library.

ISBN: 9780008803674
TPB ISBN: 9780008824747

Set in Sabon LT Pro by HarperCollins*Publishers* India



Printed and bound in the UK using 100%
Renewable Electricity at CPI Group (UK) Ltd

FSC
www.fsc.org
MIX
Paper | Supporting
responsible forestry
FSC® C013604

*To those familiar with*

*the shape*
*the sounds*
*and the smells*
*of loss*

*this book is for you*

# Part I

# Chapter One

## Breadcrumbs

Pepper wasn't supposed to be here.

Not in this part of the city. Not at this hour. And definitely not following some breadcrumb trail of the impossible.

The streets were louder than she expected for past midnight, still throbbing with life, just a different kind. Dregs of students stumbled out of bars, their laughter sharp, doing nothing for her nerves. A cab honked in impatience. Music thumped through the walls of a club as she passed, the baseline dragging her heartbeat into synchronicity.

She kept her head down. Checked her phone. Walked fast.

The air had that end-of-night smell – the musk of wet tarmac and takeaway joints. Bins overflowed. Shop shutters rolled down like closing eyelids. The city was winding down, except for the parts that never really did. And while Pepper wasn't dressed for attention, she still felt a spotlight upon her. Her coat was pulled too tight. Her expression too fixed. Walking a little too quickly maybe. She passed a man sleeping in a doorway, wrapped in plastic sheeting, and her guilt attempted to make her stop. But she didn't. Couldn't.

Over the road, she finally stopped beneath a streetlamp and pulled out her vibrating phone. Her inbox was still open – a string of untraceable contacts and junk, with one new noticeable exception that had been flagged as urgent. Its subject line read like a threat: *Last Chance*.

Her stomach tightened as she tapped it open.

Beneath a string of coordinates was a message:

*Remember that what you're searching for has eluded many.*
*It doesn't want to be found.*
*You have to walk like you've already been invited.*
*When you get there, say hello just like I told you.*
*If it likes you, it'll let you in.*

*SilkVeins*

She checked her directions on Google Maps and took a turn.

Almost there.

Pepper continued, head down, coat drawn against the October chill, avoiding deposits of the day's rain. Music leaked from pubs as she passed. Screaming profanity over heavy rock melded into waves that made the pavement throb. Laughter echoed from doorways. Somewhere, a bottle smashed. Every instinct in her body was telling her to go home. To be smart. Sensible. She never was one to take advice, not even her own.

She could have turned back at any time. That was the worst part.

The longer she walked, the more real this became. Sketchy images from this SilkVeins person became recognisable landmarks. Cryptic suggestions they had left on internet message boards seemed to be genuine, providing secret directions that led her deeper into the city's guts, away from the light as well as the safety. The buildings leaned closer here. Cracked or broken windows stared down at her like judging eyes. She said the words that would grant her protection, fragments of a language that she had no right to speak, and crossed over a lonely road.

A group of revellers passed her on the corner – heels too high, tops too thin, cheeks pink with drink and happiness. One girl bumped into her shoulder, apologised with a voice soaked in schnapps, then vanished around the corner without waiting for a reply.

Pepper herself had barely noticed.

Her thumb danced across her phone, shifting between columns of text, images and Google Maps, checking each in turn once again, just like she had done a hundred times before. Her fingers suddenly hesitated upon the screen. Her breath was stolen, but not by the breeze.

*What if this didn't work?*

What if all this was one sad joke? A lie concocted by heartless bastards on the internet, convincing the desperate that following ley lines and whispering nonsense was a good use of a Friday night.

Even worse – what if it *did*?

What if by some goddamn miracle it all turned out to be real?

Pepper was unsure what outcome terrified her more.

She hated the quiet in her own head. It left too much space for doubt to take advantage.

Following the map, she turned down a side street slick with wet, where the amber glow of streetlights faltered and the storm drains had been suffocated by rubbish. She walked alone, cautious, coat collar drawn high, trying to shrink into the dark.

Opposite the occasional kebab shop and gloomy bar

was the corpse of a discarded factory. Crumbling fences around the car park bowed inwards like tired ribs. Layers of graffiti had faded to coloured stains. Nature had begun its reclamation years ago, pulling down obstructions with ivy, and thrusting saplings through the smallest cracks in tarmac. It was the kind of place that never gets rebuilt or put out of its misery by being torn down. It was and would forever be communally ignored.

Pepper's fingers drifted to the gold locket around her neck, rubbing it between thumb and forefinger. The chain had tangled twice today, snagged on her collar, like it didn't want her to come here. Or maybe it just knew what waited on the other side.

This was it. This was it!

*It was here.*

She looked about herself. The street was still moving, quietly alive in the way cities get after midnight – never silent, just slow and tired. Two men smoked outside a minicab office, politely arguing about football. No one looked her way.

But there was something; of that, Pepper was sure. The wind unnaturally slowed itself on approach, fighting some unseen resistance, before racing onwards. But only here and here alone.

And she knew it was time.

The fence was slanted wooden panels, fractured in many places. Beyond it: silence. Not quiet. Silence. The kind that feels horribly deliberate.

Everything pointed to this being the place. All the clues, the cryptic comments and anonymous prodding in certain directions was enough, but among the faded symbols spray painted on the road by a utility company, was something different. Geometric and unique. And it did not belong.

There was no doubt it was a marker. *The* marker.

'I must be mad,' she whispered under her breath, but madness felt easier to embrace than despair.

The gold locket skimmed Pepper's fingertips one last time before being enclosed in a fist. The jewellery was a crucial component of the job in hand. It had to be old. It had to be important. For the woman, it couldn't have been any more treasured.

She closed her eyes and repeated the words she had rehearsed dozens of times. But when Pepper spoke them, they didn't sound like magic. They sounded almost like begging.

And when she opened her eyes . . . nothing.

Nothing had changed. The run-down factory still loomed in the darkness, inconvenienced by slipped piles of debris from multiple collapses. It was simply abandoned. Just like Pepper's last hope.

She scrunched up her eyes in disbelief. Of course, it was bullshit. Of course it was! How could *any* of it be real? Was she actually insane? Why had she bought into this ridiculous fantasy that others had been feeding her?

Behind her, a delivery van honked at a teenager on a bike who crossed dangerously close, causing her to look over her shoulder. When they had finished exchanging hand gestures, Pepper rubbed at her face as she turned back.

And among the dark obstructions of her fingers were cracks to the outside. Past that were subtle happenings, like catching movement from the corner of your eyes and turning to find nothing there. The broken yard shimmered. The air grew denser with the introduction of spice and smoke. Pepper lowered her hands slowly as warm orange flares of light emanated above the ground, painting trails in the deserted space. No, not deserted, not anymore. The lights illuminated brick paths, paths that sported small tents and wooden stalls, some with white and red canvas tops, matching stretching strings of bunting. Tables, cages, crates – all bloomed into existence. Then, obstructing some of the paths, huge fabric canopies of tents shifting into view, here, there, with signage and . . . people.

Individuals chatted, haggled loudly with vendors, laughed and cheered, while others stood sentry, dressed in striking suits with elements Pepper couldn't quite discern. The delicate singing of someone caught the breeze that had now returned.

But the ordinary world behind just didn't care. The city continued its routine regardless. Laughter bubbled from a couple, private and carefree. A man barked into his phone across the road. Someone swore as they decorated the pavement with half a kebab. And not a single one who passed Pepper paid the slightest bit of notice to the grand spectacle she gawked at.

The factory yard, once lifeless, had been transformed into a festival filled with the sounds of music and excited chatter.

No, not a festival.

Pepper knew exactly what this was. And she could scarcely believe it.

Holy shit.

It was real.

*The Night Market was actually real.*

# Chapter Two

## The Night Market

The Night Market was real.

It hadn't been imagined, nor was it the fantasy of internet lunatics. All Pepper had needed was its location and the means to perceive it, both provided by her anonymous benefactor. But revealing the Night Market was one thing. Getting inside was another matter.

The sentries were on the lookout for troublemakers. People like her, most likely. Some mingled with the patrons, eyes constantly sweeping, while others stood guard at key points, suspicion etched on their faces. Getting in through the front was out of the question.

There had to be another way.

She paced the edge of the fence, boots crunching on loose grit, drenched in shadow. The dilapidated panelling worked in her favour, sporting points where the wood had simply dissolved.

There. Low to the ground, torn open like something had forced its way through from the other side. She crouched and looked about. No one was watching. Headlights from a van flashed past from the road behind her. Someone yelled something she couldn't make out. Normal city noise. It was just an ordinary night. For everybody else, maybe.

The hole wasn't large, but enough for someone determined. Pepper exhaled and dropped to her hands and knees, pushing through. Her coat snagged on a nail, tugging like the city itself had second thoughts about letting her go and had to be convinced.

She emerged from the other side of the fence behind a sagging tent, hands scuffed, coat dirtied. Shadows pressed in close, the smells of smoke and wet brick prominent. The street sounds had faded as if someone had turned the volume down, replaced with the chatter of those passing and the jangle of wind chimes.

The Night Market lay before her like a dream taking shape. Awnings fluttered over narrow walkways. Lamps glowed in colours that didn't exist during the day. Stalls stood crooked and leaning, as if drunk from attention.

For a few minutes she just watched, hidden in the dark between guy ropes and shadow, spying on its patrons, fighting the rising unease. Because to the common eye, they seemed . . . normal. But if Pepper didn't know what she did, she wouldn't have noticed the finer details that sent the hair on her neck to rise. The attire was largely casual but chic; however, a good number made statements in striking silver suits, tailored dress coats or elegant flowing gowns. Their gold and platinum jewellery shimmered, catching the light from the candles and lamps. But it was the little details that put Pepper on edge. Despite appearances, the eyes were a touch too sharp, smiles too wide. Just like she had been warned.

She knew exactly what they were. And was under no doubt that the Night Market belonged to them. And God help her should she be caught.

She brushed debris from her coat and tugged the collar

higher – this time not for the cold, but for courage. Pepper stepped out slowly, careful not to draw attention, and merged with the quiet, casual pace of those around her. Keep your head down, she told herself. Look like you belong.

Signage, some bright and colourful, others peeling and dulled, announced trade names such as MALECYST & FAMILY, HAWKINSONS TRADE CO and PAN'S CABINET OF CURIOSITIES. Some bragged about being the finest purveyors of something, but what of, Pepper had difficulty in determining. She let her eyes skim the tables in passing. Plenty on offer just looked like junk. Jars of undeclared fluid were bound with chains. Braids of what looked like hair wrapped into circlets. Various bones laid out in order of length like surgical tools. Bronze statues of animals, and things that resembled animals but were unnatural enough to defy classification. Many stalls were promoting smoky-glassed bottles, from stacked crates of the things to gaudy, gold-sealed affairs much smaller in size with somewhat concerning names like PIRATE'S REGRETS, LOOSE LIPS and GENERATIONAL WELSH.

But the further she went on, the more she realised that every stall lacked any sort of price list. No matter. Whatever the potential cost of the objects she saw, she needed something infinitely more valuable: information.

She navigated her way to one of the stalls that seemed the most comfortable to approach, whose wares were less morbid. Just bundles of neatly wrapped cloth. Hanging crests and emblems upon wooden mounts. A few racks of those small coppery bottles tied at the neck with dangling lengths of ribbon. The stallholder, a woman old enough that her wrinkles seemed carved rather than formed, caught sight of Pepper and offered a smile with an incomplete set of teeth. She wrung her creased hands together, rubbing at the knuckles.

'Hello,' Pepper said. The smile she returned was genuine. The confidence wasn't.

'Good evening!' the stallholder chirped. 'Whatever takes your fancy, I'm sure you'll find it here. Got good silks if you need that special oomph in your work. If you're unsure as to what to go for, I recommend the Monk's Wine. Sublime flavour. He was drunk when it was taken.'

The words pressed a dagger of ice against Pepper's spine to unleash a shudder, but she endured, looking casually over what was on offer.

'Sounds wonderful. Maybe some other time,' she said lightly. 'I'm after something . . . special. Don't know if you have it?'

'I'm listening.'

'I heard it can be found here, the, uh . . . the Eternal Rose, they call it.'

Pepper tried her best to act nonchalant, perusing the stock as if she was undecided. Her eyes flashed back to the stallholder after scanning a row of bottles with brown frosted glass. In fact, they were all terracotta in colour, apart from the neck. For just beneath the wax-coated stoppers, Pepper could determine there were flashes of clear glass, lending to the thought that it was the contents that gave the bottle its colour. The deep rust-red tinge . . .

'The Rose?' The stallholder froze, then exploded into a cackle sharp enough to turn a few heads. She dabbed at the corners of her eyes with thin fingers, then leaned upon the wood. 'Oh my, don't be absurd. If I had it, do you think I would be running a ratty stall in *this* dump? I mean—' She cut herself off before her mouth extended into a knowing smile. 'Ohhhh. *Ohhhhhhh!*'

Pepper glanced around. The dagger sank in, chilling the blood.

'Ohh, I *seeeeeeee*' – the old woman wagged a bony finger – 'you shouldn't *be* here. And you know you shouldn't, hmm?'

Pepper straightened in alarm. 'What do you—'

'You're not fooling me. You're out of place, and you, you *know* this. You have to tell me, dear, I'm begging to know' – she leaned even closer, hushing her voice – 'how did you even get *in*?'

'I don't know what you—'

'I'm over four hundred years old, y'know? I've had a lot of people try to pull the wool over my eyes, and you're no good of a liar, dear. You don't share that. You've got kind eyes. Fading, sure, but still kind. So, I can see right through you.'

The dagger twisted. It was not gentle. Pepper's breath faltered. Eyes became wet.

'Ah-ah. Don't run,' the woman warned. Her voice dropped. 'Stay where you are. You bolt now, and it won't be me you need to worry about. It'll be *them*. Slowly . . . look left. Toward the gate.'

Pepper did.

A crimson-suited sentry moved slowly through the crowd, eyes unblinking. Another loitered at the gate, arms folded, head scanning the crowd like a lighthouse. They didn't speak. They didn't have to.

Her heart pounded so hard it blurred her hearing.

'That's trouble,' the stallholder said quietly. 'And those, the Enforcers, they're here for people like you. The uninvited. The unlucky. You know what they are, right?'

'. . . Yeah.'

'What we *all* are?'

'. . . Yeah.'

The woman's voice softened, but her smile didn't. 'What *I* am?'

Pepper turned back to face her, swallowing hard. She nodded.

'And if you were one of us, you wouldn't be asking about the Eternal Rose. Everybody knows where that's going to be on a night like this. And that alone is a big giveaway. See that large tent over there?' She looked down the path to where lights congregated around huge, erected strips of red and black. Bodies were swarming around the outside. 'You'll find the Rose there. Being auctioned to better people than myself. Soon, actually, if you want to catch it. And this time, be careful who you speak to.'

Pepper's throat tightened. 'Why are you—'

'Helping?' The woman shrugged. 'You seem decent. I've seen decent before. Doesn't usually last long around here. A young thing like you don't want to be mixed up in all this. Not that it's my business.' The woman's tone dropped into something quieter, almost kind. 'Take my advice. Go back to where you came from. Forget all this and hold on to that life of yours. Because whatever you're thinking of needing the Rose for . . . it can't possibly be worth the hassle.'

'I can't,' Pepper replied. 'I need it.'

'I'm sure you do. I had a feeling you would say something like that.' The woman sighed. 'But needing something doesn't mean you get to have it. Especially something as valuable as *that*. Make no mistake, the one who walks away with the Rose tonight? They won't be the kind that begs. Or sneaks. They'll be the kind that *takes*, and stares right in your face while knowing full well you can't stop them. So, whatever your intentions, you need to think long and hard as to if you want to upset people like that.'

Pepper shivered. The wind wasn't any colder, but it suddenly felt like she was standing naked in it.

# Chapter Three

## The Auction

Pepper followed the swell of bodies until the tent came into view.

If it could still be called a tent.

The main structure loomed like a cathedral above the surrounding stalls. Its black-and-reds shimmered faintly as it caught the lantern light in a way that suggested that something else held it all together, not just wooden supports and canvas. Reinforced ropes anchored the thing like a ship upon a stormy sea. It didn't flap or sway in the breeze. It breathed.

Around it, a crowd had gathered, hundreds strong. A crowd that Pepper kept to the edge of, slipping into the gaps between taller figures, trying not to draw attention. Her coat was still dirty from crawling through the fence, but no one seemed to notice. Or care. Either was good. She inched forward through the standing audience until she found a patch near the side that gave her a partial view into the main tent.

Inside, the ground was set with black-stone tiles that glimmered like polished obsidian. Candles floated in tall iron candelabras, their flames steady despite the open air. At the centre of the space was a square, unmarked, but clear in its intention. At each corner of this invisible stage sat a single chair.

Chair wasn't the correct description, not really. Throne, perhaps. Carved from ancient wood and cast from metals that caught the light in uncomfortable ways, each faced inward. Their occupants – three men and a woman – made small talk to one another while flanked by a handful of unidentified individuals. Security most probably, though not all, not by how they sat, how they moved, what they wore. Some looked like they would be at home in a Quentin Tarantino movie. Others, more a church, draped in vestments of an unrecognisable religion.

Pepper, who knew nothing of their reputations, could feel it. The pull of power. The weight of it. Every exchange between them was a statement of bloodline, wealth, and most importantly, respect. The kind that was earned with fear.

An elderly gentleman in the centre waved his hands about expressively before a standing microphone, wearing robes of purple decorated with feathers that shifted in colour from lavenders to fire shades at the slightest turn. A ripple of applause moved through the audience, compelling Pepper to join in. Somewhere, a bell rang, low and deep.

Pepper swallowed, trying not to feel small. She shifted her weight, peering through the shoulders of those in front of her, careful not to press too close to anyone who might notice.

'Thank you, everyone, for your patience, and to our bidders, for your generosity. What an evening we have had already.' He bowed before extending a hand toward the only woman seated. 'Before we reveal the last item, I would like to introduce the sponsor of tonight's wonderful event: *Lady Concetta Cavendish*. Applause, please.'

The lights in the auction tent dimmed slightly, shifting the focus from the stage to the tall woman who rose and glided toward its centre.

The auctioneer stepped back without a word. He knew better.

Concetta Cavendish didn't require an introduction so much as acknowledgement. Dressed in a sweeping gown of white silk with a deep emerald sheen that caught the light like beetle wings, she moved with queenly grace. Her silver hair was sculpted into a chignon, and heavy gold earrings framed a face that spoke of years spent holding power and holding it well.

When she presented herself before the microphone, she raised one elegant hand in a soft, theatrical wave.

'Thank you, thank you,' she said warmly, her voice smooth and assured, placing her fingers upon the microphone stand, a drink of red in the other. 'Tonight is our ninety-third Night Market. Ninety-third. What an incredible number. When the very idea of the Night Market was proposed, it was said that it would never work. Look at you all. Evidence that convention can be defied. As it should be.'

A murmur moved through the tent. Some looked at one another. Others just smiled.

'Each and every time I have the privilege of arranging a Night Market, it warms my heart. The gratitude I feel never goes away,' Concetta continued. 'Some of my fondest memories have been walking these stalls over the decades, seeing many of you go from strength to strength in your enterprises. I may have even hired a few of you in light of that. The Night Market is home to talent of no equal. Providers of no comparison.'

A few chuckles rose from the crowd.

'You know what it's like out there,' she said, her tone turning contemplative. 'We don't exactly have the opportunity to be open about our culture, our traditions. So, the Night Market . . . is something special. A place where, no matter our backgrounds, our successions or birthplace, we can mingle in safety. And mutual respect.'

She paused.

'A most unique opportunity for our people in trying times.'

A few bodies away, Pepper caught someone mumble.

*'How the fuck does she know what it's like in the real world? Any of 'em?'*

And while some in the vicinity chuckled in agreement, a handful turned and fired threatening glares.

'So,' Concetta declared with a smile, 'our heartfelt thanks to every trader, business owner and the dedicated people working tirelessly behind the scenes who keep things running – my husband especially.'

She turned slightly, raising her glass in his direction. A thin man with streaks of grey through his slick-backed hair and dressed in an understated navy suit, lifted his glass in return. And when he sipped from it, Pepper found herself feeling peculiarly uneasy for a reason she couldn't determine . . .

'And all those from each family here who provide their manpower to ensure everyone's safety. A round of applause for them, if you please.'

The crowd responded with polite, genuine clapping. Even the more jaded attendees offered a few appreciative taps.

'And of course,' Concetta said, lowering her voice

slightly as the clapping faded, 'to every single one of you in attendance.'

The quiet returned, this time softer, more focused. She raised her glass, but did not drink its contents. A beat of silence. Not awkward. Just *held*. Then she smiled again, this time smaller, and offered the microphone back to the auctioneer. No flourish. No bow. She didn't need one.

'Ladies and gentlemen. It is time for tonight's main event!' The auctioneer took hold of the microphone with energy and snapped his fingers.

From behind the velvet curtains, two attendants emerged, each dressed in muted grey robes. They moved in perfect sync, carrying between them a narrow box of polished oak. The grain shimmered faintly under the lights, with unusual symbols burnt into its surface. They placed it on the raised plinth with care.

One attendant reached into his coat and produced a silver key, long and notched with teeth in strange, uneven shapes. The other untied the thick blue rope wound around the chest like a belt. As the rope fell away and the key turned, everyone in attendance seemed to lean forward. So much so that Pepper stumbled, under the impression she would be knocked down.

'It is my privilege tonight to present a piece whose reputation precedes it by centuries. One of the most fascinating, and indeed elusive, of recorded Relics. This,' he purred as the velvet cloth was drawn back, revealing the object in its glass casing, 'is *Rosam Crucis*, though most know it commonly as *the Eternal Rose*.'

Pepper's heart immediately launched itself into her mouth at the name. *This was it!*

Inside the box, nested in black velvet and secured by delicate clasps, was a glass case, faintly fogged from the inside.

At first glance, it didn't look like much. A wilted, brownish bloom, folded in on itself like a cabbage left too long in the sun. But the longer one looked, the more it revealed. Veins of opal shimmered beneath its outer leaves, pulsing with a shifting, pearlescent hue that couldn't be described as colour alone. It leaked light through as though bruised.

The attendants raised the case slowly, reverently, and turned it toward each corner of the tent where the players in this game were readying to make their move.

'First recorded in the *Alnwick Fragments* of eleven thirteen, it is believed to have been cultivated by a forgotten sect of spiritualists during the reign of Henry the First. It disappeared following the Norse-backed raid of the North, vanishing after the skirmish at Brinklow Hollow. For nearly seven hundred years, it was little more than a rumour. Then, in the nineteenth century, it began to surface again. Briefly. It changed hands quietly, and not always peacefully. It reappeared in France, its last confirmed private owner, a Mister Leon Carter, was shot dead over a misplayed hand in a Marseille card house. The assailant then fled to England with the Relic and vanished. For most of the twentieth century, it passed through one family line, their names unknown. That is, until now.'

He paused, letting the quiet swell again. The Rose was carefully returned to its velvet cradle, the case resealed, and the lid closed with a soft, final thud.

'Legend claims the Rose possesses peculiar, some say spiritual, healing properties. It is said to cure any affliction of flesh or spirit, be it illness, affliction or curse, regardless of origin or age. A bold claim, of course. And as with most myth, the truth cannot be validated – at this time. But as to how factual it may be . . .' He smiled faintly. 'I leave that for you all to decide.'

He let the silence stretch as murmurs rose from the back.

'*The Eternal Rose, ladies and gentlemen!* Whole. Undamaged. And for the *first time*, available for possession. Whether you wish to acquire it, or simply witness its presence, you are all part of something historic.' He gave a shallow bow, prompting another ripple of applause. 'We open the bidding at fifty thousand. And . . . begin.'

The first bid came quickly. Then another. No gavel. No call-and-response. Just gestures. Numbers traded like secrets between the elite in their chairs, and only them. This was clearly a spectator sport for everybody else.

From the left, a nod. From the right, a flick of a ringed finger. The numbers climbed rapidly. These weren't people guessing. These were players. For those who never had the intention of owning the Eternal Rose, they would ensure its price to be substantial. That was all part of the game.

Concetta sat with perfect composure, her expression unreadable. When she finally leaned sideways to address one of her rivals, her voice carried just far enough.

'Little too rich for your tastes, Dominic?'

The man she addressed, slightly portly with an excitable beard, dressed by old money, shook as he snorted.

'I prefer value over spectacle,' he replied. 'Besides, I'd never dream of spoiling your fun.'

'That's very considerate of you. Possibly the most sensible thing an Ode has ever done,' Concetta returned without malice, swirling the crimson liquid in her glass with idle grace. It was met with good humour.

The tension escalated again. Bids rose further. Significantly. Then, silence. Until Concetta spoke confidently again.

'Seven hundred and ninety-two.'

A pause followed. Pepper eyed each of the bidders in

turn. None seemed to have the stomach to continue. The auctioneer nodded once, eyes flicking briefly across the tent to confirm what everyone already knew.

'Final offer accepted,' he said. '*Seven hundred souls pledged, ninety-two years of bound service.* Going once. Going twice . . .'

No objection.

'*Sold!* The winning recipient of the Eternal Rose: Lady Cavendish. Congratulations.'

A burst of restrained applause followed.

Concetta didn't rise. She merely lifted her glass. Not in thanks, but in acknowledgement. This had never been a competition. Just confirmation.

Two black-suited Enforcers stepped forward from beside the winner in silence. They lifted the chest between them and moved towards an exit.

Pepper was moving too.

The crowd dispersed slowly, murmuring in tones that ranged from amusement to envy. Pepper slid between the bodies, keeping her steps measured and unremarkable. She left her fear behind, because if she didn't do this, and she didn't do it now, then the whole affair would have been a waste. There wasn't time to think. Not to worry. Too much was at stake.

The Enforcers didn't rush. That made it easier.

They took the chest through the tent's side flap, down one of several corridors extending from the main event space, and out into the Market itself. Pepper trailed behind, careful to keep a distance, stepping behind hanging fabric. She kept her head low and her ears open.

They moved to the fringe of the Market, toward a shell of a building that had been repurposed for the evening, flanked by rusted scaffolding and a crooked set of stairs. A deeply weathered steel door, fitted with massive strap hinges, served as its entrance. Everyone on the route stepped aside.

The two Enforcers stepped inside. When they came out, one took point at the door. He didn't look particularly imposing in his body language, leaning against the doorway and paying attention to those passing without urgency.

Pepper stepped behind some tents into long grass and shadow and waited.

Five minutes passed. Then ten.

No one else entered. No one left. Just the lone guard now posted outside, arms folded, attention loose. He was young. Bored. Clearly not expecting trouble. But there was a clear presence about him, the way he shifted his eyes, the unreadable expression on his face. Undiscernible as it was, it was a quality enough to be noticed.

Pepper exhaled and moved.

She shifted around the perimeter of the building, keeping low behind shattered crates and draped tarpaulin. The place looked dead from the outside, just more forgotten infrastructure folded into the edge of the Market. But up close, she spotted it: a grimy old staff toilet block bolted onto the side, its paint flaking, one of its windows shattered.

Perfect.

Pepper checked once more. No one in sight. She climbed atop a rusted bin, braced her knee against the piping, and hoisted herself up. The window was barely wider than her shoulders. Her coat tore. She gritted her teeth, twisted sideways, and shoved. A rogue blade of glass scored across her hand, causing a cut deep enough to bleed. She withheld a wince and tumbled through with a grunt, landing squarely on the lid of a toilet seat.

Plastic creaked. She gripped her injury tightly until the sting numbed enough for her to continue. It wasn't a graceful entrance. But not loud, either. The smell of damp and brick was an assault on the senses.

She slid down and eased the stall door open, where the air was cold and still.

The cubicle opened into a narrow washroom, its tiled floor cracked, a corner invaded by rampant black mould. A row of sinks sagged beneath a vandalised mirror; the remaining glass blackened with age. One tap dripped in slow, hollow intervals, the sound too loud in the silence.

Pepper crossed the room carefully with careful steps, listening out for any signs of life.

The door at the far end hung ajar.

Beyond it, somewhere behind an old conveyor belt, a single lamp buzzed above metal tables. Crumbling plaster and brick still sported graffiti. She pressed forward, stepping quietly out onto the factory floor.

The space opened wider than she'd expected; the ceiling lost in a lattice of steel beams and shadow. The lone lamp cast a thin pool of light across the concrete, leaving the rest of the building to brood in darkness. Pitted concrete all but silenced her footsteps, though the faint crunch of loose stones occasionally betrayed her. The air reeked of oil and dust, as though the decaying machines had only recently fallen silent. Along one wall, a defiant window had finally given way, and brambles were taking their time spilling through the broken frame, inching their claim across the interior.

Pepper kept to the margins, skirting a line of abandoned pallets and rusting drums, until she knew there was no danger. Then she approached the tables.

The chest might have been the centrepiece, but it wasn't alone.

To the left, several other crates and containers were neatly stacked, some locked, others sealed with thick wax and cords knotted in ritual fashion. One of them was humming faintly, like it held something alive and annoyed. Another gave off the faint smell of scorched grass.

A holding area, she presumed. A halfway place for auctioned items before they were escorted to their ultimate destinations. Everything expensive, dangerous or best kept unboxed had been stored here temporarily.

And yet, there was hardly any security. She expected at least a few cameras or something to that effect. Wasn't all this terribly expensive? Rare, wasn't that the word that was used? Why with such high-value items here, did they just put a single bored-looking Enforcer on the door? Why not an army of them? This wasn't right. It had to be a trap, surely. Or the other possibility was that they didn't expect anyone to be stupid enough to pull this kind of stunt.

Which, in retrospect, was a *terrifying* prospect.

The chest sat like it owned the space. Heavy. Waiting.

She approached carefully. Her fingers itched for the lid. The lock stared up at her, complex and ancient. No key. No time. Luckily a nearby workbench retained some dust-covered tools, including a battered chisel. She took it in hand and slipped the tip into the crease to make the wood yawn with effort. A couple of pushes and the lid began to give, but every time she expected the latch to break away, it pulled back on her tool and returned to a close. She tried again and again. *Come on.* She didn't have time for this!

A door clattered shut somewhere nearby. But just before it did so, a hand closed over her wrist, not harshly. Just firmly. Its owner having crossed the darkness in those few seconds. And quietly too.

Pepper turned sharply, eyes wide.

A figure stood half shadowed behind her, close enough to hear her breath catch.

The young Enforcer, who, just minutes before, was positioned at the door outside, loomed over her. He looked at her the way someone might regard a stray animal that had wandered into the wrong garden, glaring somewhat beneath a shock of trim black hair.

Pepper hadn't the voice to speak. He did.

'*What do you think you're doing?*' he demanded.

# Chapter Four

## Run Like Hell

There was no option. No time. The chisel slipped free from between the wood and skimmed in an arc between them, slipping out of her hand like it wanted no part of what came next. In doing so, the Enforcer flinched. Just a heartbeat. Just enough.

She yanked her wrist free, heart hammering like it wanted out of her ribs. She didn't look back. Couldn't. Just ran. Her boots scrambled over broken tile and old grit, every step exploding in a crunch, her breath sharp and loud in her ears. Behind her, shelves rattled as she knocked into them, tools and jars and unidentifiable things clattering to the ground. She didn't stop to see if he'd fallen behind. She already knew he hadn't. *She could hear him.*

The factory seemed to close in on her, walls narrowing with every turn, shadows leaping like hands trying to catch her coat. She vaulted the workbench, slipped on loose plaster, shoulder barged the toilet door open, and didn't think. Just climbed. She scrambled out the window, damn the glass, crashing down upon the bin and sending both toppling over.

It would buy her some time. There was no way he was getting through that. All she could do was run like hell.

She crashed through clusters of people, splitting conversations. One woman shrieked as Pepper nearly bowled her over. A man swore violently and stumbled against a stall, sending its wares toppling everywhere. Behind her, the Enforcer came. No longer calm, no longer quiet. He didn't push through the crowd. He cut through it like a blade. People scattered at the sight of him.

She raced through the black night, trails of lamplight streaking past like car headlights, skimming between four men whose drinks exploded as she powered on between. A trip on one of their shoes almost sent her tumbling, but she fought on, regaining her balance. Profanity spewed behind her and the group had burst into sprints to try to intercept her. She had to move faster, run faster, *fucking run!* Her legs pumped and she could feel them failing already, becoming numb with the shock of the speed demanded of them. Her throat burned raw, her chest like glass being stepped on. She was running blind now, not smart, just desperate.

The group gave chase, slipping between tents and signs like they'd done it a thousand times before, with the Enforcer at the back of the pack. Pepper ran harder, grunting with every stride, vision tunnelling. Fire burned in her throat and tears wetted her eyes in desperation. But she was here! Her escape! *She was so close now!* With a surge of power, she sharply turned into where the night congregated behind a line of tents, skipping over a guideline. And there! There in the gloom was the gap in the fence! She could see it, she could reach it, she could—

Pepper spun sideways, her feet skidding over slick grass beneath her. She was yanked aside and crashed back-first into the fencing, causing a shriek of alarm.

One of the men tossed his head back, snorting in delight, a cigarette still dangling from his lips. He had sharp bleach-blond hair, the kind that looked like it had been styled with a knife. His leather jacket was a patchwork of spikes, torn slogans and safety pins. His grin didn't reach his eyes.

'Oh, that was a fucking chase, darling.' He took a deep drag on his smoke and blasted haze from his nostrils. His lackeys flanked behind, just as unimpressed. 'Well rude to bang into folk. Spill my fucking *drink*. Not even a sorry from ya. Why you running, huh? Why would you be doing that?'

He leered, showing his teeth, his canines unusually long, making him look like a—

She lashed out to catch him across the face, but it was anticipated and restrained at the wrist. He put his attention on the cut that had scored her skin with an unusual amount of interest before the limb was tossed away.

'You know what I'm thinking, girlie?' He shot out a hand and pinched her cheeks together, voice thick with menace. 'I think you need us to teach you some *manners*.'

Pepper felt her lips quiver as her eyes shot between all four of them, trying to summon the words to say something, anything. Until, silhouetted from the lamplight of the paths, four became five, and the new shadow stretched over them all. The grip on Pepper slipped away.

*The Enforcer.*

Initially his attention fell on Pepper, who had instinctively held her breath, feeling almightily small. She watched his cold eyes shift to each of the pursuers in turn and wrinkle his fresh-featured face.

'I'll take it from here, fellas. She's mine,' he coldly demanded, striding towards her.

'What? Just like that? I don't think you get to spoil our fun. Piss off.'

The Enforcer didn't blink as he addressed the punk in the middle.

'You ain't so fresh to be unfamiliar with Market Law, and you know what happens to those who break it. So, I'll repeat myself. This one is mine.' He took a bold step forward, scowling. 'Get. The hell. Away from her.'

The punk exploded in laughter. He released Pepper's face, then plucked the cigarette away and wagged it at the interruption.

'The balls on this! Fucking Enforcers, you're all the same. Throwing your weight around to everyone else. Acting all high. We got here first. Just because you get paid to forget the chase doesn't mean we haven't.'

Pepper felt the fence press against her shoulders, but she wasn't the only one being cautious. One of the gang had already taken a tentative step back. He wasn't as bold. In fact, his eyes had widened at the Enforcer's appearance, and a tremor was running through his fingers.

'Mate, don't, that's—'

'What, 'cause he's a Family Man? Families have forgotten what life's like down in the streets! They wouldn't last a minute without their money. Don't care what fucking Family *you're* under. Silk shirt, fancy suit like that makes you just the one thing: a lapdog. No. Worse than a lapdog, 'cause at least a dog's got fuckin' *teeth*. So, I told you what we were doing, smart guy. We're having a little *fun* with this one. Eff. Yuu. Enn.' He took a bold step ahead and punctuated the last words with a pair of firm, disrespectful prods to the Enforcer's chest. 'With an emphasis on the *eff yuu*.'

'You don't want to do that,' the Enforcer warned.

'No, I suppose I don't.' He pulled the cigarette free and fired a cloud into the Enforcer's stony face. 'But I'm gonna do it, anyway.' Before outrageously grinding the cigarette to a stub on the lapel of the Enforcer's pristine and obviously expensive suit jacket.

The kick was quick, direct and to the gut, its speed catching him off-guard, so the punk flew onto his back. The Enforcer raised his guard, ready for his friends to intervene. Wisely, they didn't. The punk leaped up and threw a series of jabs, all of them crashing against the forearms like the tide. When open, the Enforcer landed a right cross straight over the jaw – enough to make the point to stop, but not enough to drop him for good. Which may have been a mistake because the next thing Pepper knew, the deafening snap of a switchblade came from nowhere and metal sailed this way and that. And while the Enforcer did a fine job of blocking each attempt of the blade meeting his chest, or the face, the punk's improvisation of driving it deep into his shoulder unexpectedly caught him. The knife was twisted and left in, its owner holding his hands out in triumph, almightily proud of his achievement.

It didn't last long.

Pepper saw it. Saw the blade sink deep into the Enforcer's shoulder, almost to the hilt, undoubtably hitting bone. Pain may have washed over his face, but he didn't cry out. And it didn't last long. Confidently, and to the punk's confusion, he yanked it free. And something else pulled free with it.

Not blood. Darkness.

'I warned you,' the Enforcer snarled, his voice sounding as if it was joined by another, deeper, guttural companion.

Blackness flooded through the wound, spreading like ink in water. It crawled over his skin, slipping into the seams of his clothes, down his neck, over his hands. His eyes, once blue, burned gold. Not bright. *Wrong*.

'Oh my God,' someone whispered. 'It's *him*.'

The Enforcer became a swelling shadow. His form ballooned, bones stretching, joints cracking. His pitch form was so dense that it seemingly sucked in the lamplight from around them.

And then, the chaos began.

The entity struck the mouthy one with a blow that launched him skyward, crashing through a canopy. One of his friends tried their luck but vanished beneath a sweep of a huge pitch arm. It snagged on tent canvas and ripped the entire thing from its position, owner and all, scattering them into the air. Glass shattered. Wood scraped. The screams began.

Someone crumpled near Pepper, contorted like a stringless puppet.

As the Market erupted into mayhem, it jerked its head to Pepper, who had begun to inch along to the fence in the hope of going unnoticed. And when the fierce gold eyes fell on her, she ran. Without the energy and strength to fuel her escape, adrenaline would have to do.

The Market blurred around her, a mess of fluttering banners and smoke-smudged lights, bodies scrambling to get clear. She joined the flood, all jostling for escape, most running for the entrance. A stall exploded in her peripheral vision as it was charged through by whatever the Enforcer had become. Wood and bottles and bone charms and blood-smeared glass scattered into the air like birds taking flight. Her boots slipped on the cobbles. The shrieks melted into a song of terror.

She saw a splash of colour ahead, gaudy signage promoting something undetermined, only to see a figure hurtle through the air, buckle the metal in half and collapse on the path before her. A second, or what remained of one, was launched into a concession stand. His head dangled limp over the counter, wrong at the neck.

*Don't look. Don't stop. Run.*

She pushed forward. Her legs were fire, quickly reducing to embers.

Enforcers on the path ahead of her frantically ran past, calling to one another. '*Control him!*' someone barked behind her. '*Laik! It's me! Stop! Get yourself und—*'

The ground shook again. A stall collapsed into itself in a spray of shattered bottles and smoke. Something screeched. Not human. Too close.

And then the world tipped sideways.

Something hit her. Hard.

She flew.

Tumbled.

The night sky spun. Her shoulder struck dirt. Then timber. Then her back slammed flat, knocking the breath clean out of her. Debris rained down. Canvas, ropes, cracked frames. A tent folded in on her like a dying animal. She gasped, but no sound came.

Her legs were pinned.

Panic rose, sharp and immediate, washing everything else out of her head. She clawed at the wreckage. Useless. Every movement sent a jolt of pain screaming up her thigh.

She cowered as the thick canvas was furiously hauled aside, the cries of fear having mostly faded, leaving a dangerous silence.

Victorious, the creature loomed over her. Shadow poured off it like raging steam. Its face, or the shifting thing that passed for one, drew closer, with flaming gold stars for eyes that did not blink, harbouring nothing but *intent*. She couldn't see it breathe, but the heat from its breath stung her face.

It wasn't looking at her.

It was looking *into* her.

Pepper whimpered. Her arms raised reflexively, shielding nothing, instead wrapping around the gold locket at her neck. This was over. The last thing she thought of was *Claire* as she waited for the inevitable. Not words – just the shape of her sister's face, frail and asleep. Her reason for everything. Her reason for this stupid crusade. And if she could, she would apologise, distraught that she was so, *so* close to fulfilling her promise.

And then nothing.

The weight in the air eased.

The shadow above her, astonishingly, began to *drain*. Like spilled ink retreating into the paper. Blackness slid backwards, revealing the person beneath – up sleeves, into skin, across the Enforcer's mouth and under his nails. The monster melted from him like he was rejecting it. Or it was letting go. What remained was the man flushed and troubled, hair matted with wet, sweat travelling over smooth skin. He fell to one knee beside her, gripping the rubble, breathing hard.

Pepper blinked through tears, through grit. Her limbs still refused to move.

He looked down at her, brow furrowed, more confused than angry. As though *she* had done something. As though she had reached inside and tore a part of him free. His voice, when it came, was hoarse. Like rocks sliding together.

'*How did you do that?*' he grunted.

# Part II

# Chapter Five

## In Servitude

*3 months later*

The lift was silent but for the soft hiss of rising air and the groaning pull of machinery that wasn't quite as smooth as the building's glamour suggested. Leroux Tower liked to pretend it was all clean lines and modern sheen, but behind it all, Pepper could still hear the tired bones of the thing. Eighty floors tall and constantly hungry.

She ignored the evening view of the falling city from the window and leaned back against the mirrored wall, phone in hand, thumb hovering above the keyboard. She read and reread the message, letting out a tired exhale.

> v tired go in 2 sleep speak l8r

Above it, the time. 11.01 a.m.
Beneath that one from herself.

> OK. Love you.

11.29 a.m. Unread.

Her fingers danced hesitantly over the screen. She tapped:

How did you sleep?

It joined the others.

10.13 p.m.

She sighed, pocketed the phone, and tried to flatten her reflection in the mirror. She adjusted the collar of her green felt coat. Smoothed her hair after catching a strand out of place. She found herself breathing sharper and closed her eyes to wrestle it back under control. Where she was going, nerves were a liability. She could only pretend so much, and the slightest mistake would doom her in all the ways people didn't speak aloud.

Floor 19 pinged past. Then 21. 27. 34.

She swallowed and watched the numbers tick upwards, each one feeling like another lock clicking into place behind her. She felt her shoulders tense and forced herself to roll them back. She knew her job. Drop the worry. Keep it simple.

She felt the lurch as the lift slowed.

The bell pinged.

Floor 50.

And when the doors slid open, he was there.

The Enforcer from the Night Market.

Only now he wasn't all black shadows and burning eyes. No monstrous second skin. Just the man beneath it – tall, pressed into a dark jacket sharp enough to cut glass, arms folded, face neutral. But the memory of what he had become clung to his presence. He stared at her as if he'd been waiting. Like he always knew exactly when the doors would open.

'You're late,' he said.

'And you're annoying,' Pepper replied, stepping out, stack of manila envelopes under arm.

'Be on time and I won't have reason to be. Or to have to come find you.' He followed along behind. 'Are you going to be much longer?'

'Depends how many of these I've got left,' she muttered, adjusting the bundle in her possession.

The legal floor was vast and almost too quiet – straight lines of glass and polished stone, where whispers carried and footsteps echoed with authority. Panels of frosted glass bore gilt-lettered department names: UTILITIES, NEGOTIATION, ANCESTRY and INFLUENCE. Through the clear sections of glass, Pepper could glimpse tailored figures moving like clockwork, some discussions mundane, others loud and direct to the point of threatening. The Cavendish Family's dealings were all wrapped in glossy civility, but she could feel the predatory undercurrent beneath it all.

A gaunt man pushed along a squeaking trolley of parcels and files between departments, completely ignoring them. The scent of hot toner, polished oak and wash of air conditioning filled the floor. Everything felt deliberate – no clutter, no sound out of place.

'Smile,' the Enforcer beside her said as they walked. By that point Pepper had learned his name was Laik, pronounced exactly like the body of water. It felt oddly fitting, though not for the reasons he probably would have preferred. There was certainly something dark beneath his surface, something difficult to measure, but mostly it just meant she'd spent the better part of their time together resisting the urge to throw stones at him whenever he opened his mouth.

'I am smiling,' she replied flatly.

'You're scowling.'

'I'm nervous.'

'Still? It's been months.'

'Yes. Months *here*. It's enough to put anyone out of sorts.'

He smirked faintly, though the look barely reached his eyes.

'You know,' she continued, glancing through a frosted pane marked LITIGATION AND HUMAN AFFAIRS, 'this isn't exactly what I imagined I'd be doing when I was brought on board. Then again, according to Viola, I'm trusted to handle such sensitive documents after being made a Domestic Affiliate, which she makes a point of saying, *all the bloody time*. Which is *weird*, isn't it? I've only been here a couple of months and already people are put out by how much I'm trusted.' She gave him a glance, one eyebrow raised. 'Why would that be, I wonder?'

'You should be thankful you're here at all,' Laik replied, scanning the corridor ahead with his usual soldier's precision. 'People like *you* shouldn't even be in this building. If anyone knew—'

He cut himself off as a woman in a slim charcoal suit turned the corner, tablet in hand. Pepper nodded courteously as she passed, prompting a returned gesture. Laik showed no such display of respect. Pepper waited until she disappeared into another office, placing a thick envelope on a shiny desk before saying quietly, 'I'm fully aware of the consequences.'

'For both of us.'

'Obviously.'

'Good,' he said, not looking at her. 'Then act like it.'

They stopped at a door labelled REQUISITIONING AND OVERSIGHT. Pepper pressed the call panel, waited for the click of locks, and stepped inside to deliver an envelope to a tall man with silvering hair and a pocket square precise enough to cut. She murmured her pleasantries, received a curt nod, and retreated into the corridor again.

The next office was labelled INFLUENCE. The frosted

glass didn't quite obscure the silhouettes within – elegant figures in hushed debate, one idly stirring something from a jug into his tea that was clearly not milk. Pepper's step lingered a moment, watching, and something about the practised calm of it all unsettled her. She cleared her throat, refastened her smile and made her delivery. Then left.

A soft chime rang down the corridor – an elevator on the far end opening to reveal another worker with a cart of files. Pepper stepped aside, clutching the last envelope to her, a chunky package of paperwork that attempted to fold under its own weight. She rubbed the aching wrist that had been taking most of the stress.

'You know these aren't exactly light. You could have offered to carry them for me.'

'And give up our pretence? Not a chance.'

She shot him a glare, and for just a heartbeat, he gave her a look of acknowledgement. It wasn't kind, exactly, but it was almost human.

They reached the end of the corridor, and she handed off the last of her envelopes to a secretary sitting behind a desk marked AUDITS AND CONTAINMENT. Pepper flexed her wrist as they walked back toward the lift.

'Finally,' she said, blowing a small sigh of relief.

He pressed the lift button. The doors parted to welcome them. He stepped inside, assuming the rigid stance of a stone sentry.

'Come on. We can talk over lunch.'

She followed him in, arms folding, suspicious. 'Why the sudden generosity?'

'You deserve a treat.'

Laik reached out and jabbed a button on the panel, causing a light to pool beneath a finger. When she noticed, Pepper frowned at him.

'Thirty-one is the restaurant,' she pointed out.

'That's correct.'

'It's *free*,' she reminded, as if this fact had somehow escaped him.

'Which is why I'm treating you. You're welcome.'

The lift doors slid closed on her exasperated sigh.

Floor 31 opened into something else entirely – not sterile glass or silent order, but a broad, open restaurant filled with warm light and muted chatter. Booths lined the walls, circular tables occupied the centre, and servers in dark uniforms moved with professional grace. Conversations hummed between the patrons: talk of contracts, acquisitions, negotiations and murder, all delivered with polite attitudes.

They stepped aside as a pair of Enforcers passed them, laughing under their breath about some recent assignment, until they noticed Laik and promptly hushed. Pepper was struck by how everyone here looked immaculate. Flawless hair, flawless skin, perfectly pressed suits.

Someone approached them with an efficient bow, offering a table for two. They followed along, the vast windows overlooking the night's glittering sprawl of the city. Outside, the lights of passing cars and the faint rise of the horizon cast a gentle glow through the glass, the view interrupted only by a man dressed in a tailored charcoal suit with an open collar. His hair was the colour of desert sand, cropped short at the sides but left a little long on top, and there was an easy charm in his smile that didn't quite manage to be convincing. The kind of man who could blend in at a business dinner and break someone's jaw before dessert.

'Evening, Swan,' Pepper greeted, a smile slipping onto her lips. 'How's the arm?'

'Better. Came out of the sling yesterday,' he replied, rolling his shoulder. 'No thanks to your brother. Need me to save you from him?'

'You're sweet. I'll let you know if he gets too much.'

'It was a tap,' Laik said. 'You got caught in the crossfire. You'll get over it. He'll get over it,' he insisted as they continued.

'Not likely!' Swan called after them, returning to his own table as the pair made their way to theirs.

'See?' Laik said. 'Water under the bridge.'

'That's a lot of water,' Pepper murmured.

'Lucky it's a bloody great bridge, then.'

The waiter pulled Pepper's chair out and offered them a pair of leather menus, then stood attentive with a poised smile. 'What can I get for you this evening?'

'Glazed duck breast,' Laik said, glancing at the menu as though he already knew. 'Medium, with plum reduction and saffron potatoes.'

'And for you, miss?'

'Gong Bao chicken and chow mein,' she said, offering the menu back. 'Without the green onions, please.'

'And for drinks?'

'Lemon gin, ice, and a side of Red Garment.' Laik leaned back in his seat, searching about for familiar faces. Swan was eating with other Enforcers, and whatever they were discussing was so funny, it made him roar with laughter.

'And for you, miss?'

'Just a Coke, please.'

'Anything to add?'

'No, thank you.'

The staff didn't react. Didn't blink. Still, Laik watched his colleague a second longer than necessary before turning back. Pepper could sense it, how Laik was always assessing risk, always thinking two moves ahead. He was untrusting, even among his people.

'Gong Bao?' Laik arched a brow as the waiter left. 'Exotic for the likes of you.'

Pepper met his gaze evenly. 'You've never met the likes of me. I'm full of surprises.'

He huffed, half a laugh. 'Yeah, that's what I'm afraid of.'

When the waiter returned with their drinks, Laik poured the miniature bottle into his glass. Its contents elegantly clouded the gin like ink through water. He tapped the last burgundy drops out on the lip of the glass, staining a red trail to their destination.

*Blood.*

Pepper didn't mean to stare as she sipped her Coke. She just always did.

'Did you want some?' he said dryly, knowing the answer.

'Don't be absurd.'

'Then stop staring.'

She traced the curve of condensation on the outside of her glass with her nail.

'It's just . . . difficult to get used to.'

'Fake it, then. Just make sure you're keeping up appearances. I don't want you to get caught out by such an obvious oversight.'

'I know, I know. I always thought you would need, like . . . more of it.'

'Common misconception, and one in your favour: you don't have to pretend to feed on some poor sucker in an alleyway, or whatever you think we do. There's kegs of it behind the bar there. An entire industry even, to provide—'

'*Alright*,' she interrupted snippily, 'I get it.'

'I'm glad you do.'

He raised his glass, and this time she didn't bother

pretending to join him. When he realised that he would be left wanting, he shrugged and leaned back in his chair. For a moment, the pair sat like that. Not enemies. Far from friends. Just two individuals looking out across the city that had been transformed by the night, a city that had decided to throw them together as the collective punchline of some sick joke. When the food came, they barely spoke, the silence sitting between them like an unfinished question while they ate. Until Laik finally became impatient enough to ask it.

'I'm guessing,' he said as he sheared through a slice of meat with his knife, 'you are still pissed at me.'

Pepper's face fell immediately, jabbing at a ball of chicken with a fork so hard that the cutlery went right the way through.

'*You told people that I was your sister . . .*' Her voice sounded pained, though hushed.

'First of all, I saved your ass; let's not forget that little fact. And yes, I did – I didn't have much of a choice, remember?'

'I don't need a stranger pretending to be my sibling. I *have* a sister, thank you very much. And she's a damn sight nicer than you.'

'So you've told me, like, a *million* times. I get it. What did you want me to say?' he hissed. 'Oh, right, I caught this human snooping around with her hands on a *Relic* of all things? How do you think that would have gone? For both of us?' Laik checked around them to make sure they weren't being too loud.

'Badly, obviously.'

'Badly. It's the only way I could get you in here, pulling a few strings, calling in a favour with Mortis. If they didn't believe the commotion was caused by me defending my sister from being attacked, we wouldn't be having this conversation now.'

'It's not like you left anyone alive who could tell different.'

'Sorry for not sharing your sentimental view of the troublemakers who were intent on killing you. But please, tell me what I should have done instead. Be my guest.'

She glared at him, lips pressed into a line, knowing full well there was no comeback. Instead, she retreated to her drink.

'Exactly,' Laik bragged. 'You're *welcome*, by the way. I've got you where you needed to be.'

'Let's not pretend it's just for my benefit,' Pepper added.

'You're right. It's not. So let's touch on that. How goes the planning?' he asked, dropping a slice of duck into his mouth.

'Not well,' Pepper admitted, twirling a collection of noodles together. 'I don't have permission to go to sixty-five and I couldn't blag a convincing excuse. If I made a straight line for it, that'd be far too suspicious.'

'Give it time,' he said. 'Sixty-five might be locked up, but you'll have your moment.'

'Yeah, but I don't *have* time, do I?'

He gave a low hum of amusement, tilting his glass. 'Who knows what wondrous opportunities will come knocking at the door?'

She gave him a look. 'You sound like an idiot.'

'I'm an optimist.'

'A positive idiot, then. You've still not told me why you need the Rose. You know my reasons.'

'What?' Laik looked blankly. 'You think I *like* having a monster inside me?'

Pepper was scraping up the last of the noodles from her plate as Laik's attention went from the flickering city skyline to a figure cutting between the tables and making a beeline toward them. Her blue uniform was sharp, pressed and precisely tailored, accented with a trailing series of flowers from lapel to hem. A pair of thin-framed glasses perched on the bridge of her nose, sharp eyes framed by shoulder-length dark hair. The eyes scanned those seated at their tables. The woman approached with purpose, heels snapping on the tiles.

Laik shifted in his seat.

'Pepper,' the woman said, looking between them. 'There you are.'

She met the woman's gaze whilst finishing off the last of the chicken. 'Here I am.'

'This is where you've been.'

Laik, still reclining in his chair, raised his glass with all the laziness of a man determined to provoke.

'She's on lunch, Viola. Do join us,' he offered, full well knowing the answer.

'We don't take lunch. Not ones of our position,' Viola said, barely flicking her gaze at him. 'You especially should know that.'

'Still on one. Sit.' He nudged the closest chair away from the table with the shove of a foot.

Pepper cleared her throat gently and leaned forward, eyebrows raised.

'Ignore him, he's being . . . him. What can I do for you?'

'Actually, it's what I can do for you,' Viola replied, stepping closer, her voice lowering into something more pointed. 'It has been determined by powers greater than myself that you are to be bestowed with a considerable honour, and I need you to come immediately with me. We have a special task to perform. And promptly.'

'Sounds ominous,' Laik muttered, sucking an ice chip into his mouth and theatrically crunching it.

'Not really. Word has come down that Pepper has been approved for integration for the upper floors. She is going to be formally introduced to the heirs.'

Laik straightened slightly, less out of surprise and more to draw breath for another barb.

'Then you could have just said that. You didn't need to be all mysterious about it. We're not the bloody Mafia.'

'Thank goodness your sister has enough tact and responsibility for the pair of you.'

'Mmmmhmm. I don't think I'll lose sleep over that.'

'Unlike you, I prefer those I work with to maintain a professional standard.'

'Was there a point to all this?' He waved his hand dismissively.

'The *point* was that I am retrieving Pepper and we are leaving at this moment to accommodate this incredible opportunity. You just happened to butt in. With that resolved, we shall leave you alone to drink. May I suggest ordering another one for your ego? Best make it a large.'

Laik smirked, raising his glass in mock salute.

'Funny.'

'I wasn't trying to be.'

Pepper rose, easing her chair back in with a squeak. She gave Laik a look with not a small amount of warning, then turned to follow Viola without another word.

As the two women disappeared back into the interior of Leroux Tower, the balcony fell quiet again, save for the faint clink of ice in Laik's glass and the low hum of the city far below.

It would have remained that way, if Swan hadn't approached him, thumbing over the screen of his mobile phone.

Laik quirked a brow.

'You talking to me now?'

Swan gave a tut, dropping his phone into his inner jacket pocket.

'You done eating?'

'Yeah?'

'Good.' Swan cracked his neck to the side. 'We've got a job.'

# Chapter Six

## The Wild One

The lift rose with its usual slow shudder, the soft whirr of cables behind the polished wood panelling the only sound as the two women stood in silence. Viola stood upright, purposeful, every inch of her oozing discipline. Pepper, on the other hand, kept her hands lightly clasped in front of her, resisting the urge to fidget with the hem of her sleeve. She swallowed her nerves down deep.

'I apologise for Laik's behaviour,' Pepper said, breaking the quiet with what she hoped was a smooth enough deflection.

'Please, you have no reason to. I've seen many like him throughout my tenure, they're nothing new. All balls, no brains . . .'

Pepper raised an eyebrow in surprise.

'Well, maybe he's a little different on account of his, um, *condition*. Which, may I ask—'

'You may not. Sorry.' Pepper offered a small, apologetic smile. 'It's not my place to say. He gets upset if I start sharing his business.'

'I understand.'

'So, what are we doing again?'

'*We* are going up to see if we can make ourselves useful. *You* are going to be meeting the heirs of the Cavendish Family in the process. I needn't tell you that protocol must be followed to the letter. Whatever you are told is in the strictest confidence, even to that ass-wart sibling of yours. Whatever they require, you source and provide. And whatever you are exposed to, you are not . . .' She paused, her tone thoughtful. 'Intimidated.'

The lift continued its quiet climb. The floor indicator ticked upward.

Pepper glanced at her reflection in the mirrored lift door. Pale. Collected. At least on the surface she looked . . . fine. But her stomach felt like it was quietly tying itself into new and increasingly inventive knots.

*Vampires.*

It was still hard to fully accept. She'd grown up with them, like anyone had – on screens, in books, dripping in melodrama and bad accents. They burned in sunlight. They were afraid of crucifixes and couldn't cross running water. Garlic was apparently lethal, and if you believed the films, they were all tragic romantics who either brooded or seduced in equal measure.

Little of it lined up with the truth.

Living among them for months had dispelled plenty. They didn't drink from chalices, didn't tear virgins apart in gory ceremonies. Not that she'd seen, anyway. Most of them just seemed . . . normal. In their own distant, slightly off-kilter way. They had routines, habits. Quirks like anyone else. For some reason she was especially surprised when she found out some of them enjoyed watching the football.

Sunlight was fatal, that was accurate at least. And they could be hurt, though recovered quickly. Aversion to garlic, she was told, was a sham to sell more produce at market in more superstitious times. The blood thing though, that still weirded her out. They did need it, that much was true, but not in the quantities she'd imagined. Just a small dose each day, like some twisted nutritional supplement. It was traded, labelled and categorised like perfume or designer wine. Shaped glass bottles. Wax seals. Looping gold script upon the label.

It unsettled her more than the idea of teeth in the neck ever could. The teeth themselves were usually retracted, protruding when necessary, like a cat extending its claws. Like an animal.

She realised she'd zoned out when she felt Viola's eyes on her.

'Anything wrong?'

'No,' Pepper said quickly. 'Just a little nervous.'

'You should be. It should be obvious to you that there are a number who believe you should not have this privilege. They have dedicated themselves to lives of service, have been with us for years in the hope of serving our betters. Some dream of just being in their presence. And yet you have gained their ambitions in the space of mere months thanks to the good word of your brother.'

Pepper hesitated, then asked, 'If you don't mind me asking, how long did it take you?'

Viola's gaze remained fixed forward, unreadable as she looked to the floor numbers scrolling past lift doors.

'That's not the point.'

'I don't need Laik to vouch for me. He's always been . . . protective. It's well natured, but annoying.'

It came out easier than she expected. Still a lie. Still strange to say it aloud. But it was cleaner than the truth, and the deception had started coming more easily now, like learning to fake an accent when the real one might get you killed.

'In this case, I doubt you would be anywhere where you are today without his endorsement,' Viola replied, clipped but not unkind. 'Despite his . . . unfortunate lapses, and numerous character flaws, he has always been in good standing with Lord Cavendish. I promise you that helped.'

The lift gave a mechanical shunt. The bell chimed.

'Ah. Here we are.'

The lift gave a final, reluctant jolt. Then the doors, peculiarly, groaned apart with a sound like someone breathing out their last.

Pepper's breath caught.

It was dark. Painfully so. There was sparse, erratic lighting in obvious need of attention, but what it provided was enough to assess what they had walked into.

The foyer resembled something from a horror movie – if horror movies had a budget for high-concept ruin. The floor was dense in places with mud and grass and actual *trees*, as if a forest had crept through an open window and forgotten to leave. It was so remarkably dense, making Pepper conclude this must have been in place for decades. Ceiling tiles sagged or hung at jagged angles, exposing electrical wires and copper pipes that slithered between lightless gaps. A lone strobe light nearby hummed a sickly buzz with every flicker.

Overgrown plants dominated the interior, vines crawling up columns, roots cracking through marble. Moss spread in patches across glass, stone and metal alike. It was beautiful, in a way, if one could ignore the creeping sense that everything here had *given up* on order a long time ago. Some insect buzzed loudly on by, making Pepper jump.

And in the centre of it all: a massive, weather-worn

Japanese torii gate. Its wooden pillars were sun-bleached and splintered, lacquer long gone, red now faded into something more like rust. The thing stood in the middle of the floor like a totem dragged from another world where the natural pathway would send them beneath.

'Remember what I said,' Viola answered, stepping out with the confidence of someone who, while used to this sort of strangeness, remained on her guard.

Pepper followed, casting one last glance behind her as the lift doors shunted closed, sealing them inside.

Everywhere her eyes landed, something was either in disrepair or transformed by slow invasion. Walls were cracked open as if punched by giant fists to let through snaking cables or furniture. One desk sat half in and half out of a ragged hole, like someone had given up on moving it all the way. Strange graffiti traced the corridors in looping symbols and jagged, angular marks that glowed faintly in ultraviolet hues under sporadic cathode lights.

A glass-walled room that may once have been an office looked more like a greenhouse now, though it had long since given up any pretence of control. Plant life clawed at every surface. Condensation streaked the inner panes in sluggish rivers, and just as they passed, a single overhead sprinkler activated with a sharp click. A blast of cold, pungent water misted the area, trickling down the filthy glass. Green mould wept along the corners. Pepper's feet took a couple of steps through something wet. Water, she hoped. She dared not look down to confirm.

Another room besides, its doorway lined with candles exhausted by overuse. Hundreds of them, maybe more. An effigy of sorts hung from the ceiling within, barely visible in the gloom. It twisted slowly on a wire, the shape indistinct and unnerving.

The deeper they moved, the more chaotic things became. Lights failed to follow any pattern. Some hallways glowed with warm yellow spotlights that burst like suns from the darkness. Others were all shadows, broken only by the occasional flicker from an exposed cathode tube.

Then Viola stopped.

Pepper almost bumped into her before noticing the sound. A soft shuffle in the dirt. The heavy snuff of breath.

Between two pillars tangled in ivy, a deer nosed its way along the edge of the floor, its hooves brushing against leaves and broken tile. Its fur was patchy, its eyes too wide, too still. It looked up and froze.

Then, in a flash, it bolted – crashing into something metal behind the undergrowth, sending a distant clatter echoing into the gloom.

'Should we be concerned about that?' Pepper mumbled.

'Only if we're told to be,' Viola replied as they pressed on.

What should have been a boardroom had been transformed into something altogether *wilder*. Candlelight fluttered against dark wood-panelled walls, casting long, twitching shadows. Tables, not one but *several*, were scattered across the space like driftwood. Some were cracked. One was lopsided. Each surface groaned under the weight of objects: stacked books bound in skin and silver, cloudy jars with pickled things suspended inside, tangles of chains, broken mirrors, candle stubs melted into their holders, a porcelain doll with no eyes, an honest-to-God *sink* filled with toy frogs. The air smelled of dust, cloves, melted wax and something acrid – burning hair, maybe, or an herbal remedy that had gone stubbornly wrong.

Clocks covered the walls in no particular arrangement. None matched. Some ticked, some buzzed, some hung still as paintings. A few had shattered glass faces, their hands spinning endlessly, or not at all.

There was no structure to any of it. No clear theme.

Except to the woman who was its architect.

She stood barefoot on a table like it was a stage, balancing with effortless grace amidst open books, cracked teacups, and what might have been a petrified bird. Her blonde hair was pinned with bone clasps, streaks of violet catching the candlelight, and her outfit was the kind of ensemble that demanded you *not* ask questions – velvet corset, green army officer jacket, and a floor-length patchwork boho skirt that had been dragged kicking out of the 1960s.

A stuffed iguana rode her shoulder like royalty, its glassy eyes unblinking.

She acknowledged the women's arrival, looking down from her place. Her smile was too wide to be innocent, and her gaze flitted about as if she were reading thoughts in the air itself. Everything about her seemed to be composed with danger and delight, and of these she was many.

Vampire.

Heir.

*Catastrophe.*

She fell from the table mid-step, landing uncomfortably effortlessly to those watching, looking eagerly between the new arrivals.

'*Visitors*. How nice,' she chimed.

Viola bowed slightly, then gestured with her arm to Pepper.

'May I introduce you to Miss Quinn Cavendish.'

'A pleasure to meet you.' Pepper gave a small curtsy, unsure if she was meant to or not. It felt old-fashioned, but this place *felt* old-fashioned in all the wrong places.

'She's curtsying.' Quinn blinked as if someone had just

thrown cold water on her. She turned sharply to Viola. 'Why is she curtsying? Is it the seventeen hundreds or something?' Then, as if struck by divine absurdity, her face lit up. 'Wait, *is* this the seventeen hundreds? Did we go round again?' She gasped, equal parts horrified and delighted. 'Oh my God, did it *work*?'

'I'm afraid it's still the same year as yesterday, miss,' Viola explained.

'Aw. Maybe next time.' Quinn pouted, looking her companion up and down. 'What's this one's name?'

'This is Pepper Montgomery.' Viola offered the explanation like a rehearsed script. 'A Domestic Affiliate assigned to the Cavendish household. One who assists in sensitive errands and internal support. And it has been agreed that she is to be at your disposal.'

'A *Domestic Affiliate*, huh? Like you?' Quinn hastily added, hunching over one of the tables, pawing over a scattering of playing cards.

Viola blinked, almost insulted at the assumption they were of the same standing. 'Ah, well, not *exactly* like me.'

'Your replacement, then?'

'Not yet, at least. And, she is Laik's sister, of all things.'

'Well, sure, I know that much. I can smell him all over yous.' Quinn pushed herself upright to circle Pepper, eyes wide, gait theatrical. 'I like your hair. Very rad.'

'Thank you, I like your, uh . . .' Pepper looked around the room, trying to pick a word that might safely sum it up, '. . . style.'

'Psh. No, you don't. It freaks you out.' Quinn pointed an accusing finger. 'Congratulations, Vee, you've brought me a liar, this one. But she's new, so I'll let her off.'

'She's trying to—' Viola attempted to explain.

'No, I get it. She's trying to keep me happy. But a good

liar is hard to find. Super rare. And you're close, but not quite there yet.' Quinn was twirling now, gesturing to no one and everything. 'Everyone tells me what I should and shouldn't do. People like *you. Her. All of them.*' She pointed at a row of bound teddy bears pinned along a display shelf, like they were attending a silent seminar. 'Do I look like I need more opinions? Got many sharing every second. I don't need to be guided into what someone thinks is the best path for me. That's boring, right?'

She turned to the preserved iguana on her shoulder, nuzzling it gently. 'Right. Telling me to do or not do this or the other. And they're not even your *thoughts*. You're someone else talking through you. I don't need more lies, get me? What we need . . . is more *deception*.'

'I'm afraid I don't follow,' Pepper stated.

'You will.' Quinn's eyes twinkled with something untamed in them.

Pepper took the plunge, honesty suddenly feeling like her only weapon.

'Your clocks are weird. This place is a shithole. Something back there stinks like it's died. And the thing over your shoulder is very distracting. I don't like it.'

Viola looked like she might explode; that was, until the young woman reacted favourably.

'Oh *finally*! Some good old-fashioned honesty.' Quinn beamed. 'Thank you. Truly. And Mister Wiggles here isn't a problem. He keeps me on the straight and narrow. Or as much as one can, am I right?'

She let out a laugh that ended in a cartoonish snort.

'Uh . . . right.'

'I wasn't talking to you.' She gently stroked Mister Wiggles' leathery head, like coaxing a kitten into sleep. 'Don't worry. They won't be staying long.'

'While the intent is to introduce you to Pepper here,' Viola interjected smoothly, 'we should also ask if we can be of any service to you, miss?'

'"Miss". That's cute. *Am I* cute? Witches got called cute before they went zipping about the stars with their jukeboxes and got burned at the stake for being not of the ordinary. Cute's dangerous.'

'I couldn't really say.'

'I suppose not. That's not a thing that happens here, is it? Not yet.'

Something crashed down the hallway – a metallic clatter loud enough to make them jump.

'Is anybody else here, miss?' Viola keenly put to her.

'Hah! Oh, I *hope* so, otherwise it'll be pretty bloody spooky, won't it? All dark and that.'

'We did see the deer.' Pepper tried to justify the commotion.

'*I have a deer now?* When did that happen?' Quinn's face lit up with genuine delight. 'Wait, hold that thought.'

She whipped around, scanning the clocks before darting toward a light switch and flipping it six times in quick succession. She paused, listening. Then, a seventh.

Another crash, deeper down the corridor, like two metal pipes violently striking one another.

'Is that normal?' Viola asked.

'Not really, it should do it on the *third* flick. I need to get an electrician to sort that.'

'May I arrange one?'

'No . . . I best find the other one first. Don't want to lose a second in here. Actually, it might be that stink you were talking about . . .' She bit at her nails.

'Then is there anything else we can help with?'

'Oh, of course, *now*'s the time you're here for that. Yes. Help. There is.'

She circled Pepper again, and this time, with a sudden flick of movement, snatched her hand and jabbed it with a pin hidden in her palm.

Pepper, unsurprisingly, yelped in alarm.

'What's the matter?' Quinn quirked her head to the side.

'You hurt me! You made me bleed.'

'And? It's just blood. Don't be so selfish. Finger, please.'

Viola's expression gave Pepper nothing – no sympathy, no instruction. Just cool, professional silence.

Pepper relinquished her hand, heart racing. Quinn squeezed a few drops into a glass filled with something dark and amber. She swirled it. Sniffed.

'If it's just blood, why do you want mine?'

'Never known someone so squeamish. Regular Edward Jenner, you are. Figure you wouldn't mind, being that red is such a good colour on you. Besides, Mister Wiggles demands you be tested. He demands *everyone* be tested, but today is *your* lucky day.'

Quinn took a sip from her glass and smacked her lips.

'Ha! Thought so. She can stay, this one.'

Viola bowed slightly in thanks, leaving Pepper utterly confused.

'I don't—'

'I know you don't,' Quinn shrugged. 'But *I* do. And that's *allllll* that matters.'

Pepper touched her finger to her mouth, soothing the sting.

Quinn, already half lost to some other thought, moved among the tables, scattering old books, incense sticks, and a pile of unboxed cassette tapes. A stone Buddha smiled from under an umbrella of newspaper-stuffed lanterns. A statue of Ganesh watched from within a birdcage.

'How is that brother of yours? He's always so busy.'

'Like you say: busy.' Pepper drew her finger away. 'Laik is in demand by many people.'

'Mmm, I suppose he is. Either way, I would appreciate him to make some time for me once in a while. Tell him to come by at some point, would you, please? I miss that smiling, pretty face of his. Brings me the sunshine, it does.'

Pepper frowned. Was there something buried in that? Or was this just another of Quinn's meandering thoughts?

'He *smiles*?' Viola asked, amused.

'Oh. I mean, *not him* smiling. I mean his *smile* smile. From his other. You know, the one with the pretty eyes.'

Pepper shivered involuntarily upon realising what she was referring to.

Viola noticed.

'Will that be all?'

'Just one teeny, *tiny* thing,' Quinn said, sweeping papers from a table in a flurry. Books thudded to the floor. She slammed her hand down on something, seized a pen, scribbled furiously on paper, stuffed it into an envelope, and turned with a flourish.

'Could you hand this to my brother personally? It is *imperative* that he receives it within the next . . .' She scanned the walls again, eyes hopping from one clock to another in deduction. '. . . twenty-eight minutes and thirteen seconds.'

She turned back to her mess, disappearing into the glow of lamplight and haze of incense. When she finally noticed them still standing there, she waved vaguely.

'Oh, we're, uh— We're done here.'

# Chapter Seven

## Eyes of the Wolf

The lift hummed as it climbed.

Pepper stood beside Viola, watching the glowing numbers tick upward one more, one after the other. The envelope in her hand felt heavier with every floor.

'So,' she murmured, 'she's completely insane.'

Viola didn't blink. 'One would think. I'm not entirely sure myself. I understand her just enough to carry out my duties. She's a handful, yes, but the fact remains, she is one of the most important individuals in the family. And importance, Pepper, always demands respect. Whether or not they make sense.'

'Of course.' Pepper twisted the envelope between her fingers, the name *Canis* in cursive across its front. 'Is the brother the same?'

Viola gave a faint breath of a laugh. 'No, thankfully not. Not as . . . spontaneous. Positively boring in comparison – but not in a bad way, no, not that. No, he's a lot more . . . he is exactly how you would expect someone of his position to be.'

Pepper wasn't sure that was comforting.

The lift gave a soft metallic sigh and came to a stop on floor 75. A gentle chime. The doors parted.

And the world changed.

It was like stepping into a magazine spread – cool whites, polished beige, and clean architectural lines that hummed wealth without ever raising its voice. Plinths held tasteful sculptures in gentle spotlight. A silent television whispered rolling news on a far wall, Vivaldi's 'Summer' played somewhere discreetly. Art – real, original art – graced the walls in subtle, casual symmetry. It didn't just look expensive. It looked *curated.*

'Quite the transition, huh?' Viola remarked as they stepped into the corridor.

'This is what I expected downstairs,' Pepper said under her breath, eyes drawn to the luxury.

'Not quite the black sheep, this one,' Viola replied with a small smirk. 'Canis is very much a creature of presence. He cultivates his image like one would a garden. He needs to. He's always on parade. Never not in the spotlight.'

'It's so impressive.' Pepper fought the urge to gawk about herself.

'Indeed, it is.'

There were guests: multiple, moneyed and indulgent, leaning on balcony railings, laughing over champagne, canapés and hushed gossip. A terrace shimmered in the spotlights, complete with a pool and flickering screens showing market reports no one seemed to be watching. A woman was in the throes of seducing a young man on a white leather sofa, paying special attention to his neck. His moans were such that Pepper couldn't tell if his life was being drained away or he was in the midst of an orgasm.

There he was.

Canis Cavendish. Standing at the far end of the room, like

the centrepiece of a gallery few could afford the admission fee of. Tall. Dressed in a white silk suit that managed to avoid pretence through sheer confidence. Hair pale gold, a waterfall of elegance falling past his shoulders. He held a glass of something amber in one hand, the other resting lightly on the shoulder of a younger man – a guest by all signs, flushed from drink or attention or both.

He turned at the arrivals.

'Ah, Viola,' Canis greeted, voice like velvet being ironed. 'Good evening. I hope you haven't been troubled by my guests?'

'Not at all.' Viola smiled, folding her hands. 'Everyone has been perfectly civil.'

'Really?' His gaze slid to the man beside him. 'Do you hear that? I must be losing my touch. If word gets out I'm not scandalous anymore, how ever will I cope?'

'I highly doubt that day will come, sir,' Viola said, and to Pepper's surprise, blushed faintly.

'You flatter me.' Canis shot a smile, then leaned toward his companion. 'Why don't you run along and join the others out on the terrace? I'll be along momentarily. Fix me something strong while you're waiting. I have high hopes for tonight.'

The young man nodded, murmured something, and left. His fingers lingered just a beat too long on Canis's sleeve before releasing. Then, finally, Canis turned his full attention on Pepper.

'And who,' he said, voice dipped in silk, 'is this rather startling creature?'

'Canis,' Viola began, 'this is Pepper Montgomery. She's recently joined us in an upper-floor capacity. General duties. She'll be assigned to floors, including yours, moving forward.'

He took Pepper's hand gently and brought it to his lips. '*Enchanté*,' he purred. 'A pleasure . . . though I don't recall seeing you about until now. And I am very good with faces.'

'She's only been with us a short while,' Viola explained. 'Elevated by your father's request, no less.'

Canis arched a perfectly manicured brow. 'Ah. That sounds highly suspicious.'

'Not necessarily. She is Laik's sister.'

'*Is* she now?' His eyes flicked up with mild interest. 'The old man does have a soft spot for his golden boy. Well. I do hope you don't share his . . . affliction.'

'Not at all, sir,' Pepper said, steady. 'My brother's burdens are his own to manage and his own alone. I'm unaffected by such a thing. Please judge me on my actions, not on his behaviour.'

'Reassuring to know,' Canis said with a warm nod. 'The last thing I need is a commotion like that rearranging my affairs. That is not to say he is not an asset, please do not get the wrong impression. My family is very grateful to have him serve. He is, unfortunately, just . . . prone to drama. How are you finding your position, Pepper?'

'I enjoy the work, sir,' Pepper replied. 'There's always something new to learn. And I take the trust placed in me seriously.'

'As you should.' He studied her a moment longer. 'And how are you finding my home?'

'It's . . . fine, sir.'

'Fine?' He tilted his head with mock injury. 'I was rather hoping that being welcomed into the innermost sanctum of the Cavendish dynasty would inspire a touch more *awe*.'

'Oh! No, I didn't mean—'

'He's teasing,' Viola interrupted, dry but smiling. 'Tell her you're teasing, Canis.'

Canis gave a slow smile. 'I'm teasing. Pay no mind, I'm simply indulging myself. So, what brings you here? Is Viola simply giving you the tour?'

'Actually,' Viola said, producing the envelope from Pepper's hands, 'we've just come from your sister. She insisted we deliver this to you posthaste.'

'Haste, huh?'

Canis took the envelope delicately, looked over its particulars, then opened it. A coil of black landed in a hand. 'A dead spider. Correction: a *flat* dead spider.' His expression didn't shift. He turned the paper to face them. There, in the centre of a piece of stained cream paper, written with perfect cursive script, was the word *Dunce*. 'Lovely.'

He sighed, but it turned into a laugh. 'That girl, I swear.'

He looked down at the spider again, returned it to the envelope, along with the letter itself, and placed it upon a side table. 'Family, eh?' he said with a genuine smile. 'What ever shall we do with them? As treasured as they are . . .'

Canis stepped through the open glass doors and onto the balcony, the throb of motion down in the streets bubbling up to meet him. The city stretched beneath them, a sprawl of twinkling lights and monolithic glass office buildings. The passing clouds soaked in artificial light presented pockets of stars.

He leaned against the railing, cradling a half-finished drink, watching the lazy blinking of a police helicopter as it went on its way.

'Will I have the pleasure of you both joining us this evening?' he asked, not bothering to look over his shoulder.

Viola let out a startled gasp. Her fingers went to the collar of her blouse, tugging at a crease that wasn't there. 'Oh, I hadn't expected . . . I mean, I'm hardly dressed for such an invitation—'

'A problem easily rectified, Viola, you know that,' Canis said with the faintest smile. Then he turned, his gaze drifting to Pepper.

She straightened instinctively, then gave a small shake of her head. 'I appreciate the offer, but I'll have to pass. My shift's nearly over, and I've somewhere I need to be.'

Viola blinked, almost insulted by the refusal, though she said nothing.

Pepper added, more softly, 'Family matters. The kind you don't miss. Treasure, like you say.'

Canis didn't press her. His expression barely shifted. 'Of course. But know the absence will be noticed. Next time, maybe.'

He turned his gaze skyward, to the upper reaches of the tower where Lord and Lady Cavendish stood silhouetted on a higher balcony, their heads close in quiet conversation. Their words didn't carry, but their presence alone held gravity, as if they were looking out across their domain, their *entire* domain, and discussing how it should be shaped. Despite being only a few floors away, they didn't acknowledge him, though noticed his presence, without so much as a wave.

In response, Canis drew a sleek phone from his pocket, tapped out a message with his thumb, and hit send. The screen cast a brief glow against his face before vanishing into the folds of his pale jacket.

'We all have our places to be . . .'

# Chapter Eight

## Dirty Work

It was late, or early – depending on who you asked – and the streets they passed through were half dead and flickering under sickly amber streetlights. Tower blocks and shuttered stores swept by the windows in the wash of headlights. The inside of the car was tight and dim, the engine a restrained growl beneath them, barely masking the tension of the city that was refusing to sleep.

Laik drove with one hand on the wheel, the other on the gearstick, knuckles tight and jaw locked. He wore street clothes – thick hoodie, black jeans, the same battered black-and-white jacket thrown over it all. Anything more formal would've given the game away. Not that anyone would've mistaken him for ordinary. Even here, where the only witnesses were fellow Enforcers and the shifting skyline, he emanated tension like static from a pylon wire.

In the passenger seat, Swan checked his phone which had pinged not seconds before, soaking his sharp features in a whitewash glow.

Laik glanced across.

'What does the old man say?'

Swan didn't look up, patiently brushing the screen with a thumb.

'This isn't from him. This is from his son.'

Laik gave a dry laugh and flexed his fingers on the wheel.

'Jesus. He's not even head of the table yet and already wants to call the shots. Think Mortis knows?'

'Nothing we do happens without him knowing,' Swan murmured, still scrolling. 'Might just be turning a blind eye.'

Laik smirked but didn't answer. The streets bled past – shuttered storefronts and closed takeaways with smeared neon, the occasional shadow lurking by a bin. He slowed as they neared the river, the car gliding over the bridge, closing in on their destination. It wasn't the best part of the city: remnants of the manufacturing boom from the 1950s that had refused to modernise, or be torn down, so were left to rot. Overlapping graffiti blistered the walls: murals, tags and gang signs so numerous no one even bothered to scrub them away anymore.

'How do you want to play this?' Laik asked.

Swan finally locked his phone and tucked it away.

'We go in and say hello. Everything else we improvise.'

'That's not a plan.'

'I wasn't pretending it was one. Alright. This is us.'

Laik pulled up just beneath a blown streetlight and killed the engine. The car settled into silence, tinted windows hiding those inside and their intentions.

From the back seat, Reese leaned forward between the headrests, sleeves rolled, red hair scruffy, and picked something from beneath her red nails.

'Please tell me we're not doing another polite knock-and-chat, boys,' she said. 'Last time we did that, I got spat on.'

'That was because you smiled,' Duncan replied next

to her, not looking up. He fastened up his jacket, but not before he checked something metal and compact squatting in an inner pocket. When satisfied, he snapped the buttons shut. 'Most of the time you look like you're going to deck someone.'

Reese snorted, falling back onto the leather. 'I wasn't smiling. I was… being civil. And I don't have a look.'

'Yeah, that look. That one right there.'

'What look? There's no *look*.'

'There's a look.' Swan caught her scowl in the rear-view mirror.

'Exactly. Stop doing that.' Duncan stated, emboldened by the validation.

Laik grabbed a pack of mints from the dash, shook one into his mouth, and offered the pack over his shoulder without looking. Duncan took one. Reese didn't.

Swan swept his hood up and pulled the door handle.

'Let's get to it.'

The four of them climbed out. The air outside greeted them with the usual cocktail: diesel fumes, rotten God-knows-what from the bins behind the kebab place, something faintly chemical. The Impreza doors clicked shut behind them, and they took to the street.

It was a fine night for a walk.

The streets were a mess of old brick, loud signs and potholes that had grown too large to ignore. People stooped in entrances, their business unspoken but understood. Rough sleepers sprawled out on benches or in nooks, or foraging through rising piles of rubbish bags. A woman screamed laughter as she passed beneath reams of scaffolding that haphazardly clung to a storefront. In the next moment, a couple of drunks threw profanity at one another, then, when the words weren't enough, fists.

They walked fast, crossing without waiting for lights, shoes crunching on glass. Swan led them down a narrow side alley that had become an obstacle course of wheelie bins and scrap wood. They emerged out the other side before an old cinema with boards nailed over the front.

The Quality Cinema was a relic from the 1930s and abandoned when local property prices began to freefall from the influx of small-time dealers. Display cases for posters were now broken and empty, but the marquee still read, COMING SOON: *TROUBLE*, as if its last movie was a premonition for tonight. The steps up had a number of empty beer bottles discarded on them, revealing a flickering neon sign which barely managed to say, SNOOKER HERE.

The lobby of the once-grand picture house was dusty, dirty and altogether unpleasant, the air polluted with stale urine and cigarette smoke, the kind that you tasted for days. Another sign pointed an arrow up a staircase with a single red ball.

'Alright. We're here to put things straight. I'll do the talking. Follow my lead. And let's not make a noise unless we have to. We're not savages.'

They ascended the stairs without further words between them. When confronted with a suspiciously well-enforced door, Swan raised a hand and knocked sharply. A slit opened in the door at the top.

'Who is it?' a voice barked.

'Buyers.' Swan glared. 'Now open up.'

'What's the password?'

Swan rolled his eyes. 'The password is *open the fucking door, else we take our money elsewhere*. That good enough?'

There was a pause. Then a heavy bolt slid aside. The door opened with a groan, revealing the haze-drenched interior: snooker tables stretched beneath dim bulbs, with men hunched over cues and drinks. Concert posters of classic rock bands were lined along the walls. The music, an old rock ballad on a tired jukebox, played just loud enough to be unpleasant. At the end, a simple bar that was already struggling with the number of empty glasses.

All eyes turned to them. Dozens of men, women, a few half naked, all halfway into something illegal or immoral. The bartender froze mid-pour. A group of gothic clubwear-clad women, seated in a corner booth, blinked up from their seats, glassy-eyed. Cue sticks lowered slightly.

A man with greasy black hair and biker patch-covered waistcoat slipped from his stool and approached far too confidently. He looked at the Enforcers in turn.

'You're all here to buy?'

'If you've got something to sell. Unless we've heard wrong.' Swan quirked his head.

'We do. Drinks first?'

'No. Just business.'

'Suit yourselves.' He shrugged his burly shoulders and led them to the booth, where the line of leather seating was decorated with bodies, all under the watchful eyes of the rest. The table was littered with half-filled glasses, orange pill bottles and tracks of white powder. The ones capable gave saccharin-sweet welcomes soaked in promise. The others seemed too high or drunk to care.

'How much you boys looking to spend?'

'We've got deep pockets. That's all you need to know.'

'Alright. There's what we've got at the moment. We've another six coming in tonight, closer to midnight. But these, they'll have whatever you want in them, and you can either send them on their way, or you can have your fun, no holds barred. As long as you don't damage the merchandise, you have free rein.'

Swan's gaze slid to the first pair of slumped young women who could barely acknowledge their presence. He stepped closer, eyes narrowing, flicking his head to Laik. One of them didn't even flinch when Laik turned her head to the side. Bite marks, old and new, covered the neck. Fresh bruises purpled the skin. He gently pulled the girl's arm out to examine the bruising. His jaw tensed. Needle tracks ran down both arms. Laik scanned the others who shared identical injuries.

'Living drug deliveries. Clever,' Swan muttered. 'Get them high, drain them later. They good to be bottled in this state?'

'I've never heard of a problem yet,' he rasped, proud.

'What if they OD?'

'Nobody cares. The girls involved in this aren't the kind who get missed, if you catch my drift.'

'Huh. You get a lot of attention doing this?'

'God, I hope so. Already known as the best provider before the river. You know, if you boys want to invest in the expansion, you can have a seat with the others. Help shape things. Get a freebie or two, even.'

It was fashionable to believe that vampires hated humans.

Centuries of blurry confrontations transformed fact into fiction, and fiction into spectacles. Vampires were reduced from horrors to pageantry on the screen, mocked as children's toys or worse. It was an easy conclusion to reach.

But, in truth, what they truly despised was each other.

Sure, tribalism was well and rife in the vampiric community, and one could meet a significant amount of prejudice for what you worshipped, when you were born, when you were turned, what customs of the era you adhered to or not.

But nothing drew their ire faster than their own behaving

like fools, something which seemed to be rampant in the younger generation. The ones bitten in the last few decades, drunk on myths and media, parroted clichés from books and films as if they'd lived them. Deluded little cliques who mistook theatrics and fiction for tradition, thinking fangs and early hours made them untouchable.

To old blood, they were an embarrassment. A liability.

And liabilities didn't last long.

Swan's eyes flashed to Laik, who silently echoed his colleague's thoughts.

'Who's in charge? I want to speak to them. Now,' Swan put to the man.

'That'll be me.' He weakly shrugged once more.

Stepping forward, Laik refuted the lie with a punch to the jaw. The man crumpled immediately. Cue sticks rose again. Glasses were put down or brandished as weapons. One smashed his bottle against the bar top and held it forward. The more lucid girls shrieked in alarm. One exploded into manic laughter.

'*He*,' Swan barked, pointing at the new mess for all to see, 'is clearly *not* who we're after! A word of advice to everyone here! Do *not* try and insult me! So, I shall say it again: where is the one running the show?'

A low growl filled the room. A bear of a man eased his stool back and straightened himself, wiping flecks of foam from his lips. He was massive. Ginger beard streaked with grey, decades of tattoos rode down thick forearms. Over six feet and built like one of the tables, the man moved with lazy menace. His black tank top stretched over muscle and gut, all but destroying a Ramones band logo. Those in his presence stepped aside to let him approach. He snorted, easily a good foot in height over Swan.

'That'll make you Hayter, I'm guessing,' Swan sneered.

Laik cracked his knuckles in turn. Duncan put up his fists, ready to get some good old-fashioned fighting done.

'S'right. Any reason you barge in my joint and start swinging?'

'I don't know, is there any reason why I hear that you fellas are causing noise? Throwing girls around left and right smacked outta their fuckin' skulls? Getting picked up by police with teeth marks all over them? Dragging 'em out the water? It's a bad look. And tell your rabble to step back,' Swan said, voice deep and dangerous. 'I see a couple of them looking like they're itching to do something stupid.'

Hayter's jaw flexed. 'Who the hell are you to tell us how to handle our merchandise?'

Laik didn't flinch. 'Representatives from the Cavendish Family. We were sent to shut down the trafficking.'

Hayter's laugh was hollow. '*Cavendish?* Really? Fuck, no wonder *she* looks like she wants to kills us.'

Reese rolled her eyes and made a silent curse in exasperation.

'This is Ode territory,' Hayter continued. 'You're out of your depth here, boys, and we are paid up with the ones who matter. You better turn around, trot on home. Daddy's gonna slap that ass when you get in. Will do when I put the call in.'

Swan stepped forward, eyes icy.

'Given what you're doing here, I'm surprised you're not shut down already. You've drawn too much attention. There're headlines already. Rumours, witnesses, bodies in ditches, for God's sake. That puts all of us, from the gutter to the towers, at risk. That's a sin we don't tolerate.'

Hayter's face turned red as he spat, 'Learn to. I'll be dead before I hand over my business to the Cavendishes.'

'We have no intention of taking over this' – Swan

coughed deliberately, looking through the smoke haze at his people inching forward slowly – '*classy operation.* Just you working discretely as you know you should.'

'Hm.' Hayter nodded in thought, before deciding, 'Well, I'm gonna keep doing what I do, the way I've always been doing. It's going real well. And there's nothing the Cavendishes can fuckin' do about it. And nothing will get that point across faster than their people dumped outside the tower *without their heads*.'

A collective breath was held. Swan, unexpectedly, let out a chuckle.

'I'm sorry to hear that. I'm guessing you're not planning on letting us leave, right?'

Hayter's teeth squeaked as they ground together. 'Obviously.'

There had to be a good thirty goons, armed with whatever they could find, each emboldened by their better numbers. They snaked their way around the tables, forcing the Enforcers to press their backs to one another. Burning eyes, borderline animalistic and filled with murderous intent, glared at them from every direction.

'*Well!* Since you want to do it the hard way.' Swan patted Laik on the shoulder, who had been preoccupied with staring Hayter down. 'Fancy showing them your party trick?'

The confidence from Hayter's men quickly evaporated as Laik shuddered.

The room seemed to dim with every breath, like the light itself sensed something wrong and tried to flee. A tremor ran through Laik's arms as shadow bled from the seams of his skin, coiling in inky threads that slithered up his neck, across his face, down his hands. He swelled, taller by inches, then feet. Broader. Denser. Eloped in a steaming, shifting mass of pitch. His fingers thickened, claw-like. The floorboards groaned under his new weight.

The shadows swallowed his face last, presenting a pair of collapsing suns where his eyes once were.

Nobody dared breathe. A good thing too, as they needed their breath for the cries.

Laik launched forward with all the weight of a charging train, slamming into the nearest pool table with such force it exploded. The air was suddenly filled with splinters, green felt, and two of Hayter's men reduced to a tangle of broken limbs and shrieks. One hit the floor with a noise no throat should make. The other was flung into the air, crashing into one of the hanging lights and ripping it free from its supports. A blur of black limbs sailed this way and that. Snooker cues snapped effortlessly as they struck him. A crack of thunder boomed from the barrel of a handgun, whose owner soon lost both the firearm and the means to hold it. It was carnage.

Swan, Reese and Duncan were already throwing punches, capitalising on the carnage. Hayter had relinquished his bravery and tried to press through others to escape somewhere through the kitchen, but Swan wasn't going to let this happen. He had tackled someone and stamped them into submission, pulled himself up onto one of the tables, sprinted its length and dived atop of him. He brought his head down onto Hayter's nose, making it erupt into a crimson spray, buying him enough time to finish the job. Teeth sank into Hayter's exposed neck. Swan was the furthest thing from gentle as he drove deeper into flesh, into muscle, before feeling the frenzied thudding in his mouth. Then, snapping his jaws together, he tore himself free, ripping away a strip of pale flesh in the process. Blood uncontrollably gushed from the wound, leaving Hayter wide-eyed in terror as his hands fruitlessly scrambled to stem the bleeding.

Swan rose, spitting the torn flesh to the floor, along with any trace of blood that had made it to his mouth. The last thing he wanted was that filth in his veins.

All that remained now, was the rest.

Swan navigated the slalom of wreckage and bodies. 'Let the Sky Fall' by Ten Years After crackled through the jukebox, the guitar's slow, mournful wail echoing through the ruined snooker hall like a bluesy funeral anthem. The beat matched his lazy swagger as he weaved between splinters and growing pools of blood across cracked floor tiles. A light hanging from a single fitting swung overhead.

The Enforcer moved behind what was left of the bar, cracked in half like a fallen tree. He slipped four bottles of beer through the broken glass of a fridge and slammed their necks against the counter, sending the caps spinning to the floor. He took the first drink slow, rolling the taste around his tongue. The jukebox crooned behind him. He nodded along, letting the music soothe his sore bones.

The first bottle went to Reese, perched on the edge of a table, dabbing at her reddened eye with her shirtsleeve, blemishing her freckled skin. The second to Duncan, sitting on some luckless bastard who hadn't moved since he went down hard, his coat torn open and shirt soaked at the collar. The third found its way to Laik, standing apart, fists still clenched, the last remnants of his other form finally retreating. His eyes were fixated elsewhere, only returning to the present with a pat on the shoulder and the drink offered.

The bottles were struck together, and they each took a mouthful in unison, surrounded by complete carnage.

Laik was the first to speak. 'The state of you,' he muttered, eyeing Swan, the blood on his jaw having dried like war paint. 'Whatever happened to not acting like savages?'

Swan snorted and wiped his mouth with the back of his hand. 'Caught up in the moment. Happens to the best of us.'

In the far corner of the room, the group of women huddled tightly into the shadows, their faces slack with exhaustion, eyes wild with terror and tears.

'What about them?' Reese gestured with her bottle.

'Not our mess,' Swan said flatly, taking another swig.

Laik stretched his shoulders with a wince, then stooped to loot a crumpled pack of cigarettes off one of the fallen. He flicked the lighter he found beside it, lit up, and patiently exhaled. 'You serious?'

Swan shrugged. 'Picked their lot.'

'Bullshit,' Duncan muttered, his voice low but firm.

Reese shook her head. 'You think they willingly came along for the ride?' She gestured again. 'They're victims.'

'Technically collateral damage. And still not our responsibility, unless they're accountable for some big bad,' Swan insisted, but it sounded hollow even to him.

Laik stood, flicking ash to the floor. 'They're people. Like you were.'

Swan scoffed as he followed. '*Were*, as you point out. Past tense. Playing saviour isn't part of the job.' He pushed the kitchen door open and took stock of the contents. He strode to the grimy cooker, flicking the hob knobs as far as they could. The sharp hiss of leaking gas was immediate.

Laik followed, stepping behind the shattered bar, and began rifling through the wreckage. He raised his voice to be heard. 'It's not about that. What's wrong with having a little humanity?' A lockbox glinted beneath a broken shelf.

He jimmied it open with a knife and flipped through the bundles inside.

Swan jammed a pair of stained kitchen towels into the cheap, chrome toaster, the lever clicking loudly as he forced it down.

'You of all people are saying that?' Swan called in disbelief, as he walked back in, the door clattering behind, 'In case the fact escaped you, *we ain't human no more*. You more than the rest of us, I would guess.'

'Yeah, well, whatever I am, an asshole ain't it.'

'Really? Why break a habit of a lifetime?'

Laik moved toward the girls with measured steps, the din of the room falling away behind him. They were pressed in the booth, curled in on themselves, coats drawn tight around shaking shoulders. A few flinched at his approach; a couple didn't even look up, suspecting themselves to be loose ends in need of silencing.

He crouched down, slow and unthreatening, like someone trying not to startle a wild animal. The cigarette in his mouth glowed faintly as he breathed in, then died as it was flicked away.

'I know,' he said awkwardly, 'all this, this here . . . you shouldn't have been caught up in it. This isn't your place and it's not your fault. None of it. This don't make up for what you saw . . .'

He placed the wad of cash from the lockbox onto the table and eased it before them like an offering.

'But this'll get you away from here. All of you find a hotel, get cleaned up. I saw one on the way here, about five minutes up the street. Get yourselves some place warm. And call someone who gives a damn. Family or a friend or whatever, or don't. Just . . . go. Go somewhere better than this.'

One of the girls, bruised and glassy-eyed, lifted her gaze and blinked slowly at him. Her lip trembled, but she said nothing. Another reached forward, hesitated, then took the money in both hands, clutching it like it might vanish if she let go.

The girls shakily moved to the door in unison, escaping the mess that had been made. Laik returned to the others, took a long pull from his bottle, and let out a breath he hadn't realised he was holding.

'See?' he muttered, not looking at anyone in particular. 'That wasn't so hard.'

Swan drained the last of his bottle and set it into the corner pocket of the nearest table. The others got to their feet, stretched their backs. 'No,' he said. 'You just make it harder than it needs to be. I think that sister of yours is rubbing off on you. Christ, if people knew how soft you were becoming . . .'

They made their way out in single file, boots scraping through broken glass and half-splintered pool cues. The front door gave a reluctant creak as Duncan shoved it open, letting the night breathe in around them. The air was sharp, damp.

Laik adjusted his collar as he stepped out, eyes flicking across the street. A stray dog ripped at bin bags for a meal. An impatient car horn was lost somewhere in the city's sprawl. The group drifted into a slow pace, their footsteps dull against the wet pavement, conversation tapering off into tired silence. Behind them, in the creases of the streets, the night sky flared orange.

The blast ruptured the quiet, a man-made thunderclap. The force rolled through the streets, rattling windows on its journey. Fire tore through the snooker hall's façade, belching smoke and debris into the street. Brick and timber buckled inward as the roof collapsed with a roar. Car alarms began in panic.

They all stopped to look back at the fire that was now taking hold of the old cinema.

Swan retrieved his phone and thumbed a message to Canis, confirming the job was done. With a stiff prod of the send button, he looked between them. They had taken a few punches tonight, but that had been expected. Enforcers rarely received a warm welcome, especially in pits like that, but it was what made the job so exciting: it got the blood pumping.

All that was needed now was to get home.

But before that, as new sirens began to leak into the air, Swan confronted a much more pressing matter. He struck his hands together.

'So . . . Food?'

# Chapter Nine

## Blood Siblings

Pepper stood in the sterile belly of the lift, alone except for the scent of disinfectant and the buzzing fluorescent light overhead. The metal walls reflected her faintly, warped at the seams, making it uncomfortable to meet her own eyes. Her hands were stuffed into the deep pockets of her coat, but one slowly crept upward, fingers closing around the gold locket that hung from her neck. She rubbed it between her thumb and forefinger with nerves.

The lift jolted once, then began its slow ascent. She exhaled in the hope to calm her racing heart. By the time the doors opened onto the corridor, she had composed herself. Mostly.

But this wasn't Leroux Tower. No glossy floors, no classical music echoing through the hallways. Just dull grey tiles, walls the colour of old chalk, and that quiet, humming kind of sorrow that only hospitals could conjure. It was late enough to ensure that the only visitors were ones whose bedside vigils were not long to last. Only the distant sounds of gurneys being wheeled and the slow, steady steps of overnight staff remained.

She walked to the secured door and pressed the intercom.

'Yes?' crackled a voice.

'I'm here to see Claire Montgomery.'

'She's family only. Relation?'

There was a pause. Pepper leaned against the cool wall, shut her eyes, and then said softly, 'I'm her sister.'

A mechanical buzz followed. She pulled the door open and stepped inside.

The ward was silent, save for the quiet beep of machines and the distant squeak of rubber-soled shoes. People slept behind drawn curtains and partially closed doors. The air was tinged with antiseptic and the echo of too many held breaths.

At the nurse's station, a lone woman in blue scrubs looked up from a dim monitor.

'Good evening.'

'You must be Pepper?' the nurse asked, flipping through a clipboard. 'She's spoken a lot about you. I'm Nurse Arleen.'

Pepper gave a tired nod. 'Yes, hi.'

The nurse found the right page and stood. 'Alright then. We're in room nine, please follow me.'

They walked side by side down the hushed hallway. A trolley squeaked from somewhere behind. Doors whispered open and shut in the distance. Nurse Arleen opened the door to a side room.

Claire Montgomery lay under a pale blue blanket, her face washed in the dim light from the hallway. An IV fed something clear and slow into her arm. The tubes and wires didn't look like lifelines to Pepper. More like they were sucking everything *from* her sister.

'How has she been?' Pepper whispered.

Nurse Arleen adjusted a hanging IV bag, marking down a number in the patient notes. 'Tired, mostly. That's to be expected at this point. She's lost a little weight but is as steady as she can be.'

'I see.'

Pepper crossed the room and settled into the high-backed chair by the bed. It had that cracked plastic texture hospitals loved so much.

'Mind if I sit with her a while?'

'Not at all. Can I get you anything? Tea? Blanket?'

'No. Thank you. I'm fine.'

The nurse smiled kindly and slipped out, closing the door with a soft click.

Pepper reached out and took Claire's hand. It was limp and cool, but reassuringly familiar. Claire snorted gently in her sleep. Her eyelids flickered.

'Hey, sis,' Pepper said softly. 'I missed you. I always miss you.'

She settled back into the chair and watched her sister breathe. The steady rise and fall of her chest. The little fluttering pulse at her throat. It was becoming difficult to prevent her voice from wavering.

'I meant to come sooner, but work has been . . . it's just been real busy. That's not an excuse, I know, but there're reasons.'

Her words lodged themselves in her throat. What would she even say if Claire woke? That she'd infiltrated a vampire dynasty? That she now lived in a skyscraper full of killers wearing suits? That she'd chased down a mythical flower in a hidden market built on old blood and older lies?

She covered her mouth as a yawn suddenly took hold.

'Guess what,' Pepper whispered, voice catching. 'I found something. Something real. And it might help. I'm sure it will, everything else has been true. It's . . . a miracle. You won't believe it. Hell, I don't believe it. But it's there. A rose, they call it, an Eternal Rose. And with it, we'll get our lives back. I promise.'

Her eyes drooped. The hospital warmth made her heavy, and her voice slurred just slightly.

'You just rest.'

Her head fell back, eyes closing.

She didn't realise she'd fallen asleep until the whisper startled her awake.

Pepper blinked, startled upright. 'Hey. Ho . . . Sorry, God, I didn't mean to—'

Claire was sitting upright, fragile, her cheeks slightly gaunter than what Pepper remembered. Her chestnut curls were greasy, draped on a pillow that was seemingly big enough to swallow her head. Claire's voice was soft. Faint. But real.

'You still snore, you know.'

Pepper huffed a tired laugh. 'You're one to talk. Honestly thought a tank was about to come bursting through the wall.'

Claire smiled. It didn't quite reach her eyes, but it was there. 'When did you get here?'

Pepper glanced at the clock, trying to make sense of the fact it was now pushing 3 in the morning. 'Nine? Something like that?'

Claire's brow lifted. 'Nine p.m.? Wow . . . They're really working you, huh? Hope the pay's worth it.'

'It's not about the pay.'

'That's just something poor people say.'

'Yeah, I forgot what it was like with us growing up. Gold mansions, Versace top to toe. I've got to keep the life I'm accustomed to, y'know?'

Clare stifled a splutter, which transformed into a series of sharp coughs.

Pepper reached for the water jug, hands trembling. She filled a cup and handed it over.

Claire took it carefully, sipping like it might run out. 'You're shaky. You should get that checked out.'

'I see too many doctors these days.'

Claire tried a grin after sipping her water. 'I was trying to be funny . . . aren't I allowed to joke anymore?'

'Of course, just get better material. How are you?' Pepper asked. It felt like a betrayal of a question.

'Like my body wants to kill me. Not in a fun way, either.'

'What have the doctors said?'

'Just the same. No donors yet on account of the rarity. The, uh . . . kidneys aren't holding up too well. I've been for some scans and got told they didn't look promising. They're talking about dialysis being on the cards. So that's fun.'

Pepper nodded. She felt it again – that familiar tightening in her chest as helplessness clamped down on her heart. Her fingers instinctively travelled to the gold locket around her neck.

Claire smirked. 'You still wear that thing?'

Pepper unclasped it and handed it over. 'Of course I do. Keeps you close.'

Claire popped it open and smiled softly at the photo of two young girls inside, angling it under the sterile light, drifting a thumb over its surface. Another two photos slipped away. An elderly woman in a chair. A middle-aged woman with tangled hair on a beach trying to keep the sun from her eyes. 'God, look at us. I look like a marshmallow.'

'You look like my whole world.'

Claire glanced up, eyes wet.

'It was hard then. It shouldn't be hard now. Not like this, Peps.' she whispered. 'You shouldn't have to—'

'You always did,' Pepper interrupted. 'When Mum passed. And Gran died. You didn't give up on us. So now it's my turn. That's how this works.'

'And how are you holding up?'

'Truthfully? Not very well . . . not, uh . . .' Pepper blinked tears back unsuccessfully, 'not well at all. But I'll cope. You did.'

Claire reached out weakly, and their hands met in the middle of the bed.

Laik strode into the lobby of Leroux Tower, brushing drizzle from his hair, thankful that the rain had managed to wash splatters of blood from his jacket. He flashed his security card at the scanner and went on through the turnstile, nodding to a colleague who, even at this time of night, stood attentive. The others had decided to hit the Kingfisher, but he had other, more pressing things to do than drink and deafen himself in a bar like that. He jabbed at the lift button for up and tapped his foot until the doors opened. As he stepped inside, he saw Pepper dart within and turn her back to him. He couldn't help but notice in the reflection of the lift's metal panelling, her eyes were red and her mouth stuck in a deep frown.

'Everything alright?' he tentatively asked.

Pepper furiously nodded, straightening herself and dabbing her nose with a coat sleeve.

And rather than press the matter, Laik stood there in silence, watching the floor numbers rise until the doors slid apart. The hush remained, interrupted only by the tapping of rubber on marble flooring. She walked ahead, not much, just enough to avoid the burden of shared glances and small talk. Laik followed. They reached the same door, Pepper first.

Laik hesitated for a breath, watching her frisk herself for her keycard a little too fast, like she didn't want to give herself the chance to think. She began rummaging through the same pockets again, impatiently now, which was when Laik decided to lean over and place his own card on the electronic lock.

A muted click. A green light. For a moment he felt that she was going to say something as her head twitched ever so slightly in his direction until she took the handle and vanished inside their flat.

He lingered in the hallway a moment longer to give her space, fighting a question he didn't quite have the nerve to ask.

Then, with a tired breath, he stepped inside and shut out the rest of the world.

# Chapter Ten

## The Morning After

Sunlight struck like a slap to the face.

Pepper groaned, face buried into the pillow. Her limbs felt heavy, not from sleep but from something denser – grief, maybe. Or guilt. The duvet had slipped off her during the night, half pooling on the floor, the sheets tangled around her legs. One bare thigh caught the fading sunset bleeding through the coated glass – a necessary fixture in a building where tenants could combust under direct sun.

It hurt to look at.

The headache, like a nail being driven into her skull, made sure of that. She groaned a broken profanity and gripped her forehead in the hope the pounding would relent.

The room looked exactly like how she felt. One drawer was half-yanked-out, a blouse half hanging from it like it had tried to escape. Her green felt coat was slumped over the back of a chair, one sleeve dragging on the floor. An empty glass by the bed joined a still-open bottle of gin. Her laptop was still awake on the desk, accompanied with reams of paperwork in binders that were dangerously close to falling onto the floor. Half of the contents of her bag had spilled out after being accidentally kicked.

Pepper lazily blinked, straining to focus on the sounds of movement outside.

She managed to sit up slowly, hair wild and shadowing one eye, threw on a worn dressing gown and tied it with a loose knot before padding out of the room. The walls provided support as best they could. Her bare feet made soft sounds on the floorboards as she closed the door behind her and wandered toward the open-plan kitchen at the end of the hallway.

The smell hit first.

Bacon. Salt, smoke and sizzling fat. It clawed at her stomach despite the rock of nausea sitting in it.

Laik stood by the stove, sleeves rolled, pan angled just so as he flipped the rashers with practised ease. His back was turned, but he looked over his shoulder when she entered, and they shared a glance across the half-lit room. Neither spoke.

Pepper dropped into the nearest chair at the breakfast table and let her spine melt against it. She stared blankly at the far wall, only half present, before letting out a staggered groan.

Without a word, Laik walked over and set a drink in front of her.

She blinked at it. The glass was tall, its contents a dense red, with a length of celery protruding. Her eyes narrowed in suspicion.

'What's this?'

'Virgin Mary,' he said, placing his own glass beside her. A darker shade – thicker, richer.

She raised an eyebrow.

'Don't worry. It's just tomato juice,' he added. 'At least yours is. It'll help.'

She eyed his glass that still sported an unmixed cloud of blood slowly dissipating. She glanced back to hers, hesitated, then took a long drink. It hit the back of her throat like a bad decision.

She coughed, winced, then gave her thanks.

He gave a small shrug and returned to his plate. Eggs joined the bacon, and he dusted them with cracked pepper from a wooden grinder.

Pepper stayed silent, hands curled around the cold glass, the scent of the food making her stomach lurch and growl in confusing unison. She played with the locket between thumb and forefinger, its weight familiar, its presence constant. It sat heavy against her chest like a clock ticking louder every day, chiming Claire's name every hour. And now, more than ever, it felt like she could hear it.

Laik didn't speak. He just ate, methodical. The only sounds were the click of cutlery, the low hum of the fridge, the ticking of a wall clock and the quiet ache of everything that hadn't been said.

Pepper glanced up, letting her eyes lazily focus on the scratches along Laik's knuckles, raw and angry and needing rest to heal. Rest which, knowing him, wouldn't be forthcoming.

'Tough night?' she asked, the words almost accusatory.

Laik didn't look up from his breakfast. 'Somewhat. Had to talk to some people who'd been doing very bad things,' he said, pushing a piece of bacon into his mouth. 'But I think you'd rather not know the details.'

His voice was cool, detached, like it was all part of a routine. Pepper didn't argue. He was right about her not having the stomach for elaboration. An Enforcer's role was varied and violent.

Laik subtly glanced her way. 'What about you?'

She stirred the drink with a lazy wrist. 'Tired,' she replied. 'Don't want to talk about it.'

'Fair enough.' He didn't push it any further.

By the time Laik had finished, Pepper was halfway through her drink, struggling with every sip.

He leaned back in his chair, setting his cutlery down with deliberate care. 'You have to talk to me at some point, you know.'

She glanced at him over the rim of her glass. 'Why would that be?'

'Because,' he said, rising, 'we're doing the thing today.'

'What thing?'

'Your thing. You said you needed to get some things from your flat.'

Pepper made a long, miserable groan and slumped back in her chair. 'I forgot that's today. Can we not?'

'As much as I'd prefer to do *literally anything else*,' Laik said, sliding the plate into the dishwasher, 'you went on enough to convince me. And I moved things around to accommodate that. It'll be pretty rude to pull out now.'

'Ffffiiiinneee.' She rubbed at the throbbing that had repositioned itself behind her eyes.

'Then get yourself dressed.' He strode away to his room, calling out, 'You've got half an hour until we go.'

Evening rain freckled the windscreen, each drop distorting the orange lights bleeding through the mist. Laik's Subaru Impreza hummed low as it idled at the lights, the wipers working a steady rhythm. The radio buzzed faintly – an old rock station with too much static.

Pepper leaned against the window, watching the streetlights smear by in streaks of amber and blue as they pulled off. She noticed the beat of the radio made him tap his fingers on the wheel.

'You like music?' she asked, breaking the quiet.

Laik didn't glance over. 'Who doesn't?'

'No, I mean . . . I just never thought about it. You've been around a fair while,' she pressed.

'That's right,' he said. His tone was dry, noncommittal.

'A while being . . .?' she prompted.

'I'm not telling you that.'

Pepper looked away. 'Fine. Then what kind of music do you like? Got a favourite band? A song?'

He shifted his head slightly, eyes still on the road. 'Dunno about favourite. It'd be Seventies, maybe early Eighties. Music had . . . more teeth then. Real edge to it.'

'Oh God, don't say that like you were at Woodstock.'

'I wasn't,' he said flatly. 'Did Isle of Wight Festival, though.'

Pepper turned to stare at him, half laughing. 'Really? Did you fight the establishment or *were you* the establishment?'

Laik sniffed, pulling around a corner. 'Nobody called it the establishment. And it depended on the day. Had to make money somehow.'

'I hear that,' she said, nodding toward the next turn. 'Left up here.'

The car rolled through the narrow streets, headlights cutting through puddles and neon signage of takeaways. Graffiti sprawled across shuttered shopfronts, and the road dipped into a quieter, grimier stretch of the city.

The Impreza came to a stop beside a corner shop with a dying sign that buzzed in the drizzle. A flickering red light cast the doorway in a soft pulse.

Laik fought the urge to make a comment as he killed the engine. A good thing too, as Pepper was expecting something and was prepared to give him a mouthful. Pepper pulled her coat tighter as she closed the door behind her. Laik looked up and down the street and double checked to make sure the car was locked.

They crossed to the side of the shop, where a narrow metal staircase wound upward between two stained brick walls. The steps clanked underfoot. At the top, she shoved a key into the stiff lock and pushed. The door caught on something – mail, mostly. She shoved it open and flicked through the envelopes. They joined a discarded pile on a simple chair.

Laik stepped inside behind her, taking in the room without comment. The curtains were still drawn, the air heavy with the smell of stale coffee and something oddly musty. Clothes were draped over the back of a sofa, dishes still in the sink, half a dozen mugs colonising the counter.

Pepper flicked on the light. The bulb flooded the room in a thin yellow haze. He wished she didn't, as everything that previously sat in shadow looked so much worse in the light.

'This explains my bathroom,' Laik said, stepping inside.

She turned sharply, already on edge. 'Don't.'

'It wasn't easy, you know?' she went on, voice tightening, arranging piles of things. 'Trying to keep a job and look after my sister at the same time. Some of us have to pay our way. We weren't all handed a fucking penthouse.' She exhaled hard through her nose, brushing a strand of hair behind her ear.

Laik didn't rise to it. He moved slowly through the lounge, eyes scanning the evidence of her past life – a dressing gown thrown over a chair, a mug by the window, a cracked photo frame leaning against the wall. A clock ticked, obnoxiously loud. The fridge rattled for a few moments before quieting itself. His fingers brushed lightly over an erratically filled bookshelf before he stopped at the photo of Pepper and

Claire. The two sisters were smiling, arms looped around each other, their faces younger, unguarded.

'How is she now?' he asked quietly.

Pepper didn't look up. She gathered a pile of clothes from the sofa and stuffed them into a black bin bag with more force than necessary. 'None of your concern.'

He set the photo back down with care. 'Suit yourself.'

He kept walking, inspecting the space as if it were a puzzle he was bored enough to solve. She went to the side door and pushed it open with her shoulder, half turning toward him.

'Oh no,' Laik said, deadpan. 'You're not inviting me into your bedroom. People will talk.'

Pepper glared. 'Where do you get off?'

'Clearly not in there,' he said, eyes flicking past her at the unmade bed. 'Judging by the mess, I've no idea what I'd catch.'

She let out a short, incredulous laugh, half amusement, half disbelief. 'Asshole.'

He shrugged, moving into the kitchen, where boxes and condiments had been left on the counter and a pot plant was in its death throes. The table pushed against the wall originally meant for dining. Not anymore.

It looked like a conspiracy theorist's workspace: dog-eared books with titles like *Vampires Through the Ages* and *Ancient Magik* stacked beside a kettle; a cluster of Blu-ray cases with brooding actors joined with equally brooding actresses leaned precariously like a game of Jenga. On the wall, emails and screenshots had been pinned over a crude city map scrawled with circles and lines in red pen. The most prominent being over a disused factory.

He frowned at the chaos. 'What's all this?'

From the bedroom came the squeak of a drawer, the thud of something being shifted.

'What's all what?' Pepper called back.

'This stuff in here. The, uh' – he gestured vaguely, even though she couldn't see him – 'little occult museum you've got going on?'

Nothing.

He leaned closer to one printout, squinting at the underlined name. 'Who's *Silk Veins*?'

There was a pause from the other room, then Pepper appeared in the doorway, carrying a bag of paperwork and something wrapped in fabric. She hesitated before answering, just long enough to betray that she'd hoped he wouldn't ask.

'Someone who pointed me toward the Night Market,' she said finally. 'And the Rose. There's a lot of murky sites on the internet that talk about vampires, most of them are crap. Thankfully she knew what she was on about.'

'Sounds shady,' Laik replied, eyes flicking back to the map.

'Yeah, well, it got the job done. I'm not gonna worry about it. I'm where I need to be.'

He picked up one of the books, letting the pages fall open to a woodcut depiction of something evil in Welsh folklore. 'Lot of reading here too. Didn't see you as the type. Thought you were more of a Netflix kind of girl.'

Pepper crossed her arms. 'I was obsessed with saving my sister. It's not every day you find out vampires are real, so I figured I should know everything about them. About *you*. Increase my chances, you know?'

Laik gave a low hum. 'Suppose that makes sense.' He set the book down and reached for the pile of movies. 'And that's what these are too?'

He held one up between his fingers – *The Lost Boys*.

Pepper gave a short, embarrassed laugh. 'Yeah. It's a classic. Considering how many films there's been, I figured there was some truth to be found in them.'

'I highly doubt that,' he mused, placing it back down.

'You're not a movie fan, I take it?'

'Not really my thing. You?'

'*Loved* them,' Pepper chimed, before reining herself in. 'It was escapism for me. Would curl up with my nana and Claire and watch anything that late-night TV had on. When we were moving about, they sort of became a comfort.'

'I tended to read more, if anything. Saw some greats like *Seven Samurai*. *M for Murder*. Oh, *Few Dollars More*. That was good. Nothing's ever interested me.'

'They're *ancient*. Did you just hibernate in a coffin and miss every good film ever made?'

'Funny. I saw that dinosaur one, *Jurassic Park*? It was alright. Just didn't care to watch much else after that.'

'Serious? What about, like, vampire movies? You've gotta—'

'Nope. Not even them. I know a bit from other people. Christopher Lee, is it? He's supposed to be good. Someone I know swore he was their grandfather and was one of us, but I don't buy it.'

Her eyes widened in mock horror. '*You don't watch vampire movies?*'

'Why would I?'

Pepper reached for the pile and presented a case with a coffee ring. A pale face stared out, sporting some strange expression that resembled a constipated smile.

'Not even *Interview with the Vampire*?'

Laik twisted his face. 'Why the hell would I? Would you watch a movie called *Interview with the Human*? What's he doing, anyway? Trying to get a job?'

'Oh my . . . oh my *God*! You *are* that guy, that Brad Pitt guy in it. The mopey one.' She threw her hands up in astonishment, then marched around the room, scanning it for something. Finally, she wrenched free the TV remote from between the sofa cushions. 'It's just sad, is what it is. That ends now. You. Sit. We're watching some.'

The television noisily flickered to life.

'Pepper, I've got no interest—' But his objections were cut off as she retrieved large bags of crisps from a kitchen cupboard.

'Ab-bab-bab. Hush. This is happening,' she said, passing by and ripping the bags open in turn. She shoved an off-brand packet of Doritos into his arms, then retrieved the movies and dropped the pile next to the television. 'You're going to watch a couple. You said it yourself; you have nothing else to do today, so you get to do this with me. Gary Oldman's *Dracula* first. And no, you don't get a vote. You get to shut up and watch. And eat.'

Pepper fell back on the sofa and patted beside her, making it clear that refusal was not an option.

Laik begrudgingly took his place.

Two films in, they were slouched so deep into the cushions that it felt like the sofa was in the process of eating them. The snacks had extended to grabbing a bottle of wine from the shop downstairs. The alcohol's effects became obvious when the pair burst into uncontrollable bouts of laughter while Laik attempted to protest *From Dusk till Dawn*'s inaccuracies (*'why do the vampires explode like there's bombs in them?', 'why does that guy have a dick gun?', 'Holy water doesn't set us on fire. It's water!', 'Jesus, this movie is basically racist to us.'*). Glasses were refilled. A bag of popcorn had somehow appeared. And as Pepper fired up the first series of *Buffy the Vampire Slayer*, Laik smiled despite himself.

But, of course, he couldn't let her see it.

# Chapter Eleven

## Guilt

The afternoon light was soft when Pepper woke, filtered through the drawn blinds of her bedroom back in Leroux Tower. Window open, the faint hum of the city below was muffled, distant, like the world had forgotten her for a moment.

Her head throbbed gently, the dull pulse of a night spent drinking cheap wine and being distracted from the obvious. The bag she'd dragged over from her flat still sat half unpacked by the wardrobe, clothes spilling from its open mouth like it had made an attempt to organise them, got halfway, and then gave up.

She rolled onto her side, groaning, and her eyes landed on the photo frame resting beside her on the bed. Claire's arm was looped around her shoulders, both of them laughing at something stupid. The kind of laugh that felt like nothing bad could ever reach them.

For a long moment she just stared. The sun, weak and pale through the blinds, caught on the glass, laying a thin sheen across their faces. Pepper could almost hear the echo of that laugh. She couldn't remember what was being shared when it was taken, but that barely mattered.

The stillness of the room pressed around her. Faint sounds of traffic bled through the window. Life kept moving, indifferent.

Her throat tightened, the ache rising sharp and sudden. That photo had survived being packed and unpacked more times than she could count, jammed into bags, kept on nightstands in places she couldn't stay long enough to call home. And still, somehow, it looked untouched.

A small sound escaped her – half-laugh, half-sob – and she pressed her lips together, trying to swallow it back, to no avail. The guilt crawled up her ribs like something living, reminding her how long it had been since she'd last seen that smile in person, how every smile now was glazed with the contribution of constant pain.

She wiped at her eyes quickly, angry at herself for slipping. Angrier still for allowing the weakness to surface. She'd promised herself she wouldn't break again – not here, not while she was this close. The photo was a reminder, a weight she carried willingly and hated all the same.

For a heartbeat, she almost turned the frame face down. But she didn't. She couldn't.

Pepper sat up, running her fingers through her hair. Her heart was tight, aching with guilt. She needed to get back to the mission, the Eternal Rose, the *only* thing that mattered. All the rest of this – sleeping in sheets that didn't smell like home, watching movies with a fucking *vampire* of all things – was temporary. She needed to get her head together. Keep her eyes on the prize. Not get distracted any further.

She pulled on yesterday's jeans and padded out of her bedroom barefoot.

Laik was there, naturally. He was perched on one of the stools by the kitchen counter, sharpening the kitchen knives with calm, precise strokes. The sound – a quiet *shhhk-shhhk-shhhk* – was smooth and dangerous. His hair was damp from a shower, his shirt buttoned crisp. He looked as unruffled as ever.

Pepper leaned on the doorframe, rubbing her temples. 'Do you ever sleep?'

Laik glanced up briefly. 'Not when I have a million things to do.'

'Figures,' she muttered, heading for the counter to pour herself a drink of water. The glass trembled slightly in her hand.

'You don't look great,' he said, nonchalantly.

She scowled. 'Thanks. Just what every woman wants to hear in the morning.'

'I meant hungover.'

'Oh, well then, that's different.' She took a sip, grimacing. 'Guess I can't keep up with you.'

He shrugged faintly, returning to his task. 'It's a perk. My body burns through it quicker. It takes a lot to get us drunk.'

'Must be nice.' She eyed him, pressing her backside against the sink, watching the blades glint with each stroke.

'I didn't do anything embarrassing, did I?'

'No, not at all. Apart from forcing me to watch some stupid movies? No.'

'Good.' She took to her drink again.

'Well, you were getting a little bit handsy during that *Dracula* film.'

Pepper immediately spluttered while taking a mouthful, the water bursting within the confines of her glass. She looked honestly shocked before realising he was having her on.

'Oh you *wish*.'

She wiped her mouth with the back of a hand and took an actual gulp this time.

'After last night, I'm not really up for this sodding party later, if I'm being honest. Last thing I need.'

'You and me both,' he muttered, depositing a knife upon the countertop and reaching for the next in line. 'But I don't think we have much of a choice.'

Pepper snorted, half laughing, half exhausted, and took another gulp from her drink. It still didn't taste any better, but at least it was doing the trick of waking her up.

'Ugh . . . Don't I know it.'

'Entertaining must be done,' Laik said, flicking the edge of a cook's knife with his thumb and eyeing up its condition. 'Otherwise, someone will whisper that the Cavendishes are turning their noses up at the other Families. And then the politics begin.'

'Oh, the hours will just fly by for me,' she replied dryly.

The *shhhk-shhhk-shhhk* returned as Laik offered the hint of a smirk. 'You'll be working. That's different.'

'Exactly,' Pepper said, raising the glass again. 'I'll be working while you'll be schmoozing and eating nice things while I'm fetching drinks and pretending not to eavesdrop.'

'I'll be on duty too, you know.'

She didn't answer. He was right. Her fingers had wandered to the locket. She stared at it, the metal warm now. Then, after a long silence, she shifted forward.

'I'm getting impatient, Laik. I need the Rose.'

'I'm fully aware. And we shall get it.'

She looked at him, eyes sharpened now. 'Are you? Because from where I'm sitting, it seems like you're letting me do all the legwork. Which, if you hadn't noticed, is a bit unfair.'

Laik slowed his motions, looking up.

'My *job* is making sure you don't get exposed and torn apart in front of the canapés. Unless you want me to neck you and give you a more convincing disguise.'

She frowned, unimpressed.

'Please. You wouldn't bite me.'

'Maybe I would do it to the end instead. Leave you dead.'

'You wouldn't do that either.'

'Why?'

'You like having me around too much.'

He didn't miss a beat.

'If I didn't bite you, it wouldn't be because of the company—'

'Lies.'

'No, it'll be because I suspect you'd taste awful.'

She huffed, drumming her fingers along the side of her glass.

'Alright. Idea. What if we use the party?' she asked, eyes flicking up to meet his. 'Could we use it as cover? Get into Floor Sixty-Five?'

Laik leaned back in his chair, waggling the knife in his hand in her direction.

'Unlikely. Not with so many from other Families around. Security will be doubled. Cameras, patrols, sniffers. Every delivery would be checked. It puts us Enforcers on edge more than usual, so we're always checking blind spots or being overzealous in sweeping floors.'

She rolled her eyes, slumping into her hands. 'Then how do we get in there?'

He shrugged.

'The elevator.'

She stared at him. 'Jesus, Laik . . .'

'I'm serious. The ducts to the floor are sealed. Windows

are reinforced, blast-proof. Even the stairwell is blocked off, literally stops on the floors over and under. It's called the Vault for a reason. The only way to get up there is by the main elevator with a security card with specific access.'

'Which would belong to . . .?'

'The Cavendishes, naturally,' he said, sliding the finished knives into a block on the countertop. 'Archivists, researchers, technicians too. But they're tight, and getting close to one risks exposure. Maintenance teams have to lease them from Security, and they're escorted by an Enforcer the entire time. Hell, I'm not even allowed to wander up there on my lonesome with what they have locked away.'

Pepper leaned in again, lowering her voice.

'So, either we get someone to let us in, or we lift a card.'

'That's about the size of it.' He went back to his sharpening.

She studied him now, really studied him. Then, with that familiar twist of edge, she said, 'Still surprised you're going to these lengths to help me . . .'

Laik met her gaze without blinking. 'I'm not helping *you*,' he said. 'I'm helping *me*. We made a deal. I get you close, you get the Rose, save your sister. Then you hand it over, and I do what I need. That's all this is. If you hadn't almost pulled it off last time, you wouldn't be sitting here. You'd be dead.'

She raised her eyebrows, tasting the rising impatience.

'Is that the vampire talking? Or the big scary thing inside you that hid away when we met? From the way I see it, neither wanted to off me.'

His jaw tightened, just a fraction.

'What was that, by the way?' she asked, eyes narrowing in mock curiosity. She pursed her lips. 'Was it me? Did I scare it? Do girls give it the willies? Maybe it just found me too pretty.'

Laik rolled his eyes and sighed deeply. But Pepper made a sudden realisation that hitched her breath, and despite the gravity of it, she couldn't help but tease further.

'Wait . . . don't tell me you don't even know *why* it got spooked?'

'Drop it.'

She shifted forward, grin sharpening.

'Oh my God. You *don't*, do you? That's actually terrifying. What the hell even *is* it?'

His voice snapped before he could help himself.

'It stopped because it doesn't *like* you! It doesn't *trust* you. There's something in you that makes it uncomfortable. It doesn't know who you are and frankly, neither do I. And the more you go on, the more I get where it's coming from.'

'Who are you to—'

'*The guy protecting your ass!* But you're always firing at me with the attitude. Making comments. You've got this thing with your sister, like I know full well, because you don't stop banging on about it. How many others out there are struggling, Pepper? How many others feel the time running out and are powerless to do anything about it? Debt, illness, homelessness? Forced to make the bad choices, shacked up to the wrong people? Plenty, I tell you. You, on the other hand, you have a chance to actually remedy the situation, and all you can do is piss off the only man in the position to help!'

Pepper shoved back from the sink, slamming her glass down, fingers tight around it.

'But you ain't a man,' Pepper stated, her voice low. 'You're something different.'

Laik patiently put down the knife and glowered.

'You drive me mad. You think I enjoy this? Things were nice and quiet before you came along and messed it all up. Do you think that I *want* to be stuck acting like friends with the likes of you?' Laik added, quieter now, but with the same venom.

She stood there, trembling with the weight of everything she wasn't saying. Then spoke bitterly.

'But we're not pretending to be friends, are we? We're pretending to be family. Which is *so much worse*.'

Before she could stop herself, Pepper launched the glass she was holding into the sink. It shattered with an explosion of noise as shards bounced around inside. Without another word, she stormed off down the hallway and threw the bedroom door shut behind her with a final, echoing slam.

# Chapter Twelve

## Keeping Up Appearances

Steam ghosted over the bathroom mirror as Laik brushed his teeth, one hand braced against the cool marble counter. His reflection stared back at him – sharp, pale and expressionless. The faint points of his fangs peeked through before receding neatly into his gums with a soft click. A practised motion for their kind, as automatic as combing his hair or straightening a tie.

He rinsed, spat, wiped the mirror clean, almost knocking over a pink bottle of deodorant. He'd noticed it getting worse over the last few weeks – make-up brushes splayed beside the sink, a half-open compact leaving traces of powder on the counter. Bottles of perfume and cheap moisturiser scattered among his razors and cologne, a Hello Kitty toothbrush leaning haphazardly in a mug that wasn't his. It was like the room itself had started to rebel against his sense of order, one product at a time.

The towel around his waist clung low on his hips as he crossed the hall into his room, its order greeting him like a habit. No clutter. No photos. Just clean lines and clear surfaces. A bed crisply made, contents of a desk aligned precisely.

The towel was placed over a chair with the same precision as everything else. He moved unhurried, retrieving underwear, stepping into dark trousers, threading a belt through its loops. Socks next, then he laced up a pristine pair of black dress shoes. While he did so, his mind remained unburdened, his movements automatic.

Laik pulled on his shirt, buttoned it methodically, then reached for his watch – the one constant that had followed him through years of doing this kind of work. The cufflinks clicked into place. Jacket next. Tie. The motions filled the silence.

He paused, then caught himself glancing toward the adjoining wall. Pepper's room.

They hadn't spoken since the argument. He could still hear the glass bursting into pieces, the tremor in her voice when she'd thrown her words like knives. They had missed their aim but somehow still managed to cut.

He'd told himself she was being unreasonable. He'd told himself she deserved his frustration. But in the stillness of his room, it was harder to believe his own excuses.

A dull thud broke the quiet – something from next door. Something falling, maybe. He sighed, rolling his shoulders back. Tonight wasn't the night for grudges. Not with the Cavendishes' guests arriving. Not with the tower full of eyes.

He adjusted his tie, smoothed his jacket, and opened the door.

The corridor lights ran cold and white along the polished floor. As Laik stepped out, the door further down swung open – Pepper and Viola emerging together.

Pepper looked transformed. Her hair swept up in a knot,

her crisp waistcoat and tailored trousers lending her an air of authority that didn't need to be spoken. She wasn't going to be there to dazzle – she was there to impress.

Viola followed, all grace and calculation. Her outfit was sharp but not severe – a tailored blazer of deep plum over a black satin blouse, paired with slim trousers and silver heels that clicked like punctuation marks when she walked. She was elegance edged in steel.

Pepper caught sight of him and paused just long enough to look him up and down, one hand busy fastening an earring.

Viola's eyes flicked between the two of them, reading the air. Then she smiled, slow and knowing.

'Well,' she said, 'for all your numerous flaws, I have to admit, at least you clean up pretty good.'

Laik exhaled through his nose, halfway between amusement and fatigue. 'Thanks. I'll try to stay this tolerable for the next ten minutes.'

'Ten? That would be a personal record for you,' Viola said lightly. 'Aim lower, so none of us get disappointed.'

Pepper smirked faintly, but her eyes didn't linger long. Laik turned to her, tone gentler.

'You look nice.'

Her reply was flat. 'Yeah, well you look like a liar.'

Viola laughed under her breath. 'Excuse me – where was my compliment?'

Laik glanced at her, deadpan, as he fixed his radio earpiece on an ear. 'Didn't realise it was an obligation.'

'It's not. Just good manners.'

Laik's jaw twitched, the only hint of irritation breaking through. He looked between them, both effortlessly composed, both ready for the stage ahead. With a dry scoff, he unlocked the front door and held it open.

'Let's go,' he said over his shoulder. 'Best we hurry. Wouldn't want to be keeping anyone important waiting.'

The women ventured out to the hall – Viola graceful, Pepper measured, flicking her eyes to him upon passing. And Laik took to his silence again, walking ahead like a man who couldn't quite decide which was harder to swallow: his pride or his regret.

# Chapter Thirteen

## Strange Company

Leroux Tower had always loomed high over the skyline like a monument to power, but tonight it glittered. Floors 25 to 30, usually curtained in shadow, now blazed with soft golden light. Valets lined the crescent driveway at the base, bowing with sharp efficiency as sleek, expensive cars glided in one after another – Bentleys, Rollses, limos, Porsches, vintage Astons, and unsubtle blood-red Ferraris filled the night with throaty purrs of their engines. Almost all sported tinted windows. Guests congregated out, dressed like they'd stepped off a catwalk, their positions granted by old money and uncomfortable secrets.

A wall of security checked names, frisked bodies, scanned invitations with devices. Nothing slipped through the cracks tonight. Anything that could be considered a weapon was prohibited. Good behaviour was mandatory.

Elevators rose, each a hushed capsule of anticipation. Inside, guests murmured behind their masks of politeness, feet shifting, cufflinks gleaming, eyes darting subtly to size up alliances and rivals. A young bellboy in a black waistcoat pressed the buttons with a gloved hand. His smile was professionally vacant.

When the lift doors slid open, the real theatre began.

Floor 25 held a low-lit lounge, scattered with high tables and lush velvet chairs. Floor 26 boasted a garden terrace behind glass, where slow-spinning heaters kept guests warm as they drank beneath orchids and moonlight. The floors above opened into salons of crystal, chrome and candlelight. Live music – a quartet of piano, violin, cello and a smoky alto singer – drifted between rooms like perfume.

The thirtieth floor, however, was not a space for the casually rich or the merely connected. Here were the heads of Families. Their Enforcers. Their closest allies. The people who didn't need to explain who they were.

It was here where Laik stood beside the bar, a quiet monolith in a tailored three-piece suit of midnight cashmere so dense that it seemed that the shadows around him appeared reluctant to leave. His hair was combed back, the usual jaggedness tempered, but his jaw was clenched in its familiar position for quiet calculation.

He scanned the room without turning his head, letting his eyes drift from one cluster of conversation to another. An oil baron from the Sable line raised a glass in toast to a tech magnate with a wrist full of arcane tattoos. Two artists – one painted with gold veins, the other with red mirrored lenses for eyes – laughed over blood-rimmed champagne flutes. Every clan, every style, some dressed like high fashion prophets, others like barefoot mystics. And vampires in between, as sharp and subtle as blades hidden in silk.

Everything appeared normal. But Laik had seen parties go sour before. He stood with arms folded behind his back, watching. Listening. Thinking. His eyes narrowed to an

Enforcer of the Ode Family who had caught his attention: a thin gentleman, leaning against a pillar, stubble-clad with wavy short hair, a tan suit with a crisp white shirt beneath. Laik had noted he had already knocked back three blood Manhattans and was trying to catch someone's eye.

*His specifically.*

Behind him, the band changed tempo – something slower, jazzier, sultry. The kind of tune you could dance to if you were in love with the wrong person. Or planning to kill someone.

Laik watched the ballroom from his post near the mezzanine rail; arms folded behind his back. Down below, Lady Concetta Cavendish floated like a queen across the ballroom, making the time for those who paid her a word, speaking niceties through power. Beside her was her husband – tall, silver-streaked hair, with disciplined eyes that his past life as an Enforcer instilled. They mingled with the elite, nodding politely, including Domonic Ode himself, who was dressed like an emperor, and with every reason to. The Cavendishes and the Odes had been on shaky ground the last few years. With most confrontations being regarded as careless mistakes, there were those who seemed content to capitalise on these misunderstandings.

The Ode Enforcer ahead flagged a waitress in passing for a fourth round. Laik tutted, hoping that this wasn't the start of trouble to come. He had the distinct impression that it was going to be a long night.

Laik adjusted the discreet earpiece tucked against his jawline, the soft crackle of Enforcer chatter being background static. Names, floor numbers, updates. He listened with practised detachment, one hand now at his side, the other brushing a cufflink into place. Then came the familiar note of mischief.

'Hey, Laik,' Duncan's voice broke in, the static fading away, 'I got your sister here.'

Laik's eyes narrowed slightly, though he didn't lift his head. A long pause followed as he watched the crowd like a hawk surveying a field.

'In what capacity?' he asked, voice low and flat.

'The one that means she's nearby,' Duncan said, half laughing. 'I'm down on twenty-two, and man, is she ever popular with our guests. If I didn't know better, I would say they were trying to whisk her away.'

Another voice inter-spliced an objection. Someone else dismissed this as being unfair.

A muscle in Laik's jaw ticked. Across the room, the Ode Enforcer caught his eye as he took to his glass. As it was lowered, they were still watching him. Still waiting for something. Laik offered no reaction.

'What's your point?'

'Point being,' Duncan continued, 'she's floating around without a drink in hand. You gonna be put out if I put one there?'

The earpiece yammered with a number of broken hoots and laughs from other Enforcers. There was a mention of danger, of trouble. Not to mention Duncan's brazenness being considered outright foolishness.

Laik's response came with all the warmth of a winter morning.

'Why should I care? She's her own person. Knock yourself out.'

Static. A faint cheer on the other end of the line.

'Copy that. Just didn't want to step on your feelings. I'll be the best brother-in-law you ever had.'

Laik didn't answer. But as the channel clicked quiet, his eyes drifted upward, toward the shape approaching, the tan-clad swagger of someone drunk, but not from an excess of alcohol, just of ego. The Ode Enforcer slinked up to Laik and drew an olive from a cocktail stick that had been swimming in his dirty martini with a crooked smile.

Pepper moved with grace beside Viola, her waistcoat crisp, trousers tailored, and hair swept up in a knot that gave her an edge of professional detachment – less of an illusion and more personal armour.

She shook hands with people who made the city tick. A politician from Mayfair here, a blood-trader from Cairo there. Viola offered names and affiliations in a murmur beside her, each introduction stitched with the grace of a woman who walked the tightrope of social affairs and had no intention to misstep. Pepper responded with smiles, nods and carefully constructed compliments.

They found Quinn and Canis on opposite sides of the floor. Quinn had carved out a corner near a neglected balcony, gesturing dramatically with a cocktail straw as she monologued to a man whose glass had long since emptied. She was vibrantly chaotic in silk layers, combat boots, and what looked suspiciously like a corset designed during a drug trip. Canis, immaculate in his white suit and open red collar, leaned beside a plinth, speaking to a small knot of guests, his anecdotes making them laugh in all the right places. He made his excuses as Pepper and Viola approached.

'Viola,' Canis said with a hint of charm, 'looking as stunningly competent as ever.'

Viola offered a half-smile and the smallest of bows. 'Only as the occasion demands.'

'Well, it should demand *far* more often.' Canis's eyes moved to Pepper. 'And here we have Miss Montgomery. Look at you. You're making quite the impression tonight.'

Pepper nodded politely. 'Hopefully the good kind.'

'The *best* kind,' he replied. 'Enjoying the evening so far?' he asked, tone smooth but watchful.

'I'm still figuring out what "evening" means here,' she replied with a dry edge. 'But yes. It's . . . pleasant.'

That earned a faint smile. 'Ah, very diplomatic. You're learning quickly.'

'Oh good, you've found each other,' Quinn announced, like a thunderclap. 'And no one's screaming yet. That's something.'

Canis exhaled a quiet sigh. 'Dear sister.'

'Brother,' Quinn replied, cradling Mister Wiggles. 'Are you entertaining the people?'

'To the extent that they require entertaining. Yourself?'

'I've been talking, but I'm not entirely convinced anyone's listening. I did find the bar, but then I lost it again. I think someone moved it?'

'I'm sure it's exactly where you left it.' Canis gave a small smile. 'Did you want a drink?'

'Oh, we're not thirsty,' she said breezily, then whispered something to her taxidermy lizard and giggled.

'I'm sure you are.' His gaze slid to Pepper. 'Would you be so kind?'

'Of course,' Pepper said with a bow of her head. 'What can I get you?'

'Surprise us,' Canis said, his voice velvet smooth.

Viola interjected, 'Make that three, please.'

Pepper bowed once more. She crossed the polished floor, weaving past polite laughter and glittering gowns toward the bar where the queue was modest. She caught shards of conversation as she leaned on the counter – a financier explaining lunar influence on trading, a bohemian poet suggesting something scandalous to a married duchess. The bartender, a sleek-haired man who would have looked right at home in a jazz club, took her order and began working on mixing the drinks.

She secretly exhaled, letting the dull ache behind her eyes settle while the noise of the room sloshed around her. Snippets of gossip, the striking of crystal and soft-stringed music, threatened to overwhelm her.

'I don't suppose,' came a voice, low and slick, 'you're taken?'

'Only by dread,' she replied dryly, mentally willing the bartender to hurry up.

'It's practically criminal to be at a party like this and not enjoy yourself.'

Pepper didn't look at him right away. 'I'm having the time of my life. Who says I'm not?'

'You are. Your posture. Your face. The absence of a drink in your hand,' Duncan had moved to her other side, ensuring he filled her vision. He effortlessly leaned against the bar in a way that implied that his life was somehow comparable to the guests' to charm her, but it had the opposite effect. 'That last one is a giveaway.'

'I prefer a clear head. Besides, you're an Enforcer, Declan. You're on the job too.'

'*Duncan*,' he corrected gently. 'And maybe so, but I wouldn't use it as an excuse to not indulge in the finer things. But I enjoy my work. I get trusted to work closely with important people. Look after them. Protect them. There's joy in that. It's honourable, I would say.'

*Oh my God, what is he doing?* Pepper wailed in her mind.

'Glad you found your calling,' she said coolly, glancing at the bartender, asking God in her mind as to why this was taking so long.

Duncan eyed the three being prepared, then tapped the bar. 'Two more of those, would you?' he told the bartender, before turning back to her. 'You're a bit of a mystery around here, you know. Especially with that brother of yours. Laik's got this reputation of not-to-be-messed-with. Been something of a lone wolf. I think he likes giving that impression. I don't think you share any of that.'

'As you know, he's an asshole,' she said flatly. 'And I'm not fun to be around. That's about the gist of it.'

'I'm sure there's more if I dug a little deeper.'

'You don't want to know me.'

'I'm game if you are.'

The bartender slid the glasses toward her. She scooped up the drinks, her fingers curling tightly around the stems.

'Unfortunately,' she said over her shoulder, 'I'm not down for playing.'

Duncan took up a glass and lifted it. 'What should we drink to?'

Pepper rushed a response that made him know this was a wasted effort. 'How about absent friends?'

And with that, she vanished back into the swell of the party, leaving Duncan staring after her, his hand still hovering, wondering what had just happened.

Pepper returned with the drinks after weaving through clusters of bodies just as Quinn was mid-theory, speaking with the confidence of someone who didn't care whether anyone was listening – only that she had something to say.

'I've never seen the need for oil,' Quinn said, accepting her drink with a nod of thanks, barely pausing in her monologue. 'So *sticky*. Bleeding the Earth never made much sense to me. But imagine a better alternative: cars running on water. Just picture it. Fuel from the *sky*. Basically unlimited. Pretty much free.'

The male guest, a polished man in simple black sporting slicked hair, offered a humourless smile. 'Maybe one can dream. But the science—'

'Oh, the science is there,' Quinn cut in brightly. 'You just use electrolysis. Split the water molecules into hydrogen and oxygen with a catalytic process using a conductive metal like platinum or iridium. Store the hydrogen, burn it clean. Boom, energy. Zero emissions. It's not magic, it's basic chemistry, silly.'

There was a moment of awkward silence.

The man blinked. 'What?'

'What?' Quinn echoed innocently, wide-eyed. 'Do I have something on my face?' She dabbed at her cheeks with her fingers. 'Anyway, water's just the prologue. It won't be a tick compared to what we're destined to use.'

The woman beside him narrowed her eyes. 'And what would that be?'

Quinn's tone dropped to a whisper of reverence. 'Why, *the dead, of course*, darling! Too many of them are just rotting in the ground where they cry. Listen to them, they're bored! Give them something to do! Hand them the reins and they'll keep on driving. Or sailing. Or flying . . .'

She glided her hand through the air in a lazy wave, like a toy plane riding invisible currents. Pepper watched in silence, trying to work her out. The strangeness was easy to mock, and clearly the couple didn't know what to make of her, but Pepper was noticing a peculiar genius beneath the chaos. One that could be beneficial.

Canis raised his glass with an interruption to smooth out any unease. 'My sister, the visionary! Logistics are not her strong suit, but every revolution starts in the minds of the imaginative. To brave ideas!'

They clinked glasses. Pepper inadvertently followed suit.

The drink touched her lips before her brain caught up to the sharp copper tang at the back of her throat.

*Blood.*

Of course it was! If Duncan hadn't interfered at the bar—

Her stomach lurched at the realisation, not from the taste but more from the horror. It was too late to flinch. Too late to do anything but swallow. It sank down her throat like a cannonball. Pepper steadied her breathing, feigning a cough, eyes flicking to the others. No one noticed as Canis turned with his signature charm, placing a hand on the individual's shoulder to guide him away.

'Now, please – tell me about this trouble with the union. Perhaps we can find a way to remedy the situation . . .' He drifted off with the couple in tow, gliding toward an altogether different conversation.

Viola leaned close and whispered, 'Can I leave you with Quinn?'

Pepper forced a dry smile. 'Absolutely.'

The crowd pulsed around them in golden light and murmured music. Pepper glanced sideways at the woman beside her, staring into the bodies and silk and smiles beneath chandeliers like she was half lost in thought.

Pepper hesitated before finally talking. 'I think it's a great idea,' she said. 'The energy thing. Using the dead. Very . . . inspiring.'

Quinn quirked her head, eyes twinkling. 'You're lying again.'

Pepper smirked. 'Alright. It's crazy. But it's bold. Like something from the future. And honestly? I've never heard anything like it. But if anyone could make sense of the impossible, it'd be you.'

Quinn blinked, caught off-guard.

'There's so much I don't know,' Pepper continued.

'About us, in general. About this place. The Families. The culture, the history. And there are people here who've been around for centuries. I'm new by comparison. I feel like I barely understand anything. Just look at my brother – he's older than me by a long shot. Knows fuck-all about stuff in general, but the, uh, vampire thing? He's just useless. And then there's, uh . . .'

She looked down, fiddling with the edge of her waistcoat. The locket around her neck shimmered in the moving light, providing inspiration for the ruse.

'I don't even know what it *is*, that, that *monster* inside him. I know he doesn't deserve it. It's terrible. On me, especially on him, because he acts brave . . . pretends that he's fine with it all, says all the right things to try and put me at ease . . . But whatever it is, I get the impression that it's killing him slowly. Eating him up from within. And it's cruel that all I can do is stand by and watch until the inevitable happens.' Pepper scrunched her eyes together, fighting the swell of guilt that gushed from a more honest place.

Quinn nodded her head, something shifting behind her eyes. 'You don't know? At all?'

Pepper looked up. 'No.'

Quinn leaned closer. The stuffed iguana on her shoulder shifted as if listening too. Her face transformed, and her eyes softened.

'Would you like to?'

# Chapter Fourteen

## Enforcement

'What the fuck do you want?'

The words dropped low and without welcome. Laik didn't turn. He didn't have to. He'd felt Horus watching him for the last twenty minutes like a heat rash.

Horus chuckled as he stepped up beside him, the crystal in his glass catching light from the chandelier above. 'Is that any way to talk to your better?'

'Not at all,' Laik replied, eyes still scanning the crowd. 'You though? Absolutely. Again – what do you want?'

'I figured we needed to talk.'

'Talk, is it?' Laik finally paid him attention. 'You've been eyeballing me all night. Assumed you were working up the nerve to ask me to dance.'

Horus let out a short, dry laugh. 'You always were a funny son of a bitch.'

'And you were always a mouth. I'm surprised you're still standing, free bar and all. Would've guessed you'd be flat on your ass by now if last time's anything to go by.'

The jab made Horus go still. His nostrils flared.

'Oh wait,' Laik added, 'that wasn't the drink, was it?

That was me. If you don't want a repeat performance, how about I advise you to fuck off? That get through to you?'

'Careful,' Horus warned, voice tightening.

'Why? You gonna glare at me some more?'

But Horus just smiled, slow and cutting, and turned his gaze to the glittering sweep of guests below, paying particular attention to the Cavendishes, who were advancing up the stairs to the upper reaches.

'Look at 'em all. You know the funniest thing about these affairs? All these so-called killers in pretty, pretty clothes? They wrap themselves up and put themselves on display. Reputations precede them. Get called ruthless . . . but how? How many here tonight *actually* get their hands dirty? Their mouths *wet*? We both know they prefer getting their nasty business done by pen or by proxy.'

He leaned in a little closer. Close enough for Laik to smell the booze on his breath.

'You and me?' Horus said. 'We know what it takes out there. Us, the real ones, the ones who aren't afraid to swallow our sins for a better world, we see these pretenders for what they are. They've forgotten what war tastes like. They're too busy sucking blood through straws . . .'

Laik shifted. 'Is this going somewhere?'

Horus ignored the barb, a deft hunger in his eyes twinkling as he leaned on the rail. 'We're killers, Laik. We scrap in the dirt because that's where the scrapping is done. Not here, looking down on the world, not among these show-offs. Vamps nowadays are too soft-hearted. *Tortured souls and weeping romantics*. It's *embarrassing*. Our kind has lost the hunger to survive, to go to battle for what we want, like the old times. Us, we spill the blood the rich are so keen to bottle. Without us working, these monuments of sloth the Families have built would come crumbling down.'

Laik's tone flattened. 'You're an Ode. Which makes you a hypocrite, don't it? Again, you wanna get to the point of all this?'

'My *point*, if you've forgotten, is the same it's always been. Same as then. Same as now. I want that thing inside you,' Horus said simply. 'You *owe* me.'

'I don't owe you shit.' Laik drew back, astonished. 'And I remember it all, thanks. I remember hearing about a fucking screw-loose company of vamps on a murder spree trying to "purify" the race. Some *grand cause*, wasn't it? And I distinctly remember you hunting me halfway across the country after you got your little hard-on.'

'I wanted to stop the massacres you caused.' Horus sneered. 'All those poor, poor people *dying*, Laik. I wanted to stop you from exposing us. Everywhere we went, we heard stories of some Welsh devil ripping apart communities it passed through. And the plan for you, like it was for every other liability we came across, was to rid ourselves of the burden.' He straightened his back. 'There were so many before we heard all about you. They were cowards as well. Godless. They're no more, making you the last putrid remnant.'

And Laik felt it. Manoeuvring through his veins, coiling in his gut. Waiting. And when he spoke, it spoke in tandem.

'Someone like you calling others godless . . . Fucking look at yourself, man. You'll put the knife to anyone who looks at you wrong, dead or no. I've kept tabs on what you've been up to under the Odes. You're not on any righteous crusade. *You're just deranged.* A maniac. A fucking *psychopath*, and whatever moron turned you undead, should have been strung up long before he burdened us with the world's biggest, longest-living asshole.'

'You're a menace, Laik,' Horus hissed back. 'Even by

our standards. Sooner or later, you'll lose control again. Funniest bit is that I don't even have to do anything to make it happen, do I? You're just a bomb waiting to go off. A fucking *danger* to everyone around you. How many innocent people will you take out next time? *The ones sheltering you who don't even know what you are?* How many more kids will end up in bin bags by the time you're through? And all the while, you'll be protected by a Family who has no option but to keep you at hand . . . because they cannot risk you serving another. That's all you are to them: a wild dog on a chain.'

A flicker passed through Laik's eyes, creeping at the edges of his vision. The thing in his belly stirred in annoyance. The laughter, the clinking of glasses, the silk-and-smoke glamour of the Cavendish party all seemed to melt away. Horus stood just a few feet away, the slick bastard reeking of cologne, confidence and condescension. And he smiled like a jackal, knowing full well he was about to get his meal.

'There he is.' Horus leaned in, whispering now. 'I see you in there. What's the matter, demon? *Am I not young enough for you to rip apart?*'

Laik's fists curled at his sides. Heat was clawing its way through his muscles, readying them for action. The presence within shifted once more, hungry, alert.

All it would take was one word. One shove. One bad blink.

And Horus knew it.

Then—

*Crackle.*

A burst of static whispered through the earpiece tucked behind Laik's ear.

'Oh man, that was embarrassing,' came a voice, low and amused.

Laik blinked, thrown by the sudden shift in tone. His focus split, part of him still clocking Horus's smirk, the other suddenly tuning in to the open radio channel connecting the Enforcers.

'Jesus, you actually did it?' another chimed in. '*What were you thinking?*'

'Drop it, fellas,' said Duncan, voice already full of regret.

'What happened?' a third Enforcer asked.

'Duncan happened,' came the reply, deadpan. 'Idiot tried to hit on Pepper.'

'*No!*'

'Really?'

There was a pause.

'Pepper who?'

'Pepper who? Hell do you mean, Pepper *who*?'

'Laik's sister. He crashed out hard. It was painful to watch.'

'I didn't—' Duncan tried.

'Laik, man,' said someone else, 'you're gonna be waiting on that wedding invite.'

'And I thought *Laik* was the hard-ass,' another snorted.

Reese cut through the voices. 'I told you I had a better chance than you, but *noooooo* . . .'

Laik stared at Horus. The thing inside him . . . paused.

The heat in his chest dropped by degrees. The tension in his jaw slackened. Somehow, of all the things that could've cut through his fury – *this* was what did it. Idiots on the other end of a radio gossiping like teenagers. He smirked at the thought of Reese's irritation, of Pepper refuting some corny line, Pepper raising a hand to his face in denial.

Of simply just Pepper.

He calmly exhaled through his nose.

Horus was still watching, eyes glinting with anticipation.

He could see Laik pulling back from the edge, confusing him.

'If I were you,' Laik said, voice quiet as the space between lightning and thunder, 'I'd hold on to what little dignity you've got left and give it a rest.'

He took a measured step closer, eyes never leaving Horus. 'Let me spell it out to you since you're having so much difficulty: *I'm not interested.* I don't think about you, Horus. You're not my nemesis or something. Not the monster under my bed. If anything, you're a dog scratching at the door, whining for someone to let you in. *Begging for a scrap of attention.* And you need to come to terms with the fact that it's *never. Gonna. Happen.*'

The silence between Laik and Horus stretched, neither willing to blink first. But then, as if summoned by the stand-off, a large hand came to rest on Horus's shoulder.

'Ah, Laik,' said Lord Ode smoothly, though his pale eyes were fixed on his subordinate. 'Horus. I trust you're not making a nuisance of yourself?'

The question hung over him like a blade. Horus hesitated.

'Of course not, sir,' he said, voice chipped.

But this wasn't believed, not even for a second. Especially when it came from a repeat offender.

Lord Ode leaned in closer, ensuring his manner remained steady, but the weight of the words unmistakable in their meaning. 'Need I remind you that we are guests tonight? And I will not have you stirring trouble for the sake of your own amusement. In fact, upon reflection, I'd like you to do me a favour.' His eyes narrowed. 'Go downstairs. Stay with the cars. Keep an eye out for . . . mischief. Something tells me you'll be more useful there.'

Horus looked momentarily stunned, caught between confusion and humiliation.

'Sir?'

'I would hate for anything to happen to them. And I need someone with considerable expertise watching out for troublemakers. That's you. Go now, please, if you would.'

Laik, as much as he wanted to, didn't smirk, though a flicker of satisfaction might have briefly crossed his face.

Horus firmly set his glass down on a table. Then, without a word more, he turned and began his retreat, shoulders stiff, pace heavy with frustration.

With his departure, Lord Ode relaxed himself, a tight smile soon appearing, then extended a firm hand. 'It's damn good to see you again, boy.'

'The pleasure's mine, sir,' Laik said, taking the hand. 'Keeping well?'

'As well as one can in such strange times.' His grin softened into something a little more personal. 'And please – Dominic. It's been long enough. I saw the commotion at the Night Market, figured you were behind it. All for your sister, or something, wasn't it?'

Now it was Laik's turn to feel trapped by this unintentional line of questioning.

'A small number of troublemakers decided they could threaten her. I stepped in. Things got a little rowdy. As you are aware, family always comes first.'

'Indeed it does, indeed it does . . . Between us, I rather think we need more like you to keep upstarts like Horus from growing too bold. Yes, yes, you have your instances, but you don't seek out altercations, at least, from what I know. So that cannot be a negative against you. But the new generations . . . this individualism, this *thirst* for stimuli, for *conflict*, it does nobody any good. They forget their place. They need to be shown the hand, see? Be educated. You know, I've always said you should come work for me.

There's space for you. More than space, in fact: opportunity. You'll get a taste of *real* power under us. And real reward.'

Laik's response was polite, but unyielding. 'That's generous of you, sir. But Mortis has been good to me. I couldn't betray that.'

Dominic's eyes glittered with something unreadable, but he nodded. 'Loyalty is a rare virtue these days. Commendable.'

He clapped Laik on the shoulder, like a proud uncle.

'But should the day come when you feel . . . disillusioned,' Dominic added, almost jokingly, 'know that my door is always open. There are many ways to serve. And who knows? In doing so, you may discover something you never knew you needed . . .'

# Chapter Fifteen

## The Vault

The elevator felt slower this time.

Quinn swiped her security card without flourish. A tiny chime. The floor button, which remained unlit to Pepper's own access card, glowed a cobalt blue, and lit up under her fingertip. The number: 65.

They ascended in silence at first. Pepper shifted slightly, fingers curling and uncurling at her side. The soft whoosh of their ascent wasn't enough to steal the awkwardness.

'Miss,' Pepper said finally, 'are you sure you're not needed at the party?'

Quinn didn't look over. Her gaze was fixed upward, watching the lights above the lift door tick away floor after floor.

'Who needs me more?' she murmured. 'The pretend faces who know me by reputation and just want to play nice? My parents who hang me like a portrait on the wall at things like these? Or my endlessly capable, endlessly *dull* brother?' She smiled, slow and cat-like. 'Or maybe the little flame beside me in the dark, trying to build a fire without knowing what she's trying to burn . . .'

'Point taken,' Pepper replied. 'I just wouldn't want to get you into trouble.'

Quinn's laugh was brief, and gone before it could catch. She rubbed the lizard on her shoulder. 'Trouble and me are bedfellows, my love. And I am far from gentle.'

The lift didn't ping. Instead, it let out a deep, resonant bong, like a cathedral bell that had been struck to mark their arrival.

The doors parted with a mechanical sigh onto a simple corridor. Smooth stone floors, pale and bare. Metal trims. No opulence. No decoration. A narrow security desk bisected the space like a confession booth. Its owner jerked upright from hunching over a monitor, looking at the arrivals.

'Patrick,' Quinn sang, stepping forward, arms loosely swaying by her sides. 'Look at you. Desk duty on a night like this? I do hope they're making the overtime worth it. The rest of us are being terribly irresponsible upstairs.'

The man, lean and cautious, stood firm as they approached. His eyes flicked from her to Pepper, then back again.

'Someone has to behave themselves, Miss Cavendish. The short straw was mine, but I'll be making up for it when I clock off,' he said carefully. 'What brings you here?'

'A little peace and quiet from the hustle and bustle.'

He looked to Pepper, uncertain. 'And your guest?'

'She's on the level,' Quinn said, without hesitation.

There was a pause. Patrick's hand hovered over a scanner mounted into the desk. 'I'll need you both to sign in, please.'

Quinn tapped her card on the reader, shortly followed by Pepper, whose motions were much more deliberate. Patrick rested a hand on his hip while the computer monitor flashed up the request, a hip that Pepper noticed sported a black holster and the chunky handle of a firearm . . .

'All this used to be done with pen and paper, once upon a time. Can you believe it? Now it's these stupid machines,' Quinn whispered, 'so uncivilised.'

Patrick watched the screen as a flash of green glinted off his eyeballs. He nodded once and reached under the desk.

'Ladies, have a good evening.'

A hiss. A thunk.

The doors ahead were huge, arched, made of something darker than wood but not quite metal. Above them, carved in deep relief, was a castle turret haloed in flames. Battlements cracked. Windows open to nothing. Fire climbing over stone like ivy.

The Cavendish sigil, representing a history barbed and burning.

'Those are bloody big doors . . .' Pepper whispered, unable to contain her observation.

The doors split apart with a hiss from pressure locks, gliding far too quickly for their weight and design. Warm light spread across the plain floor before them as Quinn paused in thought.

'Well . . .' she began to walk inside, 'they don't call it a vault for nothing.'

The air shifted cooler the moment Pepper crossed the threshold; cooler, denser. It wasn't the temperature that made her shiver; it was the knowledge of entering somewhere sacred.

And tremendously dangerous.

The floor spread out before her in two great levels, the upper balcony encircling the lower like a crown. Beyond a shallow landing, the Vault opened into a vast reading hall.

Bookcases towered fifteen feet high, black wood kissed by age and wax, packed from floor to laddered ceiling with tomes bound in everything from tooled leather to stitched vellum. Some had no visible titles. Most had no recognisable language.

The ceiling arched above, forming ribs of stone. Lanterns hung at intervals like suspended stars. They cast a golden sheen on the long reading tables that stretched through the centre of the room, each with lamps of brass and green glass that glowed low and steady.

Above, the second level balcony was lined with iron banisters and more towering shelves. Quiet movement could be seen – someone crossing with a bundle of scrolls, another seated and taking notes. They had noticed the pair, but went about whatever business they had.

Pepper couldn't define the aesthetic, struggling to identify the influences of styles that had given birth to this one. To the woman, it was utterly astounding. Like a fusion of modern and gothic.

Quinn walked a few steps ahead, her footfalls almost silent, letting Pepper take it in at her own pace. Her head turned as if following a shifting, snaking current that ran through the room, detectable only by herself.

'This,' Quinn declared with a sweep of her arms, and the crack of a high heel to the floor, 'is what we call the Vault.'

Her voice echoed slightly in the vastness, bouncing off stone and polished brass.

'A museum of sorts. Except the exhibits are real, and the curators are weirder than me. Some of our most valuable things are kept here. Important things. Fragile things. Dangerous things.' She loudly whispered, '*The dangerous ones are the best.*'

She strolled forward, arms lazily swinging, trailing her fingers along the spines of massive leather-bound tomes like a child skipping through tall grass.

'History upon history upon history. Written, rewritten,

embellished, redacted, and then written again in slightly better prose. Did you know the Cavendish line began in East Anglia? Windswept marshes became the home for a tribe of Vikings, superstitious types who relied on bloodletting, which only encouraged our arrival. While they entertained themselves with shadows and stars and smoke, we spooked them enough to abandon settlements. The Romans afterwards thought they were cursed when legionnaires went missing, but nope – just us.'

Pepper trailed behind her, eyes wide, neck craning to catch glimpses of the second floor. Two figures in high-collared cloaks looked from the upper level like perching crows.

'All our travels recorded. Bloodlines charted like constellations. Tombs mapped in ink. Famous names, infamous doings, both bound in calfskin and forgotten until someone like us comes along to peel back the covers. Look at it, Pepper.' Quinn spun slowly, arms lifted. 'Smell it. Breathe it in.'

They passed an arched entry with brass piping and a flickering sigil glowing faintly in red above it.

'A lot happens here,' Quinn said, lowering her voice to a theatrical whisper, 'but we don't like to talk about it. Everything's hush-hush. Secrets, see? Can be more valuable than anything in this world, so we make sure ours don't scurry away. Take that one—' She gestured toward the arch. 'The Hemotheca. Everything blood goes on in there. Boiling points, burning thresholds, all very spicy.'

She grinned devilishly as they passed, with Pepper catching sight of machines that would look right at home in a hospital or laboratory.

'You know why sunlight's fatal to us, right? It's not the fire. It's the betrayal. We die, and the once loving sun, the thing that *gives* life, shuns us. Our blood revolts in the process. It boils, turns against us. That's what they're studying. Poisons, tonics, serums. *Drugs*. Things to help us. Things that could unmake us. I like to go in and see what they're cooking up. Poke around. The stuffy ones get cross, but nuts to them, I say.'

They passed under another carved arch, this one colder. The OSSUARY. A dry odour lingered here, like dust and old teeth. Through the entrance she glimpsed curved walls of preserved skeletons and scrolls stored behind glass. Pepper blinked at a long shelf containing rows of preserved femurs and an ornate display of a spinal column so giant that it looked like it very well may have belonged to one.

'Oh, this, this is one of my favourites,' Quinn sighed, her voice almost reverent. 'Bits and pieces of the Family. Bits and pieces of others. Hands that can't hold, legs that can't flee, skulls that don't think no more. You'd be amazed what bones remember. They talk plenty if you know the trick of listening. They tell the future. They reveal the past. They also make a surprisingly good broth if you're bold enough to try. For obvious reasons, dogs aren't allowed in here.'

Pepper raised an eyebrow. 'People bring animals in here?'

'No,' Quinn replied simply, then added, 'I'm just saying, if they did, they wouldn't be allowed. But they don't. But if they did – no. No dogs.'

Pepper speedily read the signs for others as they passed: LIBRARIUM, RELIQUARY VAULT, HERBARIUM, RESTROOMS. Each one teasing something fantastic within, with obvious exception to the last.

And then, as if her soul had found its cathedral, Quinn stopped before the grandest arch of all. The RELIC GALLERY.

She turned in place, letting the atmosphere caress her like

the roving hands of a lover. Her eyes fluttered half closed. Her voice dropped to a breathy hush.

'You can taste the slumber,' she whispered, 'Everything in here is dreaming. Some even remember when we were still gods, and those dream the best of all. Oh, it is just divine.'

She brought a finger to her lips, a fang catching the light, subtle and dangerous, but there. She was still smiling, staring at Pepper. But there was something else within the wildness of her eyelids. A hunger. A memory. A madness.

'You can walk through here, and every step will greet you with something you could never possibly imagine. Or maybe you can! I can. I couldn't, but I can now.' She paused, then added with a smirk, 'And I'm all the better for it.'

And with that, Quinn drifted forward through the archway, her silks swaying behind her like the tail of a comet, and Pepper followed.

Rows of glass-topped cases and velvet-robed pedestals stretched ahead, bathed in the soft glow of antique bulbs. Each display was a fragment of something lost and valuable: curled papers inked in languages long forgotten, fractured stone tablets etched with dreams and warnings, masks with teeth, charms scorched by fire, and weapons whose last purpose had been vengeance. Statues of things, things on plinths, oddities suspended from the ceiling, entombed in glass. It was dizzying.

Quinn moved through the aisles, humming as she walked, low at first, and then, with a flick of her tongue, she added words to her melody:

*'And all, they say, is theirs – but love, that claim is now up for debate.*
*You turned your gaze when profit came, so your outrage comes far too late.*

*Some cry ill-gotten, when they were forgotten – your fury's a hollow mistake.*
*If you'd cared at all, about the state of it, fool, then their loss would have made your heart break.*
*You never showed interest as their caretakers.*
*Left them broken, let them be stolen – then howled as the mistake-makers.*
*Now you're bitter that they've been protected,*
*Sheltered far from where they were rejected.'*

Pepper, trailing behind, wasn't sure if the song made her uneasy because of the lyrics, or because Quinn looked far too comfortable singing them.

'All this,' Quinn said, waving a hand theatrically toward the gallery, 'was scraped from battlefields both celebrated and forgotten. Torn from the ground. Plucked from the sky. Bargained for, lost in games, rescued, gifted or bought fair and square . . . mostly.'

Pepper's eyes moved over the glittering fragments of history, unable to guess which were sacred and which were dangerous.

'These Relics, they hide in the folds of the world's history,' Quinn continued, 'brought about by epics that time may never reveal: of nations collapsing and rebuilt, of queens betrayed, hymns silenced, plagues unleashed and rebellions of yellow. And now? Now they belong to us.'

She stopped in front of a stone archway carved with interlocking runes. Her eyes glinted.

'The other Families make noises, sure. Accusations of theft, desecration, all that poetic rot. But it's always a little hypocritical, don't you think? Glass houses, and all . . . they do the same.'

They passed a tall glass case. Inside, a lavender tombstone

stood upright, beaten but intact, its surface etched with dozens of unwatching eyes.

Pepper didn't see them.

She only saw the Eternal Rose.

Her breath hitched. There, sitting alone on a low obsidian plinth, removed from its casing, unguarded, like it had simply been placed down and forgotten, was the very thing she'd risked everything to find. It looked a little different from what she remembered: fresher, if that was the best description. Its petals seemed stiffer from the weird, wilted mess that she first laid eyes on. The brown tinge seemed to have spots of pearlescence spreading. But it looked so easy to reach out and take, to run.

But she'd never make it. She'd be set upon before her fingers even lifted the stem.

'Monsters exist in this world, dear, hidden here and there,' Quinn said, snapping Pepper back to the conversation, unsure if she had been noticed paying so much attention to the Relic, 'bitten or not. Each with a purpose. Each with a root. Your brother's no different.'

'Why such an interest in him?' Pepper asked.

'You grow up in a place like this, a Family like ours, you're told everything is possible. And it is, I know it more than most! But, and think on this, if you're constantly told that the world is yours to take by money or influence, then surely you're allowed to *touch* it from time to time, right? Not so much for me. They don't let me out often. My mother worries about what I might say, or do. Fears it! Me! Like, I'll rubbish our reputation in a flash somehow. So, she insists on stuffy escorts, clinging and suffocating, hiding just out of view – ugh. Shadowing me like, uh . . . um . . .' She snapped her fingers, struggling to clarify.

'Like shadows?' Pepper offered.

'Yes! Exactly! It's for the best according to her, *but whose best*? Certainly not mine. And your brother, he's the one they rely on to keep me well behaved. Whenever I go out for a walk, or – God forbid – try and enjoy myself with whatever this city has to offer, he is always the one Mortis tasks to bring me home. Because of the noisy thing inside him. I can argue with Laik and win all day long. But his other? There's no reasoning with that. Doesn't wanna listen. Too set in their ways. But you gotta admit . . . it's sort of incredible, isn't it? Scary in that nice, tingly way when it gushes on out.' Quinn inhaled, seeming proud of herself before she got to the point. 'Frankly, your brother fascinates me. I won't pretend that I don't admire what he's conjoined with, nor deny that it is attractive per se . . . but he is *such* a killjoy. And I do so miss having my fun.'

'Have you ever tried to find out what it is?' Pepper asked, still staring.

'Out of curiosity? No. It's hardly my business. I don't need people messing in mine, so I won't meddle in theirs. Not unless it's my business already . . . in which case I cannot help it. It's already happening, see? I don't have that luxury of a choice.' She smiled to herself, drifting behind Pepper, surveying her bare neck with interest, closer than what Pepper felt was a comfortable distance. 'What is it with the pair of you, hmm? Little puzzle boxes needing a good twist to open themselves before me. What is inside you, I wonder? Whatever do I need to do to . . . find out?' Quinn looked at Pepper, half-bemused, half-bewitched.

Pepper shuddered as Quinn passed, feeling exposed enough to be threatened by the odd tangle of flirtation in Quinn's words.

'I want to know,' Pepper interrupted. 'Can I find the answers here? Work out what's in him?'

'If not here,' Quinn said, 'then I suspect nowhere else.'

'Miss Cavendish,' Pepper began.

'That's my mother,' Quinn cut in, stroking Mr Wiggles' stiff jaw. 'She's downstairs, probably disapproving of me this very minute.'

'Quinn,' Pepper said, steadier now, 'I need to ask something.'

'You may.'

'The Vault. These archives. I beg you, may I use them to . . . discover, what may be inside Laik?'

'You want access to the Vault?'

'I request, on your mercy, that in the pursuit of finding a solution for my brother, an Enforcer to the revered Cavendish Family, that I am aided to remove this—'

Pepper stopped herself, frowning at the words she had just spoken.

Remembering how Quinn reacted the first time they met.

Remembering her sister.

*Realising that this wasn't the way.*

Instead, she emboldened herself with a breath and spoke with absolute conviction.

'I want access to the Vault. All of it. Not just the surface. I want to dig, to study, to understand what's inside Laik. I want to help him. I want to identify it. Know where it comes from. Know how it functions.'

Pepper's face darkened.

'And I know, I *know*, the best possible chance of doing any of this is somewhere down here. Something will give me the insight or the means. Right. *Here*.'

Quinn entertained a small smile.

'And whatever would you do with that knowledge?'

'When I do find what it is, I will work the solution, or the cure, or however it's gonna be rectified . . . when I'm capable of doing so? I swear, I will *rip the thing from Laik's insides, with my bare hands*, and punish it for every ounce of *fucking pain* it's caused us.'

There was a stillness to the moment. Quinn's eyes drifted to the gold locket hanging from Pepper's neck and then back up again.

'Oh, girlie,' she purred with a slow grin, almost aroused by the outburst. 'For a second there, I thought you had learned nothing, and I'd have had to say no. But that . . .'

Before she could say a word more, the lights in the Vault snapped from their native tones to a deep, humming red. Noises shifted around them, doors closed, bolts shunted into housing, various clicks, clunks and hisses. The entranceway to the Relic Gallery slammed shut like an iron trap as two feet of solid steel sealed them in.

Pepper looked around sharply, paranoid that she was the cause. All there was, was the deep, slow pulsing red, and thick shadows.

'What's happening?'

Quinn remained unmoved. She sang again, softly, like a lullaby meant to unsettle.

'Lockdown. *Some-body has been naugh-ty . . .*'

# Chapter Sixteen

## Earning Your Keep

The lobby of Leroux Tower had bled into siren-light. Red strobes pulsed across polished marble like a heartbeat. Security guards were posted at the doors, guns drawn but unsure where to point them. The outside world had become a roar – distant, chaotic, climbing.

Laik walked through to the entrance, met by Swan who fell into step beside him, his coat ragged and dripping with gutter water. His left cheek was swollen and already darkening.

'Looks pretty,' Laik said, spying at the injury.

'Just adds to the handsomeness, I say.'

'Trouble on tonight of all nights,' Laik muttered, gaze cutting toward the front doors. 'They must be crazy . . . You up for this?'

'Still standing, ain't I?'

'Alright. Who are they?'

Swan spat something bloody into a handkerchief before tucking it into his pocket. 'Street vamps. They're family-less, looks like some sort of gang. Security got jumped, a couple of us Enforcers at the same time. I was out having a smoke with Duncan when it happened. Didn't get a good look at any of their markings. Don't know who they are,' he said. 'But I know *what* they are.'

He looked at Laik with a smirk. 'Dead.'

The security guards flinched as the Enforcers approached. Swan didn't slow. 'Open the doors. Lock them behind us. They don't open until we give the all-clear,' he ordered.

The locks disengaged with a reluctant *chunk*. Cold air kissed the lobby like a warning. Laik stripped his suit jacket off and tossed it onto the security station, muscle rolled beneath the fabric of his shirt as he worked the sleeves to his elbows.

Then they stepped into the night.

The street outside Leroux Tower had turned into a war zone. Glass crunched underfoot, lamplight flickering off chrome and blood. Cavendish Enforcers were already in the thick of it – some swinging, some sprawled, some not moving. The unaffiliated had come in force. Street vampires. Bruisers. Grudge-drunk with nothing to lose and too much to prove. The jealous. The manic. The dregs of their kind.

Laik didn't hesitate. He dropped into the fight like gravity had shifted direction.

The first vampire barely saw him coming. A fist across the jaw sent him to the kerb. Another grabbed Laik's arm, but Laik twisted, and shoved him against the wall, gripped by the collar. Headbutt. Once. Twice. They crumpled.

Swan tackled a brawler off Duncan's back and flattened him with a knee to the ribs, then pulled his blooded, but thankful, partner to his feet. A slap on the back got his head back in the game.

Across the street, the pack had reformed, a dozen street vamps huddled like a rugby team, fresh enough to be dangerous, old enough to be cocky. One of them, a rangy man with gold in his teeth, cracked a length of pipe in his hands against flagstones.

'Here we go, fellas!' he howled, baring his fangs like an animal. 'They had to spit out a few more because they didn't like a fair fight! Don't matter none, does it? Now we can show the Family dogs what a real party looks like!'

Laik dabbed the blood trickling from his nose and grinned. He knew their type, and it would be a joy to break this one in particular. Sure, violence was a requirement of the job, but in a situation like this, it wasn't just an obligation – it would be a delight. Instances like this convinced him that if God did exist, not only would he be watching, but Laik would be carrying out his will.

Laik heavily stepped onto the bonnet of a parked car, made his way to its roof and looked at the faces in the alleyway staring back – eyes keen, fangs already out and catching the streetlight. These didn't seem like the normal unorganised vampires looking for a scrap, but at this point he was too eager getting down to business to work out the specifics.

'I don't know what your beef is and, frankly, I just don't care! But you listen *up* and listen *good*!' Laik barked. 'You've already forfeited any chance of being allowed to walk away from this, so that leaves you two choices! You can surrender yourselves to the Cavendish Family and be brought in to be reprimanded! Or . . . you can stay as you are. But if you take the latter, I am warning you: things *will* get messy!'

'Ha!' The street vamp raised his arms. 'With just a handful? You should have brought an army with you, Cavendish! It would have made this a fair fight!'

As his companions fell in behind, Laik's face darkened with a smile so terrible it would have made the Devil shiver. When he spoke, his voice dripped with danger. There was nothing more liberating than permission.

'Funny. I was about to suggest the same to you. Have it your way!'

Duncan led the charge with seven others, roaring as they met the pack like a hammer to glass. A few of the street vamps pulled knives – flashes of metal that caught the light like warnings. Swan singled out the culprit who'd roughed him up earlier, pointed at him and stormed forward toward the violence.

They crashed together. Snarls. Yells. Somewhere, tyres screeched and a car alarm wailed as background noise. Laik raced forward, lashing out at what he could, the one with gold teeth directly in his sights. A blur of bodies in his sight skimmed and fell and was shoved before, in seconds, he was already upon what he presumed to be the one running the show.

Goldie, as Laik affectionally named their leader on account of his teeth work, swung the metal pipe wide – its radius wide enough to be dangerous, but slow enough to be easily ducked beneath. A second swing sailed overhead, leaving them open for a kick to the chest that Laik swiftly delivered. The pipe clattered on the ground. But the punk to his left was too quick with his punches. The first few landed against raised forearms until hooks to his kidneys made them lower just enough to expose him. Laik staggered, sucked wind. His jaw shuddered from knuckles. Then they had him. Two of them grabbed hold, dragging him down. Goldie, who hugged his chest to ease a cracked rib, lifted something with a metallic click.

A pistol.

'*Outta the way!*' Goldie snarled, trying to aim through the flurry of grabbing and swinging.

* * *

Swan thrust a knee into something hard that cracked beneath the pressure, pushing its owner away before scanning the mess of limbs where Laik had been pulled under. But it was too late to stop what was coming.

A flash accompanied a tight thunder crack.

Goldie admired his handiwork.

Then something shifted.

The shooter stepped back.

Swan held a breath, staring at the execution he had just witnessed. Rage began to bubble and brew, but it was being subdued by disbelief. And then, alarm.

Without warning, the two men on top of Laik were *launched*. Not shoved but catapulted away with power. One slammed into the side of a parked van, cratering the panelling. The other crashed flat against a brick wall before tumbling down in an unnatural heap.

Laik rose.

Only . . . it wasn't just Laik anymore.

His frame grew larger, casting a broader shadow. His spine had curved slightly forward, his hands swelling at the knuckles, fingertips blackened as though dipped in ink. His eyes were burning pits. A deep growl echoed out from somewhere too deep in the chest to belong to a man.

Goldie twitched to fire once more, but he was stopped from pulling the trigger. Stopped from standing, as his legs were pulled away beneath him. Stopped from seeing the world right way up. And as the colossal mass whipped Goldie over and over into the pavement, gold teeth scattering in the road, he stopped resembling anything human *or* vampire.

The thing that Laik had become shifted its gaze. The shimmering, burning pits that were his eyes bounced between the rabble.

Someone ran at him with a knife.

The creature snatched the arm mid-swing and hurled the man backwards. He hit the wall so hard, it cracked.

Swan whooped, even as he ducked a flying elbow. 'Alright! Let's go!'

The street vamps were faltering now, with the Enforcers emboldened by the transformation. A few had already fled, kicking up trash and blood as they scrambled for alleys.

The beast roared, thundering after them.

It charged, shoulder-barging into an obstructing car so hard it skidded sideways. It hit the group like a wrecking ball – bodies flung, one man lifted clean off his feet and slammed into a bin that buckled under his weight. Others were swept aside, broken.

It was too much. Swan knew the signs. This wasn't Laik winning a fight – this was the thing inside looking for an excuse to *keep* fighting.

He chased after, waving and yelling, intercepting just before the entity could bring a steel bench down on someone's head.

'Laik!' he barked. 'Hey! *Hey!* Back to me! *Remember who you are.*'

The creature snapped its head toward him. Eyes locked.

'You're Cavendish. You're an Enforcer. You have *rank*. So, let's ease it down, right? You don't wanna be seen like this . . .'

The monstrosity turned its entire mass and began to march toward him with unknown intent.

Swan felt the ground shudder on approach, starting to worry. 'Whoa, buddy! Calm! We drink together! You like bad music, and I rib you for it! And you still owe me a beer for that job in Montford. We're friends, you asshole!'

Still no change.

Swan gritted his teeth. 'You *really* want to scare someone

helping you?' he shouted. 'What do you think *Pepper* would say if she saw you acting like this?!'

That did it.

The entity flinched. The growl collapsed into a rattling breath. The hunched posture shifted. Inch by inch, the shadow inside Laik crawled back down into his being and vanished. And finally, Laik drunkenly stood beneath the streetlight, before staggering back to a wall and sliding down it. He coughed once, then winced sharply, hand instinctively clutching his chest. He looked at his trembling hands, attempting to work out which of the blood that soaked his shirt was his. Fragments of people, debris of brick and wood and bone lay around him. Fallen comrades. Still enemies. Hot blood infested the night air.

Swan kicked one of the street vamps over, gauging how dead they actually were. A shoe nudged their head side to side, checking their tattoos for any sign of gang markings. He couldn't see any . . .

'Round all of ours up,' he ordered to the Enforcers in earshot. 'If they're hurt and can walk, get 'em up to medical. As for all this trash, drag them in for questioning. Doesn't matter if they ain't moving. Someone has to be alive enough to speak. And if they do object, hit 'em until they learn better manners. And someone lift the damn lockdown!'

Swan exhaled and looked around at the ruin before squatting before Laik, spying the soaked patch of red on his shirt. 'Well,' he muttered, 'so much for the dress code. You back with us, buddy? You had me worried for a moment there.'

Laik grunted with a pained nod.

'Didn't know you cared.'

'Yeah, that's me. Real sentimental type. This is the last thing we needed. An attack on our turf, and while we're hosting company? Mortis will be out for blood. You just stay there a minute, don't push yourself.'

Laik eased the ruined shirt away from his skin and squinted at the hole. Blood-soaked, scorched around the edges. 'Pain in my bloody ass. At least it went through.' He smirked faintly before it was interrupted by a hiss. 'Didn't ruin the suit, though.'

It would be sore as anything until it was healed. Thanks to his nature, this wouldn't take long at all, a handful of days at the most, but the inconvenience was the annoyance. Yet all this was nudged from his mind as he was haunted by the obvious: *why didn't they go for a kill shot?* The heart, the head, the two vulnerable points for a vampire – they were completely exposed. He failed to believe that it was bad aim at such close range . . .

Security was already erecting barricades and rolling out lengths of hosepipe to begin washing away the aftermath. Reese strode out of the main doors, leading a gaggle of security behind her, who fanned out on her orders. With a finger pressed to her ear, she spoke to the tower in coordinating their response efforts, before addressing the pair.

'Boys. What's the damage?'

Swan didn't sugar-coat it. 'Three down, maybe more. Few got cut up, they'll need checking, but I'm predicting a couple'll be benched for a while. Duncan is out here somewhere. And he' – he gestured at Laik's chest – 'I'm surprised he's still ticking. That's a close one . . . lucky sod.'

Reese blocked the light as she bent over Laik and made a low whistle.

'Nasty. I'll get medical to check you over, there's a few down here.' She looked to the swelling on Swan's face upon rising, leaning for a better view. 'What about you?'

'Just a tap. I'll be fine.'

'If you insist.'

'We need a hard perimeter, just to make sure there're no stragglers,' Swan advised, pointing here and there. 'Start at the top of the car park entrance and cordon off the side roads. Leave just one open for the guests but make sure security don't have guns showing or anything. We don't want to scare the VIPs.'

'Got it.' Reese spoke into the radio, administering directions. Uniforms and suits broke from their set positions in the street.

Swan reached out and helped Laik up, steadying him with one arm. Laik staggered, hissed at the tug across his torso, then found his footing. Strength was already returning.

While they did, Reese had her finger pressed to her earpiece. Her face set into a frown, remaining silent. When she was finished, she addressed them.

'Guys,' she said, shifting nervously from foot to foot. 'There's something we need to see.'

Reese led them around the tower's east side, where the outer lights flickered like dying stars. Just past a line of barricades, down a slope slick with tyre-marks and oil, was the entrance to the service garage. A camera above the bay door hung crooked, yanked aside so it faced a concrete pillar instead of the entryway.

They proceeded carefully down the incline.

Laik smelled it before he saw it.

They rounded the corner, and the parking garage unfolded in grim silence. At the far end of the bay, strewn over and under valet cars like discarded mannequins, were eight bodies. Torn, brutalised, pieces missing. A torso hanging over a windshield. A severed hand resting on a hood. One figure stuffed halfway beneath a rear axle, like they'd tried to crawl away. Most of what belonged inside the individuals was dashed over concrete.

On the wall behind them, smeared in thick, arterial red, were the words:

***DO I HAVE YOUR ATTENTION NOW?***

Laik stared. Swan didn't speak. Reese spat the horror from her mouth. Behind them, other Enforcers began to gather – two exchanging a cigarette, another cradling a broken arm, all of them staring at the message like it had been addressed personally.

*For Laik, it was.*

Swan exhaled slowly. 'Jesus. Guess in the chaos, nobody noticed.'

'They must've slipped in during the fight,' Laik wheezed. 'Moved the camera, security wouldn't have caught a thing.'

'Victims?' Swan asked.

Reese manoeuvred around a corpse in overalls silently soaking in a puddle of its own fluids. The Enforcer nodded grimly. 'Valets, mechanics.'

Swan rubbed the back of his neck, then checked to see if a molar was about to come loose. 'Hate to say it, but I'm glad it wasn't guests. Can you imagine if someone important got carved up like this during the party? The fallout . . . heads would literally roll.'

'That's a very fair assumption, Swan. Can I take that as you volunteering for the job?' someone asked.

They turned in unison beneath the humming strip lights and the painted accusation.

Mortis Cavendish approached at a leisurely pace, hands in his coat pockets, eyes already sweeping the bloodied parking garage. He drew a slim, wooden cigarette case from his pocket, older than anything parked here, and lit a cigarette with the flick of an old brass lighter. The orange flare briefly cast shadows under his cheekbones, the silver in his hair gleaming like frost.

Swan straightened. 'Give me a shot, sir. I'll happily bring the culprits in.'

Reese ran a hand through her short hair. 'Provided they're not already dead.'

'No,' Mortis replied, exhaling a thin stream of smoke. 'The ruckus was just a distraction. This,' he said as he gestured vaguely to the slaughter spread out, 'the message, was the real intention.'

He stepped forward and crouched, appraising one of the corpses without touching it. His eyes narrowed faintly. Then, standing again with the sigh of someone who had seen, and approved, such massacres over his long tenure, he shook his head.

'What an absolute mess.'

Laik tried to straighten himself. 'Since when did you start smoking again, sir?'

'Since things like this started happening.' Mortis gave him a side glance. 'Don't tell Concetta. She would absolutely kill me for it. You best get that looked at, son. The last thing we need is you bleeding out.'

'I'll be going to medical after this.'

'Then make sure you do.' He looked toward Reese, plucking the smoke between his large fingers. 'Who else has seen this?'

'A handful, apparently. And them.' She thumbed behind them. 'Word hasn't travelled yet.'

'Good. Lock it down,' Mortis said. 'Get it cleaned up. I don't want this to cause a commotion.'

'Yes, sir.' Reese promptly turned to those congregating and, with her hands and a few choice words, began to disperse them.

Swan gave the graffiti on the wall a longer look, the words still glistening wet.

'You got any idea what it means, sir?' he asked.

Mortis inhaled again, eyes narrowed to slits through the smoke. 'Not yet. But the list of those who have eyes on the Family is as long as . . . Well, it's pretty long. What about you two? Any thoughts?'

Laik exhaled slowly through his nose. 'I think it may be a rogue Ode Enforcer. One with a particular grudge against me.'

Mortis's brow lifted faintly. 'Does he have a name, this troublemaker?'

'Horus,' Laik said flatly.

Mortis frowned in recollection. 'Why does that sound familiar?'

Swan scratched the back of his neck. 'He's the asshole who hijacked a blood van last month, claimed it was cutting through Ode territory when it was on the border. I had my suspicions he was involved in that Vow Runner hit but couldn't confirm it. Year before that, he tried to start something at the Night Market, said he had the right to shake down some of the stalls. Three years ago, had a brawl outside the Kingfisher. Killed three of ours solo. Almost single-handedly set off a war.'

Laik added dryly, 'Only earlier tonight he tried to start something. I knew him before I fell under your name, sir. In fact, he was the one you personally told to shove off when we first met. He's persistent and obsessive. Vindictive. Plus, he's just a *massive* twat.'

Mortis nodded faintly, amused despite himself. 'Ahh.

Aren't they all? That would make sense. And the gutter vamps here he would have paid off to do the dirty work. Classic cowardice dressed as performance. That is, if you're correct.'

He took another drag.

Swan stepped closer. 'Why so brazen? He must know this would get back to Lord Ode.'

'He doesn't think it will,' Laik said, his voice dropping. 'Or he doesn't care if it does. So, what do we do about him?'

Mortis flicked ash to the concrete. 'Nothing.'

Laik looked over. 'Sir?'

'Nothing – for now.' Mortis's voice was firm. 'Any action taken publicly would jeopardise the pact between Families. The moment we accuse one of Dominic's men of orchestrating this, we strain some already difficult relationships. We risk more than bruised egos, and I suspect that may be what the culprit wants.'

He exhaled smoke, watching it curl toward the red emergency lights still flickering overhead.

'We endure. Until we can't.'

Laik scowled, wincing at the throb in his chest. 'Sir, letting anyone get away with this is—'

'—outrageous?' Mortis finished, giving him a look. 'Yes. But wiser men than us have swallowed outrage to preserve the peace. And besides, we've a few of this rabble in good enough shape to talk. Let's see what comes from their mouths before we brandish our weapons.'

He turned to walk, cigarette burning low between his fingers.

'I won't let generations of peace be undone by one lunatic,' he added, without looking back. 'And neither will you.'

# Chapter Seventeen

## Closer

Pepper flung open the flat door like she'd been holding her breath the entire way home and could only now exhale. The moment it slammed behind her, she kicked off her heels with a graceless little hop, one landing under the shoe cupboard, the other rolling down the hall – and let out a bubbling, breathless laugh. Her security badge dangled from her fingertips before she hung it neatly on the brass hook by the door, right next to Laik's. The contrast in their photographs was sharp: his straight-and-focused kind of impression that suggested military instinct, hers, off-centre looking like she had somewhere better to be.

'*Laik!*' she called, already halfway down the hall, her voice bright and breathless. 'Laik! Oh my God, you won't believe it, you won't actually – I mean, *it's incredible*. I got it, I worked it out—'

She was practically spinning as she moved, tugging open the buttons of her waistcoat, loosening it from her shoulders. Her hair now hung wild and half unravelled from hours of tension finally allowed to go slack.

'I mean, I didn't think she'd actually say *yes*. I *thought* she might, but then she did and it just – bam – *yes*, I'm still in shock, it doesn't feel real!'

Laik was in the living room. Or, at least, a version of him was. Slouched low on the sofa, bathed in the pale lamplight that slanted across the room from the kitchen. He was quiet, still, holding a mug between his hands with the kind of reverence usually reserved for communion.

'How's about you breathe and try that again?'

He didn't look at her right away. Just took a long, deliberate sip, then winced as a pair of painkillers chased a mouthful of hot chocolate.

Pepper had already moved to the kitchen, swinging open cupboard doors and clattering cutlery. Hot water kissed a cup. Her laugh was half-sheepish, half still-fizzing. She called out from the kitchen. 'The Vault, Laik. The *fucking* Vault!'

He raised one brow, tired. 'What about it?'

'I got in.'

Laik's head lifted.

'You *what*?'

'I got in,' she said again, emerging with a steaming mug, circling around the sofa now, like a satellite finding its orbit. 'I was with Quinn – she took me down. Gave me a tour. The size of it, the things inside, it's unreal. I – Laik, I *saw* it. I saw the Rose. I stood right in front of it. *This* close! And I just have to work out how we can nab it.'

Then she stopped mid-pace, catching her breath as she finally looked at him properly.

Her eyes travelled down the state of him: dried blood on his shoulder, gauze peeling at one side, a fresh purple bruise flowering across his bare chest, its companion on the back seeping red. His knuckles were raw, and the mug trembled faintly in his grip from residual shakes. She noticed the faint sheen of sweat across his temple, the way he winced, even shifting in place.

Pepper's smile faltered.

'*What the hell happened to you*?'

Laik gave a grunt. 'That trouble tonight? There was a brawl down in the street. I was in the middle of it.'

Her eyes widened. 'The cause?'

His tone soured, a touch offended. 'No. The solution.'

'You're hurt,' she said, frowning now. 'You *look* hurt.'

'Caught a bullet, that's all.'

'That's all? That's *all*? What in the . . . people don't *catch* bullets, Laik, that's not a normal thing. You get shot, and then you maybe *die* from being—'

'You're living with a vampire,' he interrupted, deadpan.

She stopped. Blinked. Sipped her tea. 'Okay . . . sure, but it's still, like . . . bad for you, right?'

Laik gave the faintest shrug, and winced again.

'Is it painful?' she asked, softer now.

'Pretty much.'

'Okay, you're bleeding through your thing there. Like, a lot.'

'Thought I was,' he muttered, fruitlessly trying to look behind. 'I can't reach it. Any chance of you changing that for me?'

Pepper hesitated, then nodded. 'Uh . . . sure.'

She crossed the room and gently lowered herself beside him on the sofa, slipping her mug down next to some clean dressings and tape on the coffee table. Her fingers hovered before she touched him, noticing how the skin ran warm under her hands. Odd. She imagined he would have been stone cold, what with being undead and all. Another thing that seemingly defied convention.

She peeled the gauze back, grimacing at the wound beneath.

'Tell me about this plan of yours then,' he said, attempting to distract her from the gory spectacle.

'I was talking with Quinn,' Pepper said, focusing on cutting the tape, 'and the talk . . . kinda turned to you.'

'Ran out of conversation that quickly?'

'Oh shush. We started to discuss you. Or, more specifically . . . the thing in you. Your, uh . . . friend.'

'Right.'

She pressed the new patch over the wound gently and set fresh tape on each side. Then she continued. 'There's more knowledge in that Vault than anywhere I've seen. Diaries, experiments, notes on blood and bones and . . . weird stuff. It's a museum or something, a laboratory, a library, there's so much. I asked Quinn for access. And she gave it to me.'

He turned slightly, wincing. 'You convinced *Quinn bloody Cavendish* to not only get you inside the frigging Vault, but to also give you access – just like that? How the hell did you manage that?'

'I said I wanted to find out what's inside you. Find it out, get to know it, so we can remove it.'

Laik blinked. 'You . . . said what?'

Pepper pulled away. 'Yeah. You know. To cure you, I guess? Is that the right word?'

'Huh . . .' His voice trailed. Something unreadable crossed his face, and a corner of his mouth began to curl. 'That's actually—'

She waved a hand. '*A great cover story*, I know, right? It just came to me and she fell for it. It was perfect, I can't believe I just . . . Anyway, I pretend that, and I can get into the, uh—' Pepper snapped her fingers in thought.

Laik blinked again. Something behind his eyes sank, though he kept the rest of his face unreadable.

'The Relic place. Relic Gallery, I think it was? The Eternal Rose was there, I saw it. I was *this* close. I can spend some time in there, work out the security, the coming and goings, and figure out how to thieve it. Oh my God, we might actually pull this off!'

Pepper energetically struck her mug with his own. Laik lowered his head, just a little. Said nothing. Sat the drink down. Then got to his feet, turned to the windows overlooking the silhouetted city.

Pepper didn't notice. She was too busy replaying her plan in her head.

'Just make sure you get it. I have my own needs for the Rose. Don't forget that.' He surveyed the blinking lights across the jutting angles touching the sky. The outlines of grey clouds. The ladders of flat windows, both dark and aglow. Anything to not look at the reflection of the women set in the glass. And for one strange, torturous moment, Laik let himself feel the echo of something dangerously close to hope.

Before driving it back down into his being again, where the monster lived.

Pepper got up and made the mistake of approaching, the thrill of her news slowly giving way to the storm settling behind Laik's eyes.

'But look,' she said, trying to catch it again, trying to find footing on the cliff-edge she didn't realise they'd both walked toward. 'Do you know how many books there are to go through? I don't even know where to remotely start to convince people I'm on the level. Laik, you've got to give me something to go on about yourself.'

He didn't turn from the window. His arms were crossed,

shoulder stiff, the city lights painting his skin in faint orange smears.

'Like what?'

'Where did you live?'

He shifted slightly. 'What kinda question is that?'

'A normal one,' she said, voice gentler than before. 'It's simple. Where did you used to live? Where do you come from?'

She watched his reflection go still in the glass. There was a flicker – something that cracked the surface – and vanished just as quick.

'What was that?' she asked.

'What was what?'

'You gave me a look.'

'No, I didn't. Didn't at all.'

'Jesus, Laik,' Pepper muttered, 'just . . . stop being insufferable for one minute. Time is against us.'

He turned quick, volatile. 'No, it's against *you*. You've spent all this time since the moment you arrived banging on about how your sister's on the hook, how the clock's ticking. Well, guess what? *I'm not*. I've got all the time in the world. No race. I can just wait it out before I get my hands on the Rose for what *I* need to do.'

His eyes flared with heat now, his voice catching like a spark on kindling. Something sad on his face was brushed over with resentment.

'Did it ever occur to you that the world doesn't revolve around you? That other people have their own shit to deal with – and storming in and turning everything upside down based on what *you* need doesn't make you popular with anyone? You know what it makes? Nothing but a goddamn *mess*.'

Pepper blinked. Her mouth opened before the words came.

'Are you *serious*? If you've forgotten, *you* were the one who dragged me into this! *You* came up with this ridiculous lie that we're related, which, by the way, I can't believe everyone's actually fucking buying. Me showing up here is the most interesting thing that's happened in your sad life!'

Her voice cracked, sharp with fury, and she threw her arms up. 'Gee, Laik – did my arrival bring some sunshine to your mopey little existence? Sorry about that! Next time I'll remember to turn up at the Night Market when you've had your fill sitting in a corner like a billy-no-mates.'

'I *had* the Rose!' he shouted, stepping into her space. 'I *had* it, alright?!'

She stopped.

'I was protecting the collection for the auction. I pulled strings for *months*, got myself cleared, kept close to the damn thing. I was *alone* with it. And just when I finally had the chance . . . I find you, skulking around in the dark with – with your goddamn *paws* all over it. You *ruined* everything.'

There was a flicker of something in her. Regret, maybe, but it twisted too quickly into anger.

'And how was I supposed to know that?' she snapped. 'You haven't said. What were you gonna do – go on the run with it? I've not been here long, but I don't think the Cavendishes are the kind of people to let something like that lie!'

'You don't know a thing about them. Or me. Because *you ain't us*.'

'Oh, I'm *sorry*, I thought I was speaking to – to a vampire, not a child! I guess that's another mistake o' mine!' she snapped. 'Considering everyone I've spoken to thinks you're a gloomy hard-ass, I thought you would have welcomed someone around. I don't *care* about your screwups. I'm up against the wall, Laik. Unlike you, I don't get all this time you're bragging about, to spend looking all menacing and brooding for pissing *effect*.'

He slammed a hand above her against the glass, sudden and towering. His body loomed close, radiating heat, a low growl hiding in his chest. When he bared his teeth, his true nature was fully on display.

'*You've never been up against it in your life*,' he snarled. 'You're too busy taking advantage of everyone else to get what you want. Stealing from their good nature. Taking 'em for a ride. Because that's what a girl like you always *does*. You're nothing but a parasite.'

And then – pain. White-hot and sharp.

Pepper had jabbed her finger straight at the patch on his chest. The wound exploded with agony. He gasped, staggered backward, swearing.

'God-*fucking*—!'

'You don't know the *first* thing about me,' Pepper hissed, advancing now. 'And if you call me that again, I swear I'll end you.'

She jabbed her finger at his chest again, between the shield of his arms.

'If you want to talk about parasites, how about you look in the mirror, huh? Where is it? Do the thing. Have a tantrum, go crazy, smash it all up! C'mon, Laik. *Get angry*. That's all you do! Bring the big guy out! Let's see what you're made of.'

His mouth opened, furious and feral, but the growl never came. Instead, he blinked, faltered. His breath broke.

'No,' he said quietly. 'Not for you.'

She blinked too, unsure. 'What?'

'It doesn't want to,' he repeated, baffled. 'It always wants a fight. *Always*. First excuse it gets. Half the time

I'll practically invite it to go nuts. God, it'll burn the world given the chance, but you . . . with you . . .'

'What? Because I'm a girl?'

'Oh, for – please,' he muttered, pulling away and dropping onto the sofa with a grunt. 'Just stop. My God.'

He leaned back, exhaling through gritted teeth. 'Why are you the *only one* who can do that? When I lose control – *really* lose it – you can just . . . shut it down. Pacify me.'

He paused to correct himself.

'Pacify *it*.'

She folded her arms. 'Maybe I just don't scare easily.'

'No,' he said, glancing up at her. 'No, it's not that. You *push* me. Constantly. You stir the pot and pick away. Run off, then come back like nothing happened. You know what you're doing. I should've gone off the deep end five times over since you got here. But something in you . . . I just don't have the energy for it.'

He shook his head.

'I don't know what kind of things you've put up with,' she said, voice still guarded, 'but you don't get to come at me like that.'

'Same,' he muttered. 'All I see is your anger. Always testing, jabbing. I'm not your punching bag, Pepper. Not one of the ones who wronged you.'

'Says the stand-offish dickhead.'

Laik looked up, really looked at her, and for once there was no venom in his voice.

'Yeah,' he said. 'Guilty. Same to you.'

He leaned forward, resting his arms on his knees.

'When you've been around as long as I have . . . keeping people at arm's length is sensible. They'll turn on you. Use you. Sell you out if it benefits them. It's hard not to—'

'—be angry,' she finished for him.

He glanced at her. Sceptical at first. 'Yeah.'

'I've never known anything *but* struggle,' she said. 'It's always been me and Claire. Nobody else. Just the two of us, always going place to place. Scraping by. Day after day. The world doesn't care how hard you fight, or how tired you are. It just *keeps* coming. And people? They're the worst. And I don't think anyone is supposed to live like that. Funniest thing is that the only other person I've ever met who gets that isn't really . . . a person anymore.'

Her voice cracked, and she turned away, wiping at her eyes.

'All this shit. It's not fair.'

Laik didn't move. But a tear rolled down his cheek, unburdened and slow.

'Buried under it all . . .' he murmured.

'Running to the next disaster . . .' she echoed.

'The world crushing you.'

'Not stopping.'

There was silence.

Then Laik said softly, 'This sister of yours. You have family. And you love her. Don't let go of that. No matter what happens. No matter how bad it gets. You *hold* onto it.'

Pepper nodded. Her face was streaked with tears now, but there was no shame in it.

'Jesus. Just tell me how it happened. I need to know,' she said.

Terror glinted in his eyes, behind the tears.

'Please,' she added gently, stepping closer.

She reached down, and slowly, deliberately, took his hand.

Their fingers laced together.

He didn't pull away.

# Part III

# Chapter Eighteen

## Far, Far From Home

The fields smelled of fire and milkweed. Bomb craters had turned the French farmland into gouged, weeping wounds, the soil blackened and slick with oil and rain. Laik crouched low beside a broken wall of limestone and lichen, boots sunk in the mud. They'd moved through the night, across twisted hedgerows and grainfields gone to ruin, pressed in tight formation under a sky that threatened to unleash another downpour.

Six of them, left from twelve, all bone-tired and underfed. Just lads from Cardiff and Aberystwyth and Merthyr, stitched together with sandbags, rifles and half-spoken prayers. Gareth had been the youngest of the lot, and it showed. Barely needing to shave, always pushing his helmet back with a nervous flick of his thumb as though it never quite sat right, every attempt to hold a conversation ended with him shaking with nerves. He'd carried a photograph in his breast pocket — two sisters on a pebble beach — and had shown it round often enough that everyone could picture their squinting smiles from memory. One, he promised, he would marry when he returned. The young man shadowed Laik at every opportunity, even making a point of comparing him to his eldest brother back in Cardiff. After that, he seemed to settle whenever he found his place at Laik's side, as though the company steadied whatever in him the war had knocked loose. Laik hadn't encouraged this behaviour, but neither had the heart to discourage it. As long as the boy kept pace and kept quiet when it mattered, there was no problem.

A week earlier they'd been part of a larger push, pressing back the German forces as they bled toward the Seine. But something had gone wrong with the orders, or the map, or both. And now they were too deep, too far east, flanked by ruined villages and farm roads with no names. Far, far from home.

They'd taken shelter in a bombed-out cowshed, its thatched roof sporting a hole so big it was as if God himself had driven a fist through it. The bodies of three French civilians had been moved to the side of the barn – or what was left of them. A mother, a father, a boy. They had not been shot. Laik tried not to look at the necks. Even for the Germans, it was cruel. Gareth had muttered something about it being a quick end at least, but nobody believed it. Not really.

The loft provided a decent vantage point over the nearby fields. Hours began to stretch. Laik and the others took turns in providing lookout upstairs while the sergeant made his plans and the sun began to bathe the sky in citrus. When it was Laik's turn for rest, he had barely closed his eyes when the shouting started. German voices, sharp and rushed from outside. Then a crack – Gareth was the first on the ground, clutching his side with his mouth open like a scream had been ripped out of it. Laik had tried to drag him back when the sarge ordered they return fire.

Bullets tore through the air, bright as lightning, loud as judgement.

It wasn't a firefight. It was a slaughter. In under a minute, three more went down. Wood cracked and burst around them. Then silence, save for the sizzle of blood in the hay and the sound of someone wetly choking.

Laik didn't remember the bullet that hit him. Just the heat in his gut and the sky tipping sideways. He saw stars, but they weren't above. They were stitched into the earth. A glitter of shell casings and ration tins. His body crumpled against the beam of the ruined loft, half covered in rubble, propping him up. Breathing was hard. He didn't call for help. There wasn't anyone left to hear him. Instead, he let his mind retreat to the green fields of the farm in Wales. Home. The faces of his family. And the last, desperate wish to be with them once more.

He waited for the calls from the Germans to grow closer, but they didn't come.

He waited for the patrol to finish the job, but it never happened.

He waited for death to finally claim him, and it would do so in time. But not in the fashion that he hoped.

The light bled out of the foreign sky. Moonlight cut across the floorboards in sharp lines. Shadows spilled across the walls like ink, and with them came the quiet.

And then – movement.

Laik opened one eye. Something was crunching in the straw below. Low to the ground. Steady. Methodical.

His first thought was a wild dog, but the shape was all wrong. It didn't growl. And its eyes weren't right. They shone with a dull, unnatural sheen – not yellow, not green, something stranger. Something hungry. It was dragging something out of sight: the sergeant.

No breath. No voice. Just that slow, wet rip.

Laik tried to lift his head, and the shape stopped. One eye blinked up at him from the dark. It didn't flee.

He lay very still, too afraid to move, and watched as the shadow crept from one body to the next. It wanted more. There *was* more, more of them in the loft. Fresh meat.

It carefully made its way up the ladder.

Laik could barely see straight, the cold having long crept into his muscles.

Now in the loft, it stalked low over the dusty floorboards, staying in the black. When it came to Gareth's corpse, something shifted in the way it moved – a twitch, like it had caught a scent. Laik could hear it then. Breathing. Soft. *Human.*

And then the eyes turned on him.

It didn't pounce. It came slowly, and with intent.

Laik's limbs failed to obey as he tried to move, his fingers clenched slate and stone, casting one forward to try and spook it, but the effort was pathetic. The creature stalked closer, no bigger than a man, but its shadow twisted long. He saw fingers, or maybe claws. The torn folds of something like wings? Maybe a cloak? A coat? The silhouette never settled.

It knelt over him.

The mouth that opened was too wide. Moonlight caressed too sharp teeth.

Laik lacked the strength to move, the will to resist.

He didn't feel pain. Not at first. Just pressure on his neck, ice water forcing itself through his veins. Then heat. Rising up his spine, into his jaw, writhing behind his eyes. Struggle was beyond him. His body locked. His chest burned.

The creature fed, slow at first, then more urgently, bony fingers kneading into the flesh beneath his uniform in the process. Laik felt himself fading, blood leaving him by the heartbeat. His vision doubled. The stars danced again, but now they were inside him. Fireflies in his skull.

The man-shape above him froze, jerking its attention at something behind it, within or beyond the barn. Perhaps it was simply called by an instinct beyond his understanding. Fingers ran down Laik's face. In comfort? Apology, maybe? But he was weak. So weak.

And then it was gone. Just gone.

He lay there shaking, taking in the moving shadows as the moonlight passed through the hole in the roof. He felt the wet from his neck sodden the collar, dampen his chest. Time passed, and the inevitable refused to transpire. The longer the moonlight shone, the stranger the space became. Something was wrong with the dark. It bent around him. It whispered. He could hear sounds of movement, the presence of life, like the peculiar sensation of being watched from here, there, everywhere. None of the sounds were his. Every corpse had gone quiet. But he could hear them still. Feel them still.

Struggling eyelids flickered. The moonlight traced the outline of Gareth before him. The movement in Laik's hands didn't feel like his. They were weak, an instinct, the push of desperation which had abandoned him before. He slumped sideways onto the barn roof with a hollow thud, still looking.

The hand extended slowly once more. Followed by the arm. Nails bit into the board edges to drag himself forward to his companion. His jacket rasped against the coarse grain as he moved closer. And closer. And closer. Until finally . . .

*Burning.*

The sudden sensation of Laik feeling his hand had been

thrust into coals summoned him from dreaming. With a paranoid yelp, he shifted from being spread out to rip his hand back in shock, brandishing it with the other. It had blistered, with open sores hissing steam. He had seen burns like this in the unit, but there was no fire present as the cause. No boiling water to have it make sense.

*Only sunlight.*

The midday sun had leaked into the barn, shifting over the boards much like the moon did before it. Its harshness contrasted against the pitch-heavy shadows that the barn sheltered. But the things that it did reveal made Laik's stomach violently lurch, and horror fill his throat.

Spread out on the floorboards was Gareth. Torn green uniform soaked, gore and parts carelessly splashed. Gareth, thankfully, looked at peace, despite being in pieces.

Laik blubbered, fighting the shaking that was now dominating his body. He crept across the dry parts of the boards on all fours and reached a hand out into the streak of light to take hold of the dog tag, so that Gareth's death could be properly recorded. Like all of theirs could.

The burning began anew. Laik snatched his hand away, wincing at the new onslaught of pain, but this quickly shifted into confusion. Testing, he reached out once more, finding that as soon as his fingertips were illuminated, his skin flushed red and scorched.

It didn't make sense.

But then, nothing did anymore.

Not the dark, congealed trail of blood that weaved across the floorboards toward him like a serpent.

Not the weight clinging to his jacket, a tacky, rust-dark stain that soaked from collar to cuff.

And not the cold crust of dried blood flaking from his mouth, brittle along his stubble like peeling skin.

Laik stared, breath frozen. His fingers trembled as they lifted to his lips, frantically trying to scrub away the evidence of what he'd done.

He wandered when the sun had surrendered its place in the sky. Slept when its dangers were evident by its presence. All he knew was to keep moving.

The woods didn't want him. The road barely acknowledged him. By the time Laik stumbled into the village, the soles of his boots had split. His soiled jacket had been scrubbed to prevent any difficult conversations, especially ones with himself, but evidence remained; a dull stain. A bullet hole. The houses here had seen conflict, shutters fastened like the town had blinked shut. Bullet holes cracked the facades, and debris collected by the roadside. Rubble and daffodils clung to the stone walls. Dull oil lamps did their best to provide light. Headstones standing sentry around a small church had performed their duty well, some having fallen in the face of gunfire.

Cicadas serenaded him as he took the path to the church and stepped inside.

There was no one waiting. No priest at the pulpit. The absence of salvation. Just the silence, and the cracked stained-glass saints spilling ribbons of rainbow light across the nave. Candles shivered as he passed.

Laik slumped in the central pew and breathed. The scent of wax and dry wood settled into his lungs, replacing the stench of wet leaves and soil.

He whispered an apology he didn't know how to shape. To God. To the boys. To himself. All the while his clenched hands refused to stop shaking.

The door creaked behind him. The candles danced again. Footsteps, now. Laik didn't know who or what to expect.

He was mid-fifties. Collared. Calm. He paused at the end of the pew, taking in the state of the young man hunched there like an abandoned dog.

The priest recognised the uniform immediately and attentively asked what brought him here. He asked, with fragments of English, if he needed prayer or confession.

Laik shook his head. Said, in broken French, that nothing could help him now, but he could do something for others. He placed a collection of dog tags, including his own, into the priest's open hand and asked him to get them to where they needed to be.

He slept at dawn in the church's back room, curled beneath a donated coat and an onslaught of nightmares.

The hunger remained.

It stayed with him. In his gums, in his throat, deep in the pit of his gut. The bread the priest gave him tasted like dust. The water made him gag. The blessings brought no comfort. Laik wasn't just waiting out the daylight. He knew he was waiting for something to arrive. Was it forgiveness? A miracle? To be smited?

None of these came.

He slipped out without a goodbye the following evening. As the roads and the towns became filled with occupying troops, their presence ignored and patrols avoided, Laik realised that the war was over for him.

But the battle for his soul had only just begun.

# Chapter Nineteen

## Home

The hills rolled like bruised knuckles beneath a grey sky, wind rushing over them in long, restless sighs. The old farmhouse sat nestled among them, whitewashed walls smudged by weather, the chimney coughing soft plumes of smoke that curled into the wind and vanished. Grass swayed like it had something to say but no voice to say it with, and the stone path leading to the door was slick with earlier rain. Night had set the valley black, leaving the windows warm and inviting.

The world had buckled under the war, but Wales, home, seemingly remained untarnished.

Laik stood at the gate for longer than he meant to, the travel-heavy satchel hanging from one hand. His uniform was battered, boots worn thin, the cuffs of his coat stained with old dirt and older blood that could be mistaken for the former. He had imagined this return more than once. In dreams, maybe. In fits of fever. But standing here, breathing the damp air before the farmhouse was real in a way dreams weren't.

The door opened after he knocked. His mother gasped,

hands flying to her mouth, tears already in her eyes. She threw her arms around him. He barely returned the hug, the motion stiff and hesitant. Her proclamation of a miracle went unanswered. Over her shoulder, he saw his father, standing in the doorway behind, taller, broader, weathered. A man who had lived with his hands in the soil. He joined their embrace.

The warmth of the house hit him all at once: the peat smoke, the stew on the stove, all things he had fantasised about. The dog asleep in the corner sprang up and ran over for attention, but received too little, lending to the animal whining. His brother appeared from the back room, sleeves rolled up, hands still dusted with the stain of field work. Mid-twenties and thick through the shoulders, a far cry from Laik's stockiness. He froze when he saw Laik, almost convinced that a ghost was among them.

They sat down together at the kitchen table that night, the lamp casting a soft, flickering glow across their bowls. Steam rose from barley and meat, and the talk turned to the war – as it always did back then. His father boasted about the old days, pushing the Kaiser back, as if the world had only known the one war, despite the latest having been over for just a few months. His brother chimed in that nobody else from the village had made it back, suggesting that God was only looking out for Laik and none of the others. That their mother's prayers were answered.

Laik spoke little.

He held his spoon loosely, barely ate. He felt the eyes of his family too difficult to meet. Their faces would shift from joy to concern far too quickly for his liking. His mother would squeeze his hand, testing to make sure he wasn't an illusion. She left her seat and returned clutching a small wooden box. Inside was a black-and-white photo of him smiling, the first time he had worn the uniform. Inside was something metal, which he dangled from his fingers to the lamplight.

His dog tags.

An official-looking letter was the last thing inside.

They were told he had died somewhere in the south of France. Because of course they would. They weren't completely wrong.

It was hell, Laik stated. That's all.

His mother looked at him. His father did too. Even his brother, usually too rough-hewn to show much concern, fell silent. There was something off in his tone, in the way he scrutinised the tag without recognition. Something about his eyes, how they didn't quite focus, like he was watching something none of them could see.

His parents exchanged a concerned glance across the table.

Their son had come home. But clearly not all of him.

Laik slept during the day.

At breakfast, he was always absent. When asked, he said nothing more than what little sense it made: that his unit had marched at night, that he was used to the dark, that they moved under cover on account of German planes overhead and sleeping in the day was habit now, not sickness. The curtains in his room stayed drawn, the edges pinned so not even a ribbon of light could seep through. His mother fussed at first, insisting he got up, setting out bread and jam on the end of the bed, but Laik would murmur something about migraines that came back with him from France.

It sounded true. Or true enough.

But in the village, word began to travel. First in the corners of the chapel, where old women clutched superstitions tighter than reason. Then in the markets, where murmurs passed between hands exchanging vegetables and eggs. There were things whispered behind closed doors. One neighbour said she saw Laik walking through the fields past midnight, even though the rain came down hard that night. Another swore she watched him stand outside the *capel rwyfedig* on the hill, just staring at the broken steeple.

He's not the same, his mother confessed once to the priest, hands folded tight in her lap. The good Father tried to assure her, said the world was restless now, and it took time for the soul to settle.

The locals were not so forgiving.

The war takes its toll, aye, but this one, the *only one who came back*, came back wrong.

Her husband, a man of hard years and little sentiment, was less forgiving of the unknown. And her eldest son, brimming with the strength of someone who had always known where he stood in the world, didn't like the idea of danger beneath their roof.

They spoke about it. Not in the kitchen, not at the table, but in the barn, where the guilt could be abandoned. Their voices lowered, not in fear of being overheard, but because the weight of what they were saying made volume feel blasphemous.

He doesn't eat, the father said.

He barely talks, the brother added.

He watches things like they're going to crawl. Sneaks out into the night. Looks a world away.

Their mother refused to hear it. She shook her head, a crack carving through her faith. *That's your brother. That's my son.*

But the brother saw it in the stupor. The father saw it in Laik's eyes – how he didn't flinch when they found a fox dead and mauled by the henhouse. How he didn't seem to blink when they buried it, just stood there, arms by his sides, watching the dirt fall.

There's something wrong, the father said. The secrecy was a concern. The dried blood and rogue bullet hole over his army jacket confirmed it.

Evil had hold of their son, the father stated, watching his wife break down in agreement. And he told his eldest to prepare himself for tomorrow morning. At dawn they would do what had to be done. Do what God himself would condone in this perilous moment.

They would beat the Devil out of him.

# Chapter Twenty

## Sins of the Father

The cloth bag smelled of dirt and dust and pressed into his face with damp insistence. The world was muffled, like he had been held underwater on account of his skull throbbing. A deep, resonant ache echoed with each heartbeat, making his temples drum.

A hand yanked the hood off.

Laik blinked against the sudden dullness of candlelight-coated stone. He was hanging by the wrists, arms pulled taut and awkward, hooked through an iron pulley nailed into the thick crossbeam of the coal shed roof. His feet barely brushed the dust-painted floor. Rain pattered against the slate outside and drummed louder against the tin eaves overhead. Wind crawled through the boards in whispering draughts.

His clothes were wet, clinging, his boots long gone. Cold seeped through him like needles of water.

They stood in front of him – his silent father, arms folded like a presiding judge. His mother beside him, shoulders hunched, hands folded around the crucifix that had hung above the mantel for as long as Laik could remember. And his brother, eyes narrowed to mean little slits, looking like he was trying not to look at all.

The accusations weren't shouted. Not at first. His father said it plain, like reading from scripture.

He'd been seen out at night. In the fields. Stalking through the animals. Moving with the shadow. And he wasn't *right*. Wasn't normal. The Devil had him. That was the only explanation.

Laik, of course, protested. It was nonsense, all of it. He was injured. He'd been at war. He had seen hell and come home broken, not damned. But before he could string more than a sentence together, the air was punched from his lungs. A thick, meaty fist sank into the gut. He curled forward as much as the chain would let him.

The Devil be gone, his father roared.

Laik spat blood and tried again. It wasn't true. It wasn't fair. He wasn't what they thought. He was their *son. Please!*

Another blow. Another howl.

Outside, the rain never let up.

His mother wept and clutched her crucifix. Her voice trembled, asking forgiveness from something, anything. Then she turned away. She couldn't stay. She said she would pray for him. She didn't look back again.

His brother followed without a word.

And Laik was left hanging.

Eight hours passed.

The candles were nearing their ends. His father sat on the floor now, knees up, back against the wall, smoking like he meant to set himself on fire from the inside. His hands shook. The bottle rattled as he poured a finger of something brown into a tin mug. His breath went in and came out sharp.

*I want my boy back*, he said to no one. *I just want him back*.

Then he left.

But it was far from the end.

Later, the door opened with a groan. His brother stepped in. Stared at him for a long time. Said Laik had got lucky. Said he should've died out there in France. Would've saved everyone the trouble. According to him it wasn't fair. The limp in his own leg had kept him home, stuck in muck and cattle, while Laik ran off to glory, away from this shithole.

He hit him, slow at first, then again and again. The frustration spoke through his knuckles to an apologetic recipient. Laik groaned between the strikes, the chain creaking, the flesh of his back raw. At first, he pleaded for his brother to show mercy, before the sobs descended into an apology.

But it didn't matter.

It went on like that. Day. Then night. Then day again. The routine of horror. No food. No water. Just salt in the wounds and prayers in the coal shed. He sagged against the restraints. At some point, it all left him. Laik stopped answering. Stopped reacting.

*But he did not die.*

Twenty days passed.

The whispers from the village grew louder. Even the priest, once so full of words, now had only questions when visiting. The family grew quiet in the house, moving solemnly within the walls. The mother crossed herself at every opportunity. The father drank more than he spoke. The brother watched the fields with a shotgun always at hand. The priest made a suggestion. A desperate one.

A bent-backed woman of the community was summoned from the edge of the village, where the land grew wilder and the hedge flowers strangled the fences. She revealed that her grandmother had followed an ancient tradition of being something called a Sin Eater – a taker of burdens, a devourer of guilt. In those days, the dead weren't just mourned, they were unburdened. And for that, something had to carry the weight.

*A box.*

The old woman told of a box: a heavy thing she remembered dusting as a child, tucked behind other heirlooms, wrapped in linen. She'd asked about it once, curious about the strange markings that sometimes shifted across its lid. Her grandmother had hushed her and said it was for the craft. It was made to hold the worst of what people left behind. A vessel for sin, sealed tight. A cage for all things wicked.

A cage, she revealed, that could *hold the Devil himself.*

Laik hung broken, suspended, and barely conscious. The beatings were severe enough to rob any normal man of life, and an immortal one, their faith. Maybe even their sanity. He heard the conversation, her name, her promises, but by the time the words made it to his consciousness, they were jumbled and nonsensical.

The priest spoke, threw around a vial of water and began to recite from his little black book, but Laik was deaf to the words. The world was blurred and crooked from the swelling over one eye. He could see the shifting shape of his father brandishing a spade for a weapon. His brother, a kitchen knife. The weakest of these shapes, the outline in the doorway, was his hunched mother grasping something close to her chest. As a new one flooded into view, Laik simply didn't care what they had in store.

Whatever they were doing, they could all go to *hell.*

The box was placed before Laik, the sheepskin pulled away in a great reveal. The symbols on the surface twitched momentarily in what others believed to be a trick of the eye, and should they have confirmed with each other, maybe they would have had second thoughts. They lacked the knowledge of the ritual. Were unable to speak the words to syphon whatever hid in Laik and banish it to this container. So emboldened by this new tool were they, *so sure*, that when the seals on the box were cut free, they believed what followed to initially be intentional.

It only took seconds.

The lid blasted off its hinges, sending everyone recoiling. The room howled and shrank in as light was drawn from every corner, swallowed by every shifting shadow that erupted from the container and clung on to the first thing before it.

*Laik.*

It swallowed him whole, swimming over bruised and burnt flesh, taking his form, wearing his face. A wail was somehow conjured from his throat that broke into pieces, but whatever summoned it was soon put at ease. *This was a good thing*, the entity insisted. *The pain is temporary. He had nothing to fear. This was the reward for enduring so much suffering*. And in an effort to convince Laik of this being true, *it would give him a most generous gift*.

Only now did the guilty realise their terrible mistake. Instead of drawing the sin into the box, they had inadvertently let it all out. And when the bindings snapped and the ceiling rafter split, the screams began.

But for Laik it was all just . . . stolen away by the dark.

Rain patted Laik's face, making him come to.

His thoughts were muddled and thick, difficult to make sense of. His body felt distant, unwieldy, as though it belonged to someone else entirely. He was upright, somehow. Standing? But the moment he realised, his legs had no strength to them. They buckled without warning, and he collapsed to the soaked gravel like a puppet with its strings cut. The impact kicked something back into place. Not pain exactly, just the dim recognition of being alive. On all fours now, he gasped against the earth, fingers clawing wet stone, the weight of his own body unfamiliar after so long hanging.

He forced his head to lift, raindrops dripping from his fringe.

And saw his brother.

Face down in the dirt, one arm twisted unnaturally behind his back, the other stretched forward like it had been reaching for something. Blood trickled from beneath his body, washing out into the storm.

Not far behind, another shape. Mangled. And another. The old woman was twisted around herself like bound thread. His father's body, or what remained of it, had been painted across the splintered fence. His mother lay strewn nearby, tangled in the gorse bushes, head skyward, eyes wide, her crucifix abandoned. But it was the shredded and spilled remains of the priest which finally forced Laik to hunch and vomit as much as he could – which was frustratingly little.

The farmhouse loomed behind it all, ruined. Slopes of wet, broken brick, windows smashed, the coal shed itself utterly destroyed as though a train had torn through. The entire building was frozen in the state of collapse.

The rain lashed on down in waves, uncaring.

And Laik, on his knees in the gravel, surrendered to the grief and wailed until his voice gave out.

# Chapter Twenty-One

## The Last Good Days

The bottle clinked softly as Pepper set it down on the coffee table. It had been there since she had moved in – an aged, almost forgotten bottle of whiskey, its label yellowed and curling. She twisted the cap, poured a glass for herself and filled a measure into Laik's empty mug.

'I don't need that,' he said, not looking up from his place on the sofa, scratching at the bandage on his chest. Through the tinted windows, despite the quilted clouds and rain pattering the windows, the sky was lightening, indicating dawn was on its way.

'Well, I do.' She poured a little more for herself. 'You've had it rough. I mean, what you've said – that's . . . Jesus, it's just it's beyond cruel. I'm sorry you had to go through all that.'

He didn't respond at first, listening to the rain strike the glass. After a long pause, he said quietly, 'The worst part wasn't what they did to me. It was that I never got time to grieve. My family, my life just – gone. And I didn't even know if I should feel bad for it. I just . . . didn't have the time.'

He leaned forward, elbows on his knees, swirling the alcohol in the mug. 'When I left Wales, I thought I could walk the hunger off which was just . . . stupid. The more I tried to stay away from people, the more I kept running into them. And not the good kind. Saw me as an easy mark to rob, or start something with. Sometimes I'd get away before it got too bad. Sometimes . . . the other side of me took over. When it did, I'd wake to silence, and blood, and I knew I couldn't stay.'

Pepper's eyes softened.

'So, I kept walking,' he went on. 'Over the border, through forests, sleeping in barns, anywhere I could. Then I found them – a camp in the Forest of Dean. Romany travellers, maybe half a dozen families. Those old-style caravans with the painted doors, sitting around campfires with a fiddle playing almost every night. They didn't ask questions. Didn't care about what I'd been. They just told me to sit, eat and rest. Didn't judge.'

He smiled faintly, eyes flickering. 'For the first time in months, I didn't feel like a ghost. Or a monster.'

Pepper rested her chin on her hand. 'Sounds almost nice.'

'It was. They took me in like a stray. There was an older man named Luka who ran the camp – big hands, always smelled of his roll-ups which he smoked *constantly*. His wife, Miri, cooked everything over the fire. You could taste the wood smoke in everything, even the bread. They had a daughter, about ten, maybe eleven. Anya.'

Saying her name, with all it carried, still hurt. 'She was all carefree. Always barefoot, singing ditties to herself. I think she saw straight through me . . . not what I was, but, like, that I was trying to hide. She'd follow me when I went to forage or chop firewood. Never afraid to be around me.'

Pepper bobbed her head. 'That's . . . kind of adorable, actually.'

'One day,' Laik said, a shade of a smile forming, 'she gave me this daisy chain she made. Said it was for luck. I tried to tell her it'd wilt by morning, but she didn't care. She looped it around my wrist anyway, showed me she had one herself, matching. I must have smiled because, she said, uh . . .' He stopped himself, shaking his head. 'Anya said, *See? Even the Devil can smile when he's with friends.*'

Laik loudly sniffled, blinking his wet eyes.

Pepper shuffled closer whilst filling her glass half full. 'You? Smiling properly? Don't know if I believe that.'

'Hah . . . yeah, well, it happened alright,' he said, but there was a quiet warmth behind it – the faintest hint of playfulness beneath the words.

Pepper leaned closer. 'You really cared about them, didn't you?'

'I didn't know how to at first. But yeah. They were . . . good people. Wanted nothing but peace. Asked nothing of me. I slept during the day, with the excuse that I spent the nights hunting for them. Could bring back deer that roamed wild there. I could drink its blood when I caught it. Hide that side of me.' He nodded in thought. 'They taught me that maybe monsters could rest, even if only for a while.'

His tone shifted, low and raw. 'Then the strangers came.'

He set the mug down. 'Two of them – a man and a woman. Said they'd been travelling, looking for shelter. I didn't realise what they were right away. They looked too alive. But I felt something was off, just had a – a feeling. They joined in around the fires, laughed, drank, told stories. And one night, when returning to camp, I saw the man make a move on one of the boys.'

Pepper's breath caught. 'Oh God.'

'I stopped him. Fought him off. He begged for mercy, said they'd been chased for weeks by some madman and were starved. That this lunatic and his crew were hunting vampires who weren't worthy of their status. The ones who killed mercilessly, like animals. They were making their way through Wales and were looking to cross over into England.'

'A madman?' Pepper probed.

Laik spent a moment formulating the name, like he was resilient to summon it in good company.

'They called him *Horus*. Centuries old. Remorseless. A real piece of work.'

Laik's hands trembled faintly as they folded together. 'They said he had an army. That they had just wanted a place to rest while passing through. I told them they could stay – on the condition that they didn't touch anyone again.'

He took a slow breath. 'For a while, it worked. Maybe a month. We cooked under the same stars. Miri would hum while she cleaned the pots. Luka would play the fiddle till sunrise. And Anya – she'd sit beside me by the fire, talking about where they'd go next. France, maybe. Italy. The old countries, they called them. Places I hadn't thought about in a lifetime. For the first time in a long time, I believed that . . . this was what peace looked like.'

Pepper murmured, 'It sounds . . . wonderful.'

'It was. Didn't last long.'

He fell quiet for a long while before continuing.

'Those two stayed in line until they left. Didn't even say goodbye. Just packed up one night and were gone. I went down to the river to fetch water. When I came back, I could smell the blood before I saw it. The air stank of it. Six or so vampires had surrounded the camp. One of them was shouting about sheltering monsters, that it was blasphemy.

Horus, he stood in the middle of them. Spoke of confession and judgement in the same breath.'

Laik's voice darkened to a growl. 'He told them to hand me over – that it would be a *godly offering*. Luka tried to explain they didn't know what he was talking about. Horus didn't even blink. He just nodded to one of his men, and Luka's head hit the ground before I even understood what had happened.'

Pepper's eyes glistened, tossing the burning whiskey down her throat.

'I don't remember much after that. Came crashing out the undergrowth and . . . I was *angry*. And all of it, everything inside me, it all came rushing out. I remember the fire spraying everywhere. The smoke. The screams. Tearing through anyone in front of me. When everything was quiet again, I was on the ground, in such pain. Everything had been ripped apart – tents. Caravans. People. The air stank of blood and burning tarps. Everyone was dead. And Anya . . .'

He shut his eyes, jaw trembling. 'She was lying near the fire. Still had that damn daisy chain around her wrist.'

Pepper covered her mouth.

He shook his head, voice raw. A tear escaped its confines. 'And I don't even know if it was one of Horus's men who did it or, or . . .' His breath staggered. 'I tried to bury them. I couldn't even do that right. My arm was broken. Horus, and whatever remained of his people, had fallen back but it wouldn't be for long. I used the opportunity to take what I could carry and left. I kept moving, but soon enough he was hunting me. Didn't matter where I ended up, he followed. Always followed. I heard Horus called it his crusade – purifying the sinful. But it was just a fancy way to justify murder. And I became his obsession.'

He leaned back, shoulders sagging. 'I slept in train tunnels, derelict towers, abandoned farms. I don't know how long I kept up running from place to place. Years, easily. Until I was so, so sick of it. I ended up here – this city. I remember standing by the old canals, and thinking I just couldn't do it anymore. Let them come. I didn't care no more. I was done running. And he did. Horus arrived with a small army in tow. Preached his sermon to his flock. I didn't even listen. I let the monster loose one last time and let it do what it wanted. When I woke, most of his pack were dead. I was getting there. But not him.'

Laik exhaled slowly. 'He came at me. Would've finished it, too – if someone hadn't stopped him.'

Pepper's eyes flicked up in surprise.

Laik gave a faint, incredulous chuckle. 'Mortis. He had a dozen Enforcers with him, all ready to get dirty. Stood there, bold as brass, told Horus I was now under their protection. Said if he wanted to continue his little crusade, he'd have to do it outside of *their* city. Horus eventually retreated, swearing it wasn't over. Guess he meant it. He got in with the Odes, climbed the ladder . . . and hasn't stopped being a pain in my ass since.'

Pepper went quiet for a long moment after he finished, processing this. She sat forward slightly, elbows resting on her knees, eyes distant.

'What does he even want, Laik? Horus, I mean. What's all this *purging* for?'

Laik's jaw tightened. He stared down at his mug for a moment before speaking.

'He wants a world without restraint. Where vampires walk the streets like kings, not shadows. Where the strong feed and the weak serve. He says we're the next rung on the evolutionary ladder, the food chain, destined to rule it, not hide from it.' He let out a small, humourless breath. 'He thinks the only way forward is to burn the rest of the world down. And plenty out there think like him. They want impunity. To feed in the open, to treat people like cattle, to play God over whoever's left standing. Survival of the fittest, he says. But really? *He's just insane.*'

Pepper's voice softened. 'And you?'

Laik looked up, meeting her eyes. 'I know what's in me is wrong . . . But I ain't no monster.'

He leaned back, the ghost of something weary behind his expression.

Pepper was quiet for a long moment. The only sound was the rain outside and her own lingering sigh.

Then she said softly, 'Laik. I lost my mother . . . my grandmother . . . I know what it's like to lose everyone twice. All I know is my sister. All I *have* is her. And if it happens a third time, then . . . then I don't know. But I get it. I do. And I'm so sorry.'

He didn't answer. Didn't need to.

She extended her arm and topped off the drinks, feeling the whiskey's effects as she spilled a drop upon the polished veneer of the table. 'Here's to still being here. However the hell we've managed that.'

He smirked faintly, raising his mug. 'To being here.'

Pepper met his gaze, her bottom lip wobbling. 'And surviving the whole damn thing.'

Their drinks touched with a dull *clunk*. The whiskey burned warm between them.

After a moment of contemplation, Pepper said, 'Look. I know we're never gonna be friends, right? This is just for convenience. But maybe we don't have to hate each other.'

Laik wrinkled his face.

'I don't hate you.'

'And I don't hate you.'

'Weird choice of words if that's something that you apparently *don't* do.' He looked at her as she took to her drink once more, her cheeks flushed. A faint smile tugged at his lips. 'But you have a point. I suppose it could make stealing the Eternal Rose easier if there's less of the drama . . .'

'Cool. Cool.' Pepper turned to him, sliding her glass onto the table and extending a hand. 'Then, uh . . . truce?'

The rain tapped against the window, steady and constant as the first cracks of sun seeped over the lines of the sleeping buildings.

Laik took her hand in his, gentling folding his fingers around. He looked at her earnestly.

'Yeah,' he softly agreed. 'Truce.'

# Part IV

# Chapter Twenty-Two

## Exhuming Answers

Pepper jolted awake at the desk, blinking herself back into the world as she surfaced from her dreams. The high-backed chair beneath her groaned as she shifted. The latest items of research lay spread open before her: a sprawl of rough-looking books, loose maps and laminated scrap pages. Some were rolled like scrolls; others wrapped in white and red ropes. One sported a tarnished padlock.

A shaft of light cut through the air from a lamp suspended overhead, casting a glow across yellowed paper and brittle bindings. Her notes, written in the tightly regulated ledger assigned to her, sprawled unevenly at times. Questions scribbled, theories half mapped, ideas scratched out and circled again. Demons. Possessions. Welsh folk stories of creatures that had no names. The nature of blood. How to summon. Why you shouldn't.

Her handwriting had grown erratic in the last additions where she had clearly been fighting the urge to sleep, descending into a line of pen that tumbled off the page.

She checked the time with a stab of her phone. 2.27 a.m..

She rubbed her eyes, yawned and sat up, glancing around

the cavernous reading hall. All around her were bookcases taller than houses, stretching in tiered rows. She could hear the faint rustle of paper, footsteps echoing off the marble floor. Other researchers, Archivists, Alchemists, Family clerks, moved in and out of sight, some quietly comparing notes, others focused so fully on their job they barely seemed alive.

Pepper absent-mindedly gathered a few books she now deemed useless and stood with a groan. Her muscles ached from being curled in a chair for hours. She stretched, carried the tomes back to their towering shelves, and began scanning the spines for something new of worth.

'Miss Montgomery.'

She turned. Canis Cavendish stood just beyond the halo of the reading lamp's glow, dressed in a velvet blazer and trousers of midnight blue, his shirt unbuttoned dangerously low, and looking somewhat confused.

'Canis,' she said, adjusting her collar slightly and summoning a weary smile. 'Sir. How may I help you?'

'You cannot help me at all, dear,' he said, smiling faintly. 'I'm just . . . surprised to see you. You're here by yourself?'

'Yes, sir.'

'How? I know Viola lacks access to the Vault.'

'You're right. She doesn't.' Pepper met his gaze without flinching. 'Quinn graciously provided it to me. For research purposes.'

'Of course she has. Why wouldn't she?' His smile widened just enough to show teeth. 'And what, precisely, does my sister have you researching?'

Pepper hesitated a beat.

'Miss Quinn believes that by studying the thing that resides inside my brother, and exploring how to . . . remove it . . . there could be broader benefits to the family.'

'Ah,' Canis said smoothly, 'that certainly sounds like

something she'd say. Though I imagine she would relish the chance to annoy everybody here by doing the work herself. May I ask how said research is coming along?'

'It's . . . progressing.'

'Come now, Pepper. Speak plainly.'

She sighed, gesturing toward the notes scattered across the table. 'Not well. Welsh folklore history is surprisingly sparse. Even vampiric. I'm inclined to believe there wasn't a foothold there, but it sounds bloody impossible. You get plenty from the Scottish Highlands and Yorkshire. Even Cornwall. But Wales? It's a black hole. Either the records don't exist or it simply didn't happen. Which is odd, considering how old – ancient – Wales is.'

Canis nodded slowly, skimming his fingers over the books on display. 'You're not wrong. But you are missing an obvious piece of the puzzle. Wales was invaded by the English – somewhere around the thirteenth century, if memory serves correctly. Their campaign to dominate involved more than swords and garrisons. They turned castles into forts, erased histories, traditions, crushed native beliefs. Even tried to kill the language. Just like the Romans before them. You can't control a people without first making them forget who they are. Erase their identity, and they'll adopt whichever one you provide. Time, eventually, removes the evidence.'

Pepper narrowed her eyes. 'The winners write the history.'

'Exactly. And they write what they want. Heroes are turned into villains. Rebellions become genocide. Superstitions swept aside. And history books after will seldom tell the truth,' Canis replied, dry as bone. 'But you're hoping to find clues about your brother's . . . situation. Wouldn't it be easier if he just told you?'

'His memory is . . . patchy,' she said carefully. 'The trauma, all he's been through, has done a number on him, so solid details are lacking. The only clue I've had to go on is something called a, uh, Sin Eater.'

Canis blinked. 'I haven't heard that name in a long time.' He stepped closer, tilting his head.

'Sin Eaters were part of old Celtic ritual. When someone passed, they'd summon one to take on what the priest couldn't absolve. It was a ritual of consumption. A crust of bread, a bowl of ale. The meal was consumed beside the body, so that whatever clung to the dead would pass into the living. The belief was that the Sin Eater would carry the adopted sins into the afterlife, sparing the dead from damnation. Some instances of this were simply symbolic. Others were not.'

'Yeah,' said Pepper. 'That I found. But this lead I have, this one in Wales was different. They allegedly kept the Sins in some sort of chest, literally trapped them.'

Canis frowned. 'That doesn't align with the rite. Sin Eaters *absorbed* the guilt. They didn't collect it.'

'Exactly,' said Pepper. 'Which is what's confusing. Whatever was used wasn't symbolic. It was . . . physical and functional. And, dare I say, magical?'

Canis formed the beginnings of a smile as his eyes searched the air in thought.

'Any object capable of performing that would be tremendously strong. More likely than not a—'

They said it in unison.

'*Relic.*'

He revealed a row of brilliant white teeth in amusement at this revelation.

'Let's go have a look, shall we?'

Pepper kept step with Canis through the Vault, the echo of their footfalls muffled by the carpet runner that split the stone floor like a river of red. They passed under archways and between displays framed in brass, or glass, or nothing. The Relics, in all their variations, were exposed, and Pepper was assessing the layers of security in the process. Strangely, she couldn't detect a single security camera within the Vault itself, no matter how keenly she looked. Her memory returned to the lockdown: the sudden shift in light, the colossal metal door that sealed them inside the gallery, like an animal attempting to close its throat and swallow them whole, until the threat had passed. She glanced behind herself, where the slab of metal remained set in the wall, sleeping, for now, and shivered.

Canis, of course, was utterly unfazed.

'Relics,' he mused, checking the clunky gold watch around his wrist. 'Fascinating things, are they not? Not my area, truth be told. There's too much homework involved, and then there's the unpredictability . . . Some grant blessings, some spirit them away, others meddle, some . . . well, some simply exist. All share something in common: they are *expensive*. It makes sense that there is an entire industry built around their acquisition. More than a few are older than any Family we know of, and I don't say that lightly.' He glanced toward a quiet corner. 'Let's ask someone.'

At the far end of the gallery, near a case displaying a tangled wrought-iron crown half fused with bone, a lone Archivist stood at a plinth. She wore a long charcoal-grey tabard marked with faded runes across the shoulders, her hair twisted in a honey-brown braid that shimmered beneath the lights. She was pressing her gloved fingers against a mask of deep onyx with a flail of raven feathers, testing its surface for something, when she noticed Canis and turned without surprise. Her bow was deep. Her voice was clear and flat, and exact.

'Sir. A pleasure to see you here. Can I be of assistance?'

'Actually, you can. We are in need of a bit of clarity,' Canis said, gesturing lightly to Pepper. 'My colleague is seeking information on a potential Relic. Miss Montgomery?'

Pepper's mouth was dry. She laced her fingers in front of her, straightened her back, and tried to sound like someone who belonged here.

'It's . . . possibly post-war. North Wales. Last seen in the early nineteen forties. A wooden box, about yay big.' She mimed the shape in her hands. 'An elderly woman inherited it from a Sin Eater, apparently. Family heirloom. Sadly, I don't have the names, nothing concrete. But the thing was . . . it would hold the captured sins. The chest had strange markings . . . Norse-like symbols, the witness said. They, uh, moved across the surface.'

The Archivist blinked once, slow and deliberate. 'Moving script has been reported before. Not Norse, more likely proto-Futhark. Or perhaps Vedrunic. There are also Babylonian glyph-forms with kinetic tendencies, though they're rarer. Do know if the marks burned, shimmered or refracted?'

'I . . . don't know. He didn't say. I know how it sounds.'

'Don't be embarrassed,' Canis said lightly. 'Quinn tells me stories about girls living with foxes. The peculiar is the norm here. We're in good company.'

The Archivist turned, leading them deeper between the Relics, toward a computer terminal that emitted a green phosphorous glow.

'There have been records,' she said, 'of artifacts created with such intentions in mind. It is not unheard of – though it is rare. Most containment relics do not endure time well. The contents tend to resist, leading to their destruction.'

She set upon the keyboard, her fingers clicking and clattering. All the while, windows on the screen popped up and vanished to the rhythm.

'Making it more valuable, one would assume?' Canis asked.

'Significantly,' the Archivist replied, emotionless. 'One moment, please.'

Pepper glanced about, casually positioning herself before a pewter vase, dark and etched with looping thorns. It looked quite unpleasant to hold. A plaque beneath it read:

**WATER OF THE MIRE**
**CAT: GE930A**

Canis bent in closer, squinting at the wording.

'What's this happy little thing?' he asked, looking it up and down.

'That,' the Archivist said without turning, 'would be what is commonly referred to as the Assassin's Jug. It infuses any liquid placed within with an undetectable poison. Even the cleanest water becomes lethal. A gift of divine spite. We're currently tracing its usage and have already discovered evidence of its use in the death of Edward the Sixth. Some in our collection are truly fascinating artifacts . . .'

Pepper swallowed, trying not to glance too obviously at the Eternal Rose, innocently resting *right beside* on its pedestal.

'We have no listing under those parameters,' the Archivist said, turning from the terminal. 'Not yet. But it may exist outside our registry. Some relics are held privately, others are still unclaimed, with exhumers . . . Would you like me to add the description to our archive watchlist?'

Canis nodded. 'Please do.'

The Archivist did so. For a moment, Pepper's eyes shifted around her. She scanned every detail. The pedestals. The angles of the displays. No visible guards making rounds. Still no cameras visible. No pressure sensors that she could see. And the thing that bothered her most during the lockdown: there was no panic.

'While we're at it, has there been any update to GE713N?'

The Archivist tapped away at the keyboard once more. 'Ah. The Eternal Rose. Yes, actually, there were some preliminary reports that came back from initial testing.'

'Anything promising?' Canis bent forward to examine the screen.

Pepper did her best to act like she wasn't listening.

'Improvement has been made by keeping it in proximity of people, animals. Apparently, it displays an almost parasitic effect where it absorbs the life from those around it. According to this, recent hypothesis is that the Eternal Rose absorbs these trace amounts, providing its curative properties. However, there is a point being made here, that calculating size and mass, the Relic is limited in its use.'

'How limited?' Canis frowned.

'It can only be used a single time – and it'll expire in the process.'

A shock of fright bounded up Pepper's spine at this revelation.

'Considering how much we paid that is quite the disappointment.' Canis made an exasperated sigh before composing himself. 'Please add a note there and thank everyone involved for their labours. And to keep up the good work.'

Pepper's head spun. This plan of theirs, *this entire plan*, was hinging on the shared usage of the Eternal Rose, and now they would have to choose who would get its benefits? Before Pepper could comprehend this further, she thanked the Archivist for her help. Canis had begun to talk as she left the gallery.

'Anyway. Your efforts are not an entirely lost cause in my opinion. Scant progress made is better than none at all. If anything resembling this box of yours crops up, we will be in the know. And I'm sure my parents would be more than interested in the outcome.'

Most of this was tuned out, lending her to think on the lack of visible security. In a moment of absolute madness, she tested her theory.

'Thank you, Canis. You've been very generous in your—'

Near the plinth where a braided bracelet of dull red stone rested in a velvet curve, she brushed her elbow too wide, too obvious. The bracelet clattered to the ground, a sharp sound in the quiet. She stooped at once, cheeks flushed, heart hammering.

No one rushed in. No alarms. No security sweep.

Canis raised an eyebrow as she apologised profusely and righted it.

'It's not me you have to apologise to. If the Archivists had seen that . . .' He whistled quietly. 'They're protective of their toys. And not known for forgiveness. Still, no harm done, eh?'

'Thank you,' she muttered, placing the bracelet back with sheepish care.

But her thoughts were racing. It was clear that the Vault's defences were constructed with the singular intention of keeping the undesirable out. It was arrogantly presumed nobody would make it this far, evident by the lack of methods within which meant that when it came to stealing the Eternal Rose, the hard part was getting in at all. A problem she had already solved.

All she had to do was come up with how to smuggle it out.

Who got to use it after that was a problem for another day.

# Chapter Twenty-Three

## The Kingfisher

The Kingfisher always looked like it was daring people to burn it down. Someone with a grudge tried back in the 80s but it is a stubborn establishment and refused to succumb to the fire. Hidden in the backstreets, brickwork soot-stained and windows reinforced, it pulsed with the throb of distorted bass and the glow of neon spillover. The mural of its namesake bird watched over the entrance like a totem god of outrageous rock and regrettable decisions.

The queue outside was long, tense with Friday revellers. But Laik, Pepper, Swan, Viola, Reese and Duncan didn't even slow their pace. The bouncers gave a nod, one muttering a low 'Evenin'' as they stepped aside. Rank had its privileges, and Enforcers – even on a night out – didn't queue at the right places.

Inside, chaos reigned in the best way. Rock music screamed from half-blown speakers, fighting for dominance against the shouted conversations and off-key singalongs. The walls were wallpapered in decades of posters, band stickers, graffitied signatures of long-forgotten and still prominent legends. Sweat, beer and perfume hung in the air. The floor was sticky. The atmosphere? Perfect.

The others peeled off quickly, drawn to familiar faces already shoulder to shoulder in the dim haze. Viola and Swan were already exchanging hugs with a group they recognised from the accounting floor of Leroux Tower. Duncan was exchanging war stories near the jukebox with someone sporting an arm in a sling. Reese was singing along to the music with a pair of girls who had become compelled to dance with her. Laik and Pepper pushed their way to the bar.

'You need to relax,' Laik said, voice low, almost casual. 'You look nervous.'

'That's because I am nervous.'

'Exactly. And if you look it, you'll make me nervous. And when I get nervous, people start asking questions.'

He leaned across the bar toward the barman. 'Bottle of Proto and a shot of Black Tarkus, cheers.' He made a flash of a card with the Cavendish crest upon it before putting it back in a pocket.

The barman nodded, setting a glass down. 'And for you, miss?'

'Bottle of Herron cider, please.'

'Just the cider?'

'I'm being good.'

'Fair enough.'

The drinks were placed on the bar. Pepper took her bottle, the label half soaked with condensation, the drink ice-cold. She watched Laik raise the shot, the liquid inside nearly black with a reddish gleam.

'You're not adding anything?' she asked.

'No need. Some of this comes pre-mixed with the red stuff. They do it all in the back. One of the perks of drinking in the right places. They keep it discreet, nobody asks questions about the V-word.' He clinked her bottle against his glass. 'Cheers.'

They drank. She took a long sip, glancing at him over the rim of the bottle. He watched her over the lip of his shot glass, and for the first time that night, there was a flicker of actual ease behind his eyes.

They found an empty pool table tucked beneath a crooked light. Their jackets went over the side rail, Laik rolling up his sleeves like he meant business. 'You always give that look,' he said as he dug the pound coin from a pocket.

'What look?'

'The look when I drink. You get shirty about the blood thing.'

'I do not.'

'You do. You ever had a cocktail? Mixed drinks?'

'Of course.'

'Same thing,' he stated while racking the balls up.

'It's totally not,' she muttered, 'not when . . .' she leaned in slightly, lowering her voice, 'not when there's *blood* involved.'

He handed Pepper a cue and gestured for her to break.

She broke clean, one ball dropping into a side pocket with a *thunk*. She missed the next. Laik chalked his cue, lined up.

'Sorry, what did you expect to happen?' he asked. 'We throw some poor bastard on the bar and go to town? Rip him up like wolves? Or what – neck a bunch of girls in underwear? You've seen too many films.'

He sank a ball with a soft crack. Pepper made a face, sipping her cider.

'I just . . . I don't know. You're vampires. Do you know how hard it is separating fact from fiction?'

'Yeah. It's easy. Just ask. I had to.' Another shot. 'It's not like in your movies. We don't suddenly have monster faces. We don't magically learn kung-fu moves. And we don't go around top to toe in black leather, wearing sunglasses at night.'

'How do you explain that guy, then?' She nodded with her chin toward the man Duncan was in conversation with, leaning against a pillar – shades on, floor-length leather, looking like he'd lost his way to a *Matrix* convention.

'That's Enrique. That's just his style. Don't hate. You still have a lot to learn about us . . .'

They played on. The music roared, the floor thumped. Pepper watched Viola lean toward someone, laughing at something said too close to her ear. By now, Reese was buying drinks for her new friends while one of them toyed with her short red hair. Laik missed a shot.

'I don't think you and I getting off on the wrong foot helped,' she said, placing the drink back down.

'I don't remember either of us getting off.' Laik smirked.

Pepper scoffed.

'Really? I'm being serious, here.'

'If I didn't say it, you would have.'

'That's not the point. Admittedly true, but still.'

He glanced at her. 'You have a point. It was a bit wild.'

'If things had been different,' Pepper said, circling the table, 'how do you think it would've gone?'

'Between you and me? Different how?'

'Say we met normally. You didn't try and kill me at first sight. That sort of different.'

He bounced his head side to side. 'And where would this meeting happen?'

'Somewhere like here?'

The cue ball cracked as she fired it off, sinking another. Laik chalked up his cue in preparation.

'Uh-uh. The Kingfisher ain't your kinda place.'

'You don't know my kinda place.'

'I know it's not here. I think you'd prefer somewhere quieter.'

Pepper lowered herself to check the angle and lined herself up. The ivory ball skidded against cushions and spun away. She immediately retreated to the comfort of her drink, only for Laik to offer a hand.

'Hi. Laik.' He was playing along, but sported a faint blush on his cheeks at the awkwardness of it all.

She took it. 'Pepper. You're named after a body of water?'

'You're named after a seasoning.'

'Touché. How would you prefer your drink? In the bottle, in a glass, or poured over your head?'

He grinned, cue in hand. 'Another beer if you're going. I'll get the next. So, Pepper . . . what do you do for work?'

'I'm a personal assistant. Sort of.'

'Sounds important.'

'Very.' She leaned slightly on her cue, watching the table. 'I make schedules, clean up messes, lie to people with a smile. I've pulled strings and pulled people out of fires. The hours are insane, the stress is terminal, and I rarely sleep more than four hours at a time. It's my job to make sure the people I work for have all they need, regardless of the size of the task. And the two I run after now, they are . . . demanding. One's pompous. The other, kind of crazy.'

Laik raised an eyebrow.

She lined up her next shot, and sunk it clean.

'I make sure everything ticks. Keep people happy. I see the angles in the process. Head off problems before they begin. It's what I've always been good at. Damn good.'

Laik smirked.

'It sounds like you're a dog walker with better shoes.'

'Basically.' She grinned, taking a long sip from her cider.

'Any family?' Laik took a short inhale watching her as he travelled around the table.

'Yes.' She froze for a moment, eyes shimmering. Distant. 'A sister.'

A flicker of a smile battled something else, clearly shown on her face. 'She's my world. When we were all but left alone, she did everything it took to keep me safe. Worked the nastiest part-time jobs to keep us fed. We had to steal at times. I had to learn to get good at it, or we would die under a bridge somewhere. She taught me resilience. And to never give up. And now she's ill.' Pepper fought her voice not to trail off as her hand rose to the locket around her neck. 'Very ill.'

'I'm genuinely sorry to hear that,' Laik offered, pausing his motion. 'Is she in there?'

Pepper lowered her face to hide the smile. 'Yeah. I keep her close.' She blinked, giving the moment space to pass before glancing sideways at him. 'Gave me this thing to remind me that she's always with me. To stop, uh . . . to just slow down once in a while. Stop running.'

He quietly watched her.

'So,' she said lightly, nudging them back toward safer territory, 'what about you?'

'Oh. I'm a . . . a bodyguard of sorts,' Laik replied, rolling his shoulders slightly as he looked for his next shot. He winced, prodding his chest.

'Is that okay? You look like you're struggling. And it's affecting your game, unless you're naturally this bad.'

'I'm fine, thanks. Just hurt myself at work. It's almost healed anyway.'

'That happen often?'

'More than I like. Something of an occupational hazard. Doesn't matter, I got my medicine.' He took a mouthful of beer.

Pepper followed him with her eyes as he summed up his next move. 'This bodyguarding. Sounds vague and dangerous.'

He offered a faint smile. 'That's because it is. The job changes depending on the night. Sometimes I'm security, standing in corners, looking threatening. Sometimes I'm a babysitter for people with far too much money and far too little sense. Again, looking threatening. And other times . . .' he paused, lining up a shot, '. . . I'm the last thing between someone and a very bad end.'

The ball kissed the edge of the pocket but didn't drop.

'Doesn't that get tiring?' she asked, watching him with mild curiosity now.

'All the time,' he said. 'But you do what you're good at, don't you? And I'm good at keeping those needed alive. I don't ask why. Don't ask what they did to need someone like me. Just get on with it. I'm not the conscience. I'm just the wall.'

Pepper leaned on her cue, thoughtful. 'Sounds lonely. And like you're being used.'

He gave a slow nod. 'Yeah. It is. But there's a strange kind of peace in that. You stay alert. You stay sharp. You don't get attached. Don't think so much . . .'

'And yet here you are, guard down,' she said, arching a brow playfully.

Laik gave a faint shrug. 'Even walls need to kick back sometimes.'

'What about you? Family?'

'No. They died in a, uh . . . accident.'

'I'm sorry,' she returned, sincerely.

'Don't be. I'm not,' he stated, cold.

She lined up her shot, ignoring the flicker of heat in her chest. She was wiping the table clean now – ball after ball disappearing down pockets.

Laik nodded in approval. 'Very nice.'

'Thank you.' She took to her drink, cocking her head. 'And from a touch of the accent, I would say it's nice knowing another Welshie. *Ach-y-fi, boyo*, and that. Honestly wouldn't have guessed.'

'Psh. *Mae hyn yn anfoesgar*. It's not something that's ever come up. You speak it?'

'Nah, just some words here and there. It's from my mother's side. My sister and I . . . our mum passed when we were very young, our grandmother who stepped in was more old school . . . used to use the lingo. We moved a lot back then . . . got taunted mercilessly about the Welsh thing at schools, so I don't really mention it. The sheep jokes alone . . .'

Laik drained his bottle. 'Been around since I was young. Some things never change.'

'Which is how long, exactly?'

'Too long.' He snorted, watching her wiggle into position, sliding the cue back and forth on the nape of her hand. She sank the eight ball and leaned her cue against the table, victorious.

'Well, Laik' – Pepper patted his shoulder – 'you seem nice, but your pool game sucks.'

'I was going easy on you. Didn't want to ruin the first impression.'

'Were you now?' She fumbled through her jacket on the table, producing a grubby coin. 'Then let's hope you fare better this time.'

The next song thundered through the bar, a raucous drumline that sent cheers through the crowd while Pepper went to the bar for another round. Glasses clinked around her, and someone near the back let out an off-key howl to the chorus. As she squeezed her way back to the table, she spotted a flash of red lipstick and the silhouette of Viola slipping through a gap in the crowd.

'There you are,' Pepper said, over the noise. 'Thought you got swallowed by the queue for the toilet.'

Viola's smile was all teeth, her lipstick smudged a little, her hair a little less pristine than it had been. 'Just talking to people. Meeting people,' she said, a touch too breezily. Her voice carried that lilting cadence that meant *don't ask more.* 'You know how it is.'

Pepper didn't buy it but let it slide. She nodded toward the pool table. 'Well, since you're here, fancy a game?'

Viola grinned. 'Oh, and embarrass myself? Oh no, I don't think so. Pool's not my thing.'

'Aw, come on.' Pepper pouted. 'I need a challenge!'

'Oi,' Laik muttered, without looking up from his drink.

'Hush. Just one. Just give it a shot. Do you need me to tell you what we're doing?'

'I think I have the gist.' Viola surrendered and took a cue. 'Hit the white ball into the others.'

Pepper rolled the cue ball between her fingers and lined up the triangle, chalk dust rising in a pale puff. The clatter of balls broke through the low hum of conversation as Viola leaned against the table, loosening her coat.

'You're breaking,' Viola said.

'Nothing new there,' Pepper replied with a wink, cracking the cue ball clean into the formation. The balls scattered, one striped clattering into the corner pocket.

'Lucky,' Laik said.

'Excuse me,' Pepper said, slanting her hips. 'It's called skill. Something you lack.'

'Ah yes, hitting me where it hurts. My pool skills.' He raised his glass to her as she stuck her tongue out. 'Vee, take the smile off her face, would you?'

Viola leaned over to take her own shot. She fired the cue off like a bullet, kissing a ball into a corner pocket. When she leaned back, she was proud of herself. All business. Her smirk was telling. Laik tossed his head back with a single *ha*.

'What is *this*? Are you gonna *hustle* me?' Pepper chuckled, rising to the challenge.

'We all have secrets.' Viola manoeuvred around the table, working the trigonometry out for Pepper's turn.

'I wasn't gonna say, but is that what's with the hair?'

'Oh!' Viola, still fixed on the table, pressed some rogue curls back into place. 'Um. Just stepped out for some air. Got talking to someone . . .'

'Someone,' Pepper echoed, half smiling, glancing to Laik.

'I ain't saying *anything*, this is girl business.' He wisely took more from his glass.

Viola's mouth twitched. 'Don't look at me like that. I'm allowed to talk to people.'

'Didn't say you weren't,' Pepper said, softening her tone as she took her turn. 'Just . . . didn't expect you to kick back so wild. No offence, but you're always so straight. I sort of thought you only had eyes for Canis.'

'Well. I don't know if you've noticed' – Viola lowered herself in posture and tone; the cue was lined up like a weapon – 'but Canis only has eyes for himself. Always has.'

The strike was sharper, powerful, and when it cracked into a ball, it caught flight above the pocket before tumbling down into the table's innards.

Pepper wasn't smiling anymore, and when she flicked her gaze to Laik, she saw that he too had felt the seriousness. Laik took a long sip from his bottle before it was noticed that Pepper had yet to line herself up.

'Your turn,' Viola reminded.

Pepper took her turn with a clean snap, missing her target by an inch. The three of them bantered between rounds, trading cheap shots and mock applause. Pepper was losing and pretended not to care. Viola was winning and pretended she wasn't. Laik was enjoying the moxie. The rhythm between them came easy – the kind that made them forget, for a while, that the world outside the Kingfisher's battered doors could be cruel. For Laik and Pepper, there were no monsters. No secrets. No plans. Just drinks and music and imagined lives they'd never get to live. And, through it all, the pair had relaxed so much that if they were asked, they would actually confess to having a good time.

So much so that Pepper was utterly unaware of the buzzing in her pocket.

She didn't hear her phone ringing.

Didn't see the voicemail notification.

She was completely oblivious to what was about to turn her world upside down.

# Chapter Twenty-Four

## Past Catching Up

The pulse of the music from the Kingfisher gave way to the hush of the backstreets, where the city had curled up for the night and left the pavements to echo with their footfalls. Duncan had ducked into a corner shop along the way and emerged with a couple of six packs of whatever was cold and cheap. They didn't need good beer to keep the night going, just beer.

Laik led, hands in his pockets, Swan and Duncan a half-step behind swapping jokes. Viola and Pepper lingered near the back, sending each other into fits of giggles. Reese launched an empty beer can into a bin with half her body still swaying to a song in her head. She rose her arms triumphantly, taking a fresh one tossed from Duncan as a trophy as they crossed into the dark outline of a nearby park.

The playground sat at its centre, a crooked little thing of metal and wood that had seen better decades. They climbed onto its bones with a reverence reserved for royalty or ruins, claiming the roundabout, the swing set, the benches along the edge. Laik sat on the climbing frame like it was a throne. Pepper perched on a swing, half turning herself with the soles of her boots.

Duncan cracked the beers. Viola offered them out. Someone lit a cigarette, and no one minded the silence for a while. Until Swan cleared his throat like a man about to commit treason.

'Alright,' he declared, loud enough to wake a pigeon in a tree nearby. 'This is driving me absolutely nuts. I'm not gonna do it anymore. No more games, you two; birth or bite?'

Pepper blinked. 'What?'

He pointed, a beer in one hand, a grin on his face. 'You're brother and sister, right? Either by birth, or one bit the other. Which is it? Because it's all anyone bloody talks about at home and I'm sick of the guessing.'

The question landed, and everyone turned to Laik.

Laik swirled the contents of his can, half amused, half not. 'Bite,' he said. 'I turned her.'

Pepper tensed beside him, her fingers catching the swing's chain, as if she might vanish into it.

'Yes!' Swan punched the air. 'Knew it. Fucking *knew* it. Pay up!'

Groans went up around the playground. Duncan and Viola exchanged looks of theatrical betrayal before digging out crumpled notes from their jackets.

'I hate you,' Duncan muttered, handing over what was owed.

'You love me,' Swan replied, already fanning himself with the pile of winnings like a cartoon aristocrat. 'You'll feel better knowing your money is going straight to good things. Like more beer. And maybe some chips. I'm feeling the need for chips.'

Pepper frowned. 'You were *betting* on us?'

Swan shrugged, grinning wide. 'Some of us were curious. Some of us were smarter than others.'

'Even you?' Pepper asked, glancing at Viola, who smirked over the rim of her bottle.

'I had money on you biting him, actually. Figured you might be the type.'

That earned her a ripple of laughter.

'Don't look at me like that,' Viola continued, eyes twinkling. 'I was *curious*. Everyone was. The big bad Enforcer has family? There were bound to be questions. Besides, mystery man over there' – she gestured lazily at Laik – 'doesn't exactly scream approachable. People talk.'

Reese scoffed. 'Yeah, they did. When he came on board, you know how many asked me to be *introduced* to him? Plenty, I tell you. That dark and mysterious thing was doing you favours.'

Duncan chimed in, 'I mean, before you came along, everyone else thought the only one who could stand to be around Laik was the stick up his ass. Dude wasn't exactly friendly. Sorry, Laik, but you know it's true.'

Laik's expression went flat. 'Still doesn't mean you get to ask about it.'

Swan wasn't done. 'Oh, come on. Don't clam up now! I wanna know how it happened. How'd you two even meet? How long has she been putting up with you?'

'That's private,' Laik said, glancing briefly at Pepper.

Swan groaned theatrically. '*Boooo!* Not an answer!' He lobbed an empty beer can toward Laik's head. It bounced off with a hollow twang, and Viola nearly fell off the bench laughing.

Laik didn't move.

But Pepper . . . she looked around at the group, at the neon light from the corner shop flickering over the dark grass, at the faces she was slowly getting used to seeing. And maybe it was the beer or the late hour, or maybe it was the soft sting of being seen as a curiosity instead of a person, but she smiled.

'Actually,' she said, brushing a strand of hair behind her ear, 'I don't mind telling it.'

Laik looked at her sharply.

But she just looked at the others, the swing creaking gently beneath her, whilst taking a slow sip from her bottle. 'You want to know how it started?' she asked.

The others leaned in.

Pepper tucked her knees up on the swing, boots creaking against the metal slats. Her fingers curled around the rust-flecked chains as the frame rocked gently beneath her. The laughter had faded now, replaced by the low hush of wind curling through the park.

She glanced at the others. Swan still held his beer can, Duncan was hunched forward, and Viola leaned against the slide, legs crossed, watching through a curtain of her dark hair. Laik hadn't moved from where he squatted on the apparatus, cigarette between his fingers, eyes on the ground.

Pepper took a breath and lied as if her life depended on it. Because it did.

'It was winter. A bad one,' she began. 'The snow was constant. The streets never cleared. After university, I'd been moving from place to place, mostly alone. I was running from bad decision to bad decision. Couch to couch. Ended up with bad boyfriends and even worse regrets. Did whatever I liked, thought I was invincible like everyone did in their twenties. Figured if I kept going, I couldn't be stopped. But things got hard. I got sick . . . real sick. I had burned every bridge I crossed. Family had abandoned me, because why wouldn't they? And I was working a job in a town that didn't want me. My escapism was smoking as much weed as I could and riding every asshole who smiled at me right. I was a state.'

Laik's gaze didn't shift, but she felt the weight of his attention.

'I was coughing up blood in the mornings. Pain kept me in bed when I needed to be out of it. Doctors told me to try this, take that. Meds didn't do anything. Made me feel worse. I soon got tired . . . of, of everything. I remember the night well because I didn't have enough money for the 'leccy. It was so cold my fingers cracked just trying to light a joint, and I flipped out, trashed the flat. I left to meet my dealer at a nearby laundrette, barely made it through the snow. Waited a couple of hours, but he didn't show up. I was sitting on a machine, exhausted, coughing up crap in a hanky, wishing that . . . thinking bad thoughts. And then . . .'

She hesitated, taking a large mouthful from her can. By now the lie was coming with absolute ease, but there were fissures in the fiction. The parts she had to make up came instinctively. But there were wellsprings of emotion fighting their way through. And instead of hiding their existence, Pepper used them to their fullest to make the lie believable.

'Then he walked out of the dark and through the door. Looked like someone else who didn't know where he was meant to be. I thought he might be dangerous. And he was. Just not in the way I expected.'

A smile curled faintly. One part fond, one part something else.

'He noticed that I didn't have anything in the machines and asked me what I was doing. I told him to fuck off. He said that wasn't nice. So, I repeated myself. He began to smoke. I began to light up. I got the wrong impression;

thought he was trying the white knight thing. I told him I didn't need a man to swoop in and save me.' She paused, noticing him listening intently. 'So he didn't even try. We just sat there for hours. Started talking about everything from the weather, to the people, to the world. And when I coughed so hard I thought my ribs would break, he got a taxi to take me to A&E.'

Swan had stopped drinking. Duncan's elbows were on his knees, listening. Even Reese had quieted.

'He came along. I told him about the illness. Said the doctors didn't care, nobody did, and I was . . . scared. I didn't want to just be forgotten, you know? Just a headline in a newspaper people skim over. I wanted a life, and it was too early for mine to end. I told him I wasn't ready to die. And he said, maybe I didn't have to. Explained what he was, and I bought it.'

By the time she finished, the group had gone still. Viola's smirk had faded into something thoughtful, her drink resting loose in her hand. Her phone buzzed in a pocket, making her keenly pull it free and type a message.

Reese exhaled slowly. 'So . . . he bit you?'

Pepper nodded. 'I let him. I gave him a choice. Either finish it for good, or turn me in to one of you. I didn't want to make the decisions for a change. And . . . it's why I'm here now. Because of Laik's . . . decision.'

The silence thickened. But Laik stepped in then, voice low, adding to the charade.

'I thought she'd hate me for it after,' he said. 'She had that look in her eye. You know the one – where you're not sure if someone's going to thank you or stab you in the chest. It's a lot to deal with. But she's resourceful. Clever. Stronger than I expected. Smarter too. Got mouthy real fast, but I dunno what I expected.'

That drew a ripple of laughter.

Pepper shot him a look. 'I was cold. That wasn't a personality trait. That was bloody frostbite.'

Swan chuckled into his beer. 'Jesus. That's grim . . . and kinda sweet.'

Laik shook his head. 'I don't think either of us meant for it to be permanent. But she stayed. Even when she could've gone.'

Reese leaned forward. 'Under you? No offence, I would have run a mile.'

Duncan smirked. 'I feel like a dick for thinking you were just Laik's terrifying kid sister . . .'

Pepper picked at her nails as the humour faded away. 'Well . . . it's not the worst thing in the world, I suppose.'

Laik took one last drag on his cigarette, then dropped it, grinding the ember out beneath his boot.

'I don't say this often,' he said, taking a slow, patient inhale. 'But I'm glad it happened. Not the sickness, or the running. But that it brought you here. Your company ain't been bad.'

Pepper met his gaze across the dim swing set. 'I'm not sure what "here" is.'

'Neither am I,' he murmured. 'But it's not as cold as it was back then, that's for sure.'

No one said anything for a while. The city breathed around them, distant sounds of people smearing into the dark.

That was until, at the edge of the park, a black car pulled up, its engine still idling, windows tinted to ink. The headlights cast long, narrow shadows across the grass and hedges. The air throbbed with the chugging of its engine.

Laik was the first to lower his drink and assess the threat. His stomach shifted like it always did when met with something unpredictable.

Viola rose, brushing dust from her trousers. 'Alright, folks. Fun as this is, I've got to call it.'

Pepper frowned. 'That for you? Don't look like no Uber . . .'

Viola slipped her phone back into her pocket, trying to sound casual. 'Yes, I'm just—' she hesitated, smiling to herself, 'going for a walk. With someone I met earlier.'

'Do you even know his name?'

'No, but he knows mine.'

Reese burst out laughing. 'Oh my God, the *scandal*!'

'You don't walk when you're in a car, you know that, right?' Swan teased.

Laik leaned back against the frame, a smirk tugging at the corner of his mouth. 'Where I come from, "stretching your legs" isn't taken so literally.'

Pepper swatted the air in his direction. 'Behave. Wait, is that the someone from the bar?'

'Maybe.' Viola's grin was wide, and feet impatient. 'Enjoy the rest of the night.'

The group exploded into hoots. Duncan loudly wished her luck, causing Viola to quicken her steps towards her ride. The door opened. She slipped inside. The car rolled off into the dark and whatever was in store for its occupants.

For a moment, Pepper wondered if Viola had any idea what she was doing – and decided she absolutely did.

'She's ridiculous.' Laik made a dry glance, but said it fondly.

'Ridiculous? Have you worked under her? The woman is a menace. Puts me through it daily,' Pepper said, drumming her fingers on the can. 'But I'm glad she's getting a win. She deserves it. Canis and Quinn are thoroughly demanding, I can't imagine the crap she's had to put up with for . . . decades, I suppose? I thought I was kept on my toes, but that one, she never stops. What we all do, it's a hard gig. I think we need to remember that from time to time.'

She raised her drink toward the middle of them, proposing a toast.

'To stopping once in a while.'

The others all chimed and took a patient swig in unison.

As the laughter faded, Pepper absently reached for her phone from her jacket. The screen lit her face in a pale glow.

Her smile slipped. She opened the latest message. Her eyes darted over the words once, then again, slower this time. The sound around her seemed to fall away – the city hum, the rustle of trees, even the idle chatter of the group. All she could hear was her pulse.

The phone trembled in her hand.

Laik, watching from his place on the climbing frame, had noticed and frowned.

'What's wrong?'

# Chapter Twenty-Five

## Crestfallen

The lift juddered as it climbed, slow and stiff, its cabling creaking under the effort. The interior was scrawled with graffiti – names, obscenities, someone's declaration of eternal love for the colourfully named 'Gravediggers'. A single flickering light buzzed overhead like it might give out at any second.

The man she'd left the Kingfisher with was taller up close. Not broad, but contained – like the shape of something powerful hidden beneath tailored layers. He didn't smile, just gave that short upturn of one side of his mouth that ignited something in her. And, truth be told, she wasn't looking to extinguish it just yet.

Viola stood besides, shoulder to shoulder, eyeing the floor count creeping slowly upward.

'You always take girls up in lifts that look like murder scenes?'

He smirked.

'If I were going to kill you,' he said smoothly, 'it wouldn't be a cliché. Not now, not in this part of the city where people find it easy to forget. No. It would matter, done somewhere with luxury. Satin sheets. Large windows. Champagne on ice. I would give you those last moments to treasure . . .'

She laughed – that short, sharp laugh of someone caught off-guard in a good way. It was playful. Amusing. Mysterious. She liked mysterious.

'Before you stole them away,' she stated.

'Before then, yes.'

'That's good to know. I'd hate to be a boring headline.'

His tone was dry, self-aware. It disarmed her, made her smile. She liked a man with poise. He still hadn't told her his name.

The lift let out a final clunk and the doors rattled open.

They stepped out into the night. The rooftop was wide and flat, bordered by waist-high concrete ledges. Thirty floors up, the city stretched in every direction – a hundred thousand lights blinking like stars fallen to Earth, traffic threading like veins below, pulsing red and amber. The sky was dark velvet, scattered with a handful of real ones. Sure, it could be seen from Leroux Tower, but here, it was like she was smothered by it.

He offered his arm, and she looped hers through it. The rooftop was bare except for a few scattered pipes, an old satellite dish, and the night.

Viola's breath caught a little.

'Wow,' she said. 'This is—'

'Quiet,' he said. 'Up here, the noise isn't so jarring. None of the traffic. None of the troubles of people. Rare, isn't it?'

Her fingers constricted around his arm. 'You don't strike me as the kind of man who likes quiet.'

'I like perspective. It seems like the only ones who appreciate it these days are the birds. And they don't judge.'

Congregations of pigeons mumbled in their little groups as they continued.

They crossed a small bridge between roof levels – just a metal gangway, aged and rust-streaked – and came to a rooftop garden. No more than a scattering of planters and wind-battered pots, but someone had clearly put time into it. There were herbs, little sprouts in rows, a trellis bent with ivy. Planters of ivy, herbs gone wild in old crates, a battered watering can catching the moonlight.

She brushed her fingers over a crooked rosemary bush. 'This yours?'

'No. But I respect the effort.'

'Thought as much. You don't strike me as the gardening type.'

'You don't strike me as the type to go for a drive with a stranger,' he countered.

Viola smiled. 'Ah, but you're not a stranger. I think you're more like a . . . surprise in waiting. A bit like an unwrapped gift.'

'And that appeals to you?'

'More than you'd guess. I'm interested in finding out what I've got.'

The tension between them was soft, warm, growing thicker with each step. She hadn't felt this electric in ages. Not like this. With Canis it was always a dance, a smirk, a tease with no destination. This man said little, did even less – and still offered her more than Canis ever had.

They stood at the edge, the garden behind them and the city at their feet. The park below glowed softly, moonlight caught in treetops. Roads shimmered with motion. From here, the city pulsed like a living thing.

He took her hand, drawing her closer.

'You like the view?' he asked.

'I love it,' she said, not looking away. His short chestnut hair fluttered silently. 'Like you said. Nobody here to judge.'

His fingers traced hers. The wind teased her coat, and her pulse kicked up as he stepped close. When he leaned in to kiss her, it was gentle. Measured. Like he'd been waiting years for his mouth to find hers. His hand moved to her cheek, his touch comforting, and then to her jaw, brushing the line where her pulse beat strong. She exhaled against his mouth. His attention was warm and lingering, coaxing her to taste deeper, kiss faster. And then, when the excitement and the thrill became too heady, she raised her chin and exposed her neck to him.

His lips brushed the skin below her jaw. She let out a breath, eyes fluttering. The bite was soft – more pressure than pain. A curl of heat rather than a burst of fire. Her breath caught in her throat, the dizzy sensation blooming in her head. The rush. The danger. The ecstasy.

But then she felt his grip tighten.

The hand on her back. Another at her wrist. Not rough, but firm. Holding.

Viola tried to shift her weight. Tried to speak. But the strength wasn't there. The pleasure dulled, becoming distant. Something was draining out of her, quick enough to steal her voice. Her vision blurred. Her body weakened. She made a sound – not a word, but something trying to be.

She blinked, her vision tipping sideways as her legs surrendered. He held her close, still calm. She couldn't move. Couldn't speak. Her breath stuttered.

He held her just a moment longer, enough for Viola's world to become shrouded with shadow. Then, with an effortless press, he eased her limp body backward, away from him.

*And the ledge.*

Viola's eyes found his one last time as the world tilted, slipped, and raced away.

For the first time, she saw him fully.

His face indifferent. His eyes dark and knowing. The guarded composure. These weren't weapons to charm at all. They were to deceive.

And as Viola spun in nothing, the pavement raced up to greet her, until there were no more stars, no more lustful kisses, or regrets. The screams from onlookers that followed sent a shock of life through the pigeons, and they set off in a flurry into the night sky.

Her murderer dabbed the trickle of blood from his lips, looking down to admire his handiwork, poised all alone on the rooftop.

Alone, with nobody there to judge.

# Chapter Twenty-Six

## Leftovers

Pepper ran until her legs gave out. Until the burn in her lungs clawed up her throat and left her staggering, clutching a stitch in her side. A smear of blood streaked beneath her nose. One eye was tender, and the palms of her hands were raw from where she'd tripped. But she kept going, kept moving, because that's what she always did; she ran. She had run from shopkeepers with chocolate bars shoved up her jumper. She had run from the older kids who cornered her at the park and pushed her around until she bit one of them. She had run when she insulted the wrong person too quickly, too savagely. She had run from the haunting silence that lived in the quiet house she and her sister temporarily made a home out of.

She cut behind the Chinese takeaway on Sable Street, the rust-stiff door propped open like it always was. The fresh heat of the kitchen hit her full in the face – garlic, oil, soy, the metallic waft of gas burners. The noise of voices followed. Two kitchen staff darted sideways, mid-prep, as the scrappy child in a dirtied hoodie stumbled inside. Comments were exchanged, carrying this, dicing that, calling to one another on the status of the orders. But Pepper walked through, unconcerned. Someone cried out, loudly, when they almost tripped right into her.

Claire stood at the centre of the storm, brow slick with sweat, one hand on the wok tossing stir fry into the air, the other holding tongs like an extension of her arm, snapping lids on plastic containers. She spun at the noise, eyes locking on Pepper.

'Peps? What are you doing here?' Claire's voice jumped above the clatter. 'What happened to you?'

Pepper stood in the threshold, shoulders hunched, sleeves too long for her arms. Her hoodie was torn at the cuff, and she was flushed red from the cold and the running. She wiped at her face with the back of her wrist, smearing blood across her cheek like war paint, looking away with a petulant glare.

From the front counter, their boss shouted, accent thick and tone sharper than the cleaver he kept beneath the till.

'Claire! *Come on!* I'm not running a nursery, we've got a queue!'

Claire scowled, but she didn't argue. She turned back to her sister and lowered her voice. 'Go wait out front, don't go anywhere. Wait for me to finish my shift, alright? Please.'

Pepper nodded, silent, dragging her feet past plastic chairs and steamy windows into the empty front seating area. A barren fish tank bubbled quietly in the corner. She sat at a Formica-topped table and tried not to cry.

The clock ticked. Minutes dragged like hours, making the hours almost unbearable.

Menus had been read. Leaflets refolded and reread, then folded into paper animals, or the closest thing. Someone had brought her a bowl of chow mein she hadn't asked for. She'd eaten it mostly out of boredom, though she was hungry. She was always hungry. Pepper had surgically separated the lengths of charred green onion into a sad pile on a flyer advertising salt and chilli ribs.

Claire finally dropped into the seat opposite, her apron damp and streaked, a plastic bag of boxed leftovers in hand. She blew a strand of hair from her face.

'Sorry,' she said, sliding into the seat across from her. 'Boss let me off early. Mostly because he thought you'd scare off the customers. Gave us this.'

'Nice of him,' Pepper mumbled.

'What's wrong with those?' Claire eyed the pile of vegetables next to the bowl.

Pepper shrugged. 'Don't like green onions.'

Claire gave her a sideways look. 'Eat 'em. They'll help you grow big and strong.'

'Nan used to say that.'

'And now I'm saying it. She was smart.'

*Not smart enough to abandon her granddaughters*, Pepper thought, yielding. She gave her a narrowed-eye glare but dutifully forced one into her mouth with chopsticks like it was poison. The look given when chewing was the same when doing maths homework.

'Happy?'

'Only when you eat the rest.'

Claire smiled, then leaned back. 'So. Who were you running from this time? Sanjay catch you nicking crisps again?'

Pepper frowned, wiping at her nose again. 'No. It was some boys. Said I didn't have a mum. So, I told 'em, yeah, *mine* died. But *their* dads pissed off because they were stuck with *you* disappointments, and that went down about as well as you'd expect.'

Claire exhaled slowly. 'Peps . . .'

Pepper bristled. 'What?! I didn't start it.'

'No, you just set it off,' Claire said, calm and tired all at once. A hand was dragged down her face. 'People are gonna be pricks, you'll see them all your life, you can't just kick something off like that. You keep getting into trouble like this because you just don't care what'll happen, you just *act*, like, automatically. I keep saying, you need to *stop* and *think* before you open that mouth of yours. You need to slow it *down*. Stop reacting to everything like the world's out to get you. Because one day, you're gonna run when you should've stayed. Or worse – stay when you should've run. And you need to know the difference.'

'All we've done is run an' move. Mum said we were running. Nan said we were running. All we do.'

Pepper looked away, jaw set.

'I'm serious,' Claire added. 'It just causes drama. We don't need that right now. You showing up here like this, you could've got me fired. Again.'

A flicker of guilt ghosted over Pepper's face. She stared at the pile of onions. Pushed it with her chopsticks.

'You're always working,' she muttered. 'You're never around. I come home and it's just me, and I wait and wait and half the time I'm asleep before you even—'

Her voice broke. She covered her face with her hands.

'I'm sick of feeling like I'm by myself all the time.'

Claire looked at her, her lips quivering.

'We need the money,' she said. 'You know that. We can't have bailiffs turning up again. Not like last time. We're barely making it as is.'

'I don't care,' Pepper snapped suddenly, her voice high, cracked. 'I don't *care* about the money, I just want you. I hate it. I hate you not being there!'

Her voice hitched. She bit her lip hard, holding back

tears, but they were already welling. Claire blinked, stricken, her hand halfway to the plastic bag.

She reached across the table instead and took her sister's hand in hers.

'Peps. It's you and me, okay? I'm always thinking of you. Always. Even when I'm working. Especially then. You are never far from me.'

She reached beneath her collar and pulled something free from around her neck. A silver locket, precious, slightly tarnished, the hinge worn smooth from years of fiddling. She clicked it open. Inside were three tiny photos: their mother in sunglasses on the beach mid-laugh, their gran, stoic in a garden chair, and the two of them curled up on a sofa when Pepper was still in primary school.

'Take it,' Claire said. 'So, the next time you feel alone, you open it, and you *know* I'm always with you. You and me. Always. You just gotta slow down for a second to see it.'

Pepper took it in her hands like it was holy, thumb brushing the image of their younger selves.

'And remember,' Claire said, taking one of Pepper's hands into her own, 'I do this for you. Everything. Even the hard stuff, because someone has to. But you've got to meet me halfway. Just slow down enough to see I haven't gone anywhere. Stop starting fights. Stop all this running . . .'

# Chapter Twenty-Seven

## Make a Deal With God

Pepper ran.

Her breath came in shallow, panicked gasps, her boots hammering down the linoleum corridors of the hospital like gunfire. Fluorescent lights above dashed past, each one briefly illuminating the panic carved into her face. Doors and signs blurred – X-RAY, OUTPATIENTS, VISITOR RECEPTION – none of them mattered. Only forward. Only the next corner. Only Claire.

'Hey! *Hey!* No running!' a voice barked from behind a desk. The security guard was a smudge of colour, and ignored.

She careened around the next junction, catching herself on the corner with a hand that shook like a leaf in a storm. At the elevator, she smashed the call button with her fist again and again, as if force might summon it faster.

Behind her, Laik caught up. He slowed, breath steady. She heard his voice but couldn't look at him. She didn't reply. Couldn't.

The lift doors sighed open. She stepped in. So did he.

The hum of the cables. The numbers ticking upwards.

Her knuckles were white around the railing. Her throat burned. Laik said nothing.

When the doors slid open on the right floor, she was already moving.

The hallway stretched ahead like a reaching tunnel, far away and oddly still. Low lighting did nothing for the foreboding. The air was thick with antiseptic. As if death couldn't be kept out, so they tried to clean around it.

She pressed the night buzzer with a shaking hand and leaned toward the speaker.

'P-Pepper Montgomery,' she said. 'I'm here to see C-Claire.'

The door buzzed open, and she stepped through.

Even Laik, who had seen centuries of suffering, of bodies broken and bloodied, found himself faltering. The ward was hushed, the beds half lit by the soft, sterile glow of machines. Sleeping shapes in white sheets. Plastic tubing glinting like glass veins. The beep of monitors, each one measuring a life in real time.

He slowed behind her, glancing from face to face, reading stories in their stillness. Laik was fluent with death. This wasn't it. Not yet. But it waited here. Lurking at the edges of every monitor, behind every pale eyelid.

Claire's room was half lit.

A nurse stood by her bed, checking the IV line with a quiet efficiency that suggested routine, not urgency. But the machines – the slow mechanical pump of the ventilator – told another story.

'She's stable,' the nurse said softly, with a glance toward Pepper. 'But the situation has changed. She's contracted an infection which her immune system cannot take care of itself, so we're helping with that. Her oxygen levels dropped too far, so we've moved her onto full ventilation.'

Pepper's stomach plummeted.

'How . . . How long, uh, does she . . . Um . . . y'know?'

'I'm sorry, I can't discuss that, you would need to talk to the doctor on call. Would you like me to fetch him?'

'Please, yes.'

The nurse touched her gently on the arm. 'I'll be at the desk if you need me.'

And then she was gone.

The door clicked shut behind them.

Claire didn't move.

She lay still in the bed, barely recognisable from the sister Pepper had spoken to days earlier. Her skin was pale, the colour drained from her cheeks. Her chest rose and fell in sync with the quiet, relentless hiss of the ventilator. Wires and tubes sprouted from her, connected to blinking machines that made electronic murmurs so soft it felt like the equipment was whispering.

Pepper walked forward slowly, her steps uncertain. Her fingers reached out to brush Claire's hair back from her forehead, gentle, like it might snap away. She sank to the edge of the bed, bent over, and rested her forehead against her sister's arm.

'Hey, you. Sorry I'm late, but I'm here,' she said. Her voice was hoarse. 'This, uh . . . This is Laik . . . a friend from work. Wish you could meet him under better circumstances. You'd like him. Acts tough. You'll tell him off good.'

Behind her, Laik stood silent.

'She always looked out for me,' Pepper finally said, not looking up. 'Even when she shouldn't have. I was . . . wild. Angry. Always running from something. Claire used to say I was born swinging and never figured out when to stop. And she never tried to fix me. She just made space for me to figure it out. Told me that I needed to . . . I needed to see what was happening in front of me. Just let it in so everything could make sense.'

She laughed once, but it broke halfway and caught in her throat. The tears began.

'Even when we had nothing, she'd find a way to feed me. She'd take the hit if someone came knocking, and they did. She used to say I'd grow out of acting like the world is out to get me. That one day I'd have to stop running.'

She sniffed and looked down at the motionless figure, forcing a smile.

'Guess that ain't happened yet. I – I remember, once, I sprained my ankle climbing some stupid scaffolding at a builder's yard. I just wanted to see a different view than day in, day out. She carried me home two streets on her back. Didn't even tell me off. Just patched me up. When I could walk properly, we went up there together and spent the night eating chips and watching people walk by.'

Laik swallowed. His throat was tight.

Pepper looked at him now, face drawn, eyes red.

'I can't . . . it's too much, I mean . . . just look at her.'

Her hand found Claire's – cool, limp, and far too still. She gripped it tighter, pressing her forehead against the arm, the cannula tube jutting out from the hand making it awkward.

'She's not just a sister,' Pepper murmured. 'She's *everything*. The only real bit of family I've ever had. Fucking Mum died, Nan died, everyone left me, Laik, but *she* stuck around. The only one who knew how to keep me going. I love her. I love her.'

A guttural sniffle and then she pulled her head up, eyes burning, staring directly at the wall. Her breathing was deep and desperate. And when she turned towards him, she was fierce with intent.

'Wait . . . I . . . wait, what if . . . If you made her like you,' she said, standing to face Laik. 'If you turned her, made her one of you, she'd be fine, right? Is that part from the movies real? That if you make her a vampire, all this goes away? Makes her b-better. You can *do* that!'

His eyes softened. 'Pepper—'

'Don't *act* like this isn't an option! I know it cures things, I've heard about it, that part of the movies is real. You said it yourself, didn't you? Told me, like, last week or . . . some, some time! *Didn't you?* Yeah, it cures things. What's the fucking difference? Just do it, yeah? Don't just fucking "*Pepper*" me!'

Laik took a breath and stepped closer. 'It's not the solution you think it is. And it's not your choice to make. Not for her.'

'She's *dying*!'

'And if she wakes up after what we do? And she doesn't want it? What then?'

Pepper's face crumpled.

'She'd forgive me.'

'She might, true. Or she might hate you forever. You don't know what she believes. Some people . . . they go mad. Because they think God's abandoned them. Because they think becoming this is a punishment. Everything they thought was true suddenly isn't anymore. And if she can't hold on to who she is . . .?'

He didn't finish the thought. He had seen the outcome too many times.

Pepper clenched her fists. 'So, what? So, we just *wait*? We just let her slip away?'

Laik's voice dropped, almost a whisper. 'I've lost people too.'

'No, you *took* them, there's a difference!' she fired back, jabbing a finger at him. 'And you can fix this for me – but you don't wanna . . . Can't believe you would, would *stand there* and . . . you don't . . . you . . .'

The tension snapped like a thread. Pepper struck his chest with her fist – a drained, futile motion that barely rocked him – and then again, then again until they became weak and pathetic. Her face buried in his shirt, sobs breaking from her in hard, ragged gasps.

Laik caught her. He wrapped his arms around her, slow and steady. His hand cupped the back of her head, held her as her body trembled. Her howls were primal. Pained. They stayed like that, together in the hum of machines and the whisper of filtered air, until her voice shattered to a croak and tears continued to spill but not so fiercely.

'Promise me,' she choked, her voice small and scratchy. 'Fucking *promise* me we'll get the Rose and fix all this. Promise me, Laik, because I need to . . . I *need* to hear you say it.'

His voice was low. Honest. He closed his eyes and pressed his lips to her hair.

'I promise.'

And she believed him.

But lacked the nerve to reveal that should she cure Claire with the Eternal Rose, then there would be nothing left to rid Laik of the monster within.

A realisation that made her sob harder.

# Chapter Twenty-Eight

## Candles for the Lost

Three days had passed since the Cavendishes lost one of their own.

Death was normal. Death was expected. But not this one. And certainly not in this fashion.

The tower, in all its brutal grandeur, had entered mourning through the way its halls grew still, how its corridors echoed differently. Even the glass of its windows seemed to refract the skyline in a dimmer hue, as if the building itself had lowered its gaze in grief.

Below its towering frame, beneath the surface and splendour, lay the crypt. A space carved in dark marble and cold silver. Torches lit the arching walls with flickering light, casting deep shadows between the engraved tombs of those whose bloodlines had earned them a resting place here. But not all who lay in the Silent Nest had worn a Family name. Some had simply given all they had, and more.

Today, Viola joined them.

The procession was silent. The kind of silence that hummed. A tide of black coats and raven-dark dresses swept down the old stone steps. Every figure wore mourning attire. Most in black, as tradition demanded. But not all.

Four wore red.

*Concetta. Mortis. Canis. Quinn.*

From their collars to their cuffs, their mourning garments bled shades of wine and scarlet and brick. Red was not a fashion here. It was a declaration. A Family custom reserved for when grief turned to fury. When a life had been stolen, not surrendered. *We were wronged*, the red said. *And we do not forget.*

The ceremony began without fanfare. No hymns. No prayers. Only a soft tremor of organ music, and the sound of the ancient gates locking behind them.

At the far end of the chamber, beneath a vaulted arch, the casket lay draped in the family crest – obsidian and gold, the Cavendish crest of the burning tower completing it. A single white rose rested atop the lid.

Then Canis stepped forward.

He looked more subdued than usual. His usual rings were absent, his suit, shirt, tie and shoes a strong maroon, his sunny hair tied back. His eyes – always a little too bright, a little too clever – were sober now. When he spoke, he would command the room. Here, he simply let his words land where they would.

'I first met Viola in an elevator,' he said, resting his hand gently on the casket. 'Of all places.'

A few heads turned. The image seemed too mundane, too modern. But he smiled at the memory, soft around the edges.

'I'd been summoned to the upper floors,' he went on, 'for one of those meetings where you nod a lot at flip charts and numbers while fighting the urge to throttle all those involved. I, however, was tired. Hungover from socialising the day and night before with important people, still very . . . fragile. These were the early days, see, when I had yet to learn how to endure the almighty burden of being *me*.'

A few people – even in grief – allowed themselves a faint smile.

'The lift stopped halfway. And she rushed in, all flustered. No introduction. Just this whirlwind in leather boots and a charity shop jacket, clutching too many box files, staring at me, like I was the one interrupting *her* moment. She looked me up and down, visibly unimpressed. Unsurprising, being that I was barely being held up by the elevator. No doubt she was intimidated by my presence, as many are. I saw her trembling. But she spirited it away, and informed me she was to be in this meeting of mine to ensure it went smoothly. To help, she said. Before *oh so brazenly* adding . . .' He paused, lips twitching. 'That, looking how I did, *I would need all the help I could get*.'

He chuckled, then sighed.

'It was true. And unexpected. I laughed. Properly. First time in weeks.'

Canis stepped back from the casket, fingers lingering a moment longer on the wood.

'Viola forced me to wear a pair of sunglasses she had on her and insisted that she did all the talking. All I had to do was agree at the right times. When I was addressed, asked to give my thoughts, she saved me from any inadvertent embarrassment I could have caused. She stepped in when I floundered. Pushed back on someone who asked questions they had no right to be asking. Later that night, I invited her to my floor. We sat on the balcony, the two of us – her with her feet up on the rail like she owned the skyline, and me playing the piano like it was the only language we both understood. And she sang.'

Canis steadied himself.

'I don't know if any of you ever heard her sing. Most of you probably didn't. But she had a voice like wind over water. Not perfect. Not polished. But . . . *true*. No filters. No theatrics. Just Viola, giving you everything she had. And that's what she did every single day for us . . . for a hundred and forty-nine years. For the Family. Always . . . there.'

He looked up, eyes glassed but dry.

'And now, we have the honour of watching over her while she rests.'

He turned to Quinn.

'Sister, do you—'

But Quinn, dressed in a construction of blood-red silks, one leg crossed over the other, her chin resting on a closed fist, didn't answer. She simply shook her head, slowly, once. The gesture was not cold. It was final. There were, astonishingly, no words in her today.

Canis nodded and returned to his place.

Concetta rose from her seat.

If grief had a spine, it was hers. In heels and structured crimson, she looked like a general at a war memorial, her features carved from purpose. She didn't need to raise her voice to hold the room.

'Viola was a Cavendish. She was not a soldier. She was not a tactician. She never sought out blood. But she was *ours*.'

Her voice echoed, cool and resonant.

'She was fearless. She was fierce. She had a tongue that could cut stone and loyalty that never once wavered. She stood for us when others fell. She loved us when others kept their distance. And she fought for her place with every inch of who she was. She, like many here today, may not be of hallowed blood. But she *is* Family.'

She let her eyes move across the crowd.

'I don't want to hear rumour. I don't want quiet speculation about how and why and what's to come. There is a time for answers. But it is not this moment. This moment belongs to her. And we will not poison it.'

She stepped forward, closer to the casket.

'If you feel lost . . . good. That means you loved her. But don't let your mourning become your ruin. Don't forget who we are. We honour our fallen by living, and by remembering. And most of all . . .'

She reached out, her hand resting on the casket beside the rose.

'. . . by continuing what they stood for.'

And with that, Viola was slowly lowered into the Vault.

The white rose stayed in place until the very end.

There was no sobbing. No wailing. Just the quiet pull of breath. One long, collective inhale from a Family refusing to break.

The kind of silence that said: *we are still here. But we bear the scar.*

The atrium had been transformed.

Where sunlight once pierced through glass from twenty storeys above, now the chandeliers burned low and heavy. Candles glowed in every recess, nestled among silver holders and empty wine bottles like a constellation scattered across furniture. The hum of low conversation drifted among the gathered – not the drunken, boisterous kind that usually followed funerals, but the slow tempo of grief quietly melding with disbelief.

There were Enforcers by the bar, drinks in hand, half in uniform, half in black. The musicians played in the far corner, a string quartet dressed in understated suits and gowns. The violin's melody was achingly suitable. At the centre of it all stood a long table, laid with photographs, white roses and a large leather-bound book for written tributes. Viola's face adorned the largest print in the middle. Not a glamour shot, just her laughing at something off-camera, eyes narrowed, smile inviting.

Pepper stood at the table with a pen in hand. She stared at the page. Her handwriting had stopped halfway through the sentence. For long moments, she said nothing. Then, with a frown and the tip of her tongue between her teeth, she added a final line:

*Thank you for your trust. It meant more than I ever got to tell you.*

She signed her name. Just *Pepper*. That felt like enough.

Turning away, she caught sight of Laik already seated in the shadows of the velvet couches near the back wall. He had that stillness to him, that very specific, very *him* way of occupying space without demanding it. A half-drunk glass sat in one hand, a second waiting beside it. He saw her approach and nudged the other toward her.

She sank into the couch next to him with a slow exhale.

'Thanks,' she murmured, taking the drink without asking what it was.

Laik glanced sidelong at her. 'How are you holding up?'

Pepper didn't answer straight away. She looked at the drink, gave it a slow swirl.

'Not well,' she said. 'It's such a shock. I shouldn't have let her go by herself.'

'You couldn't have stopped her,' Laik said. 'None of us could've. Her mind was made up before she ever set foot in that bar. She was going to have a good time.'

Pepper's mouth twisted. 'That's what gets me. Wishing I'd said something different, y'know? One different word, one minute earlier . . . maybe it changes the whole thing.'

Laik took a slow sip of his drink. His voice was low, but sympathetic.

'Yeah. I know.'

He paused. Then added, 'Reese is on the investigation team. Told me they haven't found anything solid yet. It looks like . . . just some psycho. Street vamp, no affiliate, probably. Just someone twisted looking for kicks.'

Pepper rested her head in her hands. For a long moment she stayed like that, breathing slowly through her fingers. Then she glanced up – and caught sight of Quinn. She was standing alone in the line to sign the memorial book, a storm behind her eyes. The crowd ahead of her recognised her presence and peeled back, allowing her to pass without a word. She stared down at the table, unmoving. Then she hurriedly scrawled something with a flourish in the book, turned and paced away in a swirl of crimson.

'God.' Pepper watched Quinn leave with an escort forming behind and muttered, 'All this makes me wanna be sick.'

Laik looked at her. 'Has there been any word about your sister?'

Pepper pulled out her phone, checking the screen even though she knew there'd be nothing.

'No,' she said. 'Called earlier. No change.'

He shifted slightly, guilt flickering across his features. 'Sorry. I didn't mean to sound—'

'No, it's okay,' she interrupted, pocketing the phone. 'You were just asking. Doctor said . . . months. Best case. But she's not exactly sprinting toward it, y'know?'

She gave a bitter smile that didn't last long.

Laik hesitated, then in a quiet, awkward motion, reached

out and gave her knee a gentle pat. It was clumsy. A half-formed gesture from someone who didn't do reassurance very well. But it was real.

Pepper looked at him. Then, slowly, she leaned sideways, resting her head against his shoulder. The drink balanced on her lap. Her breath came shallow, and there was something fragile in the way she folded in on herself. She didn't say anything. Neither did he.

Around them, the music swelled. The violinist sent her tune dancing through the space, not joyful, not mournful. Just . . . full. A string of candles flickered as someone passed, their perfume that of rosewater.

They sat in silence.

Not because they lacked the words.

But because in that moment, words weren't enough.

# Chapter Twenty-Nine

## Babysitting

The car rumbled beneath them like something alive, prowling through the skeletal remains of the city's nightlife. Groups of weekend revellers had reduced to dregs. Some wanted to keep the party going; others were looking for other ways to enjoy the night. Streetlights skimmed past in rhythmic procession, casting flickers across the dashboard. Rain threatened above but hadn't yet found its courage.

Laik drove one-handed, finger tapping on the wheel in annoyance. The Subaru's engine hummed low – not showy, but ready to bite if asked. Swan sat slouched in the passenger seat, nodding along to some heavy synth wave with punchy vocals. The song felt perfect to play at this time, like the city was providing its own soundtrack.

'You're quiet,' Swan said, voice low as soon as the track had finished.

Laik didn't look at him. 'I hate babysitting.'

'You hate a lot of things. I'm amazed this one even makes the list.'

'You know what I mean. You've seen her when she's on one. She's as dangerous as it gets and it's never anyone else.

It's always me who picks up the pieces.' Laik gripped the wheel tighter, turning. 'Never anyone else. Just me. How come Mortis—'

'Our *boss*,' Swan reminded him.

'—allows her to get in this state time and time again? He should just lock her up and throw away the key. For her own protection.'

'I remember the exact same thing said about you once upon a time.'

'I think you remember wrong. I dunno. I'm just not getting Mortis at the moment. All this drama with Horus and he's just letting it happen. It's not him out on the streets. We're the ones who face the other Families. Calling him soft, and that. And when work needs to be done, I'm reduced to playing bloody taxi . . .'

Swan smirked, brandishing his phone. 'Alright. Point made. So would you rather someone else do it? I can put the call in and we can turn back right now. It's no problem.'

It took a couple of glances for Laik to deduce whether his partner was serious. He was.

'Well, we're almost here now . . .' Laik grumbled, shifting himself in his seat.

The tyres hissed over wet tarmac. They passed beneath an overpass, its underside dripping and tagged with graffiti that no longer meant anything to anyone. The city was both empty and watching, like a stage after the final curtain.

'You ever think about getting out?' Laik asked suddenly.

Swan raised an eyebrow. 'Of the car? I didn't piss you off enough to throw me out while we're moving . . .'

'No. Getting out of this. Of all of it. The job. The Families. The night crawling. Just . . . giving it up.'

Swan inhaled through his nose as he gave it thought. 'Don't tell this to anyone. But yeah, once. A long time ago, must have been the Seventies, I think. All that business with Vietnam made me see things a bit different.'

'Really? What made you change your mind?'

'People like us don't get to just walk away, mate. We're an asset until we're not. Then we become nothin' but loose ends . . .'

They drove in silence for another minute. The glow of the Kingfisher's interior rose ahead, humming its electric fatigue against the alley's quiet.

They parked down the alley from the Kingfisher, tucked between a shuttered pawnshop and a fried chicken place still glowing in LED-blue. The bar's heartbeat pulsed faintly through the backstreets, a 90s anthem powerful and raw. A couple staggered past, hand-in-hand, laughing breathlessly. Someone threw up behind a skip.

The alley was still slick from earlier rain. Their boots echoed across cobblestones as they approached the familiar figures of the door staff, nodding to the muscle in black jackets who gave them a look and a grunt. The venue was winding down.

'Evening, boys,' a slab of meat rumbled, nodding.

'Any trouble tonight?' Swan asked.

'Just some scraps. Your girl's just inside. Lucky for you.'

'Lucky for her,' Laik muttered under his breath.

Inside, the Kingfisher was winding down. Only the drunk, the desperate and the romantically doomed remained. A few lone figures took time to finish their drinks, or tried to flirt with bar staff that had long ceased to care.

Pepper stood near the entrance, arms crossed, biting at her nails. The stress in her eyes was obvious. The relief seeing the pair of them walk inside, more so.

'Thank *God*.' She exhaled. 'I didn't know who else to call.'

'You did the right thing. Where is she?'

They followed Pepper's gaze to the far end of the bar.

Quinn Cavendish was drunk. Not dancing-on-the-bar drunk. Not charmingly oversharing drunk. She was the kind of drunk you only got to when a bad break-up resulted in declaring war against people happier than yourself. She was slumped sideways on a stool like her spine had forgotten what posture was. Her hair was a mess, eyes heavy and unfocused, lips slightly parted as if still mid-sentence from hours ago. Her boots were mismatched. Her coat was half on, half off, and someone had written their phone number on her hand in biro. The infamous stuffed iguana protruded from the safety of an arm.

'She left the tower without bringing any protection,' Pepper murmured. 'Thinking she'll have a few drinks, be crazy, go home. This guy called me to come and collect her. When I got here, I realised this was more than a one-person job . . .'

Laik lowered himself and looked over her face with concern.

'Quinn? You alright there, princess?' he called. 'You can't sleep on a stool all night.'

She stirred, eyes fluttering.

'Laik . . .' she mumbled, attempting to lift her head. 'Hey, sinner . . . Are you here for an operation as well? They say I got a monster in me too, so I may not make it . . . *they're gonna make it look like an accident* . . .'

'Uh-huh. What happened? Can you tell me that?'

'I just . . . wanted a good time . . . I didn't want to see her, y'know? I didn't ask her to go away. I really did like her . . .' She pouted suddenly, blinking wet eyes.

'What's she had?' Swan asked, turning to the bartender. He filled in the gaps.

'Cider, vodka, lager, schnapps. Shots of Jailbird. That's what I know.'

'Did she drop anything? Take anything?' Laik added with a scowl.

'Hey man, I got a business here. I can't sit and watch every little thing going on with one crazy girl—'

Pepper, Laik and Swan rotated their heads in unison in his direction, their stare drilling deep. It was all it took to make him swallow his retort and answer their question.

'I dunno, I didn't see. She spoke to a lot of people tonight, you know how she gets – friend to everybody. If she wasn't talking, she was arguing, if she wasn't that she was dancing. She danced, she cried, she made out with a few, might have threatened to marry someone. Some of the things she was coming out with an' all . . .' He shook his head, as if the mere memory burdened him. 'You need to keep that one in control. Whenever she comes on in, it's always drama.'

'You're lucky we come in at all. You'll take our money and be a damn sight nicer to the ones who keep you in business.' Pepper narrowed her eyes. Anything else and she would eat him alive.

'Ever seen a magpie with a scalpel?' Quinn smacked her lips. 'Buggers can fly . . .'

'So, this is normal for her? Drunk normal? I honestly don't know when her crazy turns into something we need to be concerned about.' Swan looked to Pepper who gave a shrug.

'Yeah, it's basically just this most of the time.'

'Okay,' Laik grunted, rising. 'Time to go.'

With practised ease, Swan and Laik each hooked an arm around her and hoisted her to her feet, her limbs rubbery and uncooperative. Outside, her boots skidded against the pavement as they guided her through the alley, the Kingfisher's fading music still echoing faintly behind them. Pepper followed close behind. Quinn stirred, brows furrowing, eyes glassy with confusion.

'Wait, where's . . . where's Mister Wiggles?' she mumbled, squinting at her empty hands as though they'd betrayed her.

'Got him right here,' Pepper said gently, lifting the slumping animal in her arms as they kept walking. 'He says not to worry.'

'Liar,' Quinn huffed, slurring the word as she turned her face into Laik's shoulder. 'He didn't tell you a thing.'

'And why not?' Pepper humoured her.

'Because he's dead, *stooopid*.'

Swan glanced back, muttering under his breath, 'We are not paid enough for this.'

'You better not throw up in my car, Quinn,' Laik warned her.

'Don't worry about that. I'm only sick if I'm running.' She made a struggling smile. 'Wait . . . you always been so handsome, or am I dying?'

'Little of both, I'm guessing,' Pepper replied with surprising edge.

They hit the ring road ten minutes later. The Subaru carved its way like a silver bullet, eating up the road before it. The city gave way to stretches of blur and lamplight, half-empty lanes ribboning ahead. The motorway lights cast long golden streaks across the windscreen, illuminating Quinn passed out in the back, cheek smudged against the window. Swan had pulled her coat around her and rested her head, so she didn't bang it with every bump. Even if this wasn't the case, he doubted that it would stop her snoring.

Pepper sat in the passenger seat, watching the citrus strobes wash over them in sequence. Her eyes flicked to Laik's knuckles on the wheel, then to his face. She tried to keep her voice as low as possible so Swan couldn't hear her over the road.

'Thanks. For coming.'

'It's nothing,' Laik mentioned.

'No,' she said quietly. 'It really isn't. It helped me out of a pinch.'

'That's what big brothers do, right?'

Pepper moved her head to look out her window.

'Jackass.' She covered her smile with her hand.

'You think it's real what she's doing?' Swan suddenly piped up, leaning between the seats.

Laik frowned. 'What?'

'Quinn. Getting drunk like this. Upending everything.'

'I guess the Viola thing rattled her more than she let on.' Pepper sighed. 'Viola served for over a century . . . Very few people tolerate Quinn's presence as she's so off the wall. To lose someone so routine in her day-to-day probably can't be easy to process with her . . . condition.'

'When you talk to her, she's not always there, y'know? When I first came, I thought she was like a, uh . . . Greek oracle. This huge supernatural force channelled into a body that knows things. Now I can't tell if that's the case or if she's just nuts.'

'Probably both.' Laik flicked his eyes to meet the mirror. It had caught a light from behind growing too quick for his liking.

'I think there's a method to it all.' Pepper nodded slowly, thinking on their conversations. 'There was this time when she—'

'What's this joker doing?' Laik interrupted, his tone shifting immediately to the defensive.

A car, black and sleek, surged forward in the fast lane, but with an unusual urgency before matching their speed and staying alongside. The tinted windows did nothing but set Laik's instincts into overdrive.

The driver's window slid down.

Horus stared across the divide.

His face was unreadable, save for the ghost of a smile, not of joy, but of satisfaction – the kind born from inevitability. As if all of this had unfolded exactly as he had envisioned. That it was fate.

In his free hand: a pistol.

'*Down!*' Laik barked.

He reached back instinctively, shoving Pepper low while Swan lunged across the back seat to drag Quinn down by her coat. The crack of gunfire burst through the air like limp fireworks at this range. In doing so, the Subaru momentarily jerked left, smashing into the side of Horus' car. The impact made teeth clack and heads jolt. Horus retaliated, ramming back. Mercifully, the Subaru was heavier, hardier, and had the advantage. But that mattered little when a series of bullets cracked the passenger windows, with Pepper's bursting into a shower of shards, letting the wind in. Another slam, this time sheering the Subaru's wing mirror off in the process.

Another shot rang out. Metal punctured metal.

'*Who the hell is that?*' Pepper shouted, crouched low, looking between the seats.

'Bloody Horus! Asshole must have been waiting for us,' Laik growled, eyes locked on the mirror. 'Swan, call it in.'

Swan was already digging under his coat, trying to reach for his phone, but it was chaos, motion, veering lights and swerving lines. He jabbed and prodded at the screen as best as he could. Quinn had her head covered. '*What is happening*?' she cried out, genuinely afraid.

Horus pulled up again, this time on the passenger side, so close they could hear the rubber shriek against the concrete. Their headlights tangled. A flash of Horus's face was illuminated by the muzzle flare of another shot.

The Subaru jerked violently.

Laik cursed, metal grinding as he twisted the wheel hard. They skidded across two lanes, clipped the side rail. Sparks danced along the steel like fireflies. He shunted back, left with no option but to swerve hard to take the next junction. Tyres squealed. The Subaru bucked in protest, but he gritted his teeth, wrestling it back under control. Horus pulled close again behind, bumping against their rear panel with a steel kiss meant to provoke.

Another turn. Laik weaving through traffic this way and that. A delivery van swerved, horn blaring. Horus followed, clearly sensing the desperation. A bridge loomed. Laik turned sharply beneath it, only just keeping on the road and a fringe from clipping a passing truck. Horus mirrored him. He was always there, in the mirror, when he pulled around a corner, blasting past red traffic lights, sending other traffic into a panic. He was *always* there.

Another shunt from behind, then another, with the third being enough to send the Subaru into a skid. Laik overcorrected – they spun, bounced the kerb, smacked into a lamppost which launched them across wet grass in a ferocious spin.

Panicked screams were silenced by the windscreen exploding and a deafening hollow crunch as the car crashed into the side of an oak tree, finally coming to a stop for good.

# Chapter Thirty

## Stand Alone

Steam hissed up from the car engine, spluttering its final breath before giving up for good. One headlight pulsed faintly like a dying eye.

Inside, Laik gasped, forcing himself upright, blood trickling from his forehead in a hot line. His hand instinctively went to the graze just below his ribs – a bullet had found a mark, though it hadn't gone in, just took a little meat on its journey. It hurt – of course it hurt – but he could worry about the pain after. Which felt like the right mindset to have, but as every inch of him ached, it was easier said than done. Laik blinked, the blood having reached an eye. The airbag hadn't deployed. Smoke curled from the dashboard, inciting a splutter.

'Pepper?' Laik rasped, snapping his seatbelt free and frantically reaching for her in the dark, feeling the shape of her body to urge a response.

Laik helped as she fumbled for her seatbelt release, 'Ugh . . . Hnnn . . . Oh God . . . Laik . . .' she whimpered, unable to finish her sentence.

'I know. Me too.' He pulled himself around to look to the

back seats. Quinn was already moving, resting her forehead against the back of the driver's seat, raggedy hair obscuring her face. Her breathing was a toilet having finished a flush.

'I . . . threw up in your car.' She gurgled. 'I'm *sorrrrrryyyyyyy* . . .'

'Swan?' Laik scanned the crumbled mess that was half sprawled across the back seats. 'Hey! *Hey!* Swan!' He reached through and pulled at his jacket, rocking him about. He could just about make out Swan's lifeless rolls from side to side. The smoke was sharp and acrid, clawing at the back of the throat as it settled.

Laik looked through the cracked windshield. About fifty yards away the headlights of another car were fierce and frightening. It had pulled up onto the pavement and came to a stop.

'Everyone out!' Laik managed, wrestling with the driver's side door, which needed a few weak kicks to be convinced to open. He tried his best to pull Pepper on through over the gearstick and the driver's seat, the weight and effort taking them down onto the ground in a gasping, groaning heap on top of one another. Amidst the swearing and the tears, Pepper revealed that she may have broken something, or some *things*, plural, and the rising shock was making her tremor uncontrollably. Wet grass soaked her clothes as she involuntarily lay upon it, fighting to summon the energy to move something, *anything*.

Laik had staggered to the passenger side and escorted Quinn free, who, it miraculously seemed, was largely unscathed from the impact. She fell too, still heavily drunk, exclaiming that the stars were not in alignment tonight and this was a bad omen: an observation that went ignored. Laik called for the women to get away, as the steam from the engine had evolved to smoke, and licks of flame glittered beneath the concertinaed bonnet. Pulling Swan out was an effort, his mobile phone sporting a fierce crack across the entire screen. Lord knows if he managed to alert the Family, but that barely mattered now. The vehicle gave him up, and the Enforcer slithered lifelessly to the ground. The smoke from the car was worsening now, smothering the tree and illuminating its bark. Laik and the girls staggered as much as they could with Swan in tow, before all collapsing once more.

Ahead, the black vehicle throbbed before the lights went dark and the engine cut.

Then the driver's door opened.

And a silhouette stepped out, framed against the orange haze of streetlight. Tall. Purposeful.

Laik's breath caught with effort as he fought to his feet, wiped the blood from his vision. 'Stay here,' he said to Pepper, voice flat with resolve. 'Look after Quinn.'

'What are you gonna do?' She made a pained grunt.

He didn't answer.

Laik's vision narrowed to him. The rest – the debris, the smashed lamppost, the city sounds, the faint ringing in his ears – faded into meaningless background. Horus hadn't moved from the amber pool of a streetlamp, as still as a sculpture. Just watched. *Waited.*

Laik stepped forward, teeth clenched, his fangs in full view. His jacket hung open and shredded, flapping as he advanced. He staggered a step; one hand pressed to his ribs where a bullet had scored him. His other hung at his side, trembling.

'You're *dead*, Horus,' he growled, voice like gravel. 'You hear me? A *dead man walking*! The Families are going to—'

'Oh, the *Families*,' Horus sighed, like he was already bored. 'Save me, from the wrath of aristocrats and trust fund tyrants. From their games, their pacts, their pride and their silly little egos. *Save me from the fucking Families.*'

He stepped forward slowly, conversational even as his boots crunched over broken glass. His eyes shone like dark glass. 'Do you think I care for *any* of that? I was already old when their grandfathers were playing with sticks in the mud. Civilisations came and burned to ash, and I *watched*. Kings murdered by their own sons. Queens tossed to wolves. Blood meant something back then. *Power* meant something. And now? We've traded swords for signatures. We drink our blood from decanters and call it progress. Civilised. But we lost something, Laik. We lost the *feral*. We lost the wildness that made vampires feared. And the Families? They're the ones who convinced everyone it was for the better.'

Laik kept moving, body rigid. 'You sound like a lunatic.'

'I sound *liberated*. There's a difference.' Horus's eyes gleamed. 'Why would I concern myself with what they could punish me with? I am not part of their world, Laik. I'm the one to tear it all down.'

'And the Odes?'

'A means to an end, obviously.' Horus laughed. 'You never *listened*. I told you this was coming. You kept ducking me. Ignoring my messages. And I know you got the last one. I basically addressed it to you personally.'

Laik blinked.

His blood ran cold.

He didn't shout it. He couldn't. The air had thinned, robbed from his lungs by the weight behind those words. Horus had said it with that calm detachment, that hideous sense of inevitability, like it had already been written. Like the woman's fate was just an insignificant footnote in some grander plan.

He finally spoke. 'Viola . . .? You did *Viola*?'

For a moment, there was nothing. No thoughts. No blood. Just stillness between them.

But something invisible moved. Slithered about his belly. Coiled up his arms, gripping the bones. And right now, Laik wanted nothing but to surrender to it. Out here, in unknown streets, where anybody could see the transformation happen, he wanted it to consume him fully and shred Horus to pieces. All this carnage was the perfect excuse. Why hold back? Did Horus ever show restraint at any point? Mortis demanded there be no escalation, but where did that leave them? Clinging to the edge of oblivion, where one of theirs had already been tossed in. If he was given permission to hunt Horus down after the attack on Leroux Tower, none of this would have happened and Viola would have still been with them. *Idiot!*

No, Horus was right – they'd become soft. Controlled. Chained to meaningless pacts and venomed words.

'Believe me when I say it wasn't personal. But it *was* necessary. And look: it got us talking. It worked.'

Something cracked. Not a bone, but something older. Something in Laik's foundation, and all it supported came tumbling, tumbling down.

The Sins he carried erupted from within. They could smell their kind on Horus, taste the depths of his wrongdoing, and they would take them as their own. Or it would have, until Laik breathed in sharply, looking behind to the wreckage. Swan still hadn't moved. Pepper was groaning, clutching her arm. Quinn sobbed softly, hands pressed to her mouth, still staring at the night.

Amazingly, *they hesitated*.

The fury was there, boiling, but something else was rising with it. Guilt. Confusion. The sight of Pepper, hurt, shaken. Quinn, fumbling to right herself, terrified. Swan . . . whatever state Swan was in. He reached inward once more: summoned it. Cursed it. Begged it, even. But it *shifted*, like an animal refusing the leash.

A flicker of gold flashed in Laik's pupils. The rage was real, the grief too but also a reluctance. Why? *Why now of all times?*

They squirmed in his chest, not dormant, not gone, but *uncertain*. Not out of fear. But something else. Something that had been growing and Laik had never even noticed.

And Horus saw it. Watched him falter.

'There it is . . .' he whispered. 'That beautiful little thing you carry inside you. Something that instils real, tangible fear in the Families. And fear, my lad, puts us on top of the food chain. Could give it *allllll* back. Of all the evil things in our world, Laik, you possess the worst I know, and quite possibly the last. It's the reason why you're avoided in every room you walk in. Spoken of like an impending disaster. The Families fear you, demon. Even the one who has you on their leash. They're terrified of that nasty little thing scurrying about inside you. But I am not. No. I am not.'

He pulled a knife from his coat – black-handled, curved like a talon.

'And I'm cutting it out of you, tonight.'

Laik lunged.

The clash was violent and raw. No posturing. No elegance. Just fists, teeth, desperation. Laik threw punches like hammers. Horus responded with surgical brutality. Elbow. Knee. A sweep to the leg. Laik hit the pavement but rolled away, scrambling to his feet.

They circled.

Laik spat blood, his vision swimming. He strained to

wrench the Sins to the surface, his flesh gasping trails of curling black smoke.

'*Come on!*' Horus roared. 'What are you holding back for, huh? There's nowhere to run to, Laik! Bring it out!'

Horus slashed. The knife grazed Laik's ribs, drew red. Laik screamed and barrelled into him, tackling him into a parked car. The alarm blared. They grunted, tangled. Laik got a knee up. Horus reeled. Laik punched. Again. Again.

Then the blade bit.

A line across Laik's side. Too shallow to kill, deep enough to steal his voice. He gasped, dropped to one knee, stumbled, trying to rise but finding one leg useless. The blade came down one final time, but a forearm stopped its descent, mere inches from his face. He gripped Horus's wrist with the other hand, yanked it away, forcing the knife to fly free. Laik's reward was a flash of knuckles to the temple.

And behind them, the wrecked Subaru *detonated.*

The thunderclap sent up a ball of fire, lighting up the street in a corona of orange and red. Shards of glass flew. A wing mirror cartwheeled down the tarmac.

Quinn shrieked. Pepper was sprawled forward from the blast wave. Somewhere, a car alarm barked.

Laik panted, eyes blurred, gazing at the new inferno, Pepper pleading through red eyes in horror, in fear, and every gradient between. His ears rang. His side screamed with pain. He reached for the anger again – for the thing in his blood to get its shit together and make itself useful – but it wouldn't come. It *trembled.* It feared something.

Horus dusted himself off. Cracked his head side to side.

Laik rose, legs shaking. His fists clenched. He was done. He knew it. But he stood anyway.

'I always did think you were stubborn,' Horus said. 'But stubborn is just another word for *foolish.*'

The only punch Laik could throw was easily brushed aside. Hands found him. A grip too tight to wrestle from. There was no grace in it. Horus hoisted him like a ragdoll, bent his head back with too much ease, and drove his own fangs into Laik's neck.

A flash of agony burned and spread and then, strangely, nothing. Laik thrashed, or thought he did. His limbs barely responded. His fingers scratched weakly at Horus's arm, finding only cloth and flesh that did not yield, before slipping away.

Horus drank thirsty and deep.

And Laik felt himself going.

Not just the blood, but everything. Thought, memory, will. It was all unravelling like loose thread.

*This was it.*

*He was done for.*

*No grand cause to be sacrificed to. No heroic final stand. Just the will of a madman in the gutter.*

*What a pathetic end.*

But it had been hidden beneath the grunts of effort, the whooshing and roaring of the flames, until it swelled until it could not be ignored anymore. A sound. Thin, at first. A cry, somewhere beyond the noise of the fire.

It grew. Louder. Rawer.

A wail.

A nameless, wounded *wail* that pierced Horus enough to make him falter. He released Laik. Let him drop to the ground, immobile. Turned toward the sound.

Her dress torn, her cheeks wet. Her arms shaking. Her scream broke on her lips, returning as a howl now. Not just for the wreckage or the blood or the chaos, but for what the woman watched:

*The shrivelled, blackened figure of a stuffed iguana being consumed by the fire.*

Quinn Cavendish howled distraught, over and over. And the howls ascended into an encompassing, terrible grief that broke at the height of her voice.

Then – it all went quiet.

When Quinn rose, the glow of flame rippled upon her skin, the trace of her dress shifting unnaturally as it moved. Fire danced in her eyes, its partner something far more primeval.

A slow, silent silhouette against a backdrop of the end of the world.

The woman, who had been a drunken mess only minutes ago, was gone. What remained was all teeth and commitment. Quinn's jaw twitched. Her fangs bared. She drew the back of her hand across her face, leaving a smear of ash and tears, indicating that the sorrow was over.

*And Horus had absolutely no idea what he had just unleashed.*

# Chapter Thirty-One

## Vengence

Quinn Cavendish stood in the firelight as it bathed her, composed, and unnervingly quiet. Her eyes glowed with heat. She moved like a lioness before the pounce, pacing slowly in the flickering light of the wreckage, each step smooth and full of dangerous intent.

Horus watched her, the shimmering orange dancing off the blade in his hand. He didn't flinch. But there was a subtle shift in the way he stood that suggested that this was something to be wary of.

'Well now,' he said, almost admiringly. 'I'm surprised you're still breathing! Gave you enough booze to drown a rhino back at the bar, but here you are.'

Quinn said nothing. She continued circling, gaze shifting from Horus to Laik, still collapsed, blood smeared across his throat. Was he dead? She couldn't tell. Her expression tightened at the sight of him – her fury sharpened into a weapon poised to be drawn.

Horus turned with her as she moved, amused. His own boots sank into the soft grass. 'You don't spook me, girl. I don't shiver at your Family name.'

'You may find yourself unable to fear the Family,' she said softly, her voice low, every syllable coiled in threat. 'But you have every God-given reason to fear *me*.'

As the words left her lips, every streetlamp in view exploded in a cascade of glass confetti, one by one, swallowed by the void. The night folded in on itself. Darkness grew thicker, collapsing in from the edges of the street. No depth. No distance. The fire behind her was now the only light left, casting monstrous shadows that danced and contorted along the buildings until they too faded into nothing.

Horus paused.

The knife still hung in his hand, but the confidence in his grip faltered. His gaze flicked sideways, then over his shoulder. The skyline, the surroundings had been erased – no stars, no sky. Nothing but black. The city was gone.

There was just the void, the fire and them.

Horus didn't smile this time. He straightened slightly. 'Cute trick. But I'm also not scared of the dark.'

'Nobody fears the dark. They're only ever afraid of the things hiding in it. And I have no intention of doing *that*.' Quinn stopped her pacing, baring fangs.

'This one is mine,' she said, eyes flicking to Laik. 'I had *plans*. You had *no right* to lay a finger on him.'

'I've been hunting him a long time, little miss,' Horus said. 'Way before you ever came into the picture.'

'And yet, you will still be leaving here empty-handed,' Quinn vowed, each syllable dipped in venom.

The burning car behind relinquished its fire. The blaze responded like a loyal pet – stretching along the tarmac, slithering onto the verge like liquid amber, coiling toward her heels. Horus stepped forward with care now, eyes narrowing.

'Do you really think I'd hesitate to kill a Cavendish brat? Even with these tricks?' he asked.

'Hesitate? No. Not at all.' Quinn cocked her head. 'I just don't think you've got the balls to get down to it.'

He surged forward, knife raised—

—but hit nothing. Quinn was no longer there. Just empty space. Like her form was made of smoke, or she hadn't stood there at all. She reappeared to his left, hair fluttering from motion, one hand raised.

'Missed me,' she said.

He turned and slashed, again nothing.

'Missed again.'

He kept this up, convinced a strike would land, attempting to predict where she would be next, slashing and slashing in the void, over and over, until her voice whispered at his neck.

'*My turn.*'

In an instant, flame leaped from the ground like a summoned beast, curling around her arm, licking her skin without consequence. She flicked her wrist, and a tendril snapped toward Horus like a whip. He spun to face her, but not fast enough. A puff of embers erupted from his scorched jacket as he staggered back, putting his arms up. A second strike caught him across the side, this time burning right through. Embers burst outward in a puff of heat. The flame swam and crawled over Quinn, who had no intention of holding back.

They moved in a blur – Horus lunging, Quinn evading, fire trailing behind her like an interchangeable extension of her body. Quinn was everywhere and nowhere. An illusion in the smoke. Her onslaught was ravenous, lashing again and again and again, putting Horus on the back foot each time. His counters met nothing, his dips and dodges were horrendously quick after centuries of honing them, but even these were only partially successful.

She lashed again, striking his hand. The knife spun from his grip, clattering onto the tarmac. The blaze sauntered up an arm and perched on her shoulder, waiting. Quinn dragged fingers back and forth through its form as if rubbing it in comfort.

Sweat beaded on Horus's brow. Oddly, he laughed, low and grim.

'Never been a fan of tricks like this. Not the first time I've seen them,' he muttered.

Then he opened his mouth and spoke a language that tasted of salt and spoil – ancient, twisted, wrong. Something that vampires rarely acknowledged, let alone shared. The fire quivered, recoiled, like it had been slapped. Quinn reeled and doubled over, clutching her ears, teeth gritted, as Horus finished the chant. A torrent of heat slid from its host, weakly pooling around her feet.

'When you've lived as long as I have, walked all the corners of the globe, you see many things,' Horus hissed, stepping close, 'and as a result, nothing surprises you anymore. I learned that no matter the situation, it always pays to be prepared. Especially when it comes to a *Witch* . . .'

He bent and reclaimed the knife, standing over the shaking woman. The weapon was taken in both hands and driven down upon her.

But Quinn's eyes flew open, blazing. She had whispered the same tongue back, rising to a shout – only cleaner, richer, a ringing chord to his amateurish incantation. Flame surged from beneath her and slammed into his chest, sending him flying backward like a leaf caught in a gale. By the time he stopped tumbling onto the hard ground, he had regained his equilibrium to stand, but his coat was now in tatters, lapel smouldering, his shirt scorched with holes. But Quinn's efforts bore a price, and the squall of flame evaporated into nothing.

'You speak that language like you own it?' she growled as if he had committed an atrocity. 'Boy, *I was there when it was written!*'

Only darkness remained. No street, no sky, no world. Just Quinn and Horus, standing on nothing but scorched tarmac and steaming damp grass.

Horus coughed, face smeared with ash. 'What even *are* you?'

Quinn raised her hands, shifting into a fighting stance, toes light on soft mud. The way her weight shifted was precise and undoubtedly deadly.

'I thought you knew already,' she said, a smirk curling one corner of her mouth. 'I'm *Cavendish*.'

A shock ran down his spine. Instead of heeding its warning, he screamed and charged.

Quinn vanished.

Then came a flurry of attacks. She reappeared with clawed fingers, raking his cheek. She disappeared. Reappeared again through the murk to gouge at the thigh. The shoulder. To score a cheek.

The realisation that Quinn was actively toying with him shattered Horus's tempered assault into something wild and unpredictable. He slashed blindly at every approaching breath and feel of breeze until – success! The edge of the knife provided resistance. Quinn stumbled, gripping the wrist of a hand that sported a cut across the palm. She recoiled, surprised.

And that was all it took.

Horus advanced, knife glittering. Quinn backed up, blinking fast now, slower to vanish. She misjudged once, barely avoiding a stab that could have sunk into her shoulder. Twice he almost landed in her gut. She danced backward, sweat now lining her brow, the ghost of panic in her face.

'I've got you. I've got you!' Horus roared, his thrusts gaining speed, sending her this way and that, sensing blood in the water. '*I'VE GOT YOU!*'

She was a breath too slow, half a second imperfect in her reappearance, Horus had sensed it. His final lunge was powerful and precise, as Quinn threw her hands skyward and took a step backwards.

And then the world shifted.

The stars exploded into being above him. The buildings rushed back into place like a panoramic photo of the street being thrust into his face. Air and cold and noise flooded his senses as the veil dropped, and he stepped off the kerb and into the road.

A rapid flare of headlights. A shriek of tyres.

The black car slammed Horus over its bonnet with such force its windscreen cratered as it catapulted him up. The vehicle was just inches from Quinn who felt its speed by the horrendous sucking of the air between them. By the time Horus had landed, the car's brakes had screamed, dragging it sliding to a stop.

But it wasn't alone. A convoy of cars all came to a dramatic halt. Doors slammed. Enforcers in sleek dark coats fanned out into the street. Dozens of boots pounded the ground. Firearms drawn.

Horus groaned, coughed blood, but made no move. Weapons were already trained on him, their owners warning him not to move else they would end him right there and then. He pretended to go for something in his coat so they would make good on their threat, but, instead, was knocked out with the butt of a rifle.

Quinn stared at the development, breathing hard, eyes wet. She didn't show any signs of emotion on her face. Reese approached, muttering into her earpiece to confirm that the culprit was in their custody and, more importantly, the esteemed daughter of the Cavendish Family was unharmed. Mostly.

'Miss? Quinn? We're here to take you back. You good?' Reese asked.

Quinn blinked back to reality and made a staggered exhale.

'Um . . . wow, yeah, I . . . I guess so.' She looked about the Enforcers busying themselves with the injured. Swan and Laik were already being checked over, the Enforcers buzzing with new orders to carry them to the cars, something Quinn watched with her thoughts absent.

'Are you sure?' Reese asked, lowering her pistol. 'What about your hand?'

Quinn absently turned her palm over, acknowledging the red running from a clean cut across the surface.

'Would you look at that?' She twisted it before her, then gave it a single patient lick, examining it as if detached from her own bodily sensations.

'Can you tell me what happened?'

'I don't know,' Quinn said, eyes distant. 'Funny thing, the night . . . It holds such wild secrets, doesn't it?'

Quinn Cavendish turned to the blackened remains of the vehicle crumpled around the tree, coughing tracings of smoke but void of actual flame. Her eyes narrowed as if she were trying to remember something, something deeply important, but the details escaped her and she thought nothing more of it as she was escorted to a waiting car.

But while doing so, she looked to the Enforcers surrounding someone on the damp grass. Pepper, who, whilst receiving help, clutched her arm and matched Quinn's uneasy glassy gaze with her own.

Her reward was a playful wink.

Pepper, who, from her place on the ground, had witnessed *everything*.

# Part V

# Chapter Thirty-Two

## Licking Wounds

The sterile hum of Leroux Tower's medical floor was a steady chorus of soft machinery, distant footsteps, and the faint hiss of antiseptic sprays. Pepper sat propped on a narrow bed, one arm loosely hugging her midsection. Her skin bore the evidence of the crash – shallow cuts from shattered glass, watercolour bruises beneath her ribs.

A young doctor with half-moon glasses and an immaculate coat stood over her, tapping details into a tablet.

'The good news is that your scans are clear,' he said, tone even but not unkind. 'No breaks, no cracks. You do have a contusion along the abdominal wall – bruised muscle, some inflammation. Painful, but not dangerous. And most importantly, no internal bleeding. I'm prescribing ibuprofen for inflammation and a muscle relaxant for the tightness. Ice the area when you can, no heavy lifting, and try not to twist too much. You'll be sore for a week or two.'

Pepper nodded, half listening. The words *you'll be fine* meant less than he thought they did. She flexed her fingers, the tremor still there. She gave her thanks. The doctor gave her a polite smile before moving on to the next room.

When the door slid shut, the silence felt too loud. She sat there for a while, staring at her reflection in the black of the powered-down monitor opposite her bed – dishevelled hair, dried blood on her forehead, the faint tracks of tears she didn't remember shedding.

She sniffed. Took a breath. It emerged staggered.

Then came the sound of slow, uneven footsteps – deliberate, dragging slightly with each step.

Laik appeared in the doorway, his right arm resting upon his abdomen. His black button-up shirt hung open, revealing his chest as well as his injuries; his midriff was bound tight with bandages and there were sutures upon his ribs. The collar of his shirt was stiff with blood from his neck wound, and the gash on his head was stitched. An eye was partially closed and the socket swollen and purple. But despite the staff begging him to rest further, Laik had demanded that he saw her.

He gave a lopsided grin that barely held together.

'Hey.'

She managed to formulate a shaky smile.

'Hey.' She sniffed.

Laik drummed his fingers on the doorframe. 'You wouldn't believe it, but I crashed my car. There was this woman in the passenger seat who was going on and on and—'

'Can we *not*?' Pepper weakly lifted her head to him, desperately trying to keep it together. It cut him off, mid-sentence. 'Not, like, do whatever this is? Just for the moment?'

Laik abandoned the pretence and strode in with the ghost of a limp, before wrapping his arms around her. She leaned forward, resting against his chest.

'Are you alright?' he asked.

'I just . . . hurt my stomach, is all.'

Laik paused, his question muffled by her clumped hair.

'That's not what I meant.'

'No,' she sniffled, unfazed by his body's warmth against her face and the scent overwhelming her, 'I'm not. You?'

'Same. They want me to stay for a couple of nights, keep an eye on me. I got worked over pretty bad. Still here though.'

Pepper nodded against him.

Neither spoke further. They stayed that way for a while, holding on to one another, both pretending they didn't need it as much as they did. His grip wasn't tight, but there was a weight to it, the kind that said *I'm here* without making promises it couldn't keep. Her fingers pressed against his warm skin indicated she had no intention of leaving. He closed his eyes as he caught the scent of her shampoo. Her attempt to withhold a sigh woefully failed.

When Reese poked around the doorframe, the pair quickly detached, with Pepper scrubbing at her eyes and Laik unsure where to put himself. Her short hair was pulled back and eyes softened by something that might've been concern.

'Finally,' she said, a crooked grin tugging at her mouth. 'Glad to see you in one piece. I figured it'd take more than a wreck to put you out of action.'

Laik took a deep breath, massaging a sore wrist.

'Thanks.'

'I wasn't talking to you, dumbass.' Reese pouted. 'Anyhow, I figured you would both like to know he's awake.'

Reese led the way, throwing glances back at them every so often to make sure Laik wasn't about to collapse. Pepper walked beside him, her arm looped through his without comment. He didn't shake her off. Together they moved down the corridor, her free hand pressed lightly against her abdomen.

The door to Swan's room was half-open. The smell of disinfectant and stale coffee drifted out.

Inside, Swan sat propped up in the bed, the upper half of his head wrapped in a neat bandage, one eye slightly puffed but still glinting with that unkillable spark. A drip was in an arm, a machine measuring the dosage beeping to itself. When he saw them, there was a look of obvious relief.

'Well,' he rasped, voice roughened by the impact and whatever they'd given him to dull the pain, 'ain't I lucky to get visitors? What's up, Laik, you disappointed to see me kicking so you can't rob my watch?'

Laik smirked, lowering Pepper into a chair beside the bed. 'Hardly. I wanted to see what it took for you to miss all the drama. How bad is it? Or was it just your ego that got broke?'

Reese moved past them both and poured a glass of water from the jug on the bedside table, handing it to Swan. 'Doctor says you'll live,' she said. 'Unfortunately.'

'Tragic,' Swan muttered, taking a sip. He handed the cup to her and winced as he leaned back.

'Just glad it wasn't worse,' Laik flatly added, making it known if he wanted a follow-up then he'd be disappointed.

'Talking of worse, you look a state.'

'Yep. All kinds of pretty. Might get a couple of new scars if I'm lucky.'

When Swan finally looked Pepper's way, his grin faltered. The woman sat quietly. Her face was pale in the sterile light, and she hadn't said a thing since they'd entered. In fact, she seemed a world away.

'You alright, kid?'

She nodded, but it wasn't convincing. 'I . . . I don't know.'

Reese crossed her arms, putting her weight against the counter. 'You took a hit. Shock'll do that. Give it time.'

They all waited.

'What do you both remember about the crash?' Pepper put to them all.

'Him shooting. Barging me into the barrier.' Laik leaned on the chair back for support, wincing.

'And then?'

'Horus, uh . . . getting the better of me.'

Pepper folded her hands together.

'And Quinn?'

'Nothing really. I heard them scrapping but I was pretty out of it.'

'Same,' Swan added, 'busy sleeping. Why?'

'I saw it,' she said finally, the words brittle. 'I was on the grass. I couldn't move, it was hard to breathe – but I saw everything. Quinn and Horus.' Her voice wavered slightly. 'She . . . she wasn't herself. The things she did . . . I don't even know how to describe it. It wasn't fighting. It was something else. Like she'd pulled the night into her hands and just – bent it. Swallowed everything in black and was just . . . everywhere one minute, nowhere the next . . . vanishing. And the fire was . . . was just . . . moving. Horus, he – he couldn't hit her, he had this – this knife and he always missed. She was, like, toying with him, I'm sure of it.'

'I think that's the concussion talking.' Reese glanced at Laik with concern, but his eyes stayed on Pepper. She became defensive when she noticed.

'No. Have you never seen Quinn like that? Is that not a normal thing?'

'I don't know what *that* actually is, you're not making much sense . . .' Reese looked just as confused as concerned.

'What are you trying to say?' Laik's words firmed.

Pepper wrapped her arms around herself, the movement small, uncertain.

'She frightens me,' Pepper whispered. 'She really does.'

Laik shifted forward. 'I don't doubt you. I don't know what you saw, or think you saw. I'm not judging,' he said quietly. 'But she did save our lives. We should focus on that for the time being.'

'I know what I saw, Laik.'

'I get that.' He looked to Reese who seemed to have most of the answers. 'Which room is Quinn in? I'll go and say hello.'

Reese was cautious. 'She's not. She wasn't treated down here. Medics said she refused help, went straight upstairs. Presumably back to her floor.'

Swan exhaled through his nose. 'So, she's walking around, after all that?'

'Apparently.'

'Good,' he said. 'I guess.'

The room fell quiet, save for the faint rhythmic beep of the equipment by Swan's bed – steady, insistent, like a clock counting down to something none of them wanted to face. Swan's eyes shifted in realisation before he asked.

'What happened to Horus?'

# Chapter Thirty-Three

## The Envoy

High in the bone-white crown of Leroux Tower, behind stone and reinforced glass, beneath chandeliers that shimmered like dawn frost, the Cavendish Family prepared to receive their guests.

The meeting chamber was an old tradition, redesigned in modern dress: arched ceilings, columned shadows, the floor polished until it bore the room's reflection more clearly than memory. While its name might have elicited discussion, its true purpose was to entertain negotiation. Enforcers lined the edges – suited, sharp-eyed, armed beneath dark jackets. Their presence wasn't for show.

Pepper stood just off the central stairwell that curled upward to the main balcony, her back half turned to the cavernous room and the gathering below. The marble banister beside her was cold beneath her fingertips, a static kind of cold that didn't thaw with time. Swan stood a pace to her right, his coat draped unevenly over his good shoulder, the other arm still tucked in a sling. The wound had paled his face, but not softened it. He had returned to his duties the moment he was given the all-clear by medical. A Cavendish didn't take kindly to showing pain.

'Feels weird, don't it? Like waiting for someone to throw a match before everything burns. Oddly calm,' he stated, voice hushed.

Pepper didn't answer immediately. She was watching Mortis on the balcony above, rigid beside Concetta, both of them exchanging words. Then her gaze drifted across the Enforcers among them. A wall of white collars and cold stares, they weren't here to talk. They were here to measure.

'Nothing calm about it,' she said finally. 'Everyone's pretending not to notice how close we are to snapping. There's a difference between expecting carnage and wanting to start it . . .'

Canis Cavendish, ever composed, drifted between them like the host of an evening soiree rather than a war council. A tulip-shaped glass of red wine caught the low light, swirling lazily in his fingers. Despite appearances of aloofness, his mood was unreadable. He approached upon noticing them.

'Ah, good evening. How are you both?' he asked.

Swan stood tall despite the bruise across the temple, straw-toned hair slicked back.

'Just a bang on the head, sir,' Swan said. 'I'm embarrassed that it was enough to take me out of action. I think . . . if that wasn't the case, things would have transpired differently.'

Canis gave a small chuckle, just a shade above a hum. 'They transpired exactly as they were meant to. To my understanding, it was you who alerted the Family to the danger occurring. My sister's survival is undoubtedly down to your actions. Has she thanked you, yet?'

Swan blinked. 'Uh . . . no, sir.'

'Then I will offer my manners where hers are either

lacking . . . or simply misplaced. Thank you for your sterling efforts.'

'Happy to serve, sir.'

Canis turned now, his gaze catching the woman beside him. Pepper stood with her arms loosely crossed.

'And you,' Canis said, voice dipping into dry amusement. 'I'm starting to wonder if trouble follows you or if you chase it.'

'It very much finds me,' Pepper said. 'But I do also tend to walk away from it. A couple of aches and a sore arm. I'll live.'

Canis studied her over the rim of his glass, then sipped. 'I imagine that's what the reaper thinks, right before he changes its mind.'

'Has any decision been reached about Horus? He can't go unpunished for this,' Swan asked.

'That,' Canis said, gesturing lazily toward the upper tier where Concetta and Mortis stood staring out at the sea of city lights, 'is for people more prestigious than you or me to decide.'

'I've never known you so quiet. What's on your mind?' Concetta asked the man at her side. Her dress of white satin layers was cut at the knee, with a cape desperately clinging on to the shoulders that was so thin it was nearing transparency. When she moved it always seemed a second behind.

'Do I need to be troubled to be silent in your presence?' He leaned his weight on his forearms across the banister.

'No.' She tapped her pale nails against a rail. 'But it's obvious that something is weighing on you.'

Mortis's voice was soaked with a sip of scotch from a crystal tumbler. 'I'm just remembering when the world was smaller. Just you and me, in a town not worth remembering. Before this tower became a fortress. Before whispers followed us into every room.'

'They never were simpler,' she determined, finger to her chin. 'You just found them easier to swallow. You didn't need to think then. You just acted.'

'That's true,' Mortis murmured, breaking into a soft smile. 'It's easier when you're the sword, not the hand that holds it. Everything's just heavier these days. I don't know how you do it.'

'Experience, dear,' she said. 'Plenty of it, and a natural talent for getting matters to bend in my favour.'

An Enforcer dressed in a gunmetal grey suit made a bow on her arrival.

'Lord and Lady Cavendish. He's arrived.'

Mortis rolled his shoulders, straightened his back, took one last look at the skyline, and a mouthful of courage, setting the empty glass on the rail. He offered his arm.

'Well, let's see how much you can bend this one then, shall we?'

The doors opened.

Dominic Ode entered like an unwelcome king, walking too tall, too quickly not to seek a confrontation. He was flanked by twenty Enforcers, each marked by purple collars, silver-threaded cuffs, and eyes that were in the process of measuring every soul in the room. They fanned across like oil spreading on water, creating a clear divide between the two Families.

Concetta descended the stairs slowly, Mortis beside her. As they reached the bottom, those in the room subtly bent around them to provide space.

'Dominic,' she greeted, unhurried. 'It's a pleasure to see you once again.'

He didn't smile.

'No, it's not. Far from it. This *entire* situation has been a balls-up from the get-go, and now you call me in an effort to play nice? I am only here so I can tell you, in person, to your faces, what I wish to say.'

'Then by all means,' Concetta replied. 'Do speak freely.'

'I demand you release Horus to me. *Now.*' Dominic narrowed his eyes.

'Out of the question,' Mortis frowned.

Concetta lifted a hand for calm. 'Mister Horus is in our custody on charges of attempted murder – of our Enforcers, of staff, and most damningly, of my daughter. Your man is not a guest. By his actions, he has made himself a prisoner.'

Dominic's laugh was short, dry. 'His version differs. According to my people, Horus checked in when he was pulled up alongside and attacked by your man Laik, who initiated a chase that only stopped when he lost control of his vehicle.'

'And you believe that, do you?' Mortis put to him.

'I believe your household is long overdue for humility. I believe it's not unreasonable to believe that a Cavendish Enforcer was out looking for trouble and mine happened to push back harder than he liked. You've always had trouble keeping them in check. Just the other week I got word that a place over the river was outright destroyed by Laik in particular. That's our territory, isn't it? Not exactly respecting the pacts, is it?' Dominic looked between them both, brow scrunched together.

Swan, momentarily looking uncomfortable, returned a tip of the head to Canis.

Concetta's eyes sharpened. 'That's terribly naive of you. Or problematic.'

'I call it probable,' Dominic said. 'Is it an impossibility

that after decades of the Cavendishes acting like unjust royalty, the egos within are out of control?'

By this point, Mortis was struggling to retain his composure. Nobody had ever dared be so outspoken before him for longer than he cared to remember. Previously, the fortunate ones were carried out after such an exchange. The unfortunate: mopped up.

'Are you even *listening* to yourself? Word is, one of your Enforcers is openly courting war between the families for reasons of his own. Emboldening the unaffiliated to work against us. Operating under his own loose discretion. And you are not only willingly turning a *blind eye*, but attempting to put *blame* on us? With rumours like that circulating, what would you do in our place, Dominic? Lie down and wait for the next knife in the back? Yours, maybe?' Mortis had folded his arms across his chest.

'You mistake restraint for tolerance.' Concetta ensured her words were not strained with frustration.

'And you mistake power for entitlement. Where you see difficulty, we see opportunity.' The words lingered, thick, unpleasant. 'I like to reflect on Horus's benefits rather than focus on his missteps. His experience is unmatched. His counsel, illuminating. These past few decades have revealed more than you'd like to admit. You know of our ventures in the energy sector, and the advantages they yield. But I suspect your real concern lies in the ground we've gained. It threatens you. For all your storied history, all your so-called victories . . . it's taken just *one* of my men to rattle the Cavendish Family to its core. And what's the consequence?'

He circled, looked at the spectators with his arms out, before finally locking eyes with Concetta.

'You *panic*. You scramble for answers and, more urgently, solutions to a predicament that you yourselves have created. The Cavendishes have spent far too long under the impression that they are untouchable. So, please do tell me: how does it *feel*, Concetta?' He glowered beneath his brow. '*To finally be touched?*'

Before Mortis could deliver an expletive-laden retort, an interruption came from one of the onlookers.

'Crass, even by your standards,' Canis fired, looking into his drink, pulling the room's attention to him. 'I don't think your Family should be the one lecturing on standards when it comes to debauchery.'

'The Playboy speaks! I was wondering when *you* were gonna shove your oar in,' Dominic sneered.

'Yes, as you well know, I'm familiar with matters of *shoving my oar in*.' He flashed his eyes to a young man in his company, who immediately burned red. 'An arranged marriage is simply one not yet partaken, so I am absolved of any guilt. Word was, you were simply going to buy another wife for the boy, but good luck having the dear reach the bar that I set. Tell me when the date is and I will send a fitting wedding gift. I believe a ladder would suffice?'

Lord Ode was not so restrained and instead stepped ahead with his fist drawn with every intention of knocking Canis to the ground. But the instant the arm went back, a bevy of firearms were yanked from their holsters, the space was filled with the snapping of buttons set in leather and the clicking of safety catches. Pepper momentarily recoiled, whereas Swan, even with his injury, had drawn his pistol.

The stand-off tiptoed along a knife edge, with the attention set on those within its squall, their servants eager for a command or sign to permit negotiation to give way to wild, furious violence. Canis, still nursing his glass, looked at his fingernails as he continued.

'What I am hearing is that you believe to be . . . hard done by. If your intention was to simply antagonise us beneath our roof, then you've succeeded. I have returned in kind. But now what? I believe you came to us with legitimate concerns, which we *are* willing to hear, though one would argue they could have been presented in a much better fashion before things escalated to this point.'

Dominic stepped forward into the wash of chandelier light, his shoes echoing faintly across the polished marble. The two lines of Enforcers stood motionless on either side of the chamber.

'Things are strained, you're correct there. The streets harbour danger, the new blood runs wild. But your Family incites trouble, which I, and the others, react to accordingly. *Your boy, Laik*. We all know the danger he presents. We all see him for what he truly is.'

'Enlighten me,' Mortis stated.

'A deterrent.'

Canis arched an eyebrow as he sipped from his glass once more.

Dominic continued, his voice sharp now, 'A human-shaped reminder of repercussions for those who dare go against you. Your power doesn't come from respect anymore. Hasn't for a long time. It's from fearing you may just decide to point him – *or the thing inside him* – in our direction. What surprises me is that I don't think the poor bastard even knows it himself. Maybe you should tell him, Mortis. Come clean for a change. Or, even better, be rid of him for good, so you can restore the status quo.'

Concetta's voice, when it came, was smooth as velvet but with an unmistakable edge beneath. 'Laik has been a valuable asset since the day he came to us.'

'And the fact he turns into a hulking monster doesn't factor into that at all.' Dominic gave a dry laugh. 'Come on,

Concetta. Things are like they are because of decisions like these. You parade yourselves as the bastions of vampire-kind, when you are no more elevated than any other Family.'

'Then what do you propose?' Concetta asked snippily. 'What would satisfy you?'

Dominic Ode snorted through his nostrils.

'It seems to me that we're at an impasse. You refuse to surrender your wildcard to show commitment to the peace. I am unwilling to hand over my most competent Enforcer for what he may or may not have done. I propose . . . we let the situation resolve itself.'

'Meaning?'

'Let Horus and Laik settle their dispute once and for all. Put them in a ring, and let it be done. We are hosting the next Night Market in a couple of weeks. I daresay we could even make it an . . . event.'

Mortis pinched the bridge of his nose, feeling the onset of a headache. 'Let me clarify what you're proposing. After the targeted harassment and indeed death of members of this Family, you are suggesting that we yield an Enforcer of ours to a fight to the death to . . . *resolve bad blood*?'

Dominic shrugged his shoulders with a small smile.

As the volley of words echoed through the vaulted chamber, Pepper bit at her nails. On paper, Dominic's proposal was clean – public, decisive, theatrical. In the marrow, it was monstrous. Laik could be terrible when the Sins inside took him, but his violence was directed and fleeting. Horus, however, was a zealot in love with his own doctrine, and it would take nothing short of Laik's destruction to satisfy him – for the moment. Together, the fight wouldn't be a settling of accounts. It would be an execution for one, and for all her unspoken admiration of Laik, she was unsure whether the conclusion would be in his favour.

But that wasn't something she could allow herself to be concerned with.

The flickering candlelight from the chandelier above lent her a bronze halo, though her face remained pale, drawn with focus rather than fatigue. This was all going sideways. Her focus *had* to remain on getting the Eternal Rose out of the Vault; she couldn't afford any distractions. It was a pity that it couldn't be exhibited in some fashion at the Market itself, as an exhibition piece in some capacity. It was so easy to get close to last time, but no matter how many times she thought it over, there was no justification for the Rose to travel.

The idea came, sudden. Insistent. A whisper of realisation drifted from between her lips.

'Hold the Market here . . .'

Canis turned to her as she leaned in closer, her voice low.

'Come again?'

She met his gaze. 'Sir. It would make perfect sense. If we held the Night Market in Leroux Tower, we could keep a close eye on everything transpiring. We control the ground. We know the exits. Nobody would dare cause a commotion. More importantly, let Laik and Horus fight.' The moment Pepper spoke their names she feared her voice would break. Instead, she found something harder in its place. She had sworn she would do anything –

*Anything* – to steal the Rose and save Claire, no matter the danger, or the cost. And that conviction was carried in her words. 'It can be held on one of the floors. We can ensure there's no wrongdoing, and we'll call any bluffs that the Odes may have planned. If they want to settle things in such a fashion, we'll hold the venue – but they can still foot the bill. We save face, look gracious, even. If they object, then they show themselves to be untrustworthy to the other Families.'

Canis smiled slowly, deliberately.

'You sly fox.'

He turned back toward the circle of family heads and approached.

'If I may be so bold,' he said, voice cutting clean through the air, 'I've had a flash of inspiration. Why not hold the next Night Market right here, in Leroux Tower?'

Mortis attempted an objection, but Concetta silenced him with a flick of a wrist. Her son continued working his audience.

'You're right, Dominic. Trust has been suffering as of late. That's why so many vampires remain disillusioned, shun traditions and any proposed unity. But we, *we can all*, earn it back, with one glorious night of commerce, indulgence . . . and sport. By joining hands.'

He sipped his drink and slowly walked in a circle around Lord Ode, formulating details as he did so. With an ebb of a hand, the Enforcers serving his family slowly lowered their weapons.

'Instead of having the Night Market somewhere out in the city, with all the hassle of enchanting the site, we Cavendishes will graciously provide the location. You will, of course, still pay for the logistics of the thing; your name will be the headline. But just imagine the gossip. The *acclaim*.'

Dominic considered him.

'And the fight?'

Canis was in full swing, motioning with energy.

'Not a fight. Fight conjures shirtless drunks scrapping in the gutter. This . . . is a *magnificent contest* being held between two excellent and tested combatants. A duel would be the proper term. The spectacle of it all! Braying crowds. Money changing hands. The pumping blood, the palatable excitement.'

His voice lowered as he closed in, features dark and seductive.

'Lord Ode. *Dominic.* You would become known as the man who offered the city its most incredible spectacle in generations. And be revered for it . . . for *decades* to come.'

A slow, reluctant smile touched Ode's mouth.

'Revered, you say . . .'

Canis gave a solemn nod. 'Oh, yes.'

Concetta watched the play unfold and finally nodded. 'Quite the proposal, and one I am not averse to. It would certainly cater to concerns. Dominic, if you believe it to be suitable, this could be arranged.'

Dominic extended a hand. Concetta shook it, as did Canis. Mortis did not. The Ode Lord didn't seem to mind.

'I'll return and make the announcements,' he said. 'I can't see the other Families objecting. I'll have my people make contact with yours, and they can argue the particulars. In the meantime, I must insist that Horus is returned so that he may prepare himself accordingly.'

Concetta gave a slow nod. 'So be it. But make no mistake; he is still under charge for his crimes and will be judged accordingly. *If* he survives the duel, of course.'

Dominic's eyes gleamed. 'I have no qualms about that. If he survives, I'll deliver him to you myself.'

Dominic and his Enforcers peeled away toward the lifts. Canis turned on his heel, climbing the stairs with practised grace. Mortis followed after, teeth bared in quiet fury; only the keenest caught his hissing reprimand of Canis, which would no doubt escalate in private.

Concetta trailed behind, hands laced behind her back. Pleased.

Swan watched them go, face hard.

'This is going to be a nightmare,' he muttered in

irritation, baring his teeth to Pepper. 'Why the *hell* did you suggest that?'

'Because,' she said softly, unfazed after witnessing her plan bloom into existence, 'it's the only way to end this stupid feud before it gets everyone killed.'

Far from a suitable answer, Swan stormed off.

Reese passed by Pepper with narrowed eyes. 'You've just opened our doors to every goddamn vamp in the city. Most of them hate us. I sure hope you know what you're doing.'

She gave Pepper's shoulder a parting squeeze and vanished.

Pepper stood alone in the half-lit quiet, watching the reflection in the floor. A hand drifted to her neck to coil around the locket brandishing the photo of her sister.

'I do,' she whispered.

And this time, she meant it.

# Chapter Thirty-Four

## Ordinary Things

The flat had fallen into a hush, broken only by the gentle throb of distant city traffic from a cracked window and the whirring of the air-con shifting through its evening rhythm. Somewhere, far below, an ambulance siren cut across the skyline – not unusual, not even worthy of attention.

Laik sat on the edge of the sofa with a throw blanket gathered across his lap and a fresh gauze bandage stretching across his side. He still moved as if he expected pain to surprise him, and it did in sporadic flares, but his kind healed quickly, and the worst was now behind him. There was a careful stiffness in his movements as he reached for things on the coffee table before him, keen not to antagonise the injuries. The lights were low. Two floor lamps provided a pool of warmth and not much else.

He was bored.

A couple of books were spread on the coffee table before him. One by George Henry Borrow and his travels through Wales, one on the life of the Forest Poetess Catherine Drew and a worn hardback of Paul Tinto's *Trouble in Spiritland*. He had started each of these when the previous failed to ensnare his restless mind, only making it a few pages in before moving on to the next.

He was just leaning back, eyes half-lidded and drifting, when the flat door swung open with a shove of one boot and a muttered, 'Oh *shit*, nearly dropped it.'

Pepper backed her way inside, balancing a pair of pizza boxes in one hand, her phone tucked between her shoulder and ear. To make matters worse, a cloth bag with a few bottles of wine dangled from her fingertips on the other hand, joined by a second protruding paint brushes and stems of plastic flowers. Her coat was sliding off, and her hair was half falling out of a messy knot.

Laik straightened up. 'Are we under attack again, or . . .?'

'No,' she said, nudging the door closed behind her with a hip. She set the wine and the boxes on the table. 'You're about to be, though. You've got pepperoni and peppers, but mine is goat's cheese and caramelised onion.'

'Onion? What on earth did I do to deserve that?'

Pepper smirked at him, the phone still pressed to her cheek. 'Yes, hi, it's Pepper Montgomery again. Just checking in on Claire. Uh-huh. No, I'll hold.' She covered the microphone as best she could. 'Do you want me to read you the list?'

She made a beeline for the bedroom, already tugging off her coat, tossing the bag of craft materials onto the bed and kicking off her shoes as she went. The door stayed ajar, her silhouette changing in the dim light as she peeled off her day like a second skin.

Laik leaned back, trying not to wince as the bandages around his arm tightened. 'You look like a girl who's just buried a body.'

'That would have been a damn sight easier. Trying to

organise the makeover for the Night Market is a nightmare. Meetings, budgets, meetings, signoffs and more meetings. Now I'm free, I'm *desperate* to do something normal,' she called from inside. 'You know. Pizza. Wine. A night of absolute denial.'

She emerged a moment later in pink flannel pyjamas, barefoot and scrubbed clean of make-up, her eyes tired but clear. She collapsed beside him on the sofa like it owed her rent.

The phone call came back. 'Yes? Oh, okay. No, that's good.' Her voice softened, low. 'Right . . . well, that's better than . . . the alternative. Thank you. I'll be visiting tomorrow. Okay, thank you. Bye.'

She hung up and dropped the phone onto the sofa, blowing out a slow breath.

'Claire?' Laik asked.

Pepper nodded, tucking her feet under herself. 'Yeah. Still no movement. Still breathing. Doctor said her vitals are "holding steady" – which is a polite way of saying nothing's improved, but on the bright side, things aren't degrading. If there is a bright side, but, y'know.'

'I'm sorry.' He reached for a bottle of rosé from the bag and snapped the cap loose with one hand.

'Don't be. I think if I have to deal with any more people today, I'll start throwing chairs.'

He poured two glasses and handed hers over with a small toast. 'To surviving.'

Pepper clinked her glass to his gently. 'God, I hope so.'

They both took a mouthful, then cracked the boxes open and took a slice of pizza each. Pepper flopped back onto the sofa with a dramatic sigh. Her legs stretched lazily over Laik's lap, which he very much noticed but didn't respond to.

'Aw yeah, that's the stuff,' she said, mouth half full. Even Laik found it difficult not to sigh in delight. Most of what he had eaten on the medical floor was 'nutritionally balanced' to aid recovery.

'How you holding up?' she asked, eyes lingering on the patchwork of dressings somewhat longer than he expected.

'It's just annoying. Happens every time I take a few knocks, I'm just impatient to get things done.'

Pepper gestured to the wounds and the spotted purpled flesh.

'This counts as a few knocks, does it?'

'Pretty much.'

'I would hate to see what gets you laid up in bed for a time, then.'

Laik fought the urge to follow that up, and instead reached for the pizza.

'You, uh . . . gonna be okay for the fight?'

Laik's chewing slowed before he finally nodded.

'Yeah, of course,' he bragged. 'No problem at all. Right as rain. Takes more than this to put me down for good.'

'That's good, then. I'm just worried that you aren't being careful, pushing yourself too much to get better. I think you need to be at your best for, for Horus, 'cause he, uh . . . I mean you, you *should* be careful, being that, he's like—'

'I get what you mean,' Laik mercifully interrupted.

'Yeah?'

'Yeah. Thanks.'

Pepper blushed and hastily drowned any further attempts of embarrassment with wine.

They ate in such peace that Laik barely trusted it. The kind of peace you found in the eye of the storm and didn't dare look too deeply into in case it vanished, and the wind and rain began anew.

'I have an idea of what we should do.' Pepper got up, still sore from the crash, making her rising require a little more effort – and ibuprofen. After a minute she emerged from her bedroom and waved a thin blue box before him.

'No,' he stated, unimpressed. '*No, no, no*. Absolutely not.'

'Absolutely *yes*. It is a *classic*,' Pepper retorted.

'I don't care if watching it is the only thing stopping the world blowing up, I'm not going to endure watching *Interview with the bloody Vampire*.'

'That's because you're afraid you'll like it.'

'You are pushing me, woman.'

She snapped the case open with a careless shrug. She made good on her threat.

'And I'm also pushing the disc in. So unless you can get your ass from *that* sofa, all the way over *here* so you can eject it, then we're doing this – and you are not going to complain.'

Laik softly cursed, watching her circle back round to the sofa and take the remote control. 'Fine. Alright. You win.'

'Yes I do. And I'll accept your apology graciously when the time comes.'

She passed him his glass with a devilish smile, placed her legs over his once more, and started the film. Before long she was launching popcorn into her mouth with the accuracy of a sniper. And Laik found his attention being pulled from the screen to the woman opposite. Watching her silently mouth the dialogue that had been ingrained in her memory. Elaborate on why a line was so perfectly delivered. And explain how a young Kirsten Dunst acted way past her years.

He smiled despite himself.

'What?' she said, catching him.

'Nothing. You just—'

'Don't ruin it,' she muttered, looking back to the TV, but there was colour in her cheeks. She judged the weight of the remote in her hands, thoughtfully. Then, she softly asked:

'What happened back there?' she asked. 'At the crash. The big bad in you didn't show.'

Laik's jaw worked before he spoke. 'It wouldn't come. I tried, believe me. I *needed* it. But it just . . . didn't wanna know.'

Pepper blinked. 'You mean it refused?'

He nodded. 'It's like something held it back. Or maybe it was afraid.'

Her brow shifted.

'I used to be angry all the time,' he said, quieter now. 'Angry at what happened to me, angry at how the world saw nothing wrong in it. Then people would come at me like they had something to prove. Heard a reputation of something nasty and wanted to see if it were true. Didn't matter who I was . . . they just wanted a fight. So, I gave them one. I stopped holding back. Let the thing take over, as if I didn't have to sweat about being responsible for the outcome. It was simpler that way. Just took everything out on the poor sods who put themselves in front of me. Basically justified what I did. They got what they wanted. Didn't like the results, though.' He paused, shifting his weight, like the memories itched under his skin. 'When Mortis took me in, he said I could be useful. Pointed me at the right people, and the thing inside . . . rampaged.'

'The Sins . . .' Pepper dragged her nail along the circumference of the glass.

'Yeah. Doing what it does best. But I hated that, being all I was known for, this explosive, uncontrollable monster dwelling beneath the surface. That ain't me, you know? It *never was*, not before my parents . . .' he swallowed hard, blinking in the gloom, 'not before they made me this way. And now, that fury I relied on? It doesn't come as easy anymore. I think it knows I'm so, so tired. Tired of needing it. Of carrying it around like some awful inheritance. I never asked for it. It was forced on me. And I . . . I hate it.'

She looked at him with damp eyes.

Laik took a long pull from his glass, the wine catching the light.

'They say the Rose can cure anything. Illness, curses, the supernatural . . . It's the only shot I've got to be rid of it for good. I don't know for sure if it'll work, but I have to try. I *need* to know who I am without this thing in me. You use it to save your sister, and then it's my turn. After that . . . maybe we both get something that looks like peace.'

Lost in thought, Laik didn't see the look of dread on Pepper's face, which had struck her like a lightning bolt. Her stomach wrapped into a tight knot and yanked, hard. Should she tell him? She had to. He had a right to know. She had overheard from the Archivist that the Eternal Rose could only be used just the once, meaning they would have to make a painful, unfair decision.

*Laik's salvation versus Claire's life.*

And she wanted so desperately to confess what she knew.

Would he be furious? Would he hate her for already knowing, for waiting for some imaginary perfect time to impart this information? God, she didn't know. *She didn't know.*

The words nearly spilled out. Her lips even parted. Her fingers gripped the hem of her pyjamas as if to brace herself.

But she looked at him again – his bruised face, the tired softness in his expression painted by the luminescence from the TV screen. The flicker of hope he barely dared to hold on to.

And she couldn't do it. Not now. Not tonight. She didn't want to be the thing that broke him. Couldn't.

So she swallowed the truth like a blade and forced a smile that the light mercifully hid the details of.

'We'll do this,' she said, her voice almost steady. 'It'll work. And we'll look back on it all, and we'll laugh.'

And God help her, she wished it could be true.

They sat together in the glow, passing popcorn, murmuring jokes, rolling eyes at awful one-liners, until sleep grew pressing. Eventually, Pepper's head found his shoulder. He didn't move away.

By the time the credits rolled, both of them were fast asleep, resting against one another, empty glasses forgotten on the coffee table.

And for now, in that moment, in that precious, fleeting tranquillity, the disaster waiting just beyond the horizon felt a world away.

# Chapter Thirty-Five

## Make it Hollow

The blow caught him square on the jaw.

Laik reeled back with a grunt, the padded edge of Reese's glove scraping past his cheekbone. He spat bloodless air through his teeth and readjusted his footing on the mat. It had been just over three weeks since the confrontation with Horus and his joints still ached. Not enough to aggravate, but enough to remind him not to push it too much. That was his excuse, at least, whenever he tasted the mat.

Reese grinned through her mouth guard. 'Come on, Laik! Head in the game! Horus isn't going to take it easy on you, so neither will I.'

Laik shrugged. 'I thought you were a friend.'

Reese adjusted her guard. 'You hear this? I thought you didn't *do* friends, mate! Thought things like that just held you back. You changed your tune now?'

Laik took a breath, adjusting his gloves. 'I'm just saying it's not a terrible idea.'

Reese circled him, light on her feet, like she was born to it. 'A friend would tell you to keep your damn guard up. I could drive a lorry through that gap.'

The two of them exchanged a tight flurry – gloved jabs, shoulder rolls, calculated slips. Laik blocked most, absorbed a few, then ducked under a cross, and spun. Reese kicked high, but he caught the leg mid-air, swept her grounded foot, and sent her to the mat with a solid thud.

'Oof,' Reese hissed, blinking up at him in surprise.

From the sidelines, Duncan chuckled and folded his arms. 'I'm just impressed that he asked for help to spar at all. I never see him downstairs with the rest of us in the gym. Way he brawls, it doesn't surprise me. It's a mess! I'm telling ya, relying on that monster over the years has done a number on him. Not saying he's slow, but he scraps like he's invincible. Look – doesn't keep that guard tight. Hands! What did she say, huh?' Duncan barked. 'Christ, you're gonna need a miracle.'

'Look, it works. That's the main thing.' Laik extended a glove to Reese.

'Barely,' she muttered, taking his hand and rising. 'Ugly technique.'

'I'm not trying to win a trophy,' he replied. 'Just avoid a funeral.'

Duncan leaned on the barrier, watching. 'There's some kickboxing in there. Shoot fighting, maybe. It's all very technical, Laik, but it doesn't mean squat when the big guy comes out. Why even bother training properly when you can just turn big and bust the place up? You know you're going to smush him like a bug.'

'That's not the plan.' Laik rotated his shoulders in turn. 'He doesn't get off that easy.'

'Sounds more like you're doing it the hard way – not that I'm one to judge.' Duncan picked at his teeth. 'Where's he been, anyway? Swan said he was a no-show, and I can't remember the last time I saw him.'

'Like I said, not on the table.' Laik flexed his hand inside the glove. 'This is just going to be between Horus and me. It's how I want it.'

Reese cracked her gloves together, raising a brow. 'Aw, what's the matter? A little performance anxiety?'

Laik steamed forward again – a flurry of tight jabs, sharper hooks – grabbed her wrist mid-punch and threw her again, harder this time. She grunted, winded, laughing despite herself.

'Alright, alright, oww . . . you know we're only sparring, right?' Taking his hand once again to pull her up.

Duncan looked about the arena, half dressed with tiles missing and ribbons of cables jutting from walls that were waiting to be ran. He dropped a piece of gum in his mouth and loudly chewed.

'I still can't believe you agreed to this fuckin' shit-show. Way too flashy. That and the possibility of getting your ass kicked in front of hundreds of people. I tell you, if the old man threw me to the wolves like this, I would have told him to kiss my ass.'

'Thanks for the vote of confidence. The difference between me and you, is that I'm aware of what's at stake. Horus is already out of control. He gets another taste of blood and who knows where it ends? Or what that does to those who look up to him. I'm trying to prevent a bigger mess by taking him out of the picture for good.' Laik took a mouthful of energy drink, passing one over to Reese who desperately sucked the nozzle.

From the shadowed entrance of the partially constructed arena, a slow, deliberate clap broke the moment.

Mortis Cavendish stepped forward, amused.

'A noble idea. And quite unrealistic.'

The floor fell quiet as the older man approached, hands

behind his back, gaze pinning each of them in turn. Duncan burned bright red, unsure where to put himself.

'He agreed to this *shit-show*, as you so eloquently put it, because he understands the significant risk to our Family,' Mortis continued. 'This isn't about fists and glory. It's about face. The name. The respect. All things elevated above the individual.'

He looked Laik up and down, giving a smile of approval.

'You're looking good, son. I was concerned that the crash may have hindered you for longer.'

'Nothing a rest didn't fix, sir.' Laik wiped sweat from his brow, breathing steadily. 'I'll be doing us proud. Do you really think Dominic Ode believes in this "peace" of his?'

Mortis gave a humourless smile. 'I think Dominic believes in himself. And that's enough. Men like him . . . they don't see the pitfalls when they're drunk on their own legacy. They're more than happy to dance along the edge. Oblivious to the danger.'

He looked over the arena – the rising scaffolding installing new seating, lighting panels being installed, the black Cavendish banners draped over the balconies to provide a majestic background of the proceedings.

Mortis turned back. 'If they're up to something, all this will show their hand. That's why you're not just fighting, my boy. You're bait.'

'Sir?' Laik lowered his drink.

'One of the vamps we pulled after the tower scuffle . . . young, stupid thing. Didn't have much fight in him when the questions were being asked. He spoke like he knew the end was already coming, rattled off something dramatic, saying that something was stirring in the streets. Mutters of a reckoning, the Families falling. All very theatrical.' Mortis looked up, his gaze steady. 'But he also said Horus has been planting seeds for years. Whipping up the unaffiliated like he was building something.'

Laik frowned. 'And you think Dominic's part of it? I've seen him talk about Horus myself. He's far from a fan.'

'I think Dominic Ode doesn't do anything without five layers of intention. And if Horus is making a power play behind his back, Dominic would crush him. Ego would make sure of that. But if Dominic knows and willingly lets it happen . . .' He let the idea hang in the air. 'Then we have a bigger problem.'

'You said I was bait.'

'Yes. Let's say all is true and Horus is planning something. He's dangerous, but pride is his weakness. You beat him in front of an audience – not kill him, but humiliate him – and he'll bleed influence. That will fracture the illusion Dominic's been holding up. If he's playing us, the cracks will show.'

Laik tensed. 'So I keep Horus alive. That's the plan?'

'Correct.'

Laik found his next words surprisingly thornier than what he was used to.

'And what if he doesn't return the favour?'

Mortis noticed this and stepped closer, voice low and measured.

'Then you make sure he remembers who he's dealing with. I don't care what state you leave him in. But you *don't* kill him unless I say so. Make it loud. Make it impossible to ignore. Show the city – and Dominic – that whatever they're planning . . . it won't go unanswered.'

Laik's knuckles cracked beneath the gloves. 'You're telling me to hold back after he almost butchered us, Quinn included. And . . . *And Viola?* I've known Horus for a long time, he chased me halfway across the country. This whole thing between us started long before I was even part of this Family—'

Mortis's eyes narrowed. 'But you are part of this Family *now*. A petty grudge is inconsequential. What rests on your shoulders, lad, is more than individual survival. It's reputation. Legacy. If the Cavendishes appear weak, we lose more than ground – we lose trust. Keep that in mind when the time comes. Like you said: do me proud.'

And with that, Mortis turned and walked away, his coat sweeping behind him, shoes echoing sharp and certain on the arena floor.

Laik stood in silence, fists at his sides, processing what just happened. His breathing drew staggered, as though he had been struck harder than any blow Reese could have landed.

Reese glanced at Duncan, then at Laik in concern. 'You okay?'

He didn't answer, just moved back into position, skimmed a foot behind him and raised his fists in stance. His face fell to complete seriousness.

'Let's go again.'

Laik walked the corridors of Leroux Tower with a slow, automatic stride, too deep in thought to notice the world around him. The floors were humming with activity – Enforcers barking into radios, Market crews ferrying pallets of lighting and sound rigs across marble. He shared an elevator with half a work crew that gave a few shy stares. He didn't comment on their bright hardhats. They neglected to draw attention to the bruises and K-tape on display from his training gear. He got off on his floor.

He kept his head down. Hoodie pulled over, hands in his pockets, shadows in his eyes.

Mortis's words wouldn't stop playing in his head.

*You're bait.*

That was the phrase. Flat, uncaring. Tossed like meat into the middle of a pack of hungry dogs. He may as well have laughed when he said it, like it wasn't some joke at his expense.

He passed a glass wall where the city pressed in, glittering and enormous, night spilling like ink across the skyline. Tower lights pulsed, mirrored in the flat, wet rooftops. Rain slapped the glass.

He wasn't angry. Not exactly.

But he was tired. Bone-deep tired. Not from training, or from the ache in his ribs, but from the gnawing question in his gut that he couldn't let go.

*Was that all he was to them? A tool? A threat dressed up in polite family colours?*

It hadn't bothered him, not really. Not for years. Mortis gave him orders. He followed them. Life was easier that way. And the Sins . . . well, they did what they wanted. He just pointed them in the right direction. Everybody won.

But lately, something had shifted.

Maybe it was Pepper. Maybe it was the thought that he could want something more than survival. That he could want to live on his own terms. Without the thing inside him. Without being weaponised. Feared. *Used.*

He stepped into a quieter hallway, away from the noise of the Market set-up. The carpet here dulled his steps. Paintings lined the walls, showcasing old glories. None by the hands of the Cavendish Family themselves. Always someone on their behalf.

This wasn't the Cavendishes' fight. It was *his*.

He reached the door to the flat, slapping the keycard against the reader. The lock clicked open.

Laik pushed open the door and stepped into the low-lit hallway. The smell hit him instantly – chemical and sharp. Glue, paint and something he suspected to be burning. The corridor was half lit, warm with the glow of ceiling spots. He kicked the door closed behind him, slung his kit bag onto the bench by the wall. His breath still came heavy from training; his skin glistened beneath the cling of his vest. But every inhale carried the pungency of . . . something.

He wandered down the corridor. The scent grew stronger the closer he got to the dining room. Rounding the corner, he stopped short.

The place was a mess.

Paint pots sat open across the table, their rims crusted with dry pigment. Scraps of cloth and newspaper soaked with test brushstrokes littered the floor. Brushes leaned drunkenly out of mugs filled with cloudy water. Scissors, paints, a few layers of materials he wasn't sure of, silks or satins, maybe, wire, lengths of green plastic. A glue gun seemed to still be on, and oozing. A lamp cast a sterile white glow on the chaos below and seated in the middle of it all was the culprit.

Pepper was perched on the edge of the chair, sleeves rolled, fingers stained red and silver. A half-empty bottle of craft glue balanced precariously beside her elbow. She leaned back just as he entered, stretching her arms above her head, satisfied.

'Perfect timing,' she said brightly, breathless from whatever detail she'd just applied. 'Waddya think?'

Laik looked blankly.

'I think it's a bloody mess.'

She reached behind her and held something up.

The shape made his breath stall. A flower half wilted,

petals as delicate as silk, red with a crimpled copper dusting across the ridges. Veins of pearlescence delicately ran through its stem and traced the leaves. It shimmered, like light through stained glass. The Eternal Rose!

Laik stepped forward in disbelief, eyes narrowing. 'How on earth did you get—'

He stopped himself as she grinned uncontrollably.

'That's not the real one.'

'No, but it had you going for a moment.'

She set it gently on a linen square at the centre of the table like a jewel centrepiece.

'It did. It's . . . spectacular,' Laik bent over her shoulder, 'I could have sworn that you nabbed the real thing.'

She said, voice half-proud, half-mischief. 'A day's work, a few memorised details from seeing it in the Vault, and a *lot* of YouTube tutorials on floral modelling.' She beamed at him. 'Not bad, right?'

'What are you going to do with it?'

Pepper snorted. 'Obvious, ain't it? I'm going to swap 'em.'

'You're going to *what*?'

She repeated herself, slowly, firmer.

'*Suh-whar-p. Th-em-muh*. Jeez, clean out your ears. During the Night Market,' she said, like it was the most natural thing in the world. 'I walk in, take the real Eternal Rose, drop this in its place, and walk out with the prize in my pocket.'

Laik stared, dumbfounded.

'Just like that?'

'Just like that.'

'You cannot *seriously* believe that's going to work. It's insane.'

'Why?'

'Because it doesn't even count as a plan. It barely constitutes an idea.'

She lifted her shoulders. 'That's why it's genius! It's so simple and direct nobody would ever expect it. I've been in there, how many times? The Relic Gallery is as open as anywhere else. There're no cameras inside. No pressure sensor thingies. Laser whatevers. Just one big-ass security door that closes the Gallery off in a lockdown. Security's made to keep people from getting inside, not to stop something getting *out*. Presumably because nobody would be that stupid to do so—'

'Clearly they hadn't met you.'

'Exactly – hey!' She swatted him on the arm.

He shook his head, pacing slowly around the edge of the table. 'Your big scheme . . . is just replacing the Rose. And you think the Archivists aren't going to notice?'

'They will, just not right away. They won't know what they're looking at unless they run further tests. And by the time that happens, it'll be long gone.'

He stopped, arms folding across his chest. His gaze shifted from the fake Rose to her face. She looked tired. Not physically, but somewhere deeper.

'I hope you're right,' he murmured. 'Because if you're not, this is going to get very messy, very fast.'

Pepper didn't flinch. 'You'll just have to trust me.'

He gave a quiet scoff, rubbing the side of his jaw. 'I do. That's what's terrifying.'

The hum between them settled into a tense silence, not quite discomfort, but something close.

'And we have a diversion,' he said at last. 'A proper one. Something big enough that no one's got eyes where they shouldn't.'

Pepper cocked her head. 'The fight?'

'Mm-hmm. Mortis thinks Dominic's bluffing – playing nice to stall, maybe even laying the groundwork for something worse. I don't know. But Horus is clearly up to something. There's tension brewing, you can feel it in the air. The Families will be watching. Everyone will be. If it's all a ruse and it cracks, we'll have all the cover we need.'

'I suggested the same thing to Canis. Looks like it was taken to heart.'

'Mortis wants me to humiliate Horus out there and nothing else. Apparently, it'll be enough to make them flinch.'

'After all he's done? That was his daughter Horus tried to off, and—'

'I know. But it's what he wants.'

'Then what do *you* want?'

Laik's eyes glimmered. 'I have had this asshole on my tail ever since I became what I was. I can't remember what it's like not to expect him around every corner. But I want to. I want to put him in the ground for everything he's done. Me, you, the Romany people, the Family . . . Viola . . . And I don't want it to be clean.'

'Oh.' She blinked at his candidness. 'I mean, it makes sense.'

He exhaled, dragging a hand through his damp hair.

'God, let this all work. I can't wait to have this thing out of me,' he said, voice quieter now. 'Y'know . . . didn't think I'd ever let myself imagine it. Figured it was just . . . part of me now and forever. Till you came along.'

His gaze dropped to the Rose again. 'I didn't let myself hope. Not properly. Not until now. We'll do this, get it out of me, save your sister. And this plan of yours? I don't gamble. I do sure things. And . . . it's gonna work. You know how I know?'

Pepper looked at him, lips parted like she wanted to speak, but held back whatever she intended to say. Instead, she simply shook her head, looking away.

'Because we both want it too much to fail.'

# Chapter Thirty-Six

## The Night Market Returns

The chow mein was going cold, but Pepper still picked through it, absently curling noodles around her chopsticks as though the next bite might delay the inevitable. The tiny Chinese takeaway was steadily busy, the din of the kitchen muted behind a swinging door, while customers waited for their takeout. Rain gathered on the window beside her, streaking through the yellow glow of the streetlamp outside.

Her phone screen lit up. Her last three messages to Claire had gone unread. Unsurprising, but still painful. She stared at them, thumb hovering. Then, with no ceremony, she tapped out one last line and hit send.

Love you. Thank you for being the best sister anyone ever had.

She sat with it for a moment – just a moment – then pushed her chair back, stood, and nodded a quiet thank you to the woman behind the counter. The bell chimed overhead as she stepped into the drizzle.

The wet city met her in that cold, indifferent way it always did. Traffic murmured like a low tide. Pedestrians moved in shoals, ducking under umbrellas or jackets, heads bent against the dark. Not one of them had the slightest idea what was about to unfold.

Pepper's collar was up against the wind. Her boots struck the slick pavement with purposeful rhythm as she turned onto the wider road. The rain wasn't heavy, just persistent and needle-fine, a minor annoyance if she bothered to pay it attention. She moved through the streets, a ghost of her former self, remembering her first Night Market and the strange blend of sounds, smells and unfamiliar faces. And danger. Back when everything had felt like an impossible coincidence.

And then she saw it.

Leroux Tower loomed over wet concrete and brick like a cathedral of glass and steel, defiant and luminous. Light bled from its windows, catching passing rain and transforming it into gold wire. Cars passed behind her, one hissing through a puddle and splashing up onto the kerb, forcing her to step aside. She didn't blink. Her eyes were on the tower. It loomed over the city like a promise waiting to be broken.

Pepper confidently reached for the locket around her neck. She whispered the secret words beneath her breath – three syllables charged with all the weight of intention she was taught – and the world responded.

It began as a shimmer. A faint warping in the air, like heat off tarmac. Then, with a sudden flicker, colour bled into the scene like ink in water. Strings of red and indigo lights burst into being, draped from lampposts and walkways. Bunting raced along from surface to surface as it fizzled into existence. The yard and all the passages surrounding Leroux Tower bloomed into existence as the Night Market unveiled itself, stretching not only around the building but up it – banners unfurling from the upper floors like flags upon some ancient monastery.

The last Night Market had been hidden in a ruin at the edge of the city.

Tonight, this one was in the heart of it.

It was extraordinary.

And she barely noticed.

Her boots tapped onward as stallholders scrambled in the shifting light – some stringing paper lanterns, others laying out their wares with reverent precision. Spices. Trinkets. Bottled drama and mirror charms. Music flitted on the air, the sound of flutes and the thrum of distant drums.

An old woman seated beside a cart of coloured bottles did a double take, lips parting as she tracked Pepper's stride. Her eyes widened in stunned recognition – the same woman who had warned her from dabbling in such affairs. But Pepper didn't slow. Her mind was elsewhere, beyond the smells of cardamom and firework smoke, past the shimmer of illusion and soft glamour. She was walking into something now. Something final.

The great glass doors of Leroux Tower were open to all who approached. Inside, the cavernous atrium had been transformed into a hall of celebration and spectacle. The same aesthetic continued inside: lanterns and banners, stalls built into side alcoves, lit candles everywhere, peculiar glowing symbols occasionally blinking into existence on some surfaces before shifting to others or vanishing entirely.

Security flanked the edges of the space in heavy clusters. Enforcers stood silent, eyes sharp. Near the front, Duncan nodded as she flashed her security badge. He didn't smile. No one did. Not tonight.

Escalators glittered beneath strings of lights, ferrying

guests to upper floors where more rooms had been converted for trade and entertainment. Pepper took the main floor slowly, eyeing the makeshift booths already brimming with rare and peculiar items: books that whispered, amulets that pulsed, little jars that flickered with trapped lights. Conversations in twenty languages hummed around her. The very air tasted like mystery. Before this point, she would have felt like a pilgrim in an unholy land. Tonight, she moved like she owned the space, the event, and all that would transpire.

In the centre, high above the crowd, stood a platform artfully framed in obsidian stone and pale gold lattice glowing under the soft light of floating lanterns. It looked more like a temple altar than a podium. Fitting perhaps given the night's pretence of unity.

Concetta Cavendish and Dominic Ode stood side by side, their silhouettes stark against a golden backdrop of a suspended spiral mural. The crowd around them gathered like a storm, anticipation charging the air as vendors paused their selling and conversations fell quiet. On an upper level, Mortis watched the spectacle unfold, looking vigilant.

The murmuring crowd fell into hush.

Concetta Cavendish stepped forward.

She wore her signature silhouette, but with a difference; instead of white silks, deep red velvet shaped like flowing blood, embroidered in bronze thread, shimmered with movement. Her hair was pinned in soft, deliberate waves. Every gesture was precise; every breath paced for attention. She didn't need to ask for silence. It met her the moment her heel touched the edge of the platform.

'Welcome, everyone,' she began, voice warm, rich. A cultivated hush fell even deeper, like everyone had leaned forward at once. 'It has been a long time since the

Cavendishes have opened their doors in this fashion. That fact is not lost on us tonight.'

She let the statement linger. Let it land.

'Traditionally, the Night Market is held in neutral territories – a gesture of mutual respect for the pact of peace I, and others, have signed. A promise that no Family shall rise above another. That all crafts, all voices, all bloodlines are given their due.'

Scattered nods followed.

'But tonight . . .' Her voice softened, intimate now. 'Tonight is different. Tonight, we agreed that unity should not just be spoken of – but shown. We live in strained days. Days where messages are lost beneath old grievances, and misunderstandings flourish faster than truth. We are not immune to the fractures of the world. But if our kind is to endure, then we must be more than simply survivors.'

She raised her hands slightly – an open-palmed gesture that invited belief. 'We must be one. And so, the Cavendish Family offers this tower, this home of ours, not as a symbol of standing – but of shared trust. This place is not just our home tonight. It is *yours*.'

A subtle pause. A tilt of the head.

'Let this night be a start. Let it be the first brick in a new bridge we've long needed to build.'

With graceful finality, she turned slightly and gestured behind her. 'And now, allow me to hand over to Lord Dominic Ode, whose commitment and grace has made this evening possible.'

The applause that followed was respectful, well mannered, but thinner than expected. A few claps trailed behind before falling into silence again as Dominic stepped forward.

Where Concetta was warmth wrapped in theatrical

civility, Dominic cut a leaner, more measured figure. His suit was tailored midnight, his shirt the deep violet of Ode heraldry. Sharp edges. Coiled composure. He stood with his hands behind his back, surveying the gathering with the weariness of a man who'd seen enough of the world to know how little changed. He lived for spectacles such as these, embiggened by the respect shown.

'My thanks to the Cavendish Family,' he said. 'For Concetta's outstanding generosity in allowing us within these hallowed, secretive walls.'

There was a pause. A note just a little too dry. He smiled faintly to soften it.

'This evening marks something . . . rare. Something the younger blood among us may not fully appreciate. We talk often of tradition. Of legacy. But rarely do we speak of survival.'

He glanced across the space, eyes skimming past the vendors, the elders, the Enforcers stationed like statues along the edges of the atrium.

'It is no secret that we are not united. We have squabbled, accused, jostled for influence with the tenacity of dogs in winter. And yet – look where it has driven us.' He lifted his chin slightly. 'To a moment. A gesture. A possibility. One night. One home. Shared.'

There were a few murmurs of agreement now. A tentative rise in tension.

He took a step forward, voice gaining bite. 'We must learn to work through our disagreements. We must show the next generation that it is not strength alone that keeps us thriving – *but the wisdom to know when not to use it.*'

And then, in a final rise of volume, he declared: 'Let tonight be a triumph. Not of one Family. Not of one name. *But of all of us!*'

The applause came harder now. Scattered at first, then swelling. Some genuine, some obligatory. But applause, nonetheless.

And yet, from where she stood beside a gallery of imported artifacts, Pepper didn't join the applause.

Not because she doubted Dominic's sincerity. But because she knew sincerity wasn't going to stop what was coming. The crowd pressed in with their cheers. Something was going to break tonight. The pressure had built too long, the stakes too brazen, too big, and Laik was going to be right in the centre of it.

What unsettled her most was how little she was thinking about the risk. The danger didn't frighten her; she'd made her peace with that long ago. No, the *real* fear wasn't that tonight would go wrong. It was that it would go *exactly* as planned. Laik would unwittingly play his part of sacrifice, and she'd be left standing afterward, victorious, with her prize, wondering when she'd started to care enough for the betrayal to hurt this much.

As much as she fought it, the feeling refused to leave.

And in her bones, in the quietest corner of herself, Pepper resigned herself to their fates, accepting that no matter whether she retrieved the Eternal Rose or not, there was a good chance neither of them was going to leave here alive.

# Chapter Thirty-Seven

## No Tomorrow

The air inside Leroux Tower was heavy with incense and promise. The Night Market had taken hold like ivy on stone – climbing every stairwell, curling into corridors. Its music pulsed faintly beneath the marble floors, a low rhythm, seductive and strange. Vendors barked their trades. Enchanters flicked ash into crystal bowls. Children of the night laughed and bargained and danced. You wouldn't have known the city was on the edge of something terrible.

Pepper didn't feel here. Not really.

Her steps were slow, uncertain, each one echoing in her chest. Every face she passed felt like it saw through her. A merchant with a tray of teeth. A vampiric tailor with scissors that gleamed like silver talons. A trio of Ode Enforcers, standing like statues, their eyes following her just a beat too long.

A deep breath in. Out.

Then, before she could slip out of the hall and vanish into her plan, she was intercepted.

'Miss Montgomery. Just the person.'

Pepper's spine locked straight at the voice.

Canis Cavendish emerged from the crowd wrapped in a maroon-red coat trimmed in bands of bronze. He looked as if he'd walked out of a painting and into the present. He smiled like he always did – as if nothing in the world had ever truly troubled him.

But the woman close by, who cocked her head at Pepper as if deciding whether she remembered her – or whether she was worth remembering – made her mouth uneasily dry. Initially, she presumed they were just another one of Canis's indulgences, a metal-head better suited to a mosh pit than among money and suits, who looked almost bored to be there.

Her body was bare in all the right places: a tight-cut leather crop top clung to her shoulders and ribs, leaving her abdomen exposed. Buckled shorts rode low on her hips, chains draped from belt loops to thigh straps, metal flashing in the ambient glow. The sweep of a tartan sash fell from one side, torn deliberately, clashing with the pattern of black fishnets. Combat boots laced to the shin. Black eyeshadow framed her gaze like parallel stars in the night; her hair sculpted into scruffy black spikes with shaved accents replacing an unruly blonde forest. Silver studs in her ears caught the light like splinters. She was a riot of skin and style and menace, bound in a black bomber jacket sporting a collar of white fur. All topped off with a red score on the palm of a ring-covered hand.

Pepper blinked.

If it wasn't for the storm-cloud eyes, Quinn Cavendish would have been unrecognisable.

The Cavendish heir, notably, said nothing. Her eyes were unreadable, all trace of her manic fire tempered into something distant, something looming. It was very unnerving.

'Good evening,' Pepper said with a faint incline of the head. 'I . . . I trust you both have everything you need?' She tried to keep her tone light, but her fingers twitched at her coat sleeve. 'I'm actually in the middle of—'

Canis's voice fell firm, low.

'Whatever you may be busy with at the moment, Miss Montgomery, I assure you that nothing can be more pressing than what we have to discuss.' Canis stepped past her, implying that refusal was not a possibility, eyes serious and drawn. 'Come. We'll need somewhere suitable to talk. And it is illuminating, wouldn't you agree, sister?'

Quinn mechanically shifted her gaze back and forth. No wild laughter. No riddles, no twitching fingers. Just a roll of her tongue tip over a fang-point and a quick nod.

They led the way to the elevators. Pepper followed, her thoughts moving faster than her steps. *They know. They know something. They're not here to talk. They're going to expose me.*

They ascended via a velvet-curtained lift, moving through the tower's spine until they reached a high balcony overlooking the arena floor. The architecture here was more refined. The seats below were beginning to fill. A low buzz of anticipation filled the air. The arena had once been an auditorium, built for announcements and power plays, but tonight, it had been transformed into something more primal.

The sleek tiles had been replaced with smooth, matte stone flown in from the north – dark, iron-veined, faintly reflective beneath the low light but known for its exceptional strength. A broad circle marked the combat space, etched with runic designs that seemed to faintly hum. Gilded railings wrapped the upper walkways, where guests were already seated, their laughter and wagers hanging like smoke above the blood to come.

Soft incantation-lamps ringed the ceiling, pulsing with a violet hue that made the shadows seem thicker, more expectant. Two pillars on either side of the arena held crests – the black-gold sigil of the Cavendish on one, the violet-grey of the Ode Family on the other. The gulf between them, a no man's land.

And whether by design or chance, this wasn't a fight pit. It was theatre.

Canis rested both palms on the railing, looking down at the arena where Laik stood speaking with Reese, pointing at this and that, the two of them half shrouded in shadow. His voice was too calm for Pepper's liking.

'Do you remember that little thing we did in the Vault?' he said. 'I put word out to try and locate a proposed Relic you were troubled with. Some little box, I believe it was. Ring any bells?'

Pepper didn't answer. Her fingers were tightening around the strap of her bag. Apprehension was screaming for the woman to move. To run. But she didn't. What she could manage was a nod.

'Well, I have news. Earlier today I received word from the Archivists,' he said. 'This box of yours. The one that imprisoned the thing Laik carries? It's been found. And a lot more besides . . .'

He drew out his phone.

'It surfaced last in the hands of a Relic retrieval company outside of Bath. From there, it was stuck in a warehouse gathering dust. One would presume on account of its unremarkable appearance, there was little incentive to discover the story behind it. That's the problem with the plain and ordinary. Ordinary rarely excites. Or sells. What *is* particularly surprising is this part.' Canis prodded his phone screen, bringing up a diagram with multiple names at each junction. 'There was success in tracking the previous owners of said Relic, down through the years all the way back to the seventeen hundreds. Are these names familiar: Bethan? Eluned? Briony?'

Pepper's mouth fell open. No sound came.

'Because,' Canis calmy continued, setting his eyes upon her, 'they share the same surname as you: *Montgomery*. A surname that was never replaced for generations, even in marriage, on account of its *weight*.'

Pepper's eyes flickered at the revelation.

'Briony was my mother. Eluned, my grandmother. But the other—'

'Bethan. Your *great*-grandmother according to this. And last known possessor of your lineage of the Relic. Seems like they had dug up a fair bit on her.'

Quinn interrupted, speaking just as flatly.

'Apparently, your surname was synonymous with parts of Wales. Traditions, hereditary talents passed on and taught to other generations. Not famous at all, but popular enough to make a mark. They got paid to lift curses, bless good fortunes, all that. And this Bethan, well, she didn't exactly have the same knack. Made mistakes along the way. Sold fake spells on all accounts, no idea as to the why, but – and this is the interesting part – her own grandma *was a notable Sin Eater*. One who shunned convention and *stuffed people's wrongdoings in a box*.' Her eyes narrowed as Pepper attempted to process this. 'That's what's in Laik, isn't it? The fetid remains of her doing, *swimming around in his guts*.'

The tonal shift was unnerving. Gone was the manic hurricane who once howled through rooms like a banshee chasing ghosts. What stood in her place was quieter. Not reined in, but refocused. Her perpetual chaos had either been tempered into behaving or abandoned her completely. Pepper couldn't tell which.

Pepper's mind raced. 'Canis knew that it—'

'But I fuckin' *didn't*,' Quinn snapped. 'It's barbaric, and if I *had*—'

'Sister, calm. You're winding yourself up.' Canis stepped between them. 'This is hardly Pepper's fault. All she is doing is tugging on a piece of string. And anyway, now she has confirmation, it would seem that the onus is on her.'

'What do you mean?' Pepper asked.

Quinn sharply inhaled, leaning back on the rail, studs striking the metal.

'These troubles that your relative saw fit to steal away do not *dissipate* without the correct behaviour. They don't just sit still in a box to be taken out like toys. They fester and ferment. *They rot.* And they have been rotting in Laik for a loooooong time.'

Her eyes flashed with something dark. 'You, *Pepper*, are a descendant of the one who took the sins of others as their own without considering the consequences. The Montgomery line carries the rite – *you* carry the rite – swimming in your blood. A grim inheritance that leaves you responsible for its behaviour.'

Pepper fought not to slump in one of the seats or upon the rail.

'Responsible, how?'

Canis was watching her now, not unkindly, but without the usual glimmer of amusement he so often wore as Quinn continued.

'What do you even think blood is? A simple stream of wet to keep the flesh? No. It's more than that. Illnesses, genetic disorders, things that science can measure, these backpack through generations, riding on the red, you get me? But there's plenty that cannot be seen that does the same, plenty that humanity dismisses. Calling it magic, or superstition or fate or whatever. Blood carries memories and contracts. Benefit and blight. Even purpose. It always remembers. Your Sin Eater descendant collected the sins of others totally unaware that she wasn't just constraining them in some poky box – she was forever binding them to her. And that contract, she was writing, was forged in the blood. Leaving their ownership to be passed on to your grandmother. To your mother. And then finally—'

Quinn theatrically paused, letting Pepper come to the horrific discovery.

'To me.'

The steel railing vibrated as Quinn gave it a slap.

'*Now she gets it!* Every single fucking one of them willing to do whatever you say because they *have* to. Hundreds, maybe thousands of snippets of wrongdoing – some small, some grand – function like a shoal of fish. And fish always follow the food.' She extended a ringed finger sporting a blood-red nail. 'That makes *you* the carrier of a big bucket of worms. Toss them in to keep them happy. Starve them if you feel the need. Rile 'em up. Make 'em *angry*. Put 'em out their misery. Either way. The control is yours.' She pulled a crumpled packet of cigarettes from a pocket, drew one between her teeth and lit it with a silver lighter.

'*Control it?*' Pepper stared. 'I don't even fucking *understand it*.'

'You don't need to.' Quinn's face held none of its usual erratic twitch, as she scissored the cigarette away with her fingers, 'You just have to choose what happens next. Blood gives life. Sustains it, sure, our kind knows that more than most. But in your instance? It's red venom.'

Pepper stood at the edge of the overlook, arms folded tight, trying to hide the way her stomach was churning. Below, the arena waited in silence, its great black floor ringed with a low iron guard and crimson lights smouldering underfoot like embers. Laik moved along one side, exchanging quiet words with Reese. From this distance, he looked like a man preparing for war, yet completely unaware he was already in one. He was unaware that the Eternal Rose could only be used once. Now, she unwittingly held the leash of the monster within.

The striking of a bell ran from ceiling speakers. A voice crackled above them, making her jolt. It announced that those wishing to witness the duel should journey to the arena as it would begin in twenty minutes, and as soon as it began, entry would be barred until it was over.

She wasn't breathing properly. Too shallow. Too quick.

Her family.

Her blood.

Her fault.

She couldn't breathe. The walls of the balcony seemed to press in, the murmurs of the crowd thinning to a single pulse in her ears. Pepper muttered something about air – about needing a moment – and turned before either Cavendish heir could answer. Her boots struck the marble, echoing down the corridor like falling coins.

The deeper she went, the quieter it became. The scent of incense lingered – pungent, suffocating, impossible to escape. Her reflection followed in every dark panel she passed: a ghost in a green felt coat, a pale face beneath a halo of light.

Her chest tightened. Her stomach rolled.

Each step felt looser, the world swimming slightly at the edges.

Two vampires in crisp suits brushed past, their voices soft and perfumed with wine. One gave her a courteous nod; the other simply watched her go, eyes dark with curiosity. She forced herself onward, pulse pounding in her ears, until she reached the restroom door and pushed through.

She barely made it to the sink before the nausea caught her. Her palms slapped the rim, body folding as the first wave hit. Bile scorched her throat as she retched, the sound harsh and desperate in the hollow room. The taste was acid and metal, a ruin of nerves and fear. It came again, urgently, sharper each time, until there was nothing left but the dry convulsion of breath.

Water. She turned the tap with shaking fingers, let the stream run cold and clear, rinsing the sink before splashing her face again and again until her skin burned.

With slow, suffocating clarity, it was dawning on her: if Claire was going to live – if all of this was going to mean something – then she would have to do the one thing that clawed at every decent instinct she had.

The thoughts came: clear and merciless, cutting through the dizziness like a blade.

*You're going to betray him.*

*You're going to make it run rampant.*

*You're going to feed him to that thing.*

*You're going to get him killed.*

*Just so you can have your distraction.*

*He doesn't deserve that.*

*And you know it.*

Her reflection blurred behind drops of water. She hardly recognised herself – eyes bloodshot, skin too pale, mouth trembling. She scrubbed at the tears beginning to fall, telling herself there was no other choice, that this attack of conscience was fleeting and needless. The gold locket swung from her neck like a pendulum, catching the light each time she shook.

Footsteps snapped outside. Pepper straightened, forcing her spine rigid. She wiped her mouth, smoothed her blouse in a hurry, and turned away as the restroom door opened to a trio of women discussing something so important that they didn't even acknowledge her standing there.

Then she turned, one trembling breath later, and walked back into the corridor. Each step rang sharp and final, carrying her toward what she already knew she could never forgive herself for.

But she'd do her best to pretend.

# Chapter Thirty-Eight

## If We Make it to the Morning

Leroux Tower had never known such noise. From the balconies above, the crowd surged with feral delight. Vampires from every bloodline, every allegiance, hungry for bloodshed, spectacle and scandal. Music boomed, lights pulsed like heartbeats, and beneath them, faces glistened with thrill and greed.

In the centre of it all: a perfect rectangle of polished obsidian. A space stripped bare of pretence, glamour, or escape.

And there, poised on a balcony for the Families to spectate, stood Lord Dominic Ode flanked in a three-piece suit of violet, sporting cufflinks worth a fortune. His smile was slim, sculpted. His voice, when it rose above the roar, was proud, but stitched with arrogance.

'Ladies and gentlemen,' he began, drawing the words out like a sword from its sheath, echoing through the speakers, 'what a privilege it is to welcome you tonight to a historic undertaking. One beneath a roof so high that those who owned it may have had perpetual nosebleeds from looking down upon the rest of us!'

A wave of laughter rippled. Some clapped. The Cavendish seats did not.

Dominic paced slowly, hands clasped behind his back, a sermon from a pulpit.

'For decades, the Night Market has been a symbol of trade, of shared fortune, of . . . unity, even. And yet, in recent years, that unity has frayed. Scepticism of our own kind is rampant. The new blood finds it difficult to adopt tradition. Brothers turn against brothers. These are issues we whisper in secret for fear of being judged. But tonight – tonight – we abandon secrets. Tonight, we confront that harsh truth.'

The crowd leaned forward. He was feeding them.

'On this hallowed floor, we settle blood with blood, and show the next generation that strength needs not one to be conniving, and grudges need not be shielded by tradition. You will witness what our kind has always done best: resolve what cannot be spoken, through what cannot be ignored.'

He turned now, gesturing grandly to one side below him.

'Representing the Cavendish Family: their hound, Enforcer, and bearer of a terror magnificent . . . *Laik Hewer*!'

Cheers, a few jeers, and murmurs of anticipation rocked the floor.

Laik stepped from the shadow of the tunnel and into the spotlight. No gloves. No headgear. No sanctuary. No mercy. His bare arms were marked with yellow bruises from training. A faint sheen of oil slicked his muscles, more prominent on the back where multiple scars collected, most caused by his own family. He said nothing, acknowledging the crowd only with a raised fist. He wasn't here for their praise. He was here to bury the past as deep as it would go.

'And from the House of Ode,' Dominic continued,

'a paragon of loyalty, our sharpest blade and stalker of history's fiercest battlegrounds. The battleaxe of the ages: *Horus Carr*!'

The applause was near deafening now. Horus appeared slowly, calm as thunderclouds. His chest was bare, criss-crossed with scars and old damage, his fists freshly taped. He cracked his neck from one side to the other as if the whole ordeal bored him already.

Laik narrowed his gaze.

Horus smiled.

'Combatants, to the centre!' Dominic called.

They both approached one another, undeterred. Horus was clearly the bigger of the two both by height and thickness.

'Finally. Nowhere to run this time,' he said, stretching his arms with a pop of the shoulder. 'When I've broken every part of you, and our audience here are cheering for me to finish it, I want you to remember one single thing: nobody's saving you this time, monster.'

Laik threw up his guard and took a stance. 'I'm done with your bullshit.'

The bell rang.

They collided.

The opening was savage. Not an exchange but an eruption.

Laik surged forward, aiming low – sharp, technical. Quick kicks. Disruptive elbows. He slipped beneath a wide swing, struck the ribs, then danced back, avoiding the answering knee. He moved like he was thinking ten seconds ahead, footwork honed, rage, and the thing within, held in check.

Horus barely blinked. He took the hits like they meant nothing. Like they were warming him up.

It was a testing display, finding openings in guards, challenging reactions. Barring a couple of heavy swings from both sides, it was clear this wasn't going to be quick and brutal. Those that landed lacked bite – for now. The bell rang, and they retreated to their corners.

Reese had volunteered to work the corner, feeding him water and testing the swelling over an eye. She compared his footwork, suggested how to follow up, pointed out the feint every time Horus threw a left cross, but Laik wasn't listening to a single word of it. He watched his opponent with fierce eyes, and Horus did the same. By the time the rest was over, they were keen to get back to it.

They circled each other like wolves. The crowd brayed for more. Above it all, Dominic smiled as if orchestrating a disaster. By round two, blood had been drawn. A cut above Horus's brow. A bruise forming across Laik's ribs.

In the third, Laik was starting to flag. Not from lack of skill, but from restraint. Mortis's words kept ringing in his skull – *Don't kill him. Just humiliate.* He could feel the oppressive gaze of Mortis on him even he wasn't facing the Cavendishes. Even incensed to get this done, he wasn't fighting freely. He was pulling back, shackled by his vows to the Family. And Horus could feel it.

Horus pressed forward, sensing the weakness. He feinted once, then cracked him hard across the cheek.

Laik staggered.

'Are you *toying* with me?' Horus shouted, grabbing Laik by an arm and slamming him against the barricade. 'Bring him out! Call that thing inside you! I want you to take this seriously!'

He followed it up with a front kick to the ribs, drawing a painful grunt. Blood trailed down Laik's lip, but he smiled anyway.

'I don't take orders from you.'

'No. You take them from everyone else. That's all you've done – run to someone stronger, someone meaner, to protect you. Why are you holding back, huh? Did someone tell you? Your man up there, maybe? What's wrong with you? After everything we've – *agh* – God damn you! Do you not feel *anything*? Anything at all for the hell I've put you through? Your people? That bitch I offed?'

Laik straightened himself against the barricade as the world snapped into focus once more. The Sins within rolled over at the name, sensing the upsurge of resentment, riding it like a tide, but instead fought to travel to a deeper part of its host. They didn't want any of this, not while—

A thunder crack of anger erupted within Laik, pulling him up by heavy muscles. The crowd noise dulled to a muffled roar, like sound trapped under glass.

*Viola . . .*

Horus smiled, slow and ugly, knowing that he had finally got beneath Laik's skin. 'Oh, Laik . . . It was such a laugh. You should've seen the look on her face. Her scream was like a song—'

Laik was suddenly upon him. The first blow cracked against Horus's jaw, the second against his ribs. A third caught him clean across the face, spraying blood across the tiles. Laik drove him backward into the barricade with a snarl, hitting him again and again, each strike heavier, wilder, fuelled by both old and new grudges.

The audience erupted. The air throbbed with the rhythm of fists on flesh. Horus tried to parry, but Laik barely registered it; his hands were a blur, every thought burned away by rage.

And that rage made him sloppy. Horus caught him

off-guard with an elbow to the temple, staggering him back. His grin returned – split and crimson. 'There it is,' he hissed, spitting blood. 'Knew you had it in you. Bring it all out, don't be shy. We're just getting started.'

Laik dabbed his lip with the back of a hand and turned sideways on, breathing steadily, ready for another go.

'You seem confused,' Laik growled. 'I think you're under the impression that the monster inside me gets to bury you. But you'd be wrong.' Laik's fangs slipped free from their confines as his features darkened. 'Because *I do*.'

Horus spat to the ground in disgust. 'How can you *possibly* think you stand a chance like this? I almost killed you the last time, before we were interrupted.'

'Let's find out.'

Laik launched.

What followed was chaos. Unrestrained and unrelenting.

Their bodies slammed, twisted, exchanged blow for blow. The crowd screamed for more. Sweat flew from their shoulders with every impact. Knuckles split skin. Shin met thigh. Horus dropped to one knee from a brutal right hook and Laik backed away to bark:

'*Get up!*'

Horus wiped blood from his mouth, dazed but laughing.

'Ohh, this might be interesting after all.'

Laik didn't hesitate. He surged forward, using every drop of anger he'd buried. The Sins stirred, twisted, being wrenched upward. It was cracking through his skin, a midnight black seeping from his marrow, but refusing to rise further.

He caught Horus on the side of the skull, felt the cartilage give. He fought for Swan, for Reese, for Duncan, the Cavendishes who took him in. He fought for Pepper – for everything she might still become. For the innocents who sheltered him in the Forest of Dean – their reward, a murder by association. For Viola, whose future was stolen.

For his own hopeful fate.

The punches quickened. The rage became overpowering. He furiously drove his fists until his knuckles bled, until the pain failed to register anymore, grabbed two fistfuls of Horus's hair and drove a knee into the nose. It cracked loudly enough to be heard.

Horus stumbled back, dizzy, blood pouring freely.

He hunched, blinded for a second, dazed. He snorted and spluttered broken laughter. Laik was already on him – shoulder into the gut, driving him into the wall. But the flesh turned to concrete as Horus slammed an elbow down deep in Laik's spine. The grip gave and Horus pulled him aside, yanking the arm backwards, and throwing him onto his back. Horus drove a foot upon the shoulder.

Laik felt a flash of pain as something popped under the impact. He cried out.

The bell furiously rang. It had done so seconds before, but neither had heard it.

They separated.

Laik got to his feet, gripping the burning limb, clearly struggling.

Horus spat blood on the floor, looking all business. '*Ooooohhhhkayyyy*. You've had your fucking fun,' he hissed. 'Now I get to go to work.'

Pepper didn't wait for the end of the round. She didn't wait for the bell, or the murmurs rising through the crowd like a tide of static. She was already moving.

From her place above the arena, on the upper balcony, the fight had stopped being entertainment somewhere in the last brutal flurry. She'd seen the way Laik had reeled, how he'd limped away with his shoulder hanging too low, his face a broken mess of swelling bruises. That final stamp Horus delivered had been calculated – not for flair, but to maim. To end it slowly. Surgically.

She could no longer sit and watch him be dismantled.

Elbowing her way through the first line of gawking spectators, she ducked beneath a velvet rope and hit the stairwell at pace, the clack of her boots lost beneath the roaring above. Security along the route shouted her name, their hands out in warning, stepping aside when she threatened them with insubordination.

Down the stairwell, then the wide hallway that curved beneath the stands, cold with poured concrete and humming with electricity. Fluorescent lights buzzed overhead as she hit the double doors with both palms and shouldered through, emerging into the side of the pit.

The stench hit first. The reek of sweat, the tang of blood. Then came the noise: the crowd above hadn't stopped roaring, a storm of glee and expectation.

Laik was seated on a bench near the wall. Reese knelt beside him, her hands busy with gauze, tape, and a stained towel. His chest was dotted with blood, one eye swollen shut, his right shoulder badly askew.

He looked like a man who was moments away from becoming a corpse. This time, for good.

But that wasn't the worst of it. No, the worst was the look on his face. Laik was ready to go back in. He accepted that this was going to fare badly for him.

Reese glanced up, startled as Pepper crossed the pit floor, eyes wild.

The noise quieted into a murmur of confused tension. All eyes turned to her as she walked steadily across the black-stone tiles, ignoring Reese, ignoring the gasps from the stands, her gaze locked onto Horus with a look sharp enough to draw blood.

Up above, Dominic turned in his seat with a frown and leaned toward the Cavendishes.

Laik pushed himself upright, every breath clearly costing him. One arm hung dead at his side, and he stared at the woman with dread.

'What the hell are you doing?' he rasped, limping toward her.

She didn't answer right away. Her chest rose and fell, breath caught in something deeper than panic. This moment had arrived sooner than she'd ever wanted, yet later than it ever should have. The crowd whispered, buzzed. A thousand vampires holding their breath.

'I won't let it end like this,' Pepper said finally, her voice trembling with control. 'Not like this. Laik, you gotta—'

'Pepper, you shouldn't be here.' Laik flicked his eyes to the way she came. 'You needed to . . . y'know. That was the *point*.'

'I need to tell you something.' Her voice dropped. 'And I need you to listen.'

'But there's the—'

'Laik, just—'

'Pep, you can't—'

'Just *shut up* and *listen*!' she spat.

Laik tried to take a step toward her, but froze mid-motion as she shared her revelation.

'The Rose,' Pepper began. 'The Eternal Rose. It can only . . . It can only be used *once*.'

He stared at her like the words hadn't yet connected, making a sound of confusion.

'I found out in the Vault by accident. There were tests done, they – they discovered it has its limits and can only cure one person, just *one*. And I tried to find the right time to tell you, but it never came, and I kept holding it and I didn't know how to tell you and I'm . . . I'm telling you *now*.' She hesitated. Her fingers curled into fists at her sides as her face broke. 'And I'm using it on Claire.'

'You're *what*?'

'I have to.'

'Wait, no, that's not, that's not what we agreed. You *promised—*'

'*I didn't know then!*' she snapped. 'And I don't know how to tell you even *now*. I just know that you *need* what's inside you tonight. To win. To survive. Without it, you . . . you don't stand a chance. And I'm the reason it won't come out! So, I'm doing what I can to make sure my sister lives. And *you do too*.'

He stared at her, disbelief scrawled across his face, pained by something more than his injuries.

'My family,' she said. 'We came from North Wales. Originally. Same as you. My mother. My grandmother. My family has been running from a sordid past for generations. God, all we did was move and move and move . . . I thought it was some – some stupid story my grandma told us. We were running from our history. That our great-grandmother did something unforgivable. A tragedy we apparently couldn't even dream of. But it was true. She caused deaths. Turned the village against the rest of the family and forced them to flee. All because she accidentally cursed a boy who returned from war. Tethered something monstrous to him. All because . . . she abused *her* mother's duty . . . *as a Sin Eater . . .*'

Laik reeled as if the air had been punched from his lungs.

The words came faster now, her voice shaking.

'It's why the creature won't surface when I'm around,'

she said. 'Why it faltered at the Night Market when we first met. The crash, remember? Even then. I carry my great-grandmother's blood, and I *know* you know a thing about blood. That monster, the collective of all the wrongs you carry, it *knows* me, my lineage, or whatever. It knows I hold its leash. It hid itself so it wouldn't get my attention. But now I know.'

Pepper's voice shook. 'And that's why . . . that's why I *have* to do this. We need a distraction, remember? The biggest. *We* need chaos. *You* need to survive this. The only way that happens is if they – that *thing* – comes out now – and I can make it happen.'

He shook his head, face crumpled. 'No. No way, you don't get to—'

'I do.' She stepped in. 'Because they're *my* sins to carry now. Because this is all – all my fault, without even knowing. And because I'm asking you not to fight it. Not this time.'

She cupped his face in her hands, despite the grime and blood. 'I need you to trust me, Laik. I know it's listening. Just this time, Laik, just for me . . . step back.' She examined his eyes. Deposits of tar squatted at the edge of his eyes. His pupils flashed a spark of gold. His breathing was shallow. Something ancient stirred beneath his skin, under the bruises and bone.

His eyes welled, and hers did too.

She leaned in and kissed him. A brief touch, no longer than a heartbeat. But everything was in it. And she pressed her forehead against his and hushed him, so his breathing slowed.

'You can hear me in there, can't you?' she whispered, searching his features. 'And I reckon you know exactly who I am. You have all along. While you hide away.'

Laiks head lightly bobbed against hers, involuntarily.

'And you know what I can do, yes?' she whispered.

Another nod.

'Then I get why you've been hesitant to show your face around me. And to be fair, I would be keeping my head down too, knowing there was someone who can boss you around like I supposedly can. For what it's worth? Not my fault. Blame the one who imprisoned you. But, today, you don't get to pretend you have a choice anymore. You don't get to *sit there* in the dark and spectate, hear me?' Pepper's thumb brushed a smear of blood from Laik's cheek whilst her eyes flickered. 'I . . . won't allow it. So, I want you . . . to perfectly understand what I say to you next. Okay?'

Another shallow nod in response.

'Good. That's good.' Pepper placed her lips ever so gently on his forehead, scrunching her eyes tightly together as a tear raced down her cheek. Her face folded to seriousness as she delivered her ultimatum, 'Because you can come out on your own accord . . . *or I reach in and pull you out myself.* What's it gonna be?'

The onlookers gushed in disbelief as the Sins exploded free, a cascade of old terrors erupting over Laik like a cyclone of shadow and bone, collating into a single, terrible entity. The monster uncoiled and towering, its shadowy form blotting out the arena light, dwarfing Pepper as she stood before it, unflinching.

Its golden eyes snapped to hers.

Pepper tightened her grip on the locket at her throat, unperturbed. 'Well. I'm glad you can finally join us. I think we understand each other now, don't we?' she said.

The bell furiously danced above them, indicating the next round was to begin.

She stepped to the side, revealing Horus approaching.

'Listen. Our man,' she said, eyes still on the beast, 'has

been taking a beating because *you* decided to be shy. And that ain't right. I don't care what you did in the past to be shoved in a box . . . but whatever it was, you have a chance to make up for it right here, right now. This one – him there? – he's spent decades hounding you to see just what you're capable of. Y'know what I think? I think we should give him *exactly* what he wants.'

The Sins tensed. Its body fizzed and rippled at the words as it lowered itself down to pounce. Static charged the air.

Pepper narrowed her eyes at Horus.

'Go get 'im.'

# Chapter Thirty-Nine

## The Gauntlet

The Sins launched forward like a thunderclap, all brute force and reckless intent, the ground beneath its huge feet shaking with every bound. A blur of muscle and shadow, its roar shook the air, trembling the bones of every spectator packed around the arena's ledges and balconies.

Horus smiled.

He'd waited for this.

As the beast bore down on him, Horus planted his feet and raised his guard, arms crossed like iron as the hulking creature collided with him in a storm of momentum and mass. The impact sent him flying – spun through the air like a kicked can – but he twisted mid-flight and landed hard, boots sliding across the polished stone as he bent one knee to catch himself.

The crowd erupted, roaring their astonishment, their hunger for more.

The Sins didn't wait. It thundered after him, fists like wrecking balls slamming left and right, carving chunks from the marble barriers, shaking the arena floor. Horus weaved beneath a blow that would have shattered his spine, ducked inside the monster's reach, and drove a closed fist deep into the flesh just beneath its ribcage.

It barely flinched.

Horus's grin faltered.

Pepper took one last look at the beast she had commanded, at the bloodbath unfolding, at Laik . . . or what was left of him . . . and strode away. She slipped through the nearest exit stairwell just as another shockwave from the Sins' bellow rippled through the space.

The roar drowned behind her as the door clicked shut. The air inside the stairwell was quieter, colder, claustrophobic by comparison. Her boots clicked against the steel steps. She passed two levels before entering the main hallway again, winding through guests and Enforcers too distracted by the brawl to notice her slip past.

She snatched an unopened bottle of wine from a linen-covered table, something expensive by the label alone, and walked briskly toward the elevators, withdrawing her security card from a jacket pocket. She tapped it against the panel and pressed the glowing blue button marked with the number 65.

The lift doors slid to a close.

She exhaled once, shallow and sharp.

*This was it.*

As the lift ascended, distant rumblings from below still echoed faintly: slamming stone and gasping crowds. Laik falling. She pushed the thought aside. Not now. Focus. Just do the job.

The lift chimed and opened onto the vault floor. The lights here were different – warmer, clinical. Quiet. Sterile. She stepped out with calm, even strides, walking the length of the softly carpeted corridor toward the security post.

Behind the desk sat a familiar figure, Patrick, the poor

sod who was on duty at the last party when Quinn had shown her around.

He looked up from his monitor, frowning. 'Evening, Miss Montgomery. Not expecting any visitors tonight, what brings you here?'

Pepper kept walking, casual, like she'd been sent. 'Concetta's arguing with some Lore Council stiff about Relic classifications,' she said, rolling her eyes. 'She wants me to double-check something to prove a point. Rub fact in his face after enduring so much fantasy. You know how she gets when she's got an audience.'

Patrick gave her a look of tired suspicion.

'What is it with you and drawing the short straw?' she asked.

'Knack for it, I suppose.'

'Not a total loss.' Pepper held up the bottle of wine. 'For your trouble. Been stuck behind there all night, yeah? No use it staying downstairs unopened.'

His face softened at that. He leaned back, nodding. 'Go on, then.'

'Legend,' she said, handing over the bottle as she passed. 'Personally, I can't wait until it's all over, y'know? Too many people to make nice.'

'I wouldn't know.' He grinned, beginning to open the bottle in his lap.

The Vault doors unlocked with a gentle hiss.

Inside, the air changed again, cleaner, rushing over her as she entered. The Archivists were fewer tonight. Many had wandered off to the main floors, drawn to the commotion. Those who remained moved like ghosts, murmuring quietly, eyes deep in their paperwork or screens.

She passed them without a word. Moved confidently through the catalogue chamber, past low-lit Vault rooms, past the workshops and laboratories, directly to the Relic Gallery. She glanced at the slab of metal encased within the doorway, ready to barricade her in should it be needed.

The Relics, each on a plinth or in a case, were presented throughout the room, beneath powerful spotlights. And near the corner of the room, the Eternal Rose stood waiting beneath its dome of polished glass.

She stopped before it.

Took a slow, steadying breath.

Then, with a trembling hand, she opened her jacket and slipped out the false Rose, the replica she had spent days perfecting, every curve, every pearlescent shimmer painted with care and intent. It caught the light like the real thing. Close enough to fool the eye, but nothing else.

She glanced around once.

Nobody watching.

She reached in, pulled the real Eternal Rose free, her breath catching in her chest as nothing happened. No alarms, no flashing lights. The security door remained sleeping.

Quickly, she set the fake into place. Adjusted it. Smoothed the cloth beneath.

It was done.

She turned and made her way back down the corridor, the true Rose now tucked tight against her ribs. The door to the Vault loomed ahead. She pressed the round button to exit, waiting for confirmation from the other side. When the doors shuddered to life, Patrick stood facing her in the crack of light, finger to his earpiece, brow creased.

'Hold it,' he said.

Her heart almost stopped. The Eternal Rose felt considerably weighty against her hip, like it was becoming heavier by the second.

'Sorry, Miss Montgomery.' He pressed his fingers against

his earpiece for a moment. 'Just got word that there's a situation downstairs. That brother of yours is causing chaos. This fight he's doing is turning ugly.'

Pepper blinked. 'How ugly?'

'*Nasty ugly* on all accounts. Security is getting antsy about it. You better get down there to help. It sounds like he's been hurt pretty bad . . .'

For a moment, she forgot how to breathe. In her mind she could see it – Laik wild, consumed by the monster within scrabbling in desperation, his blood pooling beneath on the tiles, the crowd baying for more. She could almost *hear* him, an awful guttural sound that wasn't pain, but desperation. And Horus, looming over him, preparing to finish the job.

She nodded, quickly exorcising her fears, forcing her face into something neutral and managing a half-smile. 'Thanks. I owe you.'

He, in return, raised the bottle and took a mouthful.

She stepped past, toward the lift. Each footstep felt wrong, deliberate, the rhythm of betrayal. When the doors opened, she stood staring at the panel, her reflection trembling faintly in the brushed steel. Her thumb hovered over the button to the arena floor, instinctively, maybe, she didn't know herself.

Her hand hesitated over the controls.

She swallowed hard. The Eternal Rose pulsed against her ribs like a second heartbeat. She was so close now, *so very close* to the goal. This was it! This was everything the worry, the deception was for! Push the button. *Just push the damn button!*

All she could think of was Laik in those dire straits. And also, for some utterly inexplicable reason, the story he told her of his time in the Forest of Dean with the Romany people. Where experiences were shared around the campfire, witnessed by wood smoke that danced to the canopies. Of songs and compassion, and innocent offerings of daisies to devils. That small sliver of peace he obtained before it was cruelly stolen away. Stolen by Horus in his mad agenda.

And she would be doing the same.

Because the Sins in Laik were nothing compared to the weight she now carried. Pepper didn't want to face it, but she knew, in the worst part of herself, that there was never going to be a version of tonight where he walked away whole. Releasing the Sins ensured that. Horus was an executioner in all but name; she had witnessed it with her own eyes, and even if he miraculously fell, there was no way the Ode Family would let it stand. Pride wouldn't allow it. And what she knew of the Cavendishes, of their eagerness to throw Laik into the ring, everybody was expendable, especially if it involved saving face. She had just beaten them to it.

So what if she could steer the monster inside him? Control wasn't what she needed. Just time – as much as possible to perform her deception. Pepper had transformed Laik into a storm so her own bloody handprints would be washed away in the downpour.

And no storm lasts forever. Even the wildest of them.

Pepper knew what she had to do.

She jabbed the controls and finally allowed herself to exhale the fear squeezing her lungs. And as the doors whispered shut, the hum of chaos from the arena floor grew louder, and urgent.

Then, it exhausted itself on speeding past, like the tide crashing against rocks, as Pepper sank to the lobby of Leroux Tower, to serve a miracle to her sister – and distance herself from her own betrayal.

* * *

On the upper platform, Dominic Ode rose from his seat, hands braced on the carved railing.

'Get Laik back to his senses,' he shouted, twisting to Concetta. '*Stop the fight!*'

Heads turned. Chatter swelled.

Concetta remained seated, fingers interlocked, her expression unreadable. Mortis simply watched with narrowed eyes, arms folded. Swan, stationed at their side, didn't even blink.

'This is what he agreed to,' Mortis said evenly. 'You didn't seem concerned when you believed Laik to be at a disadvantage. I'm guessing you had got word that he hadn't shown his other side in a while, and assumed it to be permanent. Now that the tables are turned, you cannot simply cry foul. Unless you would like to throw in the towel for your man?'

'He agreed to a duel,' Dominic snapped. '*A fair fight.* Not an execution!'

Below and behind, the Enforcers began shifting. Ode's Enforcers moved about the waves of the crowd, some having their fingers twitch near holsters. The Cavendish Enforcers didn't follow, not yet, but you could see the energy passing between them. Ready to explode.

Quinn stood at the rear of the seating, half in shadow beneath an archway, arms folded tight against herself. She rested her shoulder against it, looking between the combatants and the rolls of motion that shifted through the tumultuous crowd.

From here, the fight was reduced to movement and colour and noise.

But her real attention was set on her brother.

She waited for Canis to excuse himself from where the rest of the Family was seated, after noticing her absence. He threaded his way up the stairs, through the press of bodies, easing past Enforcers already moving to contain the crowd.

Quinn didn't look at him. Her gaze stayed fixed on the arena, on the way the crowd had begun to fracture. Cheers had broken into shouts, awe curdling into unease.

He reached her side and leaned in so she could hear him over the noise.

'Are we leaving already? Because it feels like things are just getting started.'

'They are,' Quinn declared, finally acknowledging him. She pushed off the archway and straightened. 'We just don't want to be around to watch.'

'Are you sure? Because—'

Quinn rolled her head slowly toward him, the movement lazy, almost bored, and looked at him as if he'd suggested something truly absurd.

Canis studied her for a moment, then nodded, trusting her instincts as she knew he would – and always had.

'Alright,' he said. 'After you.'

They turned away together, moving through the corridor as the sounds behind them braided into something indistinguishable. The elevator doors swallowed the pair as they entered and left the mayhem for everyone else to endure.

Back down in the arena, the beast thundered towards Horus once more, mindless in rage. Its massive fingers gouged into the marble, dragging a wall down in its blind fury. It swung wild, massive fists cleaving air and stone alike. Another barricade exploded, sending a plume of shattered obsidian into the crowd's front row.

Horus ducked under a haymaker that would've torn him in half, aiming for one of its thick legs, lunging a foot at it. But the creature didn't stagger. It barely acknowledged the blow. A human, a vampire, these had no chance against Horus, but this thing didn't adhere to their rules. He needed to do more damage; anything he was trying just wasn't getting through.

Stone and steel rained down around them, blown free from the walls as the Sins tore the battlefield apart. A bouquet of cement-capped rebar was yanked free, skimming the ground.

Horus scooped one of the steel rods, ran for the monster and swung it like a bat.

The concrete end exploded on the Sins' jaw.

The creature reeled, head snapping sideways in a powder cloud. The crowd screamed. Some even in joy.

The beast roared in fury.

The fight became a blur of motion, Horus ducking, jabbing, driving the rod into the creature's side. But it was taking its toll. Every impact on his limbs was like the kiss of a brick. He kept moving because if he stopped, he'd never move again. A cannonball sailed overhead. The rebar was driven into the Sins' gut. It surrendered resistance and sank inside the pitch, deep enough to make contact with its host – if he was even in there.

A massive fist crashed into him.

Horus flew.

He rolled, coughed blood onto the floor, and didn't get up for several seconds.

But when he did, he was laughing through the pain.

The Sins staggered back a couple of steps, acknowledging the chunk of rebar that was now impaled within it, howling in alarm. Blood – not red but something slicker, oozing, pattered to the floor in thick, dark drops. Its initial fury was fading from its new injury.

'Finally . . . oh *God damn*, I got you . . .' Horus croaked, straightening his back. Something moved in his chest, seeping pain throughout it. A rib, maybe. But it wouldn't be enough to spoil this victory. He had waited almost a century for this moment.

'I did ask for this, didn't I? And you have certainly delivered . . . Look at this. *This is the real you, Laik*. The abomination! The thing the Families were too scared to do anything about . . . made their secret plans . . . hoping that I could make the problem go away . . . *Isn't that right, Dominic?*'

On the balcony, Dominic fed his nails into the railing, turning red. The others all looked to him. Silence fell.

'I kill you, and the Cavendish trump card is gone. I was the only one who could do the job, because we have history! But them up there? They'll keep quiet if it doesn't pan out. Just another secret. Just another lie to add to the masses. I'll be their sacrifice in the name of their peace. And if I didn't walk out of here, they'd find another patsy until it happened . . . but here's the kicker, are you ready for this? *Do you hear me, Dominic?* You, and all you other sycophantic fools? You self-elevated monarchs, acting like your word is God and smite down whoever you deem to be a heretic out of fancy? I proclaim to you this – *I say to you all now*' – sucking in breath, he raised his hand as a clenched a fist before spreading his fingers out – '*the Families have had their day*!'

Suddenly, screaming erupted from the balconies. In the crowd random, unaffiliated vampires, normal Night Market patrons dressed from finery to grunge turned on the closest Enforcer to them. Blades were drawn. Guns flashed silver. Blood sprayed across the arena steps. As panic sent the crowd in every direction, the Enforcers were hopelessly consumed by the chaos, fighting to see the enemy until it was too late. When the firing began, bullets scorched the air overhead, the innocent caught in the crossfire. The Ode Enforcers battled with leaping bodies that tackled them to the ground, and set teeth upon neck. Desperate cries mingled with calls of mobilisation. Swan directed the Cavendish Enforcers to fall in and protect the Family, but even he was watching them disappear beneath seats and bodies and carnage. The Beretta bucked in his grip as he switched to each death-drunk face that catapulted towards him, knocking them out the air.

The overhead lights snapped from crisp white to pulsing red. A powerful, rising siren cut through the air as Leroux Tower shifted into full lockdown. The screams of the escaping spectators became sharper. Panic was becoming overwhelming. Above the bedlam, fragments of words could be heard.

*'No more lies!'*

*'No more Families!'*

Dominic was still at the railing, mouth open. The encompassing chaos was closing in, stealing his judgement. Mortis grabbed him by the collar, spitting as he shouted.

'*What have you done?!*'

Dominic was wide-eyed as he tried to babble an apology. Wide-eyed as his pupils darted to the shape within the stands just outside of the balcony seating. And those eyes rolled backwards as a bullet relieved him of part of his skull with a force that tore him from Mortis's grip and sent him tumbling over the balcony, down into the arena below.

Mortis snatched Concetta by the arm, angling his body between her and the chaos. Swan handed him a firearm, and he wasted no time putting it to use by downing Dominic's killer with a single shot. Around them, the Enforcers formed a wall of bodies, an unyielding barrier pushing back both the panicked and the murderous alike, clearing a path to the elevators. They were bundled inside with as many Enforcers as could be held, leaving Swan and a gaggle of others, with their backs to the walls to buy time for their escape.

Horus's sympathisers worked their way through the crowd to set upon them.

# Chapter Forty

## The Sacrifice

While this was happening, the Sins, confused by the chaos, turned toward the sound of gunfire. Bullets began peppering its hide, forcing it back with each shot. It hunched over itself, its vast arms shielding its head.

The rebar jutted from its torso at a crooked angle, vibrating faintly with each laboured movement. Whatever passed for blood seeped from the wound in thick, smoking globules that patterned everything beneath. The creature tried to draw itself up to its full height, but faltered. One knee struck the ground, summoning a crack from the weight. It turned then, setting on Horus with a feral, enraged stare. Maybe the vampire within knew where this was going. Maybe he was oblivious of whatever force compelled his actions. Gold flared in the creature's eyes, brighter for the pain, and with a guttural roar, it came for Horus, as fast and terrible as it possibly could.

Horus bent and took hold of a chunk of slab, checking its weight in his hand.

Stone sprayed with the force of every heavy gallop as the Sins launched ahead. It sprang high, raising its colossal arms above its head and brought them down, sending a shockwave travelling around the arena, firing cracks through the large, reinforced windows, splintering the view of the city around them. Ceiling tiles fell. A rigging of lights let go of its moorings and tumbled down the seating.

Horus had slipped out of the way, kept his footing from the boom and whipped the debris forward like a missile. It slammed into the Sins' temple, snapping its head sideways with a crack that echoed across the arena. The creature reeled, one arm flailing as it fought to stay upright. It roared and swung blindly in wide, furious arcs. Horus stepped between the motions instead of away from them. Then, when the opportunity presented itself, he drove his boot hard against the exposed length of rebar.

The impact sent a violent shudder through the monster's entire frame, and staggered back, claws scraping furrows into the stone as its legs threatened to buckle. Whatever passed for blood spilled faster now.

It lashed out again, slower this time, clearly fighting against the creeping failure in its limbs. Horus answered with another kick, precise, brutal, driving the metal deeper, twisting it where it lodged. Then another. And another. Each strike stole something from the creature – first speed, then strength – until its movements became a series of hopelessly delayed reactions rather than intent.

The Sins fought against dropping to the ground with a desperate snarl. Its golden eyes locked onto Horus, the ever-present rage behind was dimmed now, and resistance all but gone. Finally, fatally, it sank to its knees, losing both the battle with itself and its opponent.

The beast hissed to Horus, who made his way forward, spying the rebar, slick with . . . whatever it was.

He didn't rush. He didn't need to. It was swaying like a tired animal.

When close enough, it had taken one final, drunken swing, but it was so limp that it was far from a threat. Horus easily slipped aside, took hold of the metal, drove it once again into the creature and pressed and pressed until it gave and slid deep.

Only the groups of huddled, terrified spectators, Horus's people and the littered corpses, witnessed its desperate howl. It thrashed this way and that, smoke billowing from its form before the Sins toppled over, clawing at the ground to pull itself away, until, finally, the efforts stopped.

Horus spat out something from his mouth, somewhat hollowed by his achievement.

He'd expected this moment to carry a certain gravity, the weight of finality. A pivotal chapter in the saga of his life, something meaningful to shape whatever came next. But the feeling never arrived.

All he saw was a tired, broken monstrosity that no longer belonged in this world, and that was that. No fanfare. No grand crescendo.

Just . . . done.

Horus checked the blood on his face as he travelled the arena. Watched the last remnants of the Enforcers battle his loyal crew up in the seating. Stood before Dominic Ode and crouched – with effort – to examine the frozen shock on his face. He lifted the head with a fistful of hair, bent down and began to audaciously feed on the vampire Lord. He tossed the lifeless head back and exhaled in delight.

From the centre of the chaos, Horus stood tall. Around him, the floor was split and broken. Above, the balconies were emptied – panicked civilians spilling away like water through cracks, and Enforcers struggling to restore order, guns still raised, nerves raw. But the message had landed. It had torn through the Cavendish Family, and the Families as a whole, louder than any speech, heavier than any negotiation.

With slow, deliberate steps, he turned from the destruction. His lieutenants – street vamps and rogues drawn from shunned corners of the city – gathered at his signal, taking to the stairwell to make their leave. No explanations were given. They obeyed.

He did not need to gloat. The silence said it all. This wasn't a conquest won with theatrics – it was a surgical strike of philosophy. A statement inscribed in blood for all of vampire-kind to read.

*They didn't need to kneel to anyone.*

# Chapter Forty-One

## Fragile Hopes and Dreams

Another lift.

Pepper was sick of lifts.

Sick of the cramped metal box, of the way they sealed her in and quietly delivered her to places she wasn't sure she was ready for. But this one, this lift – slow, humming, unhurried – she had grown to hate the most.

Her breathing was shallow. Her phone vibrated for what felt like the hundredth time, buzzing quietly against her thigh in her coat pocket, and again, she ignored it. Sweat crept at her brow, cold and anxious, collecting at the nape of her neck. Her reflection in the brushed steel walls looked ghostly. Hollowed out.

Then the doors opened with a gentle hiss.

The hospital floor greeted her with its too-bright fluorescents' stench of antiseptic. A couple stepped into the lift as she exited – him holding her gently, and her clutching a handkerchief to her face, shoulders trembling with grief. Pepper kept her eyes low, pressing on the intercom button at the ward door, and announced herself with trepidation.

The buzz gave way to a heavy click and the door swung open.

Same place. Same routine. The same brittle smiles from nurses who knew too much and said too little. Their expressions were soft, voices quieter than before. One mentioned palliative care, seeding the start of a longer conversation. Pepper pretended not to hear.

Inside the room, Claire lay as still as ever, cocooned in tubes and wires, the hiss of the ventilator tracking her breaths. Monitors pulsed softly, lights blinking in careful rhythm. Fragile. That was the word for her now. Pepper stood at the foot of the bed, suddenly unsure if her legs would keep holding her. But she made herself walk forward.

She whispered a thanks to the nurse who clicked the door to a close behind her, leaving them alone.

Pepper dropped her bag onto the chair and slowly pulled open her jacket. She reached inside and removed the Eternal Rose.

It glinted in the light.

The colours shifted faintly as she turned it by the stem, watching the pearlescent glow trace across the edges of the petals. Her fingers came away powdered in shimmer. It looked . . . livelier than she had first seen it. As if it were waking up – like it knew its time had come.

And yet, in all the chaos and sacrifice, Pepper hadn't stopped to consider *how the damn thing actually worked.*

Feed it to her? Rub it on her skin? Say some kind of enchantment? A word of power?

She muttered profanity. Racked her brain for clues as she clutched the Rose tighter, her pulse racing. What had been said about it? What did she overhear the Archivist tell Canis? She couldn't remember. *Oh God, she couldn't remember*. Something about a leech, wasn't it? But leeches steal blood, steal life, they don't return it.

She panicked for a few seconds. Then she made a decision.

Gently, she lifted her sister's frail arm and nestled the Rose against the inside of her elbow, beneath the blanket, tucking it into the warmth of Claire's body.

Pepper sank into the chair beside her with a slow exhale. Her body ached, her soul felt like it had been through a shredder, but she closed her eyes anyway.

She didn't believe in God.

Not really.

But she prayed all the same.

*Please be real*, she begged. *Please be what they said you were.*

Sleep came in fits, twisted by guilt and half-formed dreams. She woke in the early morning, her back screaming from the hospital chair. Outside the window, a pink dawn was crawling across the sky. A nurse was checking Claire's vitals, clipboard in hand. The woman glanced at Pepper and offered a soft smile and a good morning. Then she was gone, leaving behind the rhythmic hiss of life support.

Pepper leaned forward and took Claire's cold hand in her own. No movement. No flutter of eyelids. The monitors beeped.

Secretly she hoped that she had woken, and all this had been over. That, by some miracle, the Eternal Rose had fulfilled its prophecy, and her sister was ribbing her over making a fuss. They would laugh. She would cry. And they would finally go home and live a new life.

The ventilator squeaked.

There was none of that.

Just Pepper's fragile hopes and dreams.

She reached down to adjust the blanket and caught sight of the Rose.

Maybe it was the dawn light through the windows, but she could have sworn that it had dimmed. The shimmer had faded from the petals. It looked pale, muted.

Her heart dropped.

But then she spotted the chart protruding at the foot of the bed. She flicked through it eagerly, her eyes scanning the graphs and notes. And there it was. Ever so slight, but it was very much there:

*A slight uptick in Claire's vitals.*

In the days that followed, Pepper kept vigil at her sister's side. She dozed in the chair more than she slept. Someone would bring coffee she regularly forgot to drink, sustained instead by a ghost of hope. A rotation of kind nurses took vitals, but their conversations were white noise. The doctor on his rounds would never commit to anything, only emphasising the importance of Claire's stability. The only time Pepper stretched her legs was to go to the bathroom or raid a nearby vending machine. Every time she passed the windows the world beyond carried on – shifting traffic, changing weather – but inside the ward, it was purgatory. Their old flat became nothing more than a storage unit she visited to shower. She would catch herself in the mirror, expecting to see a trinket or furniture of the flat in Leroux Tower, vistas that belonged to a life she had abandoned. No, that wasn't right. She hadn't abandoned anything. She had adopted it to lead her to this conclusion. Played pretend to save her sister. That was all. Everything now could be behind her.

She tried not to think about Laik's fate. Not about the fight. Not about the terrible curse forced upon him. Not about what she had done to him. To all of them. But the guilt was a heavy thing to shift.

But on the fourth morning, everything changed.

*Claire opened her eyes.*

At first, just a flutter. Then a full blink, groggy and slow. She turned her head weakly toward Pepper, and her lips parted. Her voice was dry and hoarse, barely a whisper. But she spoke.

Pepper sobbed like she hadn't in years, collapsing forward and hugging her, careful not to crush her with the weight of relief.

The doctors were baffled. Claire was conscious. Alert. Eating. Sitting up. Her vitals were improving rapidly – far beyond what was medically explainable. The inflammation markers were vanishing. Her strength returned day by day.

The Eternal Rose was gone. Sometime during the night, it had crumbled into dust beneath her skin. When Claire asked why she had to sleep on half a flower so dead it belonged in a graveyard, Pepper had insisted that it was a good luck charm. One that Claire agreed must have worked.

When Claire was having her first shower in what felt like an eternity, Pepper scooped up fragments of the debris from the bed, dropped them into her open locket and snapped it shut. Fingers wrapped tightly around the souvenir. Her heart sank as she reflected upon the grim transaction. A life saved for a life taken.

And now . . . she would have to live with that.

Two weeks passed, and the world hadn't ended.

That, perhaps, was the strangest part of all.

Outside, the buses still came late. The neighbours still argued over bins. The kettle still whined in the morning. And inside a nondescript flat above a corner shop, two sisters lived like it was always meant to be this way: normal.

Claire was alive.

She could walk. She could eat without flinching. She could laugh again, bright and ugly and unashamed. The kind of laughter that couldn't exist when you were counting tiles on a hospital ceiling.

They watched films. Bickered over who got to pick. Drank hot chocolate like children. Pepper sat curled on the couch, knees drawn to her chest, smiling at the right times and offering sarcastic jabs when they were expected.

Sometimes, Claire would grab her without warning and squeeze, whispering *thank you* into her shoulder like it was a prayer. Pepper would smile and hug her back, breathing soft words into her hair, telling her that she would have done it all again. Because that's what family does.

And it was.

But it wasn't the whole story.

Late at night, when the television dimmed the room with a soft blue glow and the streetlight shadows crept along the ceiling, Pepper would sit silently. Claire asleep in her favourite chair, a blanket twisted up in her arms. The empty seat beside Pepper barely noticeable.

Except it wasn't empty. Not in her mind.

She could still see him there. Elbows on his knees, shoulders hunched forward, tossing her a look at the ridiculous vampire flick they had decided on. He'd mutter something dry, roll his eyes at the liberties taken and pretend not to enjoy it – even though he secretly did.

And then he'd be gone. Just like that.

Just a shape. A scent. A ghost.

A few nights later, they ordered Chinese. Claire was craving something from their childhood, and Pepper, without thinking, said she knew a place. A good one. She ordered the chow mein. The first bite was like a wound reopening.

That table. That little restaurant. She had sat there, alone, texting her sister goodbye without saying it, and telling herself she was making the right choice. Not even knowing if she was going to last the next few hours.

She smiled throughout eating. Didn't flinch. Didn't explain. Let Claire ramble about old shows and terrible takeaways, but in her stomach, the food curdled into something worse than guilt.

Sleep never came that night.

Pepper paced in the centre of her bedroom, alternating between crossing her arms and stripping her fingernails with her teeth, as if her body didn't quite belong to her anymore. The flat shunned silence thanks to the struggling hum of the fridge and the tick of a clock she hadn't noticed until now. Tonight, they seemed obnoxiously loud.

*She had done it.*

She had gone from managing dealings for secret creatures and private bars with stunning skyline views, to choosing out washing-up liquid and counting her change for coffee. She had saved her sister. She had tricked the reaper. Pulled her from the edge and brought her back into the light. She should be happy! She should feel *peace*.

But something inside her was hollow and loud, chewing at her composure no matter how much she ignored it. And it was gnawing *deep*, reaching her core.

Her eyes snapped to the small bedside table. She pulled its drawer open and set eyes upon its contents.

The phone was still there, sleeping.

It had stayed that way since the night everything fell apart. Since the night she abandoned the Cavendishes and gave Laik a fighting chance – or damned him for good. Either way, Pepper chose which life mattered more.

God, why did it have to be like that? Why did she have

to feel this way? Why couldn't she just forget it all, shove it somewhere, drown it with drink and weed and easy men like everybody else?

She picked up the tether to a dead life, stared at herself in the empty screen.

The moment it powered on, it began.

One vibration. Then another. Then a cascade.

The screen bloomed with missed calls. Voicemails. Texts. The device trembled in her palm from the sheer weight of it all. Names she hadn't allowed herself to see lit up the screen like ghosts come calling.

Reese. Canis. Quinn. Swan. Duncan. Even Mortis.

Ping. Ping. Ping.

*But noticeably, no Laik.*

She didn't dare open a single one. Didn't breathe. Because opening them meant they'd know she was alive. That she was still here. That she hadn't vanished – just disappeared from *them*.

For a moment, her hand shook. Her vision blurred with tears. And she wished, desperately, that things had gone differently. That she hadn't had to trade one life for another. And she desperately wanted someone – *anyone* – to tell her she had done the right thing.

But there was no one. Just the humming of the fridge and the ticking of the clock that would not let up. Peace was for other people. Those who deserved such a thing. And Pepper knew, in the deepest part of her that she wouldn't – *couldn't* – have that. Serenity was a prize for those with a clean conscience.

With a cry of frustration, Pepper brought the phone down hard against the corner of the bedside table, splintering the screen until the notification chimes finally stopped and the screen light flickered to darkness once again.

She sat down slowly on the edge of the bed, her hands resting in her lap, sobbing. Her shoulders slumped in defeat.

*This was what peace looked like.*

A dingy flat in a crap part of the city.

A sister dragged from the brink of death.

A future built on the unknowing sacrifice of others.

And a heart barely held together by lies.

Pepper had gotten her miracle.

But finally accepted that it had come at far too high a cost.

# Chapter Forty-Two

## The Consequences

The machines hummed quietly beneath the low lighting of the Hemotheca, casting a sterile, bluish glow over the polished floor. Quinn Cavendish sat slanted on a stool, gum cracking between her teeth, one booted foot tapping idly against the chrome stem. She eyed the technician beside her within a sea of black eyeliner, who worked in silence, dropping one measured dose of reagent after another into a series of dark, sludgy vials. Each responded differently – some hissed, some bubbled, some did nothing at all. He paused and cursed under his breath when one of them failed to react entirely.

'I'm sorry, miss,' he murmured, struggling to make eye contact.

Quinn's eyes didn't leave the vials. 'That's disappointing. Run the next batch as soon as you can,' she said. 'We might get lucky.'

The phone in her jacket buzzed, muffled beneath the heavy layer of leather. She pulled it out, flipped it open, and listened. Her face remained expressionless as she leaned against the steel counter.

'Actually, you're wrong,' she said plainly. 'I can absolutely believe it. I'm in the Vault. Come up.' And she hung up.

She slid the phone back into her pocket, told the technician to keep her informed and stepped out into the expanse of the Vault's main chamber. Archivists moved silently across the suspended walkways above like shadows in an old cathedral, recategorising records and amending huge tomes post-disaster.

Then the great doors of the Vault rumbled open.

Swan walked in with the quiet steel of a man still stitched together by pure will. A black bandage wrapped around one eye. A gash still healing traced his jaw. He didn't speak.

At his side walked Pepper Montgomery.

Her expression was composed, but Quinn saw the flicker – just the flicker – of hesitation. She was holding herself tightly, but not from fear. Something else. Maybe guilt. Maybe shame.

'Seems like another one who made it through the commotion,' Swan said quietly, eyeing Quinn. 'Hopefully she won't be the last.'

'Here's hoping,' Quinn muttered. Her gaze traced Pepper up and down, still chewing her gum. 'And there we were thinking you'd been killed by Horus's rabble. But look at you. Still kicking. Welcome back, Pepper.'

She didn't wait for a reply. 'Leave us,' she said to Swan.

He gave a subtle bow, threw Pepper an unnervingly long look, then turned and disappeared down the long hall.

'I'm sorry for your losses,' Pepper said softly.

Quinn raised an eyebrow. 'You don't know our losses. Or do you?' She turned and began walking deeper into the Vault. 'It's hard to say. Our home was infiltrated. Many were slaughtered, the innocent and our own. And a couple of weeks later, you come walking right through my door like it didn't happen . . .'

'I managed to escape,' Pepper replied. 'But I was clearly targeted by Horus's people. I went into hiding and figured things had calmed down enough to return.'

'Did you now?' Quinn said without looking at her. 'You could have let us know.'

Pepper revealed her phone, its façade covered with spiderweb cracks.

'My phone got broken in the scuffle to get out.'

'So I see. There's a convenient trickle of staff who have been returning. Ones who we thought snuffed it, turn up out of nowhere. As you can imagine, suspicion is quite high. Horus managed to sow plenty of doubt among us.'

They passed into the Ossuary, where priceless bones lay behind reinforced glass cases. The room smelled of chalk and age. Quinn walked slowly between the displays, the obscure arrangement of jutting bones staring back with hollow sockets and frozen agony.

'What actually happened?' Pepper asked, more hesitantly now.

'Horus revealed his hand when he and your brother had their little dick-waving contest. Turns out he wasn't just feeding discontent, he was bloody stockpiling it. Collecting angry, aimless vampires who were pissed at the world and wanted to get something done about it. Then he made his move . . . right under all our noses.'

Pepper swallowed. 'How many were—?'

'Killed?' Quinn stopped walking. 'Too many. We still don't have the total figure and I'm not holding my breath. Nor do I look forward to it. The damage was substantial. Let's not talk about the hit on our reputation. He's taken residence in the Odes' home, along with his outcast rabble, vowing not to stop until the Families are finished. My parents are discussing the situation with the other Families. What comes from that will be anyone's guess, but I can promise it won't be pretty.'

Pepper's voice cracked. 'I'm sorry.'

'Yes. You've said that already.' Quinn turned sharply, eyes narrowed, cracking her gum once more. 'After the smoke cleared, we started the investigation as to how this happened. Sought out the holes in our defences and whatnot. Security faults. Who went missing. Who may have turned. That sort of thing.'

Pepper's throat tightened. 'Did you find anything?'

'Plenty.' Quinn took a step closer, eyes unblinking, wild hair bouncing on her turn. 'So, let me ask: why'd you come back, Pepper? You could have vanished. Stayed gone. Nobody would have known.'

'I . . . I have a duty to the Family,' Pepper replied. 'That hasn't changed.'

'A duty? That's what you call it?' Quinn hissed. 'You walk out there during the fight and whisper some words to your brother, and suddenly he goes *apeshit*. His second comes out to play and wrecks the joint in the process, sparking an insurrection! And you call that a *duty*, do you?'

'I had to tell him something important,' Pepper stammered. 'He took it badly.'

Quinn was on her in an instant.

'He took it badly, did he? Hm.'

She slapped Pepper so hard she spun against the wall. Her fingers clenched the collar of her coat and slammed her back against the reinforced glass. The bones behind it didn't stir, but the rage on Quinn's face was primal. She spat the gum free.

'You wound Laik up like a *FUCKING TOY*, igniting

an already dangerous scene, and walked away to do *what*? Get a cup of tea? Sit down somewhere to watch it all unfold with a smile on your fucking face? No, *I* presume you did something *else*. *I* think you took the east stairwell up to the lifts, took said lift to the Vault, walked into the Relic Gallery with a fake in your pocket and switched it with the Eternal Rose! *Then* you walked right out the front door with the panicked masses while our people were getting murdered and your brother *lay dead on the ground*! Do you take me for a *FUCKING FOOL*, Miss Montgomery? Did you not have the slightest idea that maybe, just maybe *I knew exactly what you had done before you waltzed on in here*?'

Pepper stammered and shivered in dread at Quinn's previous madness forged into determination. The heir was furious, and while her words were violent, it was her fangs that Pepper feared: they had been extended in rage and were *so, so close*. At any moment Quinn could rip her throat out for this deception. And she would be right to.

Pepper whimpered. 'Laik is . . . Laik is dead?'

Quinn's face broke into something halfway between fury and heartbreak. 'What the hell did you expect to happen? Who knows, maybe we could have saved him if we had the Eternal Rose in our possession! But that chance is *long* gone!'

Tears welled in Pepper's eyes. 'I'm sorry, okay? I'm so sorry! I needed it, I needed it for my sister. *She was dying*, and I had to save her somehow. I had just one chance to save her life, and I took it. She's my only family . . . I know what you and Canis are like, you would have done the same if the situation was reversed!'

Quinn's jaw tightened. '*I* wouldn't have thrown people to the wolves! *I* wouldn't have been responsible for the deaths of *hundreds*!'

'No . . .' Pepper squeaked. 'But your brother would. He'd raze the city to the ground if it meant protecting you. I see how you are. And I know that he would understand what I did.'

Quinn's face crushed up.

She let go. Pepper crumpled to the ground, coughing and clutching her neck. She wiped at her eyes and dared to look up.

Quinn stood a few paces away, silent and still in the Ossuary's glow. The overhead lights caught on the metal accents of her imposing look, thick leather trousers wrapped in buckle straps, a heavy chain hanging from her hip like a war trophy. Her black jacket was covered in patches and subtle glyphs that had been etched into the arms. The Quinn Pepper used to know looked like she caused the chaos. This iteration was seemingly home slap bang in the middle of it.

'*Get up*,' Quinn demanded.

Pepper obeyed, limbs stiff, breath shaky.

Quinn turned and walked to a reinforced security door set flush into the Ossuary's wall. Without a word, she withdrew a key card from her jacket and pressed it against the reader. The lock shivered with a pulse of green. The mechanism clunked hard inside the wall, and with a sluggish groan, the door slid open.

A wave of warmth hit them immediately, heavy, humid and unnatural. Pepper followed as Quinn stepped inside.

The corridor beyond was dim, walls lined in sleek panelling. The air felt thick, as though it had to be chewed before breathing. The further they walked, the more oppressive it became.

Quinn removed her leather jacket, revealing the black ribbed vest beneath and a fresh tattoo down her left forearm. A spider with long, delicate legs crawled in fine ink toward her elbow, its body marked with a blood-drop red symbol. A thread of silk ran from its rear, tracing the roadmap of veins to her shoulder. Pepper wasn't certain, but it seemed to shimmer faintly in the heat. Beneath it, bizarrely, in stamped gothic lettering, was the name MR WIGGLES.

'You'll want to ignore the temperature,' Quinn said. 'It's deliberate. Helps keep the seals tight. You'll see why.'

Pepper shrugged off her coat and draped it over one arm.

At the end of the corridor, the space opened out into a wider chamber. The floor dipped slightly and was lined in red-painted metal plates. Two Enforcers stood on either side of the farthest door: Duncan and Reese.

They snapped to attention the moment they saw Quinn, but when Pepper followed a few steps behind, their expressions turned cold and dangerous.

Reese's fangs slid down, lips pulling back as she stepped in front of Pepper like a guard dog off the chain.

Quinn didn't flinch. 'Out of the way,' she ordered.

Duncan looked to her for confirmation. Reese didn't budge for a moment longer before she finally stepped aside, though her glare was chilling.

Quinn exhaled. 'Can't say I blame them,' she muttered. 'They know what you did. They know what it cost.'

They passed through the chamber, the heat now oppressive. Beads of sweat rolled down the back of Pepper's neck. At the far side was another door – thicker, heavier, reinforced with criss-crossing steel bars. Along one wall beside it, a long, narrow window ran horizontally, tinted red.

Quinn stopped and gestured toward the window. 'We put him in here for safety.'

Pepper stepped forward cautiously.

She peered into the room beyond.

Inside, bathed in the low crimson light, hung a single figure suspended by chains against the far wall. His arms were draped above him, wrists bound by heavy cuffs etched with silver symbols. His black shirt hung exposing skin cracked with soot-black veins.

'Laik . . .' she whispered, before blurting. '*You said he was dead!*'

'Look closer,' Quinn insisted.

Pepper leaned to the window and pressed her hands to the glass.

Smoke curled softly from his limbs, spiralling off his shoulders and ribs in wisps.

At first, the figure didn't move. But then, ever so slowly, his head rose. Golden light gleamed behind his eyes like molten metal. He looked directly at her, expression hollow. The smoke around him pulsed in rhythm with each breath.

Pepper staggered back from the glass, hand over her mouth.

Quinn, still behind her, finished the sentence.

'As I was saying. We put him in there for safety. *Our* safety,' she said, her voice cool. 'It would seem a little matter like dying was enough for . . . *this* to happen. I don't know if what we're looking at is Laik, or the Sins themselves, but I suspect some twisted amalgamation of the two. Maybe it kept him alive in his last moments. Maybe Laik is in there somewhere. Maybe he's lost forever. We don't know. The tests have been difficult to perform on account of his . . . unpredictability . . .'

Pepper wiped her eyes. Being responsible for his death, whatever the reason, was difficult enough to accept, but this? This seemed so much crueller.

Laik, or whatever he was now, eased his head down, hair falling over his face.

'But what I do know,' Quinn said, looking to the woman, 'is that my brother did say that little box your family was playing about with, the one responsible for *all of this* . . . has been located. And conversations have been had to acquire it.'

Pepper's mouth fell open as Quinn took out a cigarette and painted her face with a warm glow in the red ambience.

'Do you have it?'

'No.' Quinn snorted smoke from her nostrils. 'Its current owners heard about the commotion and weren't willing to let us buy it outright.'

'Why would they do that?'

'Because' – Quinn tapped ash to the floor – '*they're adamant to sell it at the next Night Market.*'

Pepper took a sharp inhale, as Quinn bared down on her.

'And you . . . You couldn't live with such uncertainty hanging over you. You had to be sure there were no loose ends. Well, there is. A big one. I watched you make your moves, paint your lies, pretend to play nice with my Family all under the pretence of robbing us, knowing all too well what was transpiring. It was never a secret. You never hid your intentions well enough. Especially since I knew you *before you even stepped foot in my home*. By setting you on your path to discover the existence of us in the first place.'

Pepper's eyes snagged on Quinn's arm as she spoke, tracking the sweep of motion: the vast tattoo of a black spider sprawled across pale skin, legs extended as if they were probing. It was large enough that the shading looked almost like living shadow.

*A spider.*

*Spinning silk.*

*Up her arm.*

*Tracing her—*

Then Pepper recoiled as if the air had been punched from her lungs, a cold shock cutting through her fear. *The Night Market.* The lure had been there all along. Hints deposited by some mysterious individual across shadowy internet message boards, tempting her deeper with every click, every late-night scroll. Those long, drunken nights when Claire was slipping away, and she was desperate enough to chase anything that might lead to a cure. Step by step, they'd led her straight to the truth. Straight into them. The anonymous hand guiding her through the dark wasn't anonymous at all. It was a perverse boast. The revelation landed horrible and neat, making an ugly, distorted sense that cleared everything into focus at once.

'*SilkVeins?* No, no, no, no! That – that person who told me everything about the Night Market? The *Eternal Rose*? *That was you?*' Pepper cried out. 'You did all this, you . . . you sent me the messages, you did the . . . you did all this? You *tricked* me?'

Quinn tilted her head back, saying nothing.

*Because that was just the start.*

From that first night they met, the lazy smile playing at Quinn's mouth when she'd mocked Pepper's squeamishness and joked about her being 'the one', even suggesting that she would replace Viola, as if it were all terribly amusing. The flattery and teasing were meant to disarm her victim. Pepper had laughed then, grateful for the opportunity of being allowed to penetrate a place so trusted in their Home. Only now did she grasp what that moment truly was: an induction to Quinn's own game.

And the things Quinn had said afterwards, those strange, half-cryptic remarks that had once felt like provocation or eccentricity, shifted in her memory, rearranging themselves into a complete, damning picture. Even penetrating the Vault no longer felt like chance. Quinn's talk of Laik, of fascination and frustration and being trapped despite all the wealth of the Family, had seemed like rare honesty then. A glimpse behind the performance. Pepper had believed she was trustworthy, her own deception paying off. But Quinn had manoeuvred herself in a position where she was not only manipulating affairs, *Pepper was welcoming them*. Conversations had been secret suggestions, deceiving Pepper into believing that she had stumbled upon sought answers of her own accord. Puzzle boxes, Quinn called her and Laik. Things to be twisted and turned until solutions presented themselves.

And then there was the confrontation with Horus, the only time that seemed like when the mask truly slipped. The fury in Quinn's voice. The ownership. *This one is mine. I had plans*. Not concern for Laik's suffering. Not outrage at his cruelty. Just rage at the interruption, of something precious mishandled before its purpose had been fulfilled.

Pepper hadn't found her way through the last few months by bravery or cleverness. She had been guided on the right path, nudged along with the vain belief she was choosing every decision herself.

*She had been played from the very beginning, at every conceivable turn.*

Her breathing quickened before she could stop it. Tears welled at the devastating understanding that even standing right here, right now, to face this, had never been a choice at all – but an *inevitability*.

'Y-you said before you never got involved in the affairs of others, didn't you? So why—'

'These *are* my affairs, Miss Montgomery. Always have been. They just so happen to involve you. That is why you returned. Your guilt brought you back to us – *as I knew it would.*' Quinn sneered. 'Your job isn't done, Pepper. Horus has ignited a great upheaval and I *need* my Enforcer *back* for what's to come. But the sins he carries makes him volatile. Unreliable. And I *cannot* have that. The clock is ticking. And you – you have a *responsibility*: get them out of him . . . and rid us of your family's foolishness for good.'

The sentence hung between them like a verdict. Pepper felt her stomach drop as Quinn leaned in, nostrils flared, voice dropping to something intimate and dangerous.

'I should kill you where you stand for all your transgressions. But it seems fate has other uses for you. After that . . .'

She let the words trail, then gave Pepper one damning look from beneath her hair, teeth dangerous and presented to remind the human of her vulnerability, in case she was stupid enough to have forgotten.

'No promises.'

# Acknowledgements

It still feels ridiculous to admit this, but *The Night Market* began as a joke.

I know, but bear with me here, it's not as bad as it sounds.

Years ago, on some godforsaken corner of the internet, I said I was going to write a vampire novel. At the time, it felt like the one thing I'd never do. The world didn't seem short of them, and I'd been badgered for years to 'give it a shot' so much that the suggestion had become a running gag. The problem was that the joke landed a little too well, and there was some enthusiasm for the idea. Letting people down was . . . humbling.

So that night, half out of guilt and half out of curiosity, I wrote a couple of hundred words and buried them in an already stuffed folder called 'Ideas'. They sat there for years until a conversation with HQ encouraged me to brush the dust from them. What followed the following weekend was a resurrection that had no business taking place. By the end of it, *The Night Market* wasn't a punchline anymore.

While most books I write take a year to form and introduce themselves, this one kicked in the back door, plonked itself down and refused to leave. I'm grateful it did. Because in the time it's been squatting in my brain, sharing its theme and characters, I just didn't have the heart to evict it.

I should point out before anybody else does, the irony of a dead concept suddenly springing to life, much like a vampire itself, is not lost on me.

To the friends who kept nudging me toward this story, you were right. Hayley and Hannah especially, your support all those years ago mattered more than you probably realised. This title wouldn't exist without it. And while I'm told I should point out that admission is not legally binding and does not entitle you to a share of the royalties, I hope the knowledge makes you wealthier in the way that only truly matters.

Again, to reiterate for legal clarification: *not monetarily*.

Emma, I didn't gently enter your life. I crash-landed into it, and you somehow made space for me anyway. Thank you for your steadiness, your patience, and for always standing beside me, especially during the stranger stretches of writing this. There's an adage that writing a book is a marathon, not a sprint. This was more like an episode of *Wacky Races*. I don't know if that makes me Dick Dastardly in this analogy. I didn't think that far ahead. Either way, you were cheering me as I crossed the finish line.

Abel, yes, I'll point out that you named a chapter for me. You did that. That's forever now. I hope when you're old enough, you'll read it and smile. It's one of my favourites. Your old man loves you.

Mike, we've both been through the wars, but in the process, I got to fight side by side with one of the best people on the planet. You've always had my back, I've always got yours. I still say you're the best thing Wales has produced. Way better than the lamb, or that train station with the really long name.

John, I have sat for the last hour trying to put into words my appreciation. The generosity, the kindness, the energy you pour into others – it changes people. I suppose this is my way of returning that love, in a form that can continue weaving its way through the world, even when I'm long gone. It's the best I can do to carry it on.

To Kupocon – every one of you beneath that banner that Alex and Allan raised – no one stands alone. You've all created something that feels like home, where community becomes family. To Nikki & Dan, Mo, Jools, Katie & Jenny, Liam, Emma & Dan, and everyone else, thank you for making that family important and treasured. Heddy, Caleb, Paul, I spoke about creativity and inspiration being a circular process. This here is my turn on the wheel.

Scott & Sam, Cero, Kirsty & Dodge & Phoebe, you've been the steady hands at my back while I built this thing. Thank you for the check-ins, the encouragement, and the moments we've talked that made things make sense. Oh, and the pizza too.

To all in the Discord, survivors of multiple Neil Breen movies, we came together for a single reason. We stayed together because of a better one. Shouts to Elusive, Minifig, Britcomrade, Igor, Tribit, Amy, Chad, Estejor, Theodore Papadopoulos, POFG, Naht, Rod, Willz, SDU, Nemb, Sisaiah and everyone else.

To everyone at HQ, especially Sophia and Georgina, thank you for seeing something in a half-forgotten premise, encouraging it to grow and steering it accordingly. Publishing is a leap of faith at the best of times and I appreciate the amount put in me. To Ellen who created the spellbinding cover, Lou and everyone in Marketing who pushed to ensure it's seen by the world, the careful scrutiny of Jon who strengthened every page, and everyone not named here – this book is what it is because of you.

And finally, to you – whether you're holding these pages, or listening to someone narrate this (please, whoever that may be, take a bow) — thank you. Time is the one thing none of us have enough of. The fact you've chosen to spend some of yours in this world means more than I can say.

Christopher Byford

## HQ

**Editorial:**
Sophia Allistone
Laoise Culloo
Priyal Agrawal
Georgina Green
Jon Appleton
Michelle Bullock

**Marketing:**
Lou Nyuar
Lauren Gardiner
Jo Rose
Occy Carr

**Sales:**
Emily Scorer
Dom Brendon
Brogan Furey
Sara Eusebi
Avery Westervelt
Lauren Trabucchi
Isobel Gavaghan
Hannah Lismore

**Audio:**
Imogen Gordon Clark

**Publicity:**
Isabel Williams

**Cover design:**
Ellen Rockwell

**Managing Editorial:**
Hannah Stamp

**Production:**
Joey Yau

**Rights:**
Aisling Smyth
Alisah Saghir

**US & Canada Teams:**
Emily Gerbner
Sophia Wilhelm
Kamrun Nesa
Colleen Simpson
Katherine Earnshaw

Dear Reader,

We hope you enjoyed reading this book. If you did, we'd be so appreciative if you left a review. It really helps us and the author to bring more books like this to you.

Here at HQ Digital we are dedicated to publishing fiction that will keep you turning the pages into the early hours. Don't want to miss a thing? To find out more about our books, promotions, discover exclusive content and enter competitions you can keep in touch in the following ways:

JOIN OUR COMMUNITY:

Sign up to our new email newsletter: http://smarturl.it/SignUpHQ

Read our new blog www.hqstories.co.uk

X: https://twitter.com/HQStories

f: www.facebook.com/HQStories

BUDDING WRITER?

We're also looking for authors to join the HQ Digital family! Find out more here:

https://www.hqstories.co.uk/want-to-write-for-us/

Thanks for reading, from the HQ Digital team

HQ